Glittering par...
passio...

Regency

HIGH-SOCIETY AFFAIRS

They're the talk of the Ton!

The Venetian's Mistress
by Ann Elizabeth Cree

&

The Gambler's Heart
by Gayle Wilson

Regency

High Society Affairs

Regency

HIGH-SOCIETY

AFFAIRS

Ann Elizabeth Cree &
Gayle Wilson

First published in Great Britain in 2005 and 2004

REGENCY HIGH-SOCIETY AFFAIRS
© Harlequin Books S.A. 2010

The publisher acknowledges the copyright holders of the
individual works as follows:

The Venetian's Mistress © Ann Elizabeth Cree 2005
The Gambler's Heart © Mona Gay Thomas 1996

ISBN: 978 0 263 86887 6

052-0410

Printed and bound in Spain
by Litografia Rosés S.A., Barcelona

The Venetian's Mistress

by

Ann Elizabeth Cree

Ann Elizabeth Cree is married and lives in Boise, Idaho, with her family. She has worked as a nutritionist and an accountant. Her favourite form of daydreaming has always been weaving romantic stories in her head. With the encouragement of a friend, she started putting those stories on to paper. In addition to writing and caring for two lively boys, two cats and two dogs, she enjoys gardening, playing the piano and, of course, reading.

Chapter One

Lady Thais Margate's long-lashed blue eyes were filled with concern. 'I did not mean to overset you. Perhaps I should not have said anything.'

Cecily Renato took a deep breath and willed herself to remain calm. 'Oh, no, you were quite right to tell me. It is just I am rather surprised.' Actually she was quite shocked, but hardly wanted to tell her companion that. 'I will speak to Mariana straight away.'

'You must not be too hard on them for it was not a very…very improper kiss, but I know you would not want such a thing to happen again. If the wrong persons should come upon them…one would hate for there to be gossip.'

'No. Of course not.'

Lady Margate rose in a rustle of fashionable blue silk. 'I must go for I have an appointment very soon, but I wished to see you the very first thing today. You may be assured that none of this will pass my lips.'

Cecily stood as well. 'I know you will not say anything.' At least she hoped she would not as Cecily hardly knew Lady Margate, who had leased a house in Avezza just over a month ago. But the lovely young widow had already impressed Avezza's residents, both Italian and English, by donating to several charitable causes as well as by heading up a committee to repair the damage done to the church of Santa Sofia during the French occupation.

Lady Margate took Cecily's hand. Although Cecily was not particularly tall, Lady Margate's fine-boned features and delicate build made Cecily feel ungainly next to her. Lady Margate smiled kindly. 'You are such a devoted mother. I have no doubt you will do the right thing, although you must not be too harsh with your stepdaughter or Lord Ballister. The very first time I saw them together I could sense a special sympathy between them. It is most unfortunate that the Duke of Severin is unlikely to allow them to marry. I have heard from Severin himself that he wishes to procure an heiress for his cousin, preferably the daughter of a peer. There is a certain earl's daughter that I have heard…but that is only a rumour.' She regarded Cecily with sympathetic eyes. 'It would not be easy for your stepdaughter to live in England. The society is so very different, as you know.'

'Yes, it is different.' Cecily attempted to suppress the twinge of resentment she felt at Lady Margate's implication that Severin would not consider Mariana suitable for his cousin. 'I will see you out.'

'That will not be necessary. You must give your lovely daughter my regards. And Signora Zanetti.' She pressed Cecily's hand before releasing it, her grip surprisingly strong. Cecily accompanied her across the small salon to the staircase, which led to the ground floor.

She watched Lady Margate depart, her thoughts in turmoil. Mariana and Lord Ballister? How had this happened when she had made certain they never met except in company? Why had she not watched Mariana more closely last night at Lady Margate's *conversazione*?

Because she had been certain that Mariana's *tendre* for Lord Ballister had faded just as she was certain Lord Ballister's initial interest in her stepdaughter had died away. So when Mariana had gone to the garden with her friend, Teresa Carasco, and Teresa's brother, Cecily had not been concerned. Nor had she worried very much when Mariana had been unusually quiet and preoccupied on the carriage ride back home.

'Why was she here? That woman?'

Cecily jumped when her sister-in-law spoke from behind her. Barbarina had the disconcerting habit of suddenly appearing and startling her.

She turned. 'Lady Margate was here to pay a visit, that is all.'

'She is not good. She brings nothing but trouble.'

'Surely not.' When Barbarina merely stared at her, she tried again. 'At least not today. I must speak to Mariana now.'

'She came to tell you that the English lord has kissed Mariana, no? You must hope that she does not tell anyone else. Such as his cousin, the Duke. Or Rafaele.'

'I have no idea why she would want to do so.' Cecily said. 'Please, Barbarina, do not eavesdrop.'

'What can I do when you hold your conversations in the salon where everyone can hear?' She shrugged and fixed her dark gaze on Cecily. 'You must send Mariana away before Rafaele learns of this. It will not please him to discover that you have allowed the cousin of the Duke to kiss Mariana.'

'Rafaele is in Verona so it is unlikely he will hear of this. At any rate, nothing more will happen.'

'You must hope not. For if Rafaele does, he will come and challenge the Lord Ballister to a duel. If that happens, the Duke will come and there will be another fight. In the end, Rafaele will send Mariana to the convent. Where you should have sent her as her mother, Caterina, had wished. Then there would be no need to worry about kisses.'

Cecily quelled the sharp pang of hurt she still felt when Barbarina compared Cecily to her husband Marco's first wife and Mariana's mother. 'I would hope that everyone would behave in a more civilised manner than that. Why do you think that they will fight if they meet? Is it because of something that happened in the past? When the Duke was here?' This was not the first time since Lord Ballister's arrival in Avezza that Barbarina had hinted at some sort of quarrel between Mariana's trustee, Rafaele Vianoli, and the Duke of Severin, who was Lord Ballister's guardian.

'It would be better if you do not ask more questions.'

Cecily bit back her frustration. Barbarina always lapsed into odd, cryptic pronouncements when she no longer wished to answer any questions. 'Very well. I won't. For now, I am going to speak to Mariana.' She walked away before she said something she would later regret. She tried to be patient with Barbarina for, before he died, Marco had asked her to watch over his older widowed half-sister. She reminded herself as well that Barbarina had never really recovered from the discovery that her beloved husband had died while running off with another woman. But sometimes it was all she could do to keep her temper. Particularly at times like this.

Mariana was in her bedchamber. She sat on a chair near the window and when Cecily entered she looked up from the book on her lap. Cecily crossed the room and pulled the small stool near the bed to the chair and sat down. 'I must talk to you.'

'Is something wrong, Mama?' From the anxious look on her daughter's lovely face, she suspected Mariana had a very good idea of why Cecily was there.

'Lady Margate came to tell me that she found you and Lord Ballister in an embrace last night. That he kissed you. Is this true?'

Mariana looked away for an instant before she answered. 'He kissed me and I kissed him back.'

Oh, dear. 'I do not need to remind you that it is most improper for young unmarried girls to be alone with a man. And very improper to exchange a kiss with any man except a fiancé or a husband. Lord Ballister should know this. He also must know that he risked your reputation by such behaviour. You are fortunate that Lady Margate discovered you and not one of the other guests.'

'It is not Si— Lord Ballister's fault. I asked him to meet me in the garden.'

'Why would you do that?'

'I...I wished to talk to him.'

'Have you met him alone like this before?'

'Only a...a few times.'

Cecily tried to hide her shock. 'Has he ever done anything besides kiss you?'

'No. We only talk. He has not kissed me before last night.'

Thank God. 'Then I must forbid you to see Lord Ballister again, except in the presence of others. I will not allow him to ruin your reputation.'

'He wants to marry me,' Mariana said flatly.

Cecily's heart stopped for a fraction. 'Did he tell you that?' she asked carefully.

'Yes. But he said he would not ask me until I am seventeen and then he will speak to you.'

Cecily drew in a breath. 'I see.' She felt as if she'd been hit in the stomach. Did Lord Ballister hope to seduce Mariana by promising marriage? He did not seem the sort of young man to do so, but then she had not thought Mariana would ever arrange a rendezvous with a young man in a dark garden.

'You will approve, will you not?' Mariana asked. A note of anxiety had crept into her voice.

'You are still young, too young to think of marriage,' she began.

'Mama was seventeen when she married Papa.'

'Yes, but they had known each other since childhood. You have known Lord Ballister scarcely a month.' She hesitated. 'It hardly matters whether I approve or not, for it is unlikely the Duke of Severin will. Or Rafaele.'

'But why not? Because Cousin Raf and the Duke have quarrelled?'

Cecily started. 'How do you know that?'

'Zia told me. But she would not tell me what the quarrel was about.'

A surge of anger shot through Cecily. Barbarina had no business telling Mariana such a thing. 'I am not even certain they did quarrel. There are other reasons, however, why a marriage between you and Lord Ballister is impossible.' Mariana stared at her, her expression stricken. Cecily took her hands. 'I am sorry, but you are scarcely more than a child. Some day you will meet a man whom you can love, someone more suited to you.'

'There will be no one else.' Mariana rose and Cecily could see she was fighting back tears. She walked to the door and stopped her hand on the handle. 'You are wrong. I am not a child.' She left, her pale quietness more alarming than if she had burst into tears and run from the room as she had in the past when angry or upset.

Cecily quelled her impulse to go after Mariana, suspecting she would only make matters worse. Mixed in with her anger and worry was fear. Fear that Lord Ballister was more to her stepdaughter than a young girl's first love; fear that if Mariana was capable of meeting him alone, she was capable of something even more rash.

Surely Lord Ballister must realise he could not marry Mariana without his cousin's consent. He must have some idea that his cousin wished him to marry an heiress; although Mariana was not penniless, she was far from wealthy.

He must know, as well, that Mariana could not marry without Raf's and Cecily's permission. Although Raf was Mariana's trustee, Marco had left Mariana in Cecily's care and had made it clear that both Raf and Cecily were to approve any potential husband for Mariana.

If Raf and the Duke had indeed quarrelled, it was even more unlikely either man would approve, thank goodness.

Then she felt guilty for even thinking such a thing when Mariana was so unhappy. For her own selfish reasons, Cecily did not want Mariana to marry an Englishman. She could not bear to have Mariana go away and live in a country that Cecily could never return to.

Lord Ballister had told Mariana he would wait until she was seventeen before speaking to Cecily. She assumed he would wait until then to speak to his cousin as well. She only hoped that, by that time, Lord Ballister would be long gone and that Mariana would have recovered from her infatuation. What if they did not? What if they decided to run off together? She knew only too well how easy it was to take such a course.

She could not entertain that possibility. She must

speak to Lord Ballister today and tell him in no uncertain terms that he was not to see Mariana alone and he was not to speak of marriage again.

Nico stood in front of the window of the small villa Simon had leased. It stood on one of the hills that gently sloped up from the town providing a clear view of the red tile roofs and green trees against the blue background of the distant Dolomites. To the right he could see the brownish-red roof of the Villa Guiliani, the villa that had once belonged to Angelina's family. He turned away, as an unexpected surge of regret and longing shot through him.

He was not in Avezza to relive the past, but to deal with the present in the form of his cousin and ward, Simon, Viscount Ballister. If Simon's friend, Philip Ashton, was correct and Simon was indeed flirting with Mariana Renato, then Simon needed to be removed from her vicinity as quickly as possible. Before Rafaele Vianoli got wind of this and decided to call Simon out. For according to Ashton, Vianoli was Mariana Renato's guardian, although Ashton had also told him Vianoli had not set foot in Avezza for months.

Vianoli would return quickly enough if he thought Simon was trifling with his ward. It was unlikely he wanted an alliance between the two families any more than Nico did.

He could not fathom why the girl's stepmother did not put a stop to this, although it was possible she did not know of the quarrel between himself and Vianoli.

Perhaps she did not care and hoped to attach herself to a duke's family through her stepdaughter. At any rate, he intended to put a quick halt to any such plans. His first order of business was to call on Signora Renato and make it clear she was to keep her daughter away from Simon. He would deal with Simon after that.

For now, he needed to find the housekeeper and have his trunk taken to his room so he could change out of his dusty travelling clothes. He crossed the room and as he did heard a woman's, *'Buongiorno?'*

He strode into the hall and saw a woman standing near his trunk. The missing housekeeper, undoubtedly. 'I will use the blue bedchamber. Tell Giovanni to take my luggage there directly. I wish to change.'

'I suggest you tell Giovanni yourself, *signor.*'

Her cool voice startled him as much as her words. He looked hard at her. She was much younger than he'd expect for a housekeeper and much too pretty with a pair of large eyes set in a delicate oval face. 'I beg your pardon, *signora*?' he said coldly.

'I said you should tell Giovanni yourself.'

'And who are you, *signora*?' She was not Simon's housekeeper; she carried herself too well and her gown, although worn and unfashionable, was made of good material. Her dark eyes met his despite the flush that stole over her cheeks. He had an impression of quiet dignity.

'I was looking for Lord Ballister. Is he at home?'

'Not at the moment. Perhaps I might help you.' Perhaps it was not Mariana Renato he needed to worry about, but this woman who seemed to be running free in his cousin's home.

'I…I doubt that. My business is with Lord Ballister.'

'Is it? Then I suspect it might be with me as well since I am Lord Ballister's guardian. First you will tell me your name.'

Her eyes widened. 'You are the Duke?'

He allowed a smile to touch his mouth. '*Sì*, and you, *signora*?'

'But why are you not in Venice?'

'Because I am here. Your name, please,

'I am Signora Renato.'

This time he started. Ashton had not mentioned that Signora Renato looked to be a scarce dozen years older than her stepdaughter. He recovered quickly. 'Signora Renato? How convenient. I believe your business is with me after all.'

'I have no idea what you are talking about.' Her slightly apprehensive expression belied her words.

'But I think you do. You have a daughter, I believe.'

'Oh, drat.'

He'd hardly expected that. 'Such a very English expression.'

'But I am English.'

Ashton had said nothing about that either. 'Are you?' He switched to English. 'Then allow me to compliment you on your command of Italian. I would have thought you spoke the language from birth.'

'I might say the same thing for you, your Grace.'

'But I have. My mother is Italian. You may come to

the library with me. I do not wish to continue this discussion here.'

'I do not wish to continue this discussion at all. My business is with Lord Ballister and since he is not here, then I will take my leave.' She turned and started towards the door.

He caught her arm. 'Any business you have with my cousin is with me. And since I came to Avezza particularly to see you, then I've no intention of allowing you to leave before I accomplish the task.'

She turned and looked up, her expressive eyes meeting his. Her soft mouth was parted slightly and he felt the faint stirrings of desire.

She swallowed before she spoke, 'Please let go of my arm. It is not necessary to take me prisoner.' Her voice was calm.

His hand fell away. 'Then you will come with me to the library.'

She eyed him for a moment. 'Very well,' she said coolly.

'Good.'

A short dark, woman bustled into the hall. Her face broke into a smile when she saw Signora Renato. '*Buongiorno, signora.*' Her smile faltered a little when she glanced at Nico. She fidgeted as he gave her brief instructions, then she curtsied and bustled away in obvious relief.

He led Signora Renato to the library, a small room off the grand salon, a pleasant room that faced south towards the green fields beyond. He indicated one of the upholstered chairs. 'You may sit here, *signora.*'

Instead of sitting, he leaned against the marble-topped table near her. Signora Renato sat on the edge of the chair, her hands locked around her reticule. She looked like a young girl herself, although he guessed her to be in her late twenties. 'I assume from the enthusiastic manner in which the housekeeper greeted you that you must be a frequent visitor here.'

'I have never been here before. Flavia's sister is my housekeeper.' She looked insulted that he would even suggest such a thing.

'Is she? Then I will get to the point of this conversation. It has come to my attention that you have been encouraging a match between your daughter and my cousin.'

She stared at him as if he'd run mad. 'I have been encouraging a match? I assure you I have done no such thing!'

Her outraged seemed genuine. Or she was a consummate actress. 'Are you denying that my cousin has an interest in your daughter?'

'I really have no idea whether he does or not. You will have to ask him.'

'I will. But first I wish to ask you.'

'You may ask as much as you wish, but I will still give you the same answer,' she snapped. From the stubborn look on her face, he doubted she'd tell him much more.

'As you wish, *signora*.' He felt his own temper rising. 'However, I will suggest that you curtail any sort of plans you have made that include my cousin.'

She stood, her hand trembling around her reticule. 'I

have no idea who told you such things but your…your informant was quite wrong. Lord Ballister is the last person I would want my daughter to marry. Good day, your Grace.' She stalked to the door. This time he made no move to stop her. At the door, she turned, her eyes blazing. 'There is one more thing. If you do anything to hurt my daughter, I will cheerfully tear you limb from limb.'

He was too taken aback to speak. She left the room, her head high, and he stared after her with the sense he'd lost the round. Tear him limb from limb? He'd hardly expected that from such a mild-looking creature. But then, nothing about the encounter had gone as planned. Certainly he had not expected her to declare in such disdainful tones that Simon was the last man she would want for her daughter.

He frowned. Was it possible Ashton was wrong and there was nothing between Simon and Signorina Renato? If that was the case, why had Signora Renato told him to ask Simon instead of telling him she did not know? He had failed as well to ask her why she had called on Simon today. Not that she would have told him. She would probably look at him with her large disdainful eyes and tell him it was none of his affair.

He was hardly finished with her. Not until he discovered if Simon indeed harboured feelings for Mariana Renato. Particularly if it turned out that Signora Renato knew about it all along.

Cecily did not slow her pace until she had passed through the pillared gates of the Villa. Anger, coupled with the irrational fear that the Duke of Severin might try and stop her from leaving, had driven her steps. Now that she was safe, she realised her legs were shaking. She started down the narrow road that led towards the village, her thoughts in turmoil.

Whoever had told Severin that she was promoting a match between Lord Ballister and Mariana? And how dare he come here and accuse her before he even knew the facts? Just thinking of the cool, arrogant way he had looked at her made her angry all over again. He was not at all what she had expected—if she thought of him at all, she had pictured him as much older, which did not make sense for he must be Raf's age and Raf was two years her senior. Nor had she expected to find him as darkly attractive. If one liked that sort of cool, male look.

Which she did not. In fact, there had been nothing about him she liked. She would never allow Mariana to marry into a family with that man in it. He would ride roughshod over her just as he had attempted to do with Cecily.

She could only hope that, in time, Mariana's infatuation with Lord Ballister would fade. Perhaps she should send Mariana to stay with her mother's cousins in Padua. Vittoria and Serefina were strict but kind, and doted on Mariana. She would send a letter off to Padua tomorrow.

If only she had someone to turn to for advice. Someone to reassure her that she need not worry about Mariana—that her feelings for Lord Ballister were the normal ones any young girl felt for her first *tendre*.

Barbarina was no help. Even if she knew exactly where Raf was, she could hardly write to him if there was any possibility at all he would quarrel with Lord Ballister or his cousin.

Perhaps she should have returned to England a year ago when her grandmother had summoned her, but the bitterness over Lady Telford's rejection of Marco and Mariana still hurt. And, despite her grandmother's adding that, of course, 'the child must come', Cecily could not put aside her pride.

Well, it was too late now. She had dashed off a chilly response, making it quite clear she neither wanted nor needed her grandmother's help and she was doing very well on her own. She was already regretting her rash words before the letter had left Italy, but she had no way of retrieving it.

She was on her own.

Chapter Two

'Nic? What are you doing here? I thought you were in Venice.'

Nico looked up and for a moment was startled to see his cousin in the doorway. Simon moved into the room, a handsome youth with a pair of startling blue eyes, and a charming smile. He was dressed in a riding coat and boots, and carried a crop.

'As you can see, I am not.' His gaze raked over Simon. 'You look well. Italy must agree with you.' In the time Simon had been away from England, he had grown. His shoulders were broader and his face had lost some of its boyishness.

'It does. I cannot imagine returning to another English winter after this. So why are you here?'

'To see you safely to Venice,' Nico said carelessly. 'Since we have not set eyes on you for the past five months, my mother and Eleanora are understandably anxious to see for themselves that you are well. They are in Milan, but will be in Venice by the end of the week.'

Simon hesitated a fraction. 'Then there's no rush. I can stay for a few more days.'

'You are not bored yet? If I recall, Avezza is not exactly filled with the sort of entertainments that you favour. And it is a two-day journey to Venice. I would have expected you would prefer to be closer.'

Simon shrugged. 'Oh, 'tis not so bad. I find I rather like the quiet. I've learned to speak a tolerable Italian and there have been enough *conversaziones*—they are rather like our routs—and the like to keep us entertained. There's going to be some sort of fête at the end of the week—rather like a miniature Vauxhall, I am told. In fact, there is to be a *musicale* tonight I had planned to attend, but since you are here... I know you detest that sort of thing.'

'You do not need to change your plans on my account. I will accompany you, of course. If you wish me to.'

'That would be splendid.' He grinned at Nico. 'You will cause a stir. I must change. Do you have everything you need?'

'Yes. I am quite comfortable. By the way, you had a visitor today. A Signora Renato.'

Simon, who had started towards the door, stopped. 'Signora Renato? Are you certain?'

'Quite. She gave me her name herself. You seem surprised that she would call.'

'I am. I have always had the impression she does not like me above half. Did she say what she wanted?'

'No, she left no message.'

'I see. Most likely nothing of importance.'

Nico thought his voice was a little too casual, but decided not to pursue the matter, at least for now. 'Will you dine here tonight?'

'Yes.' He started to leave the room and then paused. He flashed Nico a boyish grin. 'I am glad you are here.'

Nico watched him go. He'd said nothing about Signorina Renato, but then he had hardly expected him to. So Signora Renato did not like him? He wondered why, for most people liked Simon. He hoped Signora Renato and her daughter would attend the *musicale* tonight— he was now very curious to find out exactly what was going on between his cousin and the Renatos.

Cecily glanced down the dinner table, grateful the tense meal was nearly finished. Barbarina ate in her usual silence, speaking only to complain about the food. A thin woman, dressed from head to foot in black, she resembled an underfed crow although her appetite was certainly not lacking. Mariana sat next to Cecily, her eyes slightly swollen, her manner subdued. She answered Cecily politely, but refused to look her in the eye or contribute anything more than necessary to Cecily's efforts at conversation.

'There is something I must tell both of you,' Cecily said finally.

Barbarina continued to pick at her fish without looking up. Mariana said nothing.

'The Duke of Severin, Lord Ballister's cousin, is in Avezza.'

Barbarina paused, her fork in mid-air. Mariana raised her head. 'Why?'

'He should not have come,' Barbarina said before Cecily could answer. 'He brings nothing but trouble.' She forked the bite of fish into her mouth.

'I pray you will not say such things.' Cecily was in no mood to put up with Barbarina's vague, dire predictions.

Mariana's sulks had vanished. She propped her chin upon her hand, her eyes sparkling with interest. 'Because of cousin Raf? Do you suppose if Raf returns they will fight?'

'There will be no fights. I am certain the Duke means to leave very soon.' At least she hoped he would once Mariana was gone.

'If he has any sense, he will leave right away. Before there is more tragedy,' Barbarina said.

It was clearly time for dinner to end before Barbarina said something about Raf and Lord Ballister, which would only serve to upset Mariana. Cecily rose. 'I do not want to hear any more talk of fights and tragedy. We must get ready for Signora Bartolini's salon. Are you certain you do not wish to go, Barbarina? I can order the carriage be brought around.' Barbarina never went to such events, but Cecily always felt obligated to ask her

Barbarina frowned at her. 'I never go out in the evenings.'

'Do you suppose the Duke will be at Signora Bartolini's tonight?' Mariana asked. She now looked worried.

'He might be, which is why I wished to tell you.' Cecily hesitated. Should she hint to Mariana that the

Duke's purpose for coming to Avezza was to quell any romance between her and Simon?

Looking at Mariana's pretty face, she decided it would not be wise. 'Perhaps you should go and make certain the gown I had laid out for you is the one you wish to wear.'

As soon as Mariana left the room, Cecily approached Barbarina. 'Please do not say such things in Mariana's presence. I do not want to worry her.' She tried to keep her voice as reasonable as possible.

Barbarina fixed her small black eyes on Cecily. 'It is a bad sign that they both are in Avezza. That woman and the Duke.'

'You are speaking of Lady Margate?'

'Yes.'

Barbarina's conversation was proving to be more confusing than usual. 'But what does she have to do with the Duke? Why do you say he will bring more tragedy? Are you referring to his quarrel with Raf?'

'Perhaps.'

'But what did they quarrel about? Why has no one ever said a thing about it until now? Not even Marco told me.'

'Why should he? It happened before you came and has nothing to do with you. Why is it your business?'

Because she cared about Mariana and Raf, but she had given up telling Barbarina that. It made no difference that Cecily had been Marco's wife for two years and his widow for the past seven—Barbarina still considered Cecily an outsider. 'Perhaps it is not,' she said quietly, 'but I do not want Mariana upset. I must go and change. You should let me know if you need anything before I go.'

She waited a moment, but Barbarina merely grunted. Cecily left the room. She wished it were possible to plead a headache and stay home, but she had promised Signora Bartolini she would attend. She feared it would be a very long evening.

Cecily glanced around Signora Bartolini's crowded salon and was relieved that neither Lord Ballister nor his disturbing cousin seemed to be present. She spotted her friend, Viola Carasco, and her daughter Teresa sitting nearby. Viola smiled and motioned and Cecily saw two empty chairs next to her.

Viola moved over a chair so that Mariana and Teresa could sit together. She was a plump, pretty woman with a pair of sparkling, dark eyes. She leaned towards Cecily. 'I have heard the most interesting rumour. It is said that Lord Ballister's cousin has arrived in Avezza. Perhaps you have heard that also?'

'Yes.' Cecily hesitated and then decided against telling Viola about her encounter with him since she had not told Mariana or Barbarina. 'You met him, did you not?' She recalled Viola had mentioned that shortly after Lord Ballister arrived in Avezza.

'Once or twice, but the Conte's family did not spend as much time at the Villa Guiliani as they did at their villa near Treviso. They were here so much that summer because of the damage done to their primary villa when the French occupied it.'

Cecily wanted to ask more, but just then the pianist played the opening measures of an aria and soon the high clear notes of the soprano filled the salon.

The applause had just died down when two latecomers entered. Cecily paid little attention until Viola craned her head around to look. She turned back to Cecily. 'He is here,' she whispered.

She did not need to ask whom Viola referred to. Unable to resist, Cecily looked towards the door. To her chagrin, Severin's eyes fell on her and a cool smile touched his mouth. She quickly looked away. Mariana touched her arm. 'Is that the Duke?'

'Yes, but please do not stare.'

Mariana sniffed and looked indignant. 'I was not.'

Cecily found Viola staring at her. 'He seems to know you.'

Her cheeks heated. 'I did meet him. Quite by accident.' She was grateful when the next piece started. Not that she paid the least heed to it, for she was planning how to convince Mariana to leave during the interval. She certainly did not want Severin and Mariana to meet.

Her plans were thwarted by Lady Margate who appeared almost as soon as Signora Bartolini announced there were refreshments in the adjoining salon. She was charmingly dressed in her favourite shade of pale blue, her fashionable gown overshadowing the made-over and outdated gowns worn by most of the other women in the room, including Cecily. Napoleon was now gone, but nearly a decade and a half of French rule had left many of the residents of Avezza impoverished.

Lady Margate greeted Viola and then turned to Cecily. 'I must speak with you for a moment if Signora Carasco does not mind.'

'Of course not,' Viola said.

Lady Margate waited until they were out of earshot. 'I do not know if you saw the man with Lord Ballister, but that is his cousin, the Duke of Severin. Because of our conversation today, I felt I must warn you.'

'Thank you.' She did not think it prudent to tell Lady Margate her warning was much too late.

'We are old acquaintances so you must tell me if there is any difficulty.'

Out of the corner of her eye, Cecily saw Teresa and Mariana heading towards the refreshment room. She prayed Mariana would stay away from Lord Ballister. And that Lord Ballister would stay away from her.

She smiled politely at Lady Margate. 'I am certain there will be none. You are most kind to offer. I must beg your pardon—I need to speak to Mariana for a moment.'

'I do understand.'

Cecily paused in the doorway of the salon. The table in the centre of the room was filled with trays of cakes. She did not see Mariana or Teresa among the guests, but finally spotted Lord Ballister talking to Paolo Carasco, Viola's son. Thank goodness he was not with Mariana.

'*Buonasera*, Signora Renato.'

She spun around, her relief vanishing. 'What are you doing here?' Severin stood next to her, tall and far too attractive in a well-fitting coat of dark blue over black pantaloons. A small diamond gleamed in the folds of his snowy cravat. Despite his elegant attire, he looked equally as dangerous as he had this afternoon.

'As in this particular spot? Or in the house?' A slight smile touched his mouth. 'Not that it matters at any rate—my sole purpose for coming tonight was to see you. As well as meet Signorina Renato.'

'I cannot think why you would wish to do either.' Heat stole into her cheeks despite her effort to remain cool. 'Nor do I want you to meet my daughter. I will not allow you to frighten her.'

'I would not dare. Not unless I wished to be torn limb from limb. Cheerfully, I believe you said.'

'I still mean it.'

'I have no doubt that you do.'

'Severin! How naughty of you to come to Avezza without telling me!' Lady Margate glided up to them. She glanced at Cecily and arched a brow. 'Signora Renato, you have been naughty as well, for you did not tell me you knew Severin.'

'I do not know him. I met him quite by accident.' Lady Margate's tone was quite playful, but Cecily suspected matters would only be complicated further if Lady Margate discovered they had met earlier.

'Just now? You seemed to be engaged in such serious conversation for meeting so very recently.' She turned to Severin.

'We have not been formally introduced,' he said coolly.

'Then I must set that to rights. Signora Renato, may I present his Grace, the Duke of Severin? Severin, Signora Renato. She is one of the nicest persons in all of Avezza.'

Cecily found herself giving her hand to Severin. He took it, the warm strength of his fingers closing around hers. 'Then you must be if Lady Margate says so. Signora Renato, I am more than delighted to meet you.' His expression was all that was polite.

'As I am to meet you.' She kept her voice equally polite.

He released her hand. Lady Margate smiled. 'Signora Renato has the most lovely daughter. You met her when she was very young, I believe.'

Cecily stared at her, dismayed. Why would she say such a thing?

'Then I hope to become reacquainted with her very soon.' Severin's voice was bland.

'Perhaps.' Cecily gave him a vague smile. 'I am certain you and Lady Margate have much to discuss, so I will leave you. Goodnight, Lady Margate, your Grace.'

'You are not staying for the rest of the concert?' Lady Margate asked.

'No, I promised Barbarina we would return early. She has one of her headaches.'

'The poor thing. Of course you must go.'

'Yes.' Cecily made her escape before something else happened, such as Severin suggesting to Lady Margate that they meet Mariana.

Mariana was neither near the refreshment table nor anywhere else in the room. Cecily left through the door that led to the next small room, intending to return to the salon through it so she wouldn't have to pass Severin. A number of people had drifted to this room. To her consternation, Mariana and Simon stood in one corner, engaged in conversation. Neither Teresa nor Paolo was anywhere in sight.

She crossed the room. 'Good evening, Lord Ballister,' she said. 'Mariana, I have been looking for you.'

Mariana looked decidedly guilty. 'Oh, have you?'

'I fear I detained her,' Simon said in his easy way. His face sobered. 'My cousin said you had wished to speak to me when you called this afternoon.'

Mariana swung around to face Cecily, who managed a smile. 'It was nothing of importance. However, Mariana and I must leave so we will bid you goodnight.'

'But, Mama—' Mariana began.

'We must go.' She gave Mariana a sharp look. Mariana stared back at her, her expression a mixture of defiance and misery.

'Don't,' Lord Ballister said softly. 'Everything will be fine.' The tender look he bestowed upon Mariana made Cecily feel odd and, when Mariana nodded, her heart suddenly felt like lead.

Someone appeared beside her and the skin on her neck prickled. She did not need Lord Ballister's surprised, 'Nic,' to tell her who it was. How had he managed to extract himself from Lady Margate so quickly? She felt rather ill—if he saw the expression on Lord Ballister's face he would never believe the young couple were mere acquaintances.

Mariana looked up and the faint apprehension on her

face made Cecily move closer to her. 'We must go. Goodnight, Lord Ballister.' She glanced at Severin. 'Your Grace.'

'But not before you introduce me to your daughter.' The slight smile at his mouth did not quite reach his eyes.

She could not evade him unless she wanted to be insufferably rude and she knew she was coming close to it. 'Very well.' She looked up; a smile of her own on her lips although she knew it was equally as false as his. She performed the introduction, her eyes never leaving his face.

He took Mariana's hand. 'It is unlikely that you remember, but I met you when you were very young, perhaps only three.' He spoke in Italian, his voice polite, his expression surprisingly kind.

Mariana gave him a tentative smile. 'I am pleased to meet you, your…your Grace.' She glanced at Lord Ballister.

'That is correct.' Lord Ballister looked at his cousin. 'Signorina Renato was not quite certain how one addressed an English duke.'

'You did very well.' Severin released her hand and Mariana flushed, her face shyly pleased. She looked pretty and charming and vulnerable and Cecily wanted nothing more than to protect her.

She took Mariana's arm. She could see the other guests were starting to drift towards the salon. The second half of the concert was about to start. 'Come, we must take our leave of Signora Bartolini.'

'Did you walk?' Lord Ballister asked.

'Yes.'

'Then you will allow us to escort you home,' Severin said.

That was the last thing Cecily desired. 'That is hardly necessary. It is not far and we prefer to walk. Besides, I have no doubt you wish to hear the rest of the concert.'

Lord Ballister laughed. 'You do not know my cousin well. He almost always leaves in the middle of any sort of performance. Claims he does not like to sit for long.'

'Quite true. In addition, I have what I came for tonight so I have no incentive to stay.' He met her gaze, challenging her.

'Indeed. But we would still prefer to walk. I should not want to inconvenience you.'

'It will be no inconvenience.'

'No use arguing with him, Signora Renato,' Lord Ballister interjected. 'He always has his way.'

'I imagine that must be rather annoying at times.' She spoke more tartly than she intended to. Lord Ballister looked rather startled and Mariana now had the expression she always wore when she feared Cecily was about to argue with a shopkeeper and embarrass her.

Severin appeared unaffected. 'Very annoying, I have been told. My cousin will send for the carriage while we bid our hostess farewell.'

Cecily opened her mouth to protest, but Mariana tugged on her arm. 'Mama, please do not say anything more,' she whispered.

'But…' She caught a glimpse of faint amusement in Severin's eyes and suspected he had overheard Mariana's plea.

'Very well,' she said.

Signora Bartolini was quite sympathetic, although she only half-listened to Cecily's explanation. 'Ah, the headache, of course you must go. How kind of the Duke and Lord Ballister to see you home so you do not risk making it worse.' She turned to the Duke before Cecily could correct her impression. 'You have been away from here far too long. How are your dear mama and your sister? They are not with you?'

'They are in Milan visiting cousins. They are both well.'

'Very good. How long will you stay with us?'

'I have not decided.'

She glanced at Cecily and Mariana with a little smile. 'I quite understand.'

What did she understand? Oh, lord, at this rate, he would never be convinced she had not plotted to bring his cousin and Mariana together.

She could hardly wait to escape, but after leaving the salon they were forced to remain in the hall while the footman fetched their shawls. 'I did not realise you had a headache as well,' Severin said, with what she considered false concern.

'I did not earlier, but I most certainly have one now.'

'I wonder why,' he murmured. For the first time she saw genuine amusement in his face. It was quite unnerving. She pulled her gaze away just as the footman returned with their shawls. Severin took them. 'Allow me,' he said. He draped Mariana's around her shoulders with a gentle touch and then turned to Cecily. 'Signora Renato?'

'I prefer to carry my shawl.' She held out her hand.

'As you wish.' He gave it to her, his hand brushing hers. She nearly jumped at the contact and prayed he had not noticed anything amiss.

'The carriage is here,' he said. He was looking at her rather than the door.

She felt rather breathless. 'How do you know? You have not looked.'

'Are you always this argumentative?'

'Goodness, the poor soprano will have no audience if anyone else leaves!'

Lady Margate stood in the hall behind them, her gaze going from one to the other. 'I had no idea you wished to leave as well, Severin. But then I should not be too surprised, for you never do like these things!' She descended the last few steps and smiled at Cecily. 'I hope he is not being too difficult.' She tossed a quick glance in Mariana's direction. Mariana had now drifted towards the door.

'No, he is not.' It was quite apparent to Cecily that Lady Margate and Severin were much more than acquaintances. She suddenly did not want to reveal anything more about Mariana in front of the other woman.

'Then you have no more objections to accepting my offer to take you and Signorina Renato home in my carriage,' Severin said smoothly.

'He is to escort you home?' Lady Margate said. Her look of arch surprise made Cecily cringe. 'I had come out for the sole purpose of offering the very same thing after Signora Bartolini told me you had the headache.

You must allow me to do so since there would only be three of us instead of four and you would be much more comfortable.'

'You are very kind—' Cecily began, only to be cut off.

'I have no doubt Signora Renato appreciates your offer, but my carriage has already been brought around. She will be more comfortable if she does not have to wait any longer.'

Brief discomfiture flitted across Lady Margate's face and then she was smiling again. 'You are always so logical—it is quite appalling. You must not bully Signora Renato too much then, particularly if she has the headache.'

'I have no intention of doing so,' he said coolly. 'Goodnight, Thais.'

'Goodnight. And, dear Signora Renato, I will call on you tomorrow, if I may, to see how you have fared.'

'Thank you. Goodnight, Lady Margate.'

Although Severin's touch was light as he took her arm and then guided her across the hall, Cecily still felt like a prisoner. Worse, Mariana had disappeared outside; when they stepped out, Cecily could see her and Lord Ballister talking together on the steps. They quickly drew apart when Severin and Cecily appeared. She dared not look at Severin's face as he helped her into the carriage after assisting Mariana.

No one said much on the short distance down the hill to her house. Severin escorted Mariana and Cecily to the door. 'Goodnight, Signorina,' he said to Mariana. 'I trust you will not object if I detain Signora Renato for a minute.'

'No, your Grace.' She cast Cecily a hesitant look before going inside.

He waited until Mariana had gone. 'I will call on you tomorrow,' he said to Cecily.

'I cannot imagine why.'

'No? After tonight I think we have a great deal to discuss.' He braced one arm on the wall and looked down at her.

'I believe we agree that neither one of us wants a match between them.'

'Perhaps I have another reason as well.'

'And what would that be?'

'To further our acquaintance.'

Her heart slammed against her ribs. 'I…it is quite unlikely I will be at home.'

'I think you will be. Goodnight, *signora*.' The slight smile at his mouth panicked her more than anything else he'd yet said. He turned and strode towards the carriage before she could answer.

Cecily dashed inside her house and leaned against the door. Of course, he meant nothing by that last enigmatic remark. He undoubtedly wished to intimidate her by implying he had an…an interest in her. She very much feared, however, if that had been his intention, he had quite succeeded.

Reluctant to go inside, Nico leaned against one of the pillars on the portico. The night was pleasant—the sort of night he remembered. He could not fault Simon for flirting with Mariana Renato, for she had grown from a charming small child with a pair of large dark eyes and a sweet smile into a beautiful young girl with large dark eyes and an equally sweet smile. Very much like her mother, Caterina. She had died after he left Italy and he had been sorry to hear of her death for she had been kind as well as lovely. He idly wondered how Marco Renato had come to marry a young Englishwoman. Had they met in England, Italy or elsewhere?

He reluctantly decided he could not blame Marco Renato for choosing her as a second wife, for Cecily Renato was certainly as lovely as Caterina had been although in a quieter way. She was intelligent, and, from the protective, anxious way she regarded her stepdaughter, he did not doubt her devotion to Mariana was genuine.

'What do you think of Signora Renato and her daughter?' Simon asked as he joined Nico. 'But then you knew Signorina Renato when she was very young.'

'I found her a very pleasing child then and I still do. I know very little about her stepmother, however.'

'Her maternal grandmother is the Countess of Telford.'

'The stiff-necked old woman who went to school with Grandmama?'

Simon grinned. 'The very same.'

He was surprised. Not only did Cecily Renato seem an unlikely granddaughter for the cool, aristocratic Countess, he would not have expected the Countess to allow her granddaughter to marry a man such as Marco Renato. Although he was from an old Venetian family, he had not been particularly wealthy and he was not English. 'When did she marry Marco Renato?'

'She has been Mari…Signorina Renato's stepmother since Signorina Renato was seven years of age.'

Nine years if Mariana was now sixteen. Cecily Renato had indeed been young when she married Marco Renato. 'You seem well versed in their affairs. Is Signorina Renato a particular friend of yours?'

'What do you mean by a particular friend?'

'I noticed that you spent a good deal of time with her. I will own I was surprised. She does not seem the sort of girl who usually attracts you,' he said carelessly.

'No, which is why—' Simon stopped. 'Is this why you are here? Because you were informed that I have a *tendre* for Mariana?'

'Do you?'

Simon's eyes narrowed. 'No. I do not have a *tendre* for her. I am in love with her. I plan to marry her. As soon as she reaches her seventeenth birthday.'

'You are too young. So is she.'

'That does not matter.'

'You have a reputation for flirtation, so why is Signorina Renato more than one of your other flirts?'

'She has a kind heart,' he said quietly. 'I can talk to her, tell her anything and she listens. And…' he paused '…the first time I saw her I felt as if I had been waiting for her all of my life.'

'Does Signorina Renato feel the same way?'

'Yes.'

He looked at his cousin's quiet, determined face and

wanted to curse. This was much more than an idle flirtation. His cousin was in love. He should know—he had felt exactly the same way when he first laid eyes on Angelina.

Chapter Three

Cecily tugged the sole weed from the damp dirt and then leaned back on her heels and pushed an escaped tendril of hair from her face. Now she probably had a smear of mud on her cheek. Not that she cared—in light of everything else it was hardly important.

She rose and stood for a moment, looking down at the now tidy patch of flowers. The only thing that seemed tidy about her life at the moment. After seeing Mariana and Simon together last night, she knew she could not expect Severin to believe they were mere acquaintances. She certainly did not. Which was why Mariana could not remain in Avezza. Not as long as Lord Ballister was here.

Or his cousin.

What if Raf heard the same sort of rumour that Severin had and thought Cecily was promoting a match between Lord Ballister and Mariana? And what if Barbarina was right—that Raf and Severin would fight if they met?

She could only surmise that their quarrel had something to do with Angelina Guiliani. Marco had told her very little; only that Angelina had been the daughter of his uncle, the Conte Guiliani. The cousins, Angelina and Marco and Raf, had been playmates since childhood. When she was sixteen she had become engaged to the son of an English duke. Less than a week before the wedding, Angelina had died in a tragic fall. Her mother, heartbroken over the death of her remaining child, had fallen ill and, less than a year later, died. The Conte had sold the lovely old villa shortly after that and had never returned to Avezza.

Until Lord Ballister had come to Avezza a month ago, almost nothing had been said about the young Englishman whom Angelina was to marry. Cecily had been shocked when Viola mentioned Lord Ballister's guardian had been betrothed to Angelina. When Cecily confronted Barbarina, she had merely shrugged and replied it was not Cecily's business. It was only recently that Barbarina had begun hinting at quarrels and fights.

She wished Marco was here. At times like this she missed him terribly. He had not loved her the way she had loved him, but he had always been unfailingly kind and gentle. She missed his strength and the certainty that he would always know the right thing to do, whereas she often felt so much at sea, most particularly when it came to Mariana.

A bee buzzing around her head brought her back to the garden. She bent down to retrieve her basket of cut flowers when she heard footsteps on the path. She looked up and froze. The Duke of Severin stood behind her, regarding her with his dark, slightly sardonic expression. 'Whatever are you doing here?'

'I told you I planned to call on you.'

'And I said I would not be home.' His mere presence made her feel uncomfortable, and, in a faded gown and dirt-smeared apron with her hair escaping beneath an old bonnet, she felt even more at a disadvantage.

'Apparently you did not make that clear to your housekeeper. Signora Zanetti did her best, however, to convince me that not only were you not home, but that my presence in Avezza was likely to prove disastrous.'

'Oh, dear.' She had never even considered the possibility that Severin and Barbarina would meet. 'I am sorry. She sometimes entertains the oddest notions—you must not heed anything she says. She seems to be becoming more and more eccentric.'

'A fearsome thought, for she was eccentric enough thirteen years ago.' He looked down at her, a little frown on his brow. 'How did Barbarina Zanetti end up living with you rather than with the Conte Guiliani? Or Rafaele Vianoli?'

'She came to live with Marco and Mariana after Caterina died. After Marco's death she stayed on. The Conte offered her a home, but she refused. Raf is gone too much, but I am certain she would not go to him anyway. She fears I cannot bring Mariana up properly without her.'

'It is apparent your stepdaughter has been brought up very well and I suspect Signora Zanetti deserves little credit for it.'

His unexpected compliment filled her with pleasure and pride in Mariana. She smiled. 'It is really to Mariana's credit—she has been the sweetest, most loving child imaginable. She means everything to me.'

'She is very fortunate.'

'No, I am.' Her smile faded. 'But you did not come here so that I can praise Mariana.'

'No. We can sit on the bench under the arbour and talk.'

'I was going back to the house.' She bent to retrieve her basket, only to have him reach it first. His hand brushed hers, sending a warm tingle through her gloved hand. She jerked her hand back and straightened. 'It is really not necessary. I can carry it very well on my own.'

'I've no doubt of that, but I wish to do so.'

'It is rather dirty. You might soil your coat.'

He actually looked amused. 'Then you may brush off any stray dirt with your handkerchief.'

'I do not have a handkerchief.'

She felt even more stupid when his mouth quirked. 'Then I will loan you mine.'

She suspected he was teasing her, but instead of coming back with a witty rejoinder she could only make the same sort of silly remarks as a schoolgirl.

'What is it you want, your Grace?' she asked as they started along the path.

The amusement left his face. 'Last night my cousin informed me that he planned to marry your stepdaughter when she turned seventeen.'

'Oh, no.' Mariana had spoken the truth; and if Simon

had gone so far as to tell his cousin, he was indeed serious. 'This is impossible.'

'What is impossible? That he told me?'

'No, that he would even think of such a thing. That they would…. Of course they cannot marry. They are too young and you would never approve and I would never approve and…'

He stopped. 'My cousin is in love with Signorina Renato.'

'He cannot be. She is too young. Both of them are and they have known each other for scarcely a month.'

'Neither of which precludes falling in love. Have you not heard of love at first sight?' His voice was laced with irony. He began walking again.

'I have always considered it ridiculous.'

'You are not a romantic, *signora*?'

'Not at all.' She looked straight ahead. 'I have written to Mariana's cousins in Padua. I will send her there as soon as possible.'

'Have you told her that?'

'No. I wish to put it off until I receive a reply, for I suspect Mariana will not be pleased. Until then I will make certain that she and Lord Ballister have no opportunity to meet.'

'Is she in love with Simon?'

Again, he startled her. 'He is very charming and attentive and I can see why a young girl might develop a *tendre* for him, particularly if she is very sheltered.'

'I am asking about your stepdaughter, not young girls in general.'

'I am certain she considers herself to be.'

By now they had reached the edge of the garden next to the narrow strip of lawn near the steps to the house. He stopped. 'I wonder if one can distinguish between considering oneself to be and the actual thing?' he asked drily. 'I suggest neither one of us makes it too obvious that we wish to separate them, for I would not wish to drive them into each other's arms.'

'No.' She had not expected a man with his cool arrogant demeanour to be quite so understanding. As if he had once been in love. Had what she'd heard been true? Had he loved Angelina? She realised she knew nothing about him at all. 'No, that would never do.'

'Where is Vianoli, by the way?'

She looked quickly up at him, but saw nothing more in his expression than polite curiosity. 'He is in Verona, or at least I think he is. He has undertaken a commission to oversee the restoration of a church.'

'He is not often in Avezza?'

'No, not often.' She held out her hand. 'Thank you for carrying my basket. I…I can take it.'

'There is one more thing.'

'Is there?'

'You have a smudge of dirt on your cheek.'

'Oh!' Her hand flew to her face and then just as quickly fell away as she remembered her gloves were dirtier than her face.

'Now you have dirt on both sides. We will need a handkerchief after all.' He set her basket down on the top step and then reached into his waistcoat pocket and produced a snowy handkerchief. Before she could protest he had tilted her chin. 'Let me do this.'

She froze as he dabbed at her cheeks. His touch was surprisingly gentle, but her entire body prickled with awareness. 'Better,' he murmured. He still cupped her chin. 'Do you always do your own gardening?'

'It is very conducive to mulling over one's concerns.' She felt rather dizzy.

He dropped his hand. 'I did not see many weeds left. You must have a number of concerns.'

'I…yes.' Over his shoulder she saw Lady Margate standing near the corner of the house, watching them. 'Oh, drat.' She backed away from him.

Severin's brow rose but before he could speak, Lady Margate crossed the lawn towards them.

'Dear Severin,' she said with a smile. 'Must I warn Signora Renato about you already?'

'It depends on what you wish to warn her about.'

'That you are quite dangerous. For women. They are far too susceptible to your charm. I would not want Signora Renato to become a victim.'

He glanced at Cecily. 'You need not worry about Signora Renato. She seems quite immune,' he said drily.

'Then she is a rare exception.' Lady Margate smiled at Cecily.

Cecily wished she could disappear. Not only did the conversation make her uncomfortable, but she also felt even more clumsy and untidy next to Lady Margate's petite grace. She was relieved when Severin said he must depart. Lady Margate waited until he disappeared around the corner of the house before speaking.

'He really can be quite charming, but he is also quite ruthless when he wants something. You must not let him turn your head.'

'He was not trying to. You are quite mistaken if you think that.'

'My dear, you must not be so serious! I was only teasing you a little, although I must own I was rather startled to see him touching you in such a way. And on such short acquaintance!' She was smiling, but Cecily sensed she was not completely teasing.

'I had mud on my cheeks and foolishly forgot my handkerchief. He removed the mud for me. I have no doubt he would have done the same for anyone.'

'Well, not quite anyone! Do not worry, he meant nothing by it. If he does anything to distress you, then you must tell me. I have known him for a very long time so I can speak freely with him.'

'Thank you, but I am certain that will not be necessary.'

'You are no doubt right. Goodbye, dear *signora*.'

Cecily slowly walked up the steps to the house. Her cheek still burned from Severin's touch. Since her husband's death, no man had caressed her face as intimately. Not that she thought he meant anything by it, as Lady Margate had pointed out.

All of this was ridiculous. She was ridiculous. A widow of eight and twenty should not be making such a fuss over a mere touch of a hand. Nor should she allow Lady Margate's words to affect her. She needed to think of Mariana.

She realised she had no idea why Lady Margate had even called.

'Severin!' Nico, who had just passed through Signora Renato's gate, halted. Thais Margate was hurrying down the path towards him. She reached his side, her usually pale cheeks becomingly pink with the exertion. 'I was not certain whether I would catch up with you or not!'

'Your visit with Signora Renato was not very long.'

She looked up at him, her rosebud lips parted in a charming smile. 'I merely called to see how she was getting on. I will own I hardly expected to find you there!'

'No?' He felt rather bored. 'Did you walk? Or do you have a carriage lurking about?'

'I walked, of course. And now I expect you to escort me home.' She took his arm. 'Do not seem so surprised. Since coming to Avezza, I have discovered the benefits of exercise. The weather is so much nicer than at home.'

'Why are you in Italy? And why Avezza?' Nico asked as they began walking down the hill that led to the centre of the town.

'Because you are here, of course.' She flashed another smile at him. 'Do not flatter yourself. After dear George died, I realised I needed to go away. So many memories, of course, and then his family was never very kind to me. They accused me of keeping them away from George when he was ill, but I was only following Dr Johnson's orders. I have bought a little pal-

azzo in Venice for not very much. The poor family—
they had lived there for three hundred years, but now
they cannot afford it. But Venice was rather tedious so
I decided to come here—I remember it as such a peaceful place. But I am certain you do not wish to hear about
that! I should really ask—why are you here?'

'For various reasons.'

'You are being elusive as usual! Shall I guess? You
worry that Lord Ballister is becoming too fond of a certain young lady and you wish to put a stop to it, which
of course you must. I cannot imagine what Rafaele
would do if he discovered your cousin wished to marry
his cousin. He is her trustee, you know, although she is
in Signora Renato's care. What an odd coincidence that
your cousin and Rafaele's should meet and fall in love.'
She spoke in a guileless manner that made him wonder
what she was up to.

'Are you not presuming too much?'

She gave an amused little laugh. 'I do not think so.
Everyone can quite see that Lord Ballister and Signorina Renato are rather too fond of one another. Why
else would you call on Signora Renato if not to warn her
not to pin her hopes on attracting a viscount for her
daughter?'

She had always possessed the shrewd ability to sum
up a situation, but her assumption that because of that
she had the right to make it her business both amused
and irked him. As did her certainty that she knew the
motives of the parties involved. He could not help toy-
ing with her a little.

'There are perhaps other reasons I wished to call on Signora Renato,' he said deliberately.

'Really? What might those be?' She looked up at him, still laughing. 'Do not tell me you find her attractive?'

'Then I won't.'

She stopped in front of a house that sat slightly back from the cobbled street and was surrounded by a wrought-iron fence. She looked up at him with her large blue eyes. 'Why, Severin, I believe you actually do! I would not have thought she was at all your style. However, I must warn you that it will not do for you to become too attached.' Her smile was now gone. 'I have heard from several sources—several very reliable sources—that Signora Renato already has an admirer. A man who has been in love with her for an age, although it is not possible for them to marry—at least, not quite yet.' She paused as if waiting for him to ask. 'Rafaele Vianoli. Unless you want history to repeat itself, you must stay away from her.'

'Why were they here?' Barbarina spoke from her chair near the window overlooking the lane, and nearly caused Cecily, who had just entered the salon, to drop her basket.

'Goodness! You frightened me.' Cecily set the flowers on the table and went to Barbarina's side.

'What did he want, the Duke? He does not like it that his cousin wishes to court Mariana, no? Now we have only to wait for Rafaele to come and fight the Duke.'

'I will send Mariana to Vittoria and Serefina as soon

as possible. So no one needs to worry about fights. I have brought you a rose. There was only one blooming.' She realised Barbarina was staring at her with a peculiar expression. 'What is it?'

'You must leave Avezza as well.'

'I will accompany Mariana to Padua, of course. Then I will return.'

'You must stay away from the English Duke. You must not return to Avezza until he is gone.'

Cecily stared at her, a peculiar chill creeping down her spine. 'I assure you I have no desire to be anywhere near the Duke. I do not particularly like him.'

'That does not matter.' She kept her gaze on Cecily. 'For I saw the way he looked at you just now in the garden. You will be in danger as long as he is here.'

'Why would I possibly be in danger from him?'

'Not from him. Because of him.'

'That does not make any sense. What do you mean?'

'He will bring danger to you. Just as he did to Angelina.'

Chapter Four

Cecily received a reply from Vittoria a few days later. Yes, they would be delighted to have Mariana. She should come for a month, perhaps two. Cecily, of course, must stay for as long as she wished as well. Although Caterina's relations, rather than Marco's, they had always been quite kind to Cecily and their warm response made her feel guilty that she did not visit them more often.

Perhaps she should consider staying with them for an extended visit. Since the day in the garden, Barbarina's words hung heavily over her. *He will bring danger to you. Just as he did to Angelina.* Not that Cecily really thought she was in any sort of peril; she was more disturbed by Barbarina's implication that Angelina had been in danger and that Severin was somehow responsible. Did she think that Angelina's death was not an accident, but something more sinister? But Barbarina would not answer Cecily's questions and Cecily could only hope it was another one of her peculiar notions.

She wished she knew what had happened between Severin and Raf, but Barbarina was unlikely to tell her. Perhaps none of it would matter once Mariana was safely away from Avezza. She wondered if Viola would know. She had not spoken to her since the night at Signora Bartolini's. She decided she would call on her today.

Viola lived in one of the narrow streets on the other side of Avezza's small piazza. The day was fine; a dog slept in the sun near the butcher shop and across the square two Austrian soldiers lingered near the café. No one was sorry to see the French leave Venice and its former territories, but whether her new Austrian masters were an improvement was yet to be determined.

She passed the old church, now undergoing repairs, which made her think of Thais Margate and her peculiar idea that Severin might be interested in Cecily. In many ways, she was as odd as Barbarina in regard to Severin.

If only he had never come to Avezza—since his arrival, everyone and everything seemed overset.

Viola leased the top floor of one of the tall narrow houses that lined either side of the street. A maid let Cecily in and Cecily followed her up the steep stairway to the upper floor. Viola greeted Cecily with a hug. Like Cecily, Viola was now a widow, her husband killed at the Battle of Borodino while fighting under Napoleon. Along with many other men in the towns that were once part of the Venetian Republic, he had been conscripted into the French army against his will, which only made his death more tragic.

As soon as they were seated on the small sofa, Viola turned to Cecily. 'So, my dear Cecily, I have heard the handsome Duke was seen leaving your house yesterday. This following the *musicale*, when he insisted on escorting you home.'

'It was not a social call. He wishes to make sure I am not encouraging a match between Lord Ballister and Mariana.'

'Are you certain that is all? A little flirtation with you might soften his heart towards Mariana and her young suitor.'

'Even if I wished to do so, I would never think of flirting with him. At any rate, we are in agreement; neither of us wants a match between them. They are far too young.' She did not want to discuss Mariana and Lord Ballister any further, for she suspected Viola sympathised with the couple's predicament, although she had never exactly said so. 'Not only that, but Barbarina has told me if Raf finds out about any of this he will fight not only Lord Ballister but the Duke as well. She speaks of some sort of quarrel between the Duke and Raf, but will not tell me why. Have you ever heard about any sort of quarrel?'

Viola frowned. 'No, but I do remember that some people were surprised when the Conte announced that Angelina was to marry Lord St Gervase, as he was then, for everyone had always thought she would marry Rafaele Vianoli.'

'Angelina and Raf?' Cecily was truly shocked. 'Why would anyone think that?'

'Because he was the Conte's heir and it seemed only natural that they would marry.'

'Was Raf in love with Angelina?'

'I do not know. No one doubted, however, that Lord St Gervase was in love with Angelina and that she was equally in love with him. Everyone could see how happy they were together, as if fate decreed it to be. I only saw him once after she died and he looked as if his heart had died with her.'

'I did not know that,' Cecily said slowly. So Severin had loved her. 'No one has really said much about Angelina except Barbarina. She seems to be one person Barbarina truly cared about.'

'Angelina was beautiful. She reminded me of the Madonna in one of Bellini's paintings. No one said a word against her because she was always laughing and teasing and had a smile for everyone. I do not think there was anyone she disliked, even the Lady Margate.'

'She knew Lady Margate?' For the second time in the past hour Cecily was stunned.

'She was not Lady Margate, of course, but Miss…' Viola frowned a little, 'Miss Winters, I think. Yes, it was Miss Winters. She also stayed with the Conte's family that summer. Her father was a friend of the Conte's.'

'Lady Margate has said nothing of that, nor has anyone else.'

'I do not think anyone has recognised her. She was only there that one summer and she was the sort of pale, thin girl that no one ever notices. She is quite different now. It is very odd, but I did not recognise her until I saw her with the Duke at the *musicale*. There was a certain way she tilted her head when she looked at him and suddenly I remembered her doing the same all those years ago. As was every other girl that summer, she was a little in love with him. Not that he noticed, for he saw only Angelina.'

'I wonder why she has said nothing.'

'Perhaps she does not want to be remembered as she was.'

'Perhaps not.'

It was all so peculiar. Did Barbarina recognise her? Perhaps that would explain why Barbarina had regarded her with such animosity from the very beginning, but not what she had done to incur it. Why had Barbarina not told her she knew Lady Margate? So many secrets and for what purpose?

'I do not know if any of this explains why Rafaele and the Duke quarrelled unless it was over Angelina,' Viola said.

'That is possible, but if the Conte announced the betrothal it seems *he* must have approved. If he really wished Raf to marry Angelina, he surely would have tried to stop a marriage between the Duke and his daughter.'

'Perhaps you should ask Rafaele. Or the Duke.' A hint of mischief appeared in her eyes.

'Raf is not here and the Duke would send me scurrying away with a cool set-down.'

Viola laughed. 'You are not such a coward. Is Raf still in Verona? He has not been to Avezza for a long time, but should we be expecting him now that the Duke is here?'

'I certainly hope not. Yes, he is still in Verona. We have not seen him for nearly three months. Mariana misses him; we both do.' During Marco's prolonged illness and after his death, he had been like a brother to her; helping her with legal matters, holding Mariana when she cried and then making her laugh, teasing Cecily into smiles when she became too serious.

'At least he will not starve,' Viola said, always practical. 'And he still has the palazzo, no? He has not been forced to sell that?'

'I hope he will never need to. He would be devastated.' It was all that was left of his family's holdings for the French policies had impoverished a good portion of the Venetian nobility, including his family as well as the Guiliani family. After the Conte's death, he had been forced to sell many of the holdings of both families.

'Perhaps he will fall in love with a wealthy woman and then his troubles will be gone.'

'Perhaps, although there does not seem to be an abundance of such women around.' Cecily could not imagine Raf marrying for such reasons, for she suspected that his laughing eyes and cool intelligence hid a romantic heart.

Their talk turned to other matters, such as the fête at the end of the week in the gardens of Signor Palmero's villa. They agreed to share a supper box, then Cecily rose to leave.

She stepped out into the narrow street and started for home, so occupied in thought she barely noticed her surroundings. She had come away from Viola with more questions than before. Questions about Angelina and Raf, Raf and the Duke, and, to add to the confusion, Lady Margate. The only thing she knew for certain was that Severin and Angelina had been in love and were to marry, she had died, and in the thirteen years since her death he had never married.

Cecily had decided she would wait until after the fête before telling Mariana they were to leave for Padua. She knew Mariana looked forward to this affair each year and Cecily hated to spoil it for her. Mariana had been compliant and almost too subdued over the past few days. Except for a visit from Teresa, she had spent most of her time reading or sitting in the garden and Cecily was now troubled by visions of a decline.

On the night of the fête, Mariana appeared to have recovered some of her usual spirits. She wore a muslin gown in a soft rose colour. The gown itself was several years old, but, newly trimmed with ribbon and lace and set off with a new sash in a darker shade of rose, it looked quite presentable. Her black curls were gathered in a knot at the top of her head and fell in a cascade of ringlets to her shoulders and her eyes held some of their old sparkle. To Cecily's eyes, she was beautiful and she could hardly blame Lord Ballister for falling in love with her.

Cecily herself was dressed in pale peach muslin. It

was a trifle outdated—the skirt was not quite as full as the current fashion, but at least it was not very worn. She was stunned, however, when Barbarina suddenly appeared in the salon and announced she planned to attend the fête with them. Cecily was equally taken aback by her appearance. Over her black dress she wore a black mantle, instead of her plain black veil she wore one of black lace, and, if Cecily was not mistaken, she had even applied a touch of rouge.

'How pretty you look!' Cecily exclaimed and then prayed she had not offended Barbarina. Barbarina merely gave a 'hmph' but Cecily thought she looked a little pleased. She did not protest when Mariana fingered her lacy veil and told her she must wear such things more often.

Shades of purple, pink and orange tinted the sky by the time Cecily, Mariana and Barbarina arrived at the Palermos' villa. A long line of carriages already stood in the villa's drive so they were forced to dismount a small distance away. A number of other guests were doing the same. Cecily worried that the distance would be too much for Barbarina, but she managed the walk to the garden entrance without complaint, albeit slowly.

They joined the crowd drifting between the stone pillars to the garden. As they entered the grounds, Cecily wondered if Severin and Lord Ballister would be here, for this was the villa that had once belonged to Angelina's family. Would Severin find it too difficult to visit this place with its surely painful memories?

She had found herself thinking far too much about him and Angelina since her visit to Viola. Tonight, she must make an effort to put them from her thoughts or she feared she would see their ghosts everywhere, which would make for a most melancholy evening.

The gardens were behind the house itself. Signor Palermo been quite taken with a visit to Vauxhall a number of years ago and had attempted to recreate the English pleasure garden. He added a pavilion for musicians and a number of supper boxes. Although lacking a Thames river, the garden could boast of a small artificial lake with a fountain in the middle. He had left the old maze that proved to be one of the most popular attractions.

A footman showed their party to the supper box. Viola and Teresa were already there; Viola arched a brow in astonishment when she saw Barbarina. After Barbarina had been seated near the front of the box so that she could observe the crowd, and Mariana and Teresa were deep in conversation, Viola turned to Cecily. 'How did you persuade Signora Zanetti to come?' she asked in a low voice.

'I did not. She decided on her own.'

'How very strange. Has she ever been here before? At a fête, that is, for I know she stayed here quite often with the Guiliani family.'

'I do not think so. I have no idea why she wanted to come.'

'Mama,' Teresa said, 'Paolo and Frederico wish to take Mariana and me to the maze. May we go?'

Cecily saw that Paolo, Teresa's brother, and their cousin, Frederico, a pleasant-looking, plump youth, were standing just outside their supper box.

Viola glanced at Cecily. 'If Signora Renato does not object.'

Cecily hesitated. What if Lord Ballister were here and joined them? On the other hand, Severin had said they must not make it too obvious they wished to separate them. And Mariana scarcely mentioned Lord Ballister this week.

'Please, Mama,' Mariana said, regarding Cecily with large pleading eyes.

'You may go, but please stay together.'

'Thank you.' Mariana gave her a radiant smile and, after planting a brief kiss on Barbarina's cheek, left with the others. By now the evening shadows had fallen and the servants had begun lighting various lanterns and torches scattered throughout the garden, giving the garden a festive air.

Barbarina seemed disinclined to talk and spoke only to ask for a glass of lemonade from one of the waiters. The strains of a Vivaldi concerto reached them from somewhere in the garden. Viola suddenly touched Cecily's hand. 'He is coming.'

'Who?'

'Your duke. He is very certainly most handsome.'

'He is not my duke!' Cecily half-turned her face to the back of the box and pretended very hard to be studying the painting of cherubs dancing around a fountain. He most likely would walk by.

The skin at the back of her neck prickled and she knew he had come to stand next to them.

'*Buonasera*, Signora Zanetti, Signora Carasco. And Signora Renato.' He switched to English. 'A fascinating work, Signora Renato. What is it that has caught your attention? The cherubs dancing in drunken abandon around a fountain or the cupid peering from beneath the leaves?'

'There is a cupid? Where?' Then she coloured and forced herself to turn around. 'Good evening, your Grace.'

'It must be the cherubs, then, since you did not notice the cupid.'

'I was admiring the use of colour.'

'Can you even tell in this fading light?' He was openly amused, which only served to fluster Cecily more.

Viola was watching with rapt interest. 'You must join us, your Grace.'

'If Signora Zanetti does not object.'

Barbarina was staring at him with something like consternation. 'You must stay away from Signora Renato. She is not safe with you.'

Viola's mouth fell open and Cecily wanted to sink through the floor of the box. She could not look at Severin.

'What precisely do you mean by that?' he asked. His voice was level, but there was a hardness to it.

'She will not be safe with you,' Barbarina repeated.

'Have you visited the maze, your Grace?' Viola asked brightly.

'Not yet.' He glanced down at Cecily. 'Where is Signorina Renato?'

'She has gone to visit the maze. With Signorina Carasco and her brother and cousin.'

His eyes narrowed. 'Has she? An interesting coincidence. My brother has gone there as well.'

She did not like his implication. She spoke in English, hoping Barbarina would not understand very much. 'I hope you are not suggesting what I think you are. If you are so worried about that, then you should keep a tighter rein on him.'

'Just as you should keep a tighter rein on your daughter, madam. I believe I will visit the maze after all. Good evening, ladies.' He walked briskly away.

Cecily was not about to let him confront Mariana without her. She started to rise, only to find Barbarina's hand clasped around her wrist. 'Where are you going?'

'To the maze. To find Mariana.'

'You must not go with him.'

'I am not going with him. I am going by myself.'

'Then I will come with you.'

'No, you must stay here with Viola.' She gently removed Barbarina's hand. 'I will return shortly,' she said to Viola.

'Of course.' Viola looked as if she wanted to laugh.

Cecily hurried after Severin, whose progress had been slowed by a trio of jugglers. He started to move around them when he caught sight of Cecily. He stopped. 'I doubt there will be much benefit in both of us showing up.'

She gave him a tight smile. 'Then you may go else-where while I find them. I am going to find my daughter because I do not want her subjected to one of your intimidating stares.'

'I've no intention of intimidating her. You are wasting time by arguing. You may do as you please.'

He stalked off. She followed him, although she grew a trifle breathless as she was forced to trot in order to keep up with his long strides. The crowds had grown and she had a hard time weaving around them. Despite the number of lanterns the gardens were not particularly well lit and some of the paths were dark.

Most of the crowd seemed to be heading towards the grotto where the musicians played. By the time Cecily reached the maze she had lost Severin because of a crowd of people who had got in her way. She felt more than a little trepidation when she entered the first path with its tall, shadowy shrubs. It suddenly seemed very dark and foreboding despite the voices and laugher coming from within. She stopped, uncertain which way to proceed.

'What happened to you? I turned around and you were gone.'

Severin's voice made her jump. He was standing near the entrance.

'I thought that was what you wanted.'

He made an impatient sound. 'I wanted you to stay with Signora Carasco, not get lost in the dark. Despite Signora Zanetti's dire predictions, you are better off with me.'

'I am sorry that she said such stupid things to you. At any rate, I have been here any number of times. I can manage quite well on my own.' Although the maze did look quite different in the dark.

'Not unless you wish to be the object of some man's attentions.' He caught her arm. 'You are wasting time again.'

'Me?' But he was already leading her into the first winding passage between two tall rows of yews.

There were not as many people as she had expected. Once they entered the second passage she knew why. Without the benefit of sunlight or a full moon, it was nearly impossible to see much. She could still hear laughter and voices from somewhere in the maze and she froze when she heard Mariana's breathless laugh and then Simon's deeper voice.

'Oh, dear.'

'Yes.' The grimness of Severin's tone made her shiver.

He glanced down at her face. 'There is no need to look so frightened. I'm not planning to beat either of them. Just lock Simon up until your daughter is safely away from Avezza. You might consider doing the same thing for your daughter.'

'I am beginning to agree.' How could Mariana do this? Did she not know, did neither of them realise, that they were both risking their reputations? Or perhaps that is what they meant to do so they would be forced to marry. The thought made her blood run cold.

They rounded another corner and found themselves

nearly careening into a couple locked in a passionate embrace. For a horrid moment, Cecily feared it was Mariana and Simon, but realised the man was much too stocky. Embarrassed, she backed up and stepped on Severin's foot. 'I beg your pardon.'

The man lifted his head and saw them. 'You will need to find your own corner, *signora.*' His lady made a breathless little protest as her swain pulled her harder against him.

Severin steered her back around the corner. 'We've taken a wrong turn. We will have to retrace our steps.'

She nodded and followed him. By now, the clouds had covered the moon and the maze was even more dark and shadowy. The music and voices seemed far away and Cecily no longer heard anything from inside the maze. It was if they were the only ones here except for the couple they had just left behind.

Severin suddenly stopped. 'We've hit another dead end.' He ran a hand through his hair. 'You said you've been here a number of times. Do you have the faintest idea how we make our way out of here?'

He was asking for her help? Astounded, she stared at him before speaking. 'I have only been here during the day.' He was not going to like what she had to say next. She forced herself to meet his eyes. 'And I have lost my way every single time. Mariana has always had to rescue me.'

She braced herself for the derision in his voice. To her astonishment, he laughed. 'Of course. And you had hoped to find them yourself?'

'I had planned on following you.'

His mouth curved in genuine amusement. 'Next time you should think twice before you decide to follow me.'

'I doubt there will be a next time.' She rubbed her arms as a cool breeze brushed her bare arms. 'If we can find the centre of the maze, there is one path that leads directly to the back entrance near the lake.'

'If I recall, the centre of the maze is to the left.'

'How do you know that?'

He slanted a look at her. 'I have been here as well, although it has grown considerably since I was last here. The paths seemed to have been rearranged, which is why I made the wrong turn.'

'Signor Palermo changes the paths each year. He digs up some of the shrubs and then replants them so the paths are never the same.'

'Very clever. But one should be able to find the old path by observing where the shrubs have been replanted.'

'I suppose,' she said doubtfully.

'Come. We will test my theory.' He took her hand, his hand warm and strong around hers, and began to walk. She glanced at his face and then looked away, her breath catching. She was suddenly aware it was too dark, too quiet, too alone. Too intimate.

A peculiar pit formed in her stomach and she felt almost panicked. Of course they would find their way out. He had been the perfect gentleman. She could not fault him for that at all. She would be safe with him.

'This way, I think.' He tugged her around a corner. She realised she had been paying no attention at all to where they were going. In a moment they were in the centre of the maze. He dropped her hand and looked around. 'I do not recall a statue last time I was here.' He spoke almost to himself.

He had been here with Angelina. She was certain of that. 'Signor Palermo added them only recently.' Her words seemed an intrusion on his memories so she moved away.

It was then she heard the faintest rustling in the bushes surrounding the small garden. She jumped and looked around, but there was nothing. She rubbed her arms, suddenly cold, her light shawl not at all adequate.

She heard the small sound again almost as if someone was in the bushes. Her sense of uneasiness increased and, when Severin appeared behind her, she jumped. 'You have the most damnable habit of disappearing,' he said.

'I did not want to interrupt you.'

'Interrupt me in doing what?'

'Thinking.'

'Thinking?' The edge of his mouth lifted. 'I can do that any time. Shall we go?'

'Yes, we should. In fact, we should leave now.' She realised her teeth were chattering.

'Why didn't you tell me you were cold? I can give you my coat.' He started to shrug out of the garment.

'It is not that. I…I don't like it here. I wish to go back. The way we came.'

'And get lost again?' He looked at her more closely. 'You are frightened. Do not worry, I won't let anything happen to you.' He removed his coat and draped it over her shoulders. 'Come, we'd best leave before you start to imagine ghosts or other such unnatural beings.'

She managed a smile. 'I suppose I have been reading too many of Mariana's novels lately. There always seems to be some sort of spectre or headless monk.' Coupled with Barbarina's odd predictions, it was no wonder she was imagining things.

A smile tugged at his mouth. 'You should find different literature in the future. Come.'

They passed through the arch and entered the straight, dark walk that led to the artificial lake on the other side of the maze. The yews were tall and forbidding and, despite her attempts to reassure herself she had only imagined hearing footsteps earlier, she found she was increasing her pace. Severin glanced down at her once, but said nothing.

She nearly collapsed with relief when the walk opened on to a small grassy lawn with the lake beyond. A number of people strolled near the water and she even saw a few daring souls had taken out the rowboats. The normality of the scene filled her with the same relief she felt after waking up from a disturbing dream.

'You really were frightened. Why?'

She looked up at him and found his gaze fixed on her face. 'I…I had the oddest sense that someone was watching us. I was being ridiculous, of course.'

'Perhaps.' His eyes were still on her.

'I suppose we should go and find Mariana and Simon.'

'We should.' He took a step towards her. 'But first there is something else I want to do.'

'What?'

'This.' He took another step towards her. His hands slipped under his coat and caught her shoulders and slowly drew her towards him. Mesmerised, she made no protest as his lips descended on hers in a surprisingly gentle kiss.

Perhaps her nerves were still on edge, but a faint movement caught her attention just as her eyes started to drift shut. The prickle of danger she'd felt in the maze struck her with renewed force. She pulled away from him and jerked her eyes open in time to see a shadowy figure drifting towards them, the glint of metal in the raised hand exactly like one of Mariana's gothic spectres. The cry broke from her throat just as the hand plunged towards Severin's back.

He half-turned and the stiletto caught his arm. 'What the hell?' he exclaimed. The assailant fled into the shadowy maze.

He stared at Cecily, his hand going to his arm for a moment. He pulled it away and her stomach lurched when she saw the blood on his hand. 'You are hurt,' she said stupidly.

'A mere scratch. Are you all right?' he asked quickly.

'Yes.'

'Stay here. I am going after him.'

She caught his other arm. 'No, you are not. Unless you want to bleed to death in Signor Palermo's maze.'

His eyes glinted down at her. 'That is unlikely.' And then he swayed.

She managed to steady him. 'Sit down. Please.'

He did not argue. He sat down on the grass, still holding his arm. She dropped his coat from her shoulders and knelt beside him. 'Let me see your arm.'

'It is fine.'

'It is not.' She gently removed his hand and suppressed a shiver when she saw the jagged slash. 'I think it will need to be stitched. First we must stop the bleeding.'

'Use my cravat.' His voice was thick.

'Good God! What has happened?'

Cecily looked up and with some astonishment saw two men and a woman standing over them. She had nearly forgotten they were at a fête. 'He has been stabbed. I must stop the bleeding and he needs a doctor.'

'Of course.' One of the men began to shout and the other dropped down beside Cecily. 'Allow me, *signora*. I have seen such wounds when I was with the army. Your sash, if you please, *signora*. I am Signor Canelli.' He produced a handkerchief and Cecily, with trembling fingers, untied the pale green sash encircling her bodice and handed it to Signor Canelli. He formed the handkerchief into a pad and pressed it to the wound, then began winding the sash about the pad.

'Severin!' Lady Margate's voice broke through the crowd that now surrounded them. 'What has happened?' In a moment, she had dropped to her knees next to Cecily. 'Oh, dear God! Who did this to you?'

'A robber of some sort.' He glanced at Cecily as if challenging her to deny it.

'Dear God!' Lady Margate stared at him, her expression horrified.

Signor Canelli finished his task just as Signor Palermo appeared. He took charge; two burly men were assigned to assist Severin to the house; another man was sent for Signor Palermo's physician. In the midst of all this, Cecily caught sight of Simon leaving the maze, followed by Paolo. She ran to them.

'What has happened?' Simon exclaimed when he saw her face.

'Your cousin…he was stabbed, just as we were coming from the maze.' She caught his hand when she saw his face. 'His arm was injured, but nothing vital. The bleeding has been stopped and Signor Palermo has sent for a physician. He is to be taken to the house.'

'And you? You are not hurt?' he asked quickly.

'No, I am fine.'

He nodded and dashed towards the small crowd around his cousin. Paolo looked shaken. 'He was stabbed? Who would do such a thing?'

'We do not know. Mariana, where is she?'

'With Mama and Teresa. Frederico has gone to look for Signora Zanetti. When we returned to the box, not only had you disappeared, but Signora Zanetti as well. Mama said she and Signora Zanetti had gone to view the fountain and became separated.'

Barbarina was missing? She recalled the black-clad figure and a frightening thought crossed her mind. 'How long has Signora Zanetti been gone?'

'I do not know. Only that she was not there and Mama was worried because both you and Signora Zanetti had not returned. She sent Lord Ballister and me to find you.'

'I see.' No, it was not possible, Barbarina would not have attempted to harm anyone. Despite her odd ways she had never shown any signs of violence. The assailant had been much too tall, or had he?

'Signora Renato? Are you unwell?' Paolo asked.

'No, I am quite well.'

'We should perhaps return to the box.'

She glanced towards the others and saw that Severin now stood supported by the two men. Lady Margate hovered nearby and, as Cecily watched, Simon took her arm as if to comfort her. Cecily turned away, a pang darting through her. 'Yes, we should. We can do nothing more here.'

Barbarina had been found by the time she and Paolo returned. The others were horrified by the news. Even Barbarina looked stricken. Cecily tried to tell herself that surely she would not look so if she had committed such a terrible act.

Later, in her bed, she was not so certain. She went over and over the assault in her mind, but somehow the shadowy figure turned into Barbarina, no matter how hard she tried to think otherwise.

When she finally fell into a restless sleep, however, she did not dream of assailants and daggers, but of being kissed by a tall, dark stranger who bore a disturbing resemblance to the Duke of Severin.

Chapter Five

Nico sat on the edge of his bed and waited for his head to clear. He'd slept a good part of the day away if the light peeping through the curtains was any indication. His arm hurt like the devil, but at least he had only a mild headache from the brandy he had drunk last night to dull the pain while the doctor stitched his arm.

As much as he would like to, he could not afford to lie in bed. His first business was to call on Barbarina Zanetti. For a stomach-wrenching moment last night, he thought the assailant would stab Signora Renato as well. The thought continued to trouble him. What if Cecily Renato had indeed been the intended victim? The attack seemed too much of a coincidence after Barbarina's warning.

He had no idea if she actually possessed some sort of ability to predict the future. Her odd black clothes and strange way of looking at one, combined with her dire pronouncements, had prompted Raf to laughingly call her *una strega*, a witch.

Did she know something? Or had she been the assailant? The person had fled and he could not imagine Barbarina moving that quickly. It was possible her shuffling walk was merely an act.

Why would she want to hurt Cecily? It would make more sense if she tried to hurt him, for she had never wanted Angelina to marry him. But if she intended to stab him, why had she said that Cecily would be in danger?

Or was the attack completely unrelated and the assailant had some other purpose in mind, such as robbery? Or had they been mistaken for someone else?

He did not like it at all. After he spoke with Signora Zanetti, he would see Cecily. For until he found out who was behind the assault, he did not want Cecily Renato anywhere near Avezza.

'Why? Why must I go? They are old and fat and I might as well be locked up!' Mariana clutched the sheet covering her with white-knuckled hands and regarded Cecily, who sat on the edge of her bed, with an accusing, angry stare.

Cecily forced herself to remain calm. She had slept very little last night and was in no mood to argue. 'You must not speak of Vittoria and Serefina in such a disrespectful way. They love you very much and quite look forward to your visit. We will leave tomorrow.'

'It is because of Simon that you wish me to go, is it not?'

'I think it best if you are away from Avezza for a while.'

'Because you do not want me to marry Simon,' Mariana said flatly.

Cecily hesitated. 'It is not possible for you to marry Lord Ballister,' she finally said. 'I am truly sorry.' The stricken look on Mariana's face nearly broke her heart, but she could not allow Mariana to nourish any false hopes.

Mariana bowed her head and said nothing. Cecily rose from the bed. 'We must begin packing today. I hope you will collect yourself enough to decide if you wish to take any books or your sketching implements.'

Mariana lifted a tear-stained face. 'If…if my mama were here, my real mama, I know she would understand! She would not make me go away. She would let me marry Simon.'

A knife tore through Cecily's heart. Never in the seven years Cecily had been her stepmother had Mariana ever said such a thing. She silently closed the door behind her and realised her hands were trembling. Of course, Mariana was hurt and angry and wanted to lash out at Cecily any way she could. Still, her words stung.

And then there was Barbarina. When Cecily questioned her this morning, Barbarina had been no more forthcoming about her disappearance than she had been last night. She had become separated from Signora Carasco in the crowd and then lost her way. Finally Cecily had asked her if she knew anything about Severin's attack.

Barbarina stared at her for so long that Cecily wondered if she had gone into a trance. She finally spoke. 'I wanted to find you because you were with him.'

'Do you know who did this?'

Barbarina shook her head. 'I know nothing else.' She suddenly looked very tired.

Cecily was beginning to wonder if Barbarina was possibly mad. She sometimes suspected Barbarina's dire warnings and predictions were a way of making herself important, but never before had anything much come of them. Certainly nothing like this.

She slowly went downstairs. Her housekeeper met her at the bottom. 'The Duke of Severin is here, *signora*. He is in the salon.'

Severin? Whatever was he doing here? She could not imagine that after the wound she saw last night he would wish to leave his bed, let alone pay a call.

'*Signora?* Do you wish to see him?'

'Yes. Yes, I will.'

The first thing she noticed was his arm in a sling, his coat draped across his shoulders. His white shirt was tucked into his breeches and he wore no cravat.

He noticed her gaze. 'I apologise for my attire.'

She crossed the room. 'You should not even be dressed at all. I cannot imagine what you are doing out of bed.'

'I needed to see you.'

'Surely it could have waited. Or you should have sent for me.'

'No.'

His pallor alarmed her. 'You must sit down.'

'After you, *signora*.'

She took the nearest chair. To her relief he took the

chair across from her. He winced a little as his arm brushed the back. The scowl on his face kept her from expressing any sort of sympathy. 'How are you feeling?'

His eyes flickered over her and, for some idiotic reason, she suddenly recalled last night's dream. Heat crept into her cheeks and she hoped he did not notice.

'Well enough.' His gaze was still on her. 'I came to see Signora Zanetti, but your housekeeper informed me she has gone out.'

'She went to the market. Is there something in particular you wished to see her about? Perhaps I can help you?'

He looked at her for a moment. 'Tell me why you knew someone was in the bushes last night,' he said abruptly.

'I heard something…a rustling. At first I thought it was perhaps the breeze or an animal, but I saw nothing. Then I had the most odd feeling that something was not right. That we were being watched. It was so dark and no one seemed to be around and I knew we needed to leave as soon as possible.'

'That was all? Just a premonition of sorts? You did not see anyone?'

'Not until you were…we were occupied.'

'Apparently you were not so well occupied that you failed to notice a person with a dagger behind us,' he said drily.

She flushed. 'I was still very uneasy, so I could not really think of anything else.'

A glint appeared in his eye. 'Next time I will make certain there is nothing to distract you when I decide to kiss you. Not that I am complaining this time—if you had not been distracted, one of us might have been gravely wounded. Do you have any idea of who it was?'

'No, I thought…' She pulled her gaze away from his mouth and tried to concentrate on the matter at hand rather than on the idea he might kiss her again. 'No.'

He looked at her hard. 'But you do suspect someone? Barbarina Zanetti, perhaps?'

'She was missing last night. Paolo told me that when he and Simon came to find us, but by the time we returned to the box Mariana and Viola had found her. I asked her this morning where she had been, but she would only say that she had gone to look for me because I was with you.' She swallowed. 'Do you think it was Barbarina?'

'I think it unlikely. Regardless of who was behind the attacks, you need to leave Avezza. Go to Padua with your daughter.'

'You will leave Avezza as well, will you not?'

'Not right away. I have business here.'

'What sort of business do you have here once Mariana is gone? You cannot stay here after last night. For if you do, then I will as well.'

'For what purpose? To protect me?'

'If I need to.'

Surprise crossed his face. 'My dear, I am touched, but I am in no need of your protection. If you recall, Signora Zanetti said you would not be safe with me. She proved to be correct. If you had any sense, you would stay as far away from me as possible.'

'But you were the one who was injured, not I.'

He rose, although she could see it was an effort. 'Have you considered that perhaps you were the intended victim?'

She stood as well. Frustration and fear washed over her. 'I cannot imagine why anyone would wish to hurt me. But then I do not know why anyone would wish to hurt you either. Why? What has happened? Barbarina will tell me nothing! Only that you and Raf quarrelled, but I do not even know why!' She realised her voice had risen alarmingly and she made an effort to collect herself. 'I should not shout at you. You are not well... and...' To her horror, her voice broke.

He took a step towards her, the cool arrogance gone. '*Cara*, don't.'

'I think you should...should go.'

'*Maldezione,*' he muttered. The next thing she knew he had pulled her against him. 'Don't,' he said roughly. He released her, but only to tilt her chin towards him. His lips came down on hers and her mouth parted under his as reality and dream merged into one.

He finally released her; for a moment, she had no idea where she was. Her eyes shot open and she stared at him, the blood pounding in her head. He looked equally dazed and then his expression closed. 'As you can see, I pose another danger to you as well. For, if you stay, I have every intention of seducing you.'

Nothing came to her mind for a moment. 'I...I do not think I would be that easy to seduce.'

He laughed, but it held no amusement. 'That very fact would present a challenge I could not possibly resist. I've no doubt I would have you in my bed within a fortnight.'

'I think you are impossibly conceited.'

'Perhaps.' He moved towards her, standing so close his body was a hair's breath away. 'Shall we find out? I would start by kissing you again.'

'If it was like your last kiss, then I doubt I would be in any danger at all. I do not like such…such assaults. Besides, I think you only want to frighten me into doing what you want.'

'Oh, it wouldn't be like that at all. It would be like this.' This time his mouth was gentle and firm, his lips moving over hers in a slow burning caress. His body was pressed into hers, his knee gently parting her legs, then he shifted and she could feel his arousal through her thin skirts. She melted into his embrace, her lips parting beneath his.

It wasn't until he finally lifted his head that cold sanity returned. A great pounding wave of shock and embarrassment washed over her.

'Cecily?'

The use of her first name startled her. She jerked her eyes open. 'I suppose you are quite right. I am so stupid that I would allow a man I scarcely know to seduce me.' She did not look at him.

'You are not stupid,' he said quietly. 'Merely a passionate, desirable woman, which is why you had best leave Avezza.'

'Very well. I will travel to Padua with Mariana,' she said.

'Good.' He looked at her and then hesitated. 'Good-bye, then.'

'Please be careful. I…I should not want anything to happen to you.'

A sardonic smile touched his mouth. 'If you continue to say such things, then I will be sorely tempted to take you here and now. I do not think that would be wise for either of us.' He was gone.

Nico stepped into his carriage and sank back against the cushions. Why the devil had he kissed her? Because she had looked so damned distressed that he'd wanted to comfort her. Once she was in his arms, it had been only natural to kiss her.

She was right—he had intended to scare her for, despite her sweet response to his kiss, he had guessed she would be appalled if he told her he planned to seduce her. He hoped that would be enough to drive her away from Avezza. Until he had a chance to determine what was going on.

There was another reason as well. He could not allow his attraction to Cecily Renato to get any further out of hand. Not if there were the slightest chance that Rafaele Vianoli was in love with her.

Chapter Six

Cecily rose early the following morning. She had slept poorly again and, as she had the night before, spent the night in restless dreams. Most disturbing of all was the dream in which she was trying desperately to save Severin's life from a faceless murderer while she attempted to persuade him to leave Avezza.

She had woken suddenly in the night with the realisation that he had never said he would leave Avezza. What he did was none of her affair. Not even if his kisses did make her long for something she could not have.

During one of her lengthy periods of restless tossing she had convinced herself that he had only meant to scare her into leaving Avezza. She was not the sort of woman that would interest a man such as the arrogant Duke of Severin.

Her head was beginning to hurt again from all the questions to which she had no answers. It was no use lying abed any longer. She threw on her dressing gown and went downstairs. Most of their luggage was piled in the hall. Perhaps if she ate she would feel better. She went into the small breakfast room and forced a few pieces of buttered toast and a cup of steaming chocolate down her throat.

She finally stood. She must wake Mariana for their journey.

Her soft rap on the door brought no response. She pushed the door open. The bedcovers were rumpled. 'Mariana?' She approached the bed and her heart stopped when she saw that it was empty.

'Oh, dear lord,' she whispered. Then she saw the note. She unfolded it with trembling fingers.

I cannot bear being parted from Simon. Do not worry, I will be quite safe. Your loving daughter, Mariana.

Not worry? Her daughter had decided to elope and she was not to worry? Where would they even go? And how was she to find them?

She could think of only one person who could help her.

Nico had just poured himself a second cup of strong coffee when he heard rapid footsteps and an agitated feminine voice. He rose just as Signora Renato burst into the dining room.

Her hair, tied back in a loose knot, trailed down her back. Astonished, he realised she wore a night rail underneath her pelisse. 'She is gone!' she said.

'Who is gone?'

'Mariana! She…she has run away with your cousin!'

He set his cup down and took her arm. 'Sit down.'

'No! I...I cannot. Where is Lord Ballister?'

'Sit.' This time she took the chair. 'Now tell me what has happened. Calmly, if you please.'

She took a deep breath and stared up at him. 'We...we are to leave today. I rose early for I could not sleep and went downstairs to eat—I thought I might feel better—but when I went upstairs to wake Mariana, she was not there. She left this...this note.' She held out a crumpled piece of paper.

He took it and perused the contents. 'Why do you think she eloped with my cousin?'

'Because she said she could not bear to be parted from him. Why else would she write such a thing?' She stood, obviously too agitated to sit. 'Please, you must see if Simon is here. If she did not run away with him, perhaps he has some idea where she has gone!'

'Stay here. I'll find my cousin.' He strode out of the room and saw the housekeeper hovering outside the door. Undoubtedly high drama. 'Is Lord Ballister still abed?' he asked.

'I do not know, milord.'

'Can you find out?'

'*Sì*, milord.' She scurried off.

He returned to the dining room where Cecily was pacing. She turned. 'Is he here?'

'I've sent my housekeeper to find out.' He took her arm. Deep circles surrounded her eyes. 'You need to sit. You did not even take the time to dress properly.'

Colour stained her pale cheeks. 'I needed to see you straight away. I did not want to waste time dressing.'

Hell. She looked as if she had just tumbled out of bed. Her pelisse had parted slightly and he could see the nipple of one rounded breast through the thin fabric of her night rail. His body responded with a lust that was completely inappropriate at the moment. He dropped her arm just as Flavia bustled into the room. 'He is gone. His bed has not been slept in. Oh, milord, do you think it is the same person who attacked you at the gardens?'

'No. I am quite certain Lord Ballister has gone of his own accord. Did he leave a note?' Not that he expected Simon to leave a message on his pillow.

'A note?'

'Allow me to see for myself. Send Enrico to the study. I want to speak with him.' He strode out of the room, only to find Cecily on his heels.

'Wait for me in the dining room. There is coffee and I've no doubt Flavia can make you tea if you'd prefer.'

Her face closed. 'Very well, your Grace.'

Flavia was correct: Simon's bed was untouched. He saw no note, but his cousin did indeed seem to have deliberately disappeared. His small valise was gone and, although most of his clothing remained, his favourite pair of boots was missing and several shirts and waistcoats were flung over the chair as if he'd pulled them out and rejected them.

Enrico waited for him in the salon. He answered Nico's questions in his rather vague way. No, Lord Ballister did not return home last night. No, Lord Ballister said nothing about a journey. Nico dismissed him, but just as Enrico reached the door he turned. 'Ah, but the young lord did wish me to give you this.' He pulled a folded paper from his pocket and held it out to Nico. The paper was now grubby with dirt and sweat. He opened it. The ink had smeared but he was able to make out part of the message.

Gone to V... Tell Signora Renato not to worry. Mariana...

'When did he give this to you?'

Enrico shrugged. 'Last night. He said to give it to you today.'

Nico cursed and returned to the breakfast salon. Cecily stood by the window. She whirled around.

'It appears they are together,' he said.

'Oh, dear lord! How do you know?'

'He also left a note. I cannot read all of it, but he does mention your daughter's name and that you are not to worry.'

'Mariana wrote exactly the same. They must be mad if they think we will not worry!' She looked shaken, but to her credit she made an effort to collect herself. 'If they plan to marry, where would they go?'

'There is an English vicar in Vicenza who, for the right fee, is said to be amenable to conducting marriages under rather clandestine circumstances. It is possible they have gone there. He might refuse to marry them if he thought Mariana was not of age, but if they convince him that Mariana is old enough then he might. At any rate, the legality of the marriage would be in question. Not that it makes a whit of difference if this gets out. Go home, I'll find them.'

'You cannot go. Your arm!'

'My arm is fine.'

'I am going with you.'

'You are not. You've no need to ruin your reputation as well by leaving with me. At any rate, I will go by horseback. There is a shortcut I know.'

'That is quite insane. I am going with you.'

'Then you will need to make your own way,' he said carelessly. 'I doubt if you want to leave in your current dishabille, so by the time you dress and are ready to go, I will be far down the road.' He hoped to God that would discourage her.

She stared at him, her expression a mix of worry and anger. 'Very well, your Grace.' She turned without another word and left.

Cecily stood outside the villa gates for a moment. His words rang in her head. *Then you will need to make your own way.*

Very well. She would dash off a note for Vittoria and Serefina with some excuse why Mariana was suddenly unable to make the journey. Her things and Mariana's were packed, so there would be no worries there. There was Barbarina… Perhaps she could tell her that Mariana was too distraught to say goodbye.

And then, she would do exactly as he told her.

Cecily brushed a strand of hair from her forehead and then glanced up at the darkening sky. She should climb back into her carriage, but she had become restless as she sat in its musty interior waiting for the bridge to be cleared. Shortly before she arrived at the bridge, a horse pulling a loaded wagon had shied. A wheel had caught in the groove where the road and bridge met and the wagon had tipped, spilling cabbages everywhere.

Now her carriage was stuck along with a number of other carts and wagons. There had been a great deal of loud talking and shouting while everyone argued about what should be done and how best to move the wagon. The wheel had broken and someone had gone to fetch a blacksmith. She suspected it would be another hour before the bridge would be passable.

She was so close to Vicenza. Only another few miles. She had briefly considered walking except she would still be faced with the problem of crossing the stream. Now it looked as if it were about to rain. She had no idea if she wanted to cry. Or throw something. What were Simon and Mariana doing? Had they already been married? Or were they turned away and forced to go elsewhere? But where would that be? Had Severin discovered anything?

Her mind kept spinning in circles and this idleness had not helped.

She walked down the grassy slope towards the stream, hoping to see progress of some sort. No one seemed to be doing much; several men were standing in a small cluster and talking with much waving of arms. Her coachman, Figaro, was leaning against the carriage, his eyes closed.

A drop of rain fell on the brim of her bonnet and hit her on the nose. 'Drat!'

'Somehow this does not surprise me.'

She whirled around, her heart thudding. Severin sat astride a large bay horse, a sardonic expression on his face.

She lifted her skirts and climbed towards him. 'Did you find them? Were they in Vicenza?'

'No. There was no sign of them.'

Disappointment coursed through her. She stared at him and then looked away, praying she would not cry. 'I see.'

'She will be safe with Simon.' His voice was surprisingly gentle.

She looked back at him. 'I…I suppose. That is, yes, I…I know.'

Another drop of rain hit her on the nose. He frowned. 'It is too late to return to Avezza. I doubt the bridge will be repaired any time in the next few hours. There is an inn, not far from here. Your coachman will need to turn the carriage around, however. Where is your maid? In the carriage? She had best dismount.'

'I did not bring my maid. She becomes exceedingly carriage-sick.' His expression told her what he thought of that. 'I will speak with Figaro now.'

'I will do so,' Severin said. He urged his horse before she could say a thing.

She eyed the narrow road, really not much more than a lane, with some misgiving and wondered how they could possibly turn the huge lumbering coach around without becoming stuck in the soft dirt next to the road.

She walked around the back of the coach and was astonished to see that Severin had dismounted and was involved in an animated discussion with several of her fellow travellers who were pointing at the coach. One of the young boys ran forward to hold Severin's horse. But when Figaro helped him slide his good arm from his coat, her amazement turned to dismay. Surely he did not intend to help.

At first he gave directions, but when one of the heavy wheels temporarily stuck in the mud, she was alarmed to see him set his good shoulder to the coach. She bit her lip to keep from calling out to him—she doubted he would welcome her concern.

Another quarter of an hour passed before her carriage was finally facing the right direction.

Severin returned to her side. A circle of dirt stained his white shirt and a smear of mud was on his cheek. 'It is safe for you to ride inside now.' He eyed the heavy old coach. 'There are lighter vehicles, you know. Ones that do not look as if they are about to lose a wheel at any moment.'

'Since I rarely use a carriage, I cannot see much sense in purchasing a new one. This suits me very well. It has proved to be very reliable.' She certainly did not intend to spend her small portion on such a thing. She frowned at him. 'Whatever possessed you to help move the carriage? What if you have injured your arm again?'

'I haven't,' he said briefly. 'Get into the carriage. I will ride alongside you to the inn.'

She searched his face, suddenly noticing he looked rather tired. 'Are you not going to stay there? I do not think you should travel any further.'

'I am fine,' he said curtly.

She turned and mounted the carriage before he could notice her flushed cheeks. She did not look at him as he closed the door. She stared out of the window at the sky, which was darkening. She hoped it would not rain on him. But, of course, what did it matter to her? He did not want her concern.

They had gone perhaps a mile, before the wind whipped up and rain spattered on the carriage roof. She saw a flash of lightning towards the distant hills. When the thunder came, she jumped, clutching her reticule. Then the storm began in earnest as hail pelted the roof of the carriage. The vehicle ground to a halt and she saw Figaro had stopped under a clump of trees. The pelting of the hail and rain lessened. In a moment, the door opened and Severin appeared. Water dripped from his hat down his face. 'We must halt until the hail stops.'

'You and Figaro must come inside.'

He shook his head. 'We cannot. We must stay with the horses.'

'Is there anything I can do?' She did not like the idea of remaining inside while they were out in the elements.

'Stay here.'

He closed the door. She cringed at the next crash of thunder. What if they were hit by lightning? Her worries turned to Mariana, who had always been afraid of such storms. Would Simon be able to comfort her? What if they, too, were on some road, seeking shelter from the storm instead of somewhere dry and warm?

She could feel the horses' nervousness for, when they

moved, the carriage rocked. She peered out the window and saw Severin standing with his horse under another clump of trees. He was speaking to the animal, stroking its neck as water dripped down their necks. A lump rose to her throat. Not only because they both looked rather forlorn, but because she had not expected him to show such tenderness.

The thunder rumbled again, but this time further away and the rain suddenly let up as quickly as it had come.

Severin gathered the reins of his horse and led him to the carriage. Cecily opened the door. 'Are you all right?'

'Yes. And you?'

'I was not out in the rain. You must ride the rest of the way inside. Could we not tie your horse to the back of the carriage?'

'I could, but he is limping a little and I don't want to risk further injury. We are not far from the inn. I'll lead him the rest of the way.'

'But what if you catch a chill?'

'You are fussing again,' he said, his expression cool. 'Don't.'

Feeling rebuffed, Cecily sat back against the cushions, as the carriage started forward. He had made it clear he did not welcome her concern, so why she persisted was beyond her.

The sudden rain had left great puddles on the road. The carriage lumbered into the inn yard only a little ahead of Severin. By the time she had dismounted, he had arrived. His horse was indeed limping. She caught up to Figaro and spoke to him in a low voice so Severin would not hear. 'Please see to the Duke's horse. Even if he refuses to allow you, you must do so when he is not present.'

Figaro nodded. *'Sì.* I will not allow him to refuse.'

'Grazie.' To her great relief, Severin handed over the reins without argument. She hesitated for a moment and then decided Severin would most likely favour her with one of his sarcastic remarks if she appeared to be waiting for him.

The inn was old and dark and smelled of dampness and onions. From somewhere down a hall drifted the low murmur of conversation punctuated with laughter. No one appeared behind the heavy wooden counter, so she rang the bell. A man came through the door, wiping his hands on the dirty apron covering his large stomach. 'May I help you, *signora*?'

'I wish to procure a room for the night. No, two rooms.'

'Alas, I have only one, which another gentleman has requested. But since he has not yet paid and you are here, I will allow you to have it. But only if you pay now.' He named a sum that nearly sent her reeling.

Only one? Severin would need it. He could not possibly travel any further. She would think of something. Perhaps there was another inn nearby. 'I will take it.' She started to open her reticule.

'I would at least demand to see the room before handing over such a sum.' Severin spoke from behind her. He turned to the proprietor and spoke to him in rapid Italian. 'I require two rooms for the night. With a private salon. At a reasonable price.' His cool manner brooked no argument.

The proprietor, whose name was Signor Bernelli, now appeared apologetic. His prices were always reasonable; perhaps the *signora* had misunderstood. Certainly there was a second room, although it was small and, since it was over the common rooms, noisy as well, but he would charge next to nothing for it. But a private salon…! After much haggling, Severin managed to procure a private parlour for an exorbitant price. He paid no heed to Cecily's protest that it was not necessary. 'I've no doubt I could purchase the inn several times over if I desired,' he said after they were shown to the small, musty room.

'Sit down. I've requested tea to be brought to you and a fire lit.' He started towards the door.

She remained standing. 'Where are you going?'

'To the stables. I need to see to my horse.'

'I asked Figaro to do that. You must sit.'

'I have been sitting all day.'

'Sitting on a horse is hardly the same thing. Perhaps you do not recall that two nights ago you were badly injured.'

His half-smile was sardonic. 'Oh, I recall it all right.'

'Then I forbid you to go out.'

'You are beginning to sound like my sister.'

'I am beginning to think a sister is exactly what you need.'

'I do not quite envision you in that role. Don't fuss. I don't like it.' He left.

Cecily plopped down into the chair. She felt a great deal of pity for his sister. Reasoning with him was impossible, which perhaps came from him being a duke, though she strongly suspected he would be just as intractable if he were a peasant. Not that it was her affair if he chose to injure himself further except that he would be useless in looking for Mariana and Simon. She would look for them herself.

None the less, she found herself on edge until she heard his footsteps. A rather sullen maid had come in and lit the fire so the room had lost some of its chill. He entered, water dripping from the brim of his hat.

She jumped up. 'Now you are soaked as well!'

'Yes.' He removed his hat and shrugged his good arm out of his coat. 'I forbid you to say any more about my condition.' He draped his coat over a chair in front of the fire and set his hat on the seat. He stood there for a moment and then turned just as the maid returned with a tray.

Severin directed her to place it on the table. This time she smiled in quite a flirtatious fashion, and lingered to inquire if milord needed anything further.

Cecily sat back down in her chair and waited as the girl removed the covers. Severin took the chair across from her. The maid left and the room suddenly seemed too quiet despite the sounds coming from elsewhere in the inn. She glanced over at Severin. His face was drawn and his eyes had a peculiar glassiness about them she had come to associate with a fever. She had no doubt that, if she said anything, he would snap at her. His eyes locked with hers for a moment so she looked away and picked up her fork.

The food was remarkably good and she found she was actually hungry. She had eaten a good quarter of her meal when she glanced up and found Severin watching her, his plate untouched. She put down her fork. 'Are you not going to eat?'

'I am not hungry.'

'You should at least eat a few bites.'

'I prefer not to.'

'Then at least drink some of your wine.'

'You are beginning to sound like my old nanny. Or a wife,' he said deliberately.

If he hoped to quiet her, he succeeded. 'I certainly have no desire for those roles either.' She rose, her appetite suddenly gone. 'I am finished as well. In fact, I am extremely fatigued. If you do not object, I believe I will retire.'

He stood. 'Of course.'

'Are you retiring as well?'

'Yes.'

He looked terrible, but she doubted he would listen if she said anything. 'Goodnight then, your Grace.'

'I will escort you to your chamber.'

'I am certain I can find my way.'

'Not tonight.'

She bit back the sharp retort that sprang to her lips. 'If you wish.'

The room was at the end of a long passage. He waited until she stepped inside. *'Buonanotte, signora.'* He leaned heavily against the doorpost, his breathing laboured. It was then that she noticed the bright red stain on his sling.

'Your arm. It is bleeding.'

He glanced down. 'So it appears. I will bid you—'

'I need to look at your arm.'

'I assure you there is no need.' His face had that haughty duke look that made her want to hit him.

'You look as if you are about to swoon as well. You must come in and let me look at your arm. If you do not do it willingly, then I vow I will force you!'

'I rather think I might like that,' he drawled.

'Stop it! Must you say such idiotic things now? You are bleeding; if you dare tell me to stop fussing over you, I will hit you!'

'I wouldn't dream of it.' He pushed away from the doorpost and then swayed. She caught his good arm. 'Please come with me.'

'If you insist.' He followed her into the room and sprawled down on one of the chairs. 'Now what?'

'I must remove your sling.'

'I can do it.'

'Let me do it.'

He did not protest as she knelt next to him and untied the cloth from his shoulder. He wore no waistcoat under his coat, only a loose linen shirt, and her stomach knotted when she saw how much blood had seeped on to his sleeve. His shirt was soaked with sweat and, from the heat radiating from his body, she feared he was feverish as well.

'You are not about to faint, I trust.'

She looked up and found his eyes on her face. 'Of course not. I am going to remove your shirt.' She reached for the first button, only to find his hand on hers.

'I think not.'

'There is no need for modesty. I was married, you know.'

'The only women who undress me are those I plan to make love to.'

She willed herself to meet his eyes, despite the heat in her cheeks. 'Then you must make an exception this time. I am not planning to completely undress you.'

'A pity—I suspect I would quite enjoy that.'

'I am beginning to think you are delirious.'

'Only with your presence.'

Her cheeks must be as flushed as his by now. She shook off his hand. 'I am going to remove your shirt because I must look at your wound. I pray you will cease teasing me.'

'But I am not teasing you. I told you in Avezza that I would very much like to seduce you.'

She finally looked at him. 'I am about to lose my temper regardless of whether you are hurt or not. So I suggest you allow me to continue before I do something you will not like.'

'Then I had best allow you to have your way with me,' he said softly. His hand fell away.

'Yes.' She undid the remaining two buttons, pleased her fingers did not tremble despite her proximity to him and her tingling awareness. She finally rose. 'Can you raise your good arm? I can then slip the shirt over your head on one side and slip it down your injured arm without your having to raise it.'

'Very well.'

She managed to get his shirt off, although he tensed as she gently pried it from around the wound. Some of the blood had dried and, as gentle as she tried to be, she had no doubt it pulled on his skin. 'I am sorry if I hurt you.'

'On the contrary, you seem remarkably skilled at this sort of thing.'

'I often helped my husband when he was ill.' She brought the candle closer and suppressed a shiver. The wound was an angry red and the flesh around it was swollen. Although much of the blood was dried, she could see fresh blood seeping from one side of the jagged wound. 'How long have you been bleeding like this?'

'I've no idea. Hardly enough to concern yourself over.'

'I think some of the stitches have come loose, but I will have to clean the wound before I can tell.' She rose. 'I will ask Signor Bernelli for clean cloths, brandy and water. And to send for a physician. First you need to get into bed.'

'Then you will need to help me into my clothes. I've no intention of walking the halls half-naked.'

'I meant you must get into this bed.'

'Any other time I would be delighted, but I fear I cannot oblige you tonight.'

She gave him an exasperated look. 'Don't be difficult.' She picked up his shirt. 'I will see if these can be washed. By the time I return I expect to find you in bed.' She did not wait to hear his reply.

She suspected he was attempting to fob her off by his improper remarks, but she had no intention of allowing him to do so. She very much feared he had developed an infection and the thought terrified her.

She found Signor Bernelli in the taproom. She hesitated in the doorway of the crowded room but then the man spotted her and bustled forward. He listened to her, a little frown on his brow, and then his face cleared. 'You are more than fortunate tonight for at this very inn a most distinguished physician is staying. Doctor Pascali is doctor to the most prominent of personages many of them your fellow countrymen. I will inform him that his services are needed at once.'

Cecily was rather alarmed to see Signor Bernelli approaching one of the more boisterous tables and speaking to one of the men. The last thing she wanted was a man in his cups examining Severin. To her relief, the tall man with a pair of intelligent eyes in a thin face that followed Signor Bernelli, appeared sober enough. She was even more reassured after he followed her into the hall and inquired what he could do for her in a pleasant, cultivated voice and questioned the symptoms.

'Allow me to fetch my bag and then I will join you in your chamber immediately. I will have Signor Bernelli send up a basin of water and cloths.'

She returned to the room. Severin sprawled halfway on the bed, his eyes closed. She thought he was sleeping until he opened his eyes. 'I've taken your bed. My apologies, but I don't think I can leave it any time soon.'

'I would not allow it.' She resisted the urge to brush

the dark locks away from his forehead. 'A physician will be here shortly.' Someone rapped on the door. 'In fact, he may be here now.'

'You constantly surprise me,' he murmured.

Cecily opened the door and found Dr Pascali, accompanied by one of the innkeeper's pink-cheeked daughters carrying a basin of water and some cloths.

Cecily stayed back while Dr Pascali examined Severin. He finally straightened. 'Your wound has developed a slight infection and the *signora* is quite correct in suspecting that you have torn several of the stitches. We must clean your wound and put in new stitches. And then you are not to move until your fever has gone unless you wish serious consequences.' He turned to the girl. 'Kindly fetch some brandy. You, Signora Renato, will assist me in cleaning and restitching his wound.'

'Of course.'

'I would prefer she leave the room,' Severin said.'

'I will need an assistant and I have no doubt Signora Renato is quite capable.'

Severin made no more protests. He refused the laudanum, but was finally persuaded to take a small glass of brandy. From his clenched fists and gritted teeth, she could tell he was fighting pain as they cleaned and then closed his wound. By the time the doctor finished, his forehead was dripping with sweat and he was breathing heavily. He fell back against the pillow.

Dr Pascali instructed her to bathe his forehead with water to bring down his fever. She could send for him if his condition worsened. Then he departed, leaving Cecily alone with Severin.

She dipped the cloth in the basin of water and wrung as much of the excess from it as possible. She turned to the bed and, as she leaned over him, he opened his eyes. 'My apologies, *cara*.' Then he promptly closed his eyes again.

Cecily finally collapsed into the chair next to the bed. Severin had fallen into a fitful sleep, the strong features of his face unexpectedly vulnerable. She realised with shock that she had not even thought of Mariana and Simon.

Chapter Seven

'*Signora, signora.*' The soft, urgent voice jerked Cecily awake. She opened her eyes, disorientated for a moment to find Signora Bernelli, the innkeeper's wife, standing next to her chair. Her mind cleared. She was in the parlour of the inn and she must have fallen asleep while reading.

'*Signora*, the Duke has awakened and asks for you.'

She bolted up. 'Is something wrong?'

'No, no. He wishes to see you.'

'I will be up directly.' She stood and winced. If she continued to sleep in chairs, she would barely be able to move.

She followed Signora Bernelli to Severin's room, the book clutched in her hand. He was sitting up in bed. He wore a loose white shirt, which she suspected belonged to Signor Bernelli since it appeared far too big. A scowl crossed his face when he saw her. 'Where were you?' he demanded.

Any worry she had entertained vanished. 'In the parlour. I suppose you had some reason for summoning me other than ascertaining my whereabouts.'

'I did not know where you were.'

'Did you ask Signora Bernelli?'

His scowl deepened. 'I wanted to see you.'

'Did you need something?'

'What were you doing?'

'Reading, and then I fell asleep. Is there something you wanted?'

His gaze raked over her. 'No. Nothing. I apologise for disturbing you.' Now his voice was stiff.

She bit back a sigh and advanced towards the bed. 'Is your arm giving you much pain?'

'Nothing to signify. Go back to your book.'

Something was obviously amiss. 'What is it you wanted? I thought by going to the parlour I might give you a chance to rest quietly. I did not intend to abandon you.'

'I've no doubt you find sitting with me damnably tedious.'

'Do you wish me to sit with you?' It had never occurred to her he might actually want her company.

'I do not wish to bore you.'

So he did want her company. At least that is what she read into his cryptic conversation. She took the wooden chair next to the bed, vaguely noting that Signora Bernelli had left the room. 'That is quite understandable when one is ill. Marc…my husband complained of the same thing.' Until the end when he was too weak to do much of anything. 'I would read to him or we would play cards or sometimes just converse if he wished to.'

Something flickered in his eyes. 'So I do not suppose you would care to do any of those things with me,' he asked carelessly.

'If you want me to. Which do you wish? I would not recommend having me read to you unless you have a taste for Gothic romances.'

A little smile touched his mouth. 'Ah, yes. I recall you mentioned reading about headless spectres when we were in the maze.'

'It is not my romance, but one left behind by another English traveller. Signora Bernelli loaned the volume to me.'

'But you intend to read it?'

She flushed. 'I did not wish to offend Signora Bernelli by refusing it.'

His eyes held a wicked gleam. 'Of course not. Then you may read it to me. I should not want you to insult the good *signora*.'

She stared at him. 'You wish to hear a romance?'

'I suspect it will be quite entertaining.' He settled more comfortably against the pillows. 'You may begin whenever you wish.'

She eyed him, attempting to determine whether he meant to annoy her or really wished her to read to him. She could tell nothing by his expression. When she did not begin, he raised an expectant brow.

Very well. She would read *The Count of Bleakwood Forest* to him. It would undoubtedly serve him right if

he was completely bored by the end of the first chapter.
She opened the book.

Ten minutes later she glanced over at him. His eyes
were closed, which reminded her of how sleepy she felt
herself. Now that he was asleep she could attempt to
wake herself by walking down to the parlour and back.
She closed the volume.

'What does Amelia do now that her father has gone
mad?'

Cecily jumped. 'I thought you were sleeping!'

'How could I when the fair heroine is about to be
evicted from her picturesque cottage?' he murmured.
His eyes were now open.

'You were actually paying attention?'

'I would not insult you by falling asleep in the middle of such a riveting tale.'

She suspected he was amusing himself. 'I would
hardly be insulted. Do you wish me to continue?'

'A few more pages.'

'Very well.' She reopened the book and began to
read. She stifled a yawn after the first paragraph and
forced herself to go on. Her voice trailed off and she re-
focused her eyes with an effort.

Cecily's voice had grown so soft Nico could scarcely
hear her. Her head was nodding as if she were about to
fall asleep at any moment. He was not faring much better. Her sweet, soothing voice had nearly put him into a
pleasurable sleep and it was all he could do to keep from
fading away himself. He was tired, but she must be

equally so. Forcing her to read to him because he was bored was hardly gentlemanly. 'Signora Renato. Cecily.'

When she did not respond, he realised she had indeed read herself to sleep. Her head drooped to one side. He should have realised how tired she was. She had been up with him most of the night. His gaze roved over her flushed cheeks, her lips slightly parted. His groin tightened. He could almost taste her mouth under his; imagine carrying her half-asleep to the bed. She would lie beneath him, her hair tousled around her face, her eyes opening in sleepy invitation as he bent over her. He would…

He jerked his lustful thoughts back to reality. What the devil was he thinking of? No matter how desirable he found Cecily Renato, he could not afford to involve himself with her. He could not make her his mistress even if he knew she would agree, which he very much doubted. She would be too complicated and not only because of Simon and Mariana.

She turned a little and made a small sound. She must be uncomfortable. He scowled and threw back the covers. He sat on the edge of the bed for a moment, pleased his head did not spin quite so much this time. He stood and looked down at her. He doubted she weighed much. If he was careful, he was unlikely to re-injure his arm. He slipped his good arm under her arms and his injured arm under her legs. Making certain his uninjured arm supported most of her weight, he lifted her from the chair. She murmured something, but did not wake as he gently laid her on the bed. He drew the sheet up over her shoulders and then sat on the bed next to her, annoyed to find he was slightly dizzy from the exertion. He gazed down at her for a moment and he found himself wanting to plant a tender, intimate kiss on her forehead.

He rose abruptly, ignoring his spinning head. He could not afford any tender feelings towards this woman.

Cecily awoke with a start to the sound of rain pounding on the window. She had no idea where she was and could not fathom why she was in a bed, fully clothed. She vaguely remembered reading to Severin and she must have fallen asleep. She sat up abruptly and saw she was in Severin's bed. Her gaze fell on the chair next to the bed and she saw he was sprawled in it, eyes closed, his head lolling against the back.

Her confusion increased. Why was he in the chair and she in the bed? And how long had they both been sleeping? She glimpsed the sky through the window and thought it was still early evening despite the dark sky.

She swung her legs over the side of the bed. Severin did not move. He must be terribly uncomfortable. She had been cramped, but he must be doubly so with his long, muscular frame. It was a wonder he had been able to fall asleep. It occurred to her, then, that he must have carried her to the bed, for she could not remember stirring enough to make her way on her own.

Her cheeks heated just thinking about it. At the same time she wondered what had possessed him to do so in the first place. What if he had opened his wound?

Worried, she slid from the bed so that she could look more closely at him. Thank goodness, she saw no telltale red staining the rough linen of his shirt. She should wake him and insist he return to the bed. He stirred a little. Her gaze fell to his mouth and her knees felt almost weak as she suddenly remembered how his mouth had felt on hers. What would it be like to kiss him again? But this time she would want to tangle her hands in his thick dark hair and then...

She drew away, horrified at the direction of her thoughts. Whatever was she thinking of? She could not possibly be lusting after the Duke of Severin. Respectable women did not do such things. At least she did not do such things. She had enjoyed the intimacy of the marriage bed, as brief as it had been before Marco became ill, but had not thought about such things at all since his death.

He stirred again and she stiffened. He slowly opened his eyes and she jumped. 'You are awake,' he said.

'So...so are you.' She prayed he would not guess the direction of her thoughts.

'Yes.' He raised his head and winced.

'Your neck must be very stiff. I...I have no idea why you are not in bed.'

A faint smile touched his lips. 'Because you were there. I was not certain you would appreciate my joining you.'

'I should not have been there in the first place. I am not the one who is wounded.'

'You needed to sleep. In a bed. I've no intention of allowing you to collapse because you've worn yourself out by nursing me and sleeping in chairs.'

His kindness touched her. 'You should have wakened me.'

'And deny myself the pleasure of holding you in my arms?'

She flushed and decided to ignore his ridiculous comment. 'You might have reopened your wound.'

'But I did not.' He rose. 'This argument is pointless since the deed has already been done. You will be glad to know, however, that Signor Bernelli has informed me that the room next to this one is available for your use.'

'Yes. That will be nice.'

He watched her with his impenetrable expression. 'You do not seem over-enthused at the prospect.'

'Of course I am. As long as you are certain you will not need anything in the night.'

'Any needs I might have are ones I am certain you would not wish to fulfil.'

She managed to keep her voice calm. 'Then I had best move my possessions next door. Are you well enough to come to down for dinner? Or do you wish a tray in your room?'

'A tray in my room.'

'Very well.' She inched towards the door. 'I will inform Signora Bernelli, your Grace.'

She turned, but not before she saw his swift frown.

By the next day, the rain had let up and the sky was blue and cloudless. Cecily ate breakfast and then made her way out to the stables. She was forced to skirt around several large puddles, one of which seemed to be the size of a small pond. She was relieved to see the horses were in good condition, although the fetlock of Severin's bay was still a little swollen. Figaro did not seem very hopeful about the condition of the road, however, and thought it would be another day before they dried enough to make a journey at all possible.

She picked her way back to the inn, disappointed by the news. Now that Severin did not seem to be in imminent danger, she was anxious to resume the search for Mariana. She would not worry that, if she left him, he would have no one to look after him. Not that he seemed to want her anyway. He had avoided her since she had moved to the adjoining room and they had barely spoken, which was just as well—she had made every attempt to avoid him as well. He would not mind if she went on without him.

At least, she hoped he would not.

She wiped her now muddy half-boots on the old rug in the inn's hall and then wandered into the parlour. Whatever was she to do for the day? Her room, although neat, was small and cramped. She could take a short walk, but she would probably ruin her half-boots. Or she could—

'Good morning.'

She gasped when Severin suddenly rose from a chair on the other side of the room. He was dressed in one of Signor Bernelli's loose white shirts, with his injured arm in a sling, and a pair of borrowed breeches that were both too short and too loose. The ill-fitting clothes did nothing to detract from his dangerous masculine appeal and her heart thudded much too hard. 'What are you doing up?'

'Looking for you. I had almost begun to think you had deserted me.'

'Of course not.' At least not for a while. 'Why ever would you think that?'

'I have not seen you since yesterday when you woke up in my bed.'

He did not need to make it sound so…so provocative. 'It was my bed to begin with, might I remind you.'

'You are correct. Your bed, then. I have not seen you since you woke up in your bed.'

'I rather thought you did not wish to be disturbed.'

'It depends on who is disturbing me.'

'I see.' He was going to be difficult again. When was he not? 'Are you certain you should be up?'

'Quite certain. I need to check on the horses.'

'I have already done so. They are in good health, although the swelling on your bay is not completely gone. Figaro does not seem to think the roads are yet passable.'

He looked faintly surprised. 'You have gone to the stables?'

'I wished to see if it was possible to leave today.'

'I trust you intended to discuss these plans with me.' He finally moved into the room.

'Well, yes. I thought, if you were still not very well, that I could perhaps go on to search for Mariana.'

'Sit down.'

She frowned at him and then realised he still appeared rather pale. He would not sit if she did not. She took the chair near the small table and he seated himself in one across from her. 'I doubt if one more day will make much difference,' he said coolly. 'Simon will see that Mariana is safe. It is possible they are already married. If they are not, they will be. He will not ruin her, if that is what worries you.'

'I never thought he meant to ruin her. But they are so young…what can they possibly know about marriage? I know how much you object to a marriage between them and I would not want her to be unhappy because you…his family does not approve. Nor do I want your family to be unhappy because they do not approve of Mariana. One does not marry just a person; one marries their entire family. I could not bear for Mariana or Simon to be miserable because they have married like this.'

'You do not need to worry about how Mariana will be received. I suspect my mother will be more than delighted to have someone in the family who is from her own country. Her family knew Mariana's uncle's family very well.'

She had forgotten that. 'Dear Lord, what will I tell Raf?'

His expression hardened a trifle. 'I will deal with Vianoli.'

She took a deep breath. 'Is it true that you and Raf have quarrelled?' For a moment, she did not think he would answer.

'Yes,' he finally said.

'Will you tell me why? Barbarina will only talk of duels and fights, but will tell me nothing more. Raf has never said anything. I would not ask if it were not for Mariana and Simon.'

'You know nothing about it?'

'No.'

'Very well, I will tell you.' His eyes did not leave her face. 'We quarrelled, if one can call it that, after Angelina, my fiancée, died. He said that, if he ever discovered I had anything to do with her death, he would kill me. I blackened his eye.' His voice was cold, emotionless.

She stared at him, a sick feeling in her stomach. 'Why? Why would he say such a thing? Marco told me her death was an accident.'

He rose. 'She asked to meet me that day. She was agitated, upset when she left the house. Raf also knew that Angelina and I had argued the day before.' His hand gripped the back of the chair in front of him. 'Her death was ruled an accident, but there were bruises on her arm as if someone had grabbed her. The physician said they were a result of her fall.'

Dear God. Beneath his cool recital she sensed his deep anguish. She had felt a sort of general sorrow that Angelina's young life had ended so tragically, but until now had not really experienced the full impact of her death on those around her. She wanted to go to him, put her arms around him as she would Mariana, but he would reject her. Instead she said, 'It is hardly unnatural that you and Angelina argued, for people do. And unless one knew why Angelina was upset, one cannot assume it had to do with you. It does not make any sense at all for Raf to even think of blaming you.'

'Oh, but it does.' His gaze was fixed on her face, his eyes bleak. 'For Angelina had begun to have doubts about our marriage. I fully expected her to end our betrothal that day. Raf knew about her misgivings. There is one more thing, something I did not believe to be true until I saw his face that day. He was my friend; I should have known. Known that Raf, too, was in love with Angelina.'

She stood then and went to him and placed her hand on the sleeve of his coat. 'I am so sorry,' she whispered.

He stared down at her for a moment. 'Don't be.' He pulled away from her. 'I must make my apologies. I am going to the stables and then for a walk. We will leave for my villa tomorrow. It is possible Mariana and Simon are there. If not, we will continue on to Venice. You will stay with my mother until we discover Mariana and Simon's whereabouts.'

She could not manage any sort of reply. He sketched a brief bow and walked away while a little part of her heart seemed to die within her.

Chapter Eight

Nico finished tucking his shirt into the top of his freshly washed breeches and then leaned back against the dresser for a moment, biting back a curse. He was still weaker than he cared to admit, but he was determined they would leave this place today.

As well as apologise to Cecily for walking out on her in such a boorish fashion. He still saw the stricken look on her face when he pulled away from her.

He'd never told anyone why he and Raf had argued. He had never spoken the words he'd carried in his heart and mind: Raf was in love with Angelina. The compassion in Cecily's eyes only increased his guilt and, in some strange sense, made him angry. He wanted neither her kindness nor her pity—he did not want her concern stirring up the feelings he'd long buried.

Which did not excuse his rudeness. They could not afford to be on poor terms, particularly since they were most likely to soon be related—which would pose a new set of damnable complications.

'*Signora*.' Cecily started out of her reverie and looked over at Severin who sat in the opposite corner of the carriage. He had decided to stable his horse at the inn and ride in the carriage with her. He'd said little as they readied for the journey and she had been in no mood to attempt conversation. Not after yesterday. Not when he made it clear he wanted nothing from her.

'Yes, your Grace?'

'I wish to speak to you for a moment.'

'If you wish.'

'I wish to apologise to you for my rudeness yesterday when I walked away from you.' His voice was cool, but the hint of stiffness in his tone told her that the apology did not come easily.

'You do not need to apologise. I quite understand that you were—'

'I do not want your understanding. I am apologising to you, not asking you to justify my behaviour.'

'Very well. I accept your apology.' She knew her voice was equally icy, but she did not want him to guess how much his coldness hurt. She turned her gaze to the window, telling herself it did not matter. His affairs were none of her concern. He was none of her concern. Once they found Simon and Mariana they would part company and she would never need to lay eyes on him again. Except if Mariana and Simon were married, then they would be related by marriage and she would be forced to see him. She would treat him coolly and quite put aside—

'Hell. Cecily.'

'Yes?' she said, her gaze now on a passing vineyard.

'Will you at least look at me?'

She finally turned to him. 'Why?'

'Because I'd at least like to see your face when I offer you another apology.'

'I have no idea why you would wish to do so.' She was being quite childish. In fact, she was behaving very much like Mariana did when she was hurt.

'For—' He stopped. 'For being so damnably difficult.'

'I do not suppose you can help it.'

He stared at her and then laughed shortly. 'You never fail to surprise me. Do you not wish to take me to task over this?'

'I doubt that would change anything. We would probably quarrel and then the rest of the journey would be exceeding uncomfortable.'

'You are undoubtedly right.' His eyes were still on her. 'Do you think we could possibly declare a truce? I'll promise to be less difficult and you...' he paused '...you will promise to converse with me.'

'How can I tell when you are fulfilling your terms?'

'You mean to say I am always difficult?'

'Yes.'

'You are wrong, I can be very agreeable at times.'

'Most likely when you are getting your own way.'

This time his laugh held genuine amusement. 'Of

course. So, if you converse with me, I can demonstrate
how very agreeable I can be.'

Her hurt was fading and she found she was starting
to enjoy herself. 'I imagine the topics must be ones of
your own choosing as well?'

'Yes, although I might be generous and allow you to
choose one.'

'Only one?'

'It depends. Perhaps another if you meet certain terms.'

'What terms?'

'First you must call me Nico.'

'That is hardly proper.'

'But since I have been improper enough to address
you by your given name, it is only fair that you do so in
return. Say it.'

'Nico.'

His gaze fell to her mouth. 'Very nice,' he said softly.

She felt as if she had stumbled into dangerous waters. 'Which topic should we start with?' Her voice was
too bright. Too breathless.

He leaned back against the squabs. 'Tell me how you
came to marry Marco Renato.'

For a moment, she was taken aback. 'I met him when
he came to London to visit a cousin. We were married
shortly after that.'

'That hardly tells me anything.'

'What is it you want to know?'

'Were you in love with him?'

She stared at him and then looked away for a moment. 'Yes, I loved him.' But not at first. No, at first jo-

vial Marco, with his ready laugh and twinkling, intelligent eyes, was only an escape from another marriage she knew would break her heart. She did not know then that her marriage to Marco would break her heart as well.

'And your family? I cannot imagine they were pleased to have you so far away.'

'My parents died when I was fourteen. I had only my grandmother. She was not pleased when I married Marco.' She tried to smile. 'Perhaps we could choose another topic.'

'Why?' he asked quietly. 'Why was your grandmother displeased?'

'Because I was to marry someone else. I…I broke the betrothal and then I met Marco. We were married in Scotland.' She waited for his condemnation, but there was none. 'I fear my past is quite disreputable.'

'Why did you break the betrothal?' His voice was impersonally curious.

'Because the man I was to marry kept a mistress. I know I should not have been shocked and accepted it— it is not at all unusual—but he made no secret of his relationship. Once I saw them together. It was at a ball… I did not mean to see them and they never saw me.' Her cheeks heated and she stared down at her folded hands. 'After that I could not bear the thought of marrying him.' Or having him touch her. She had thought herself in love with Charles Winstead and had treasured the thought that his attentive behaviour and charming manners meant he had begun to care for her. Stumbling upon him locked in an embrace with his mistress shattered her illusions.

'He was a damnable idiot.'

She looked up, taken aback to see the anger in his face. 'He was only doing what most men do, I suppose.' That is what her grandmother had told her.

'You are wrong. Not all men would behave so despicably. Any man who would keep a mistress when betrothed to you is a fool. And wholly undeserving of you.'

She shook her head, not believing his words. 'His mistress was very beautiful and sophisticated. All the things I was not. Sometimes I could scarcely utter a sentence when I was around him. I have no doubt he found me very dull.'

'You are anything but dull. As for the other, you are quite lovely.'

'I really am not. I am very ordinary—'

'Quite lovely, as I have told you before. And very desirable.'

Something in his cool tone told her he was not paying her an idle compliment. She glanced away, feeling oddly vulnerable and a little afraid. Of what, she did not know. He had flirted with her and kissed her and she had not been half as shaken as she was now with him sitting across from her in the close confines of her carriage.

Thank goodness he said nothing more, although conversation would have been difficult for, as they continued on, the road became increasingly uneven and the carriage bumped and jolted along. She hung on to the strap and prayed the carriage would not fall apart.

The carriage suddenly shuddered and jerked to an abrupt, rocking halt.

'What is it?' she asked.

'I don't know. Wait and I'll find out.' He opened the door and stepped out. A moment later he returned. 'The back wheel is loose. We are fortunate Figaro noticed something was amiss and halted before it came completely off.' He held out his hand. 'I will help you down. You should not remain in the carriage much longer.'

'No.' She took his hand and cautiously stepped from the carriage. The road was deserted and nothing but vineyards stretched in either direction. The fresh air was welcome, but the sight of the back wheel was worrisome.

'Can you manage the horses while Figaro and I examine the wheel?' Nico asked.

'Yes.'

He gave her a brief smile. 'Good.'

She went to the horses' heads. They appeared unconcerned about the matter, the bay gelding merely blowing on Cecily's cheek while his companion stretched his neck towards an enticing patch of weeds. She heard Severin and Figaro speaking in rapid Italian, but could not quite make out the words. The late morning sun was warm on her cheeks, the sky a peaceful cerulean blue. She took a deep breath, willing her headache to go away.

Nico returned. 'The wheel is about to come off. The inn is perhaps a mile from here. We can walk while Figaro stays with the carriage or remain here while Figaro goes for help.'

'I would prefer to walk. Will Figaro be safe?'

'I doubt there are any *banditti* about now. I will leave him one of my pistols.' He looked down at her. 'Are you certain you want to walk?'

'I will be fine.' Anything was better than remaining idle along the road.

He did not look completely convinced, but said nothing more.

She waited while he gave Figaro instructions. She was beginning to wonder if they would ever find Mariana and Simon. She could only pray they were safe and trust Nico when he said Simon would not let anything happen to Mariana.

He returned to her side and then set off towards the village. The road ran along a river, which Nico said was the Brenta. A passage-boat passed them, towed by horses and across the river, through the trees, she could see the stucco roof of a villa.

The inn was located just outside the village. A grey cat sunned itself on a bench and opened one lazy eye as they approached. Inside, the stone hall was cool. Sounds of conversation and laughter came from one of the rooms. Nico turned to her. 'Sit down while I find the proprietor. I will procure rooms as I've no idea how long it will take to have the wheel repaired.'

Cecily took one of the benches just as a short, stocky man entered the hall. He came forward. '*Signor, signora.* I am Benvenuto Salvidori. How might I assist you?'

Nico told him, but when he requested two rooms the proprietor frowned. 'Two?' A slight frown crossed the man's face. 'I fear we only have one. There is a party of the English staying here a number of days. Perhaps as husband and wife you would not object to sharing a room. It is quite large and I am certain your lady would be most comfortable.'

Husband and wife? Her startled gaze flew to Nico's face. Wholly expecting him to deny it, she nearly fell off the bench when he said, 'Very well, we will take the room.'

The proprietor beamed. 'Good. Good. The room is prepared, so if the *signor* wishes to discuss the arrangements, my wife will be delighted to show the *signora* to the room.' He turned towards the door. 'Sophia!' he boomed out.

Almost instantly, a well-endowed woman who stood several inches taller than her husband burst through the door. He spoke to her in rapid Italian and she turned to Cecily. 'Of course, you must go immediately to the room and rest while the *signor* sees to the carriage.'

Cecily rose and cast an uncertain glance at Nico, but Signora Salvidori was already walking away. Cecily had no choice but to follow her.

The room was indeed large, much larger than those at the previous inn. Sunlight flooded the room with cheerful warmth. The bed was high and old.

Signora Salvidori was speaking. 'You did not bring your maid? Then I will send my Portia to you. And then you will sleep. You must remove your pelisse and boots and I will find Portia.'

Signora Salvidori bustled away before Cecily could tell her she really did not need to rest. She unbuttoned her pelisse and removed it and then sat on a chair to remove her half-boots. She rose. The bed really did look quite inviting. Perhaps she could lie down for a very short time. A plump girl who must be about Mariana's age entered the room. 'Mama wishes me to assist you,' she announced.

She did not really look much like Mariana, but Cecily felt a tug at her heart and a surge of longing for her daughter. She smiled. '*Grazie*, but I do not intend to rest for very long. I can sleep in my gown.'

The girl's face fell and Cecily relented. 'Very well. Just my gown, then.'

Portia helped her from her muslin gown and her stays with surprising alacrity. Cecily thanked her and, as soon as Portia departed, climbed into the bed. She closed her eyes, images of the carriage and Severin's face swimming before her eyes as he told her she was lovely. And desirable. Soon the images blurred together and then she faded away.

Cecily opened her eyes and for a moment, had no idea where she was and why she was in bed in the middle of the day. Then she remembered; she had gone to bed intending to take only a short nap. It appeared, however, she had been asleep for a very long time.

She sat up abruptly and nearly gasped when she saw Nico's long frame sprawled in a wing chair near the window. His head lolled against the high back and from his deep even breathing she knew he was asleep.

Heat stained her cheeks when she realised her shift had slipped off one shoulder, exposing far too much flesh. No matter that he was hardly in a state to notice, she still felt self-conscious. How was she to dress if he were still in the room?

She spotted her gown draped over the back of a chair. He seemed to be sleeping soundly; she could quietly retrieve her gown and at least put it on over her shift. She could probably manage to tie the tapes of her gown and, after Nico left the room, summon Portia to help her into her stays.

She threw back the covers and slipped from the bed as silently as possible. Fortunately, the gown was on the opposite side of the bed from Severin. She slipped it on but her attempts to tie the tapes proved futile.

She reached around and found she could not quite close the back 'Drat!'

'What are you doing?'

She gasped and her head jerked up. Horrified, she froze and the gown slid from her shoulder. Cecily tugged it up and crossed her arms over her chest to keep it from falling any more. She forced herself to meet his gaze. 'Putting on my gown.'

'The procedure does not seem to be going well. You appear to need help.' To her mortification, he stood and she backed up as he came towards her.

'I assure you I do not.'

He stopped in front of her. 'But I think you do.' He held out his hand. 'Allow me.'

'I couldn't possibly.' She took another step back.

'I only wish to return the favour.' A slight smile touched his mouth. 'I believe you helped me numerous times with my, er…personal needs over the past few days.'

'You were ill, so there was a difference. This would not be at all proper.'

'We seem to be far beyond the proprieties at this point. Turn around. I merely wish to help you into your gown, not out of it.' His voice was rather impatient.

She had no doubt he would persist. Complying now would save further argument. Besides, his voice was too impatient to imagine he had seduction in mind. She turned.

As soon as she felt his fingers at her back, she knew this was a mistake. A shiver ran down her spine and languidness crept over her as he tied the tapes. When he lifted the hair away from her neck, she thought her knees might crumble. She closed her eyes and willed her body to stay still as he did the tape at the neck of her bodice. She prayed he would step away quickly.

He did not. He stood so close behind her she could almost hear his heart beat. She nearly stopped breathing and then his hand again brushed the hair from the nape of her neck. His arm came about her, pulling her back against his chest. His mouth moved across her nape and a little moan escaped her.

His mouth travelled to her ear and to her shoulder where he pushed down the left sleeve of her gown and rained kisses upon the exposed shoulder. When his hand cupped her breast through the layers of shift and gown, she thought she would explode. Her body was on fire, the warm throbbing growing between her legs and, for the first time since Marco, she felt a pure, hot desire that shocked her.

Panicked, she forced her eyes open, her hand going to the hand that covered her breast. He lifted his head almost right away and released her. He waited a moment before speaking. 'I was wrong. I do want to help you from your gown after all. But not against your will.'

'No.' She forced herself to turn although she could not quite make herself look at him. 'Th…thank you for fastening my gown.'

A surprised laugh escaped him. 'Ah, my sweet Cecily, I have just declared my desire to seduce you and you respond by merely thanking me.'

'I cannot think of what else to say. I imagine you merely wish to…to…' Words trailed off. Last time she had suspected that he meant to scare her from following him; this time, she sensed his purpose was far different.

'Make love to you, take you to my bed, be your lover,' he said bluntly. His eyes were on her face.

'I…' Her knees trembled and she thought her cheeks must be on fire. 'I…I fear I have not been offered *carte blanche* very often. I have no idea what one is supposed to say.'

'No, in most cases.'

'And this time?' The words sprang out of their own accord.

His eyes darkened, but his words were deliberate. 'I think you would be wise to say "no" this time as well.'

'Do you?'

'It would complicate matters damnably.'

'I suppose it might.'

'It would. Believe me, sweetheart.' He moved away from her. 'I will leave you to finish dressing.' He stalked to the door. Once there he turned. 'I had hoped to reach my villa tonight, but it appears the wheel will not be fixed in time so we will put up here. You do not need to worry about tonight's sleeping arrangements. I'll sleep in the stables if necessary.'

Cecily sank down on the chair, with the sensation of having been run over by a team of horses. Had the Duke of Severin really just declared he wanted to be her lover? He was undoubtedly mad, but then so was she.

Or else completely wanton…because the idea did not shock her half as much as it should.

Chapter Nine

Cecily watched as Nico's strong lean fingers curled around his wine glass. She forced her gaze to her nearly untouched plate. It was not the first time during dinner she'd found herself covertly watching him instead of eating. What would he do if she were to tell him she wished to accept his offer—well, not quite an offer, for he only said that was what he wished to do before he then proceeded to discourage her. What would he do if she told him she actually wanted to…to lie with him?

She closed her own eyes, an embarrassing stab of desire shooting through her. No doubt dozens of women had thrown themselves at him. She would be only one of many. He probably desired many women and, due to the unfortunate circumstances of finding themselves together, he had developed some sort of strange attraction to her, which would vanish as soon as they returned to society. Thank goodness, they would reach Venice in another day.

'Are you unwell?'

She jerked her head up and found him staring at her with a slight frown. 'I beg your pardon?'

'Are you not well? Your eyes were shut and you've hardly touched your dinner.'

'I am not very hungry. But I am perfectly well. Just rather tired. In fact, I will go to my room as soon as we finish the meal.'

'I am done.'

'Are you? You have not eaten much either.'

'It appears we share a common affliction, then.' He finished off his wine and rose. 'I will escort you to your room.'

She hesitated to ask him where he planned to spend the night. She doubted from his cool, polite manner he would tell her. She had just reached the door when it opened. She jumped back and found herself face to face with a man who stood on the other side. She saw his face and gasped. 'Raf?'

Rafaele Vianoli looked equally startled. 'Cecily? So it is your carriage. I...' He caught sight of Nico. His mouth fell open. 'Domenico?'

'Good evening, Vianoli.'

Raf stared at him and then back at Cecily, his expression incredulous. 'You are with him?'

'Well, yes.'

Raf's gaze returned to Nico and his eyes narrowed. 'I trust you have a reasonable explanation for your presence.'

'I've no idea whether you'll consider it reasonable or not. Nor do I particularly care.' Nico met Raf's eyes, his own hard. 'At this moment, I am taking Signora Renato to her room. She is tired.'

'She is coming with me.'

'She is under my protection. She stays with me.'

'I must contradict you. She is under my protection.'

'The hell she is.' Nico's hand closed over Cecily's arm. 'Step aside, Vianoli.'

'Release her.'

Horrified, Cecily saw Raf point a small pistol at Nico. 'Raf? What are you doing?'

Raf paid no attention. 'Let her go or I will shoot you.'

Nico dropped her arm. 'Go ahead.'

Furious, Cecily placed herself directly in front of the pistol. 'You will have to shoot me before you shoot him. But if you so much as touch him, I will spend the rest of my life making you pay.'

'Cecily, stay out of this,' Nico said.

Raf stared at her and lowered the pistol. He looked back at Nico, his expression cold. 'So you have seduced her. Why? Revenge? Because of Angelina?'

'You bastard,' Nico said softly. 'Put down the pistol. I want an equal chance to kill you for insulting Cecily and suggesting I would dishonour her in such a despicable way. I'll send you to hell before I let you near her.'

Raf dumped the pistol on the table near the door. 'You are accusing me of insulting her?'

'Yes, damn you.'

Raf lunged at Nico. They both went down, crashing into the table, sending it and its contents to the floor.

'Stop! Stop!'

They were oblivious to Cecily's shouts as they tumbled over each other like a pair of deadly, snarling dogs. She was terrified Nico's wound would open and equally terrified they would succeed in killing each other. They rolled into an elegant wing chair, Rafaele hitting his head, and then he had his hands around Nico's throat. Then Nico's hands were around his.

'No!' She snatched the pistol from the floor and pointed it at them. 'Stop! Or I will shoot you!'

They paid her no heed. She looked around and her eyes lit upon a vase filled with flowers. She snatched it up and dumped the contents over the nearest man. Raf reared back in shock as water and flowers poured down his neck.

'Maledizione! What are you doing?'

'Stopping you from killing each other.' With a shaking hand, she pointed the pistol at them. 'If either of you moves, I will shoot you.'

Nico had managed to sit and was now slumped against the wall. Water dripped from his head and he was breathing heavily. None the less, a corner of his mouth twitched. 'Do you even know how to use that thing?' he managed to ask.

'I can swear she does not. She refused to allow my cousin to instruct her.' To her astonishment, Raf looked amused. 'You had best give me the pistol before you do shoot one of us.'

'No, for I think you have both gone mad. How dare you accuse him of seducing me? He was ill most of the time!'

'Cecily, I did not mean…' Raf held out his hand. 'You are upset. At least give me the pistol.'

'No!' She backed up and stepped on something soft and slick. Her foot slid and she was falling. She attempted to regain her balance and then was pitching forward on to the floor. A sharp pain shot through the side of her head and for a moment the world spun around her. She closed her eyes.

Someone knelt next to her. 'Cecily. Damn it! Can you hear me?'

Nico. He touched her cheek.

'Swearing at her less might help.' Now Raf was next to her.

She forced her eyes open and attempted to roll to her side. She could not allow Raf to hurt Nico. 'No. Stop.'

Nico's face hovered over hers, his eyes dark with worry. 'Don't talk, sweetheart.' He slipped one arm under her head and the other under her legs and rose with her in his arms. The movement made her head hurt and she moaned.

'I am taking her to her room. Tell Signor Salvidori to send for a physician. Send Signora Salvidori to her as soon as possible.'

'Yes.' Raf's voice sounded equally grim. 'I will go now.'

'You cannot carry me. Your arm.'

'My arm is fine. Don't argue.' He strode from the room and she could do nothing but close her eyes while he carried her up the stairs and down the passage to the room. Somehow he managed to unlock and open the door and set her gently on the bed. She winced when her head touched the pillow. To her surprise he sat on the bed next to her. 'Where does your head hurt?'

'Only on the right side.'

'Let me see.' Despite his gentle touch, she jumped when his hand brushed over the spot.

'There is a small cut and you will undoubtedly have a nasty lump.' He drew back and she saw the bruise across his cheekbone.

'You are hurt.'

'Not as badly as Vianoli, however.' He took her hand. 'Do not do such a foolish thing again. Give me your word you will never step in front of a pistol again.'

'I did not want him to kill you,' she said softly.

'Cecily,' he said hoarsely. He lifted her hand to his lips.

'Perhaps I should call you out after all.' Raf had entered the room.

Nico jerked back and dropped her hand. 'As you wish.'

Cecily shot up and her head spun for a moment. 'No! I will…will strangle both of you if you even say such a thing again!'

Raf's expression was hard to interpret, perhaps due to his swollen lip. He, too, sported a bruise across one cheekbone. 'I was only teasing, *cara*. I assure you I have no wish to have another vase of flowers thrown at me.'

Nico scowled at him. 'I suggest you do nothing more to distress her. Unless you want a bullet through you.'

'Nico, please.'

He looked back down at her, his expression softening. 'I am sorry. I promise no more fights.' Nico stood just as Signora Salvidori bustled in, carrying a basin of water with several cloths draped over one arm.

She went directly to Cecily. 'Ah, the poor *signora*!

What have you done?' She set the basin on a table and looked at accusingly at Rafaele and Nico. 'Go, I will attend to the *signora*, for she needs a dry gown. Doctor Tartelli will be here soon and after he sees the *signora* I will have him see you.'

Raf glanced at Nico. 'We both need to change and then we will talk.'

'Yes.' Nico's expression had hardened.

'Raf!' Cecily said desperately.

He moved to the side of the bed. 'What is it?'

'Promise me you will not fight him again.'

He observed her for a moment. 'I promise I will not.'

He bent and brushed a kiss across her forehead. When he straightened, she caught a glimpse of Nico's face. His bleak expression made her shiver. He met her eyes and looked away.

Doctor Tartelli came shortly after that. He cleaned and dressed her cut and said it was not very deep, but she must rest for a few days. He closed his bag and announced he would see to the *signori*. He promised Cecily he would examine the Englishman's arm. She could only hope Nico would allow that.

Signora Salvidori had just left the room when she remembered Raf did not know about Mariana and Simon. She sat up, dizziness overtaking her. She would probably faint if she attempted to get out of bed to look for him. She could only pray Raf would not find out until she had a chance to talk to him. For she dreaded to think of what Raf would do when he learned they had run off together.

* * *

Doctor Tartelli finished applying a plaster to the cut on Nico's forehead and straightened. 'There is one more thing. The *signora* asked me to look at a wound on your arm.'

Nico rose from the hard-backed chair. 'It is not necessary.'

'She was quite adamant, *signor*.'

'Then I suggest you allow him to do so,' Raf said. 'Unless you wish to distress Cecily further.'

The slight amusement in Raf's eyes hardly helped Nico's temper. 'There is no need for you to stay.'

'Except to ensure you comply.'

'I will, damn you. Go.'

Raf merely raised a brow. Nico slid his coat off one shoulder and then winced as it brushed against his injury. He nearly cursed when he glanced down and saw the small red stain on the sleeve of his linen shirt.

'We will need to remove your waistcoat and shirt, *signor*.'

The waistcoat came off easily enough, but raising his arm to allow the physician to help ease his shirt over his head made his arm hurt. He sat back down and then scowled when Raf crossed the room to his side and watched in silence while Dr Tartelli examined the wound.

'A stitch has come out, but I do not think it will be necessary to restitch it. The bleeding has stopped and there are no signs of infection. You would do well to restrain yourself from doing battle until the wound is properly healed.' He put his implements away, shut his bag and, after saying he would find someone to help Nico dress, left.

Nico saw Raf staring at his arm, his expression grim. 'When did that happen?'

'At the Villa Guiliani,' Nico said shortly. 'During the local fête. Cecily was with me. The attack occurred just outside the maze. She came very close to taking the knife instead of me.'

Raf's eyes hardened. 'What was she doing with you?'

'We were looking for my cousin and Signorina Renato. We thought they were in the maze together.'

'And were they?'

'Yes.'

'Do you have any idea where they are now?'

Nico eyed him, his eyes narrowing. 'No. Do you?'

'Yes. They are in Venice. At the Ca' Cappelletti.'

'Damn you,' he said shortly. He rose and reached for his shirt. 'Have they wed?'

'Not yet. They will as soon as you and Cecily reach Venice.'

Nico tugged the shirt over his head and winced. 'Contrary to your suspicions, I have not run off with Cecily for nefarious purposes. We hoped to stop them.'

'In Cecily's carriage? I am surprised you made it this far.'

'Her carriage has been the least of our problems.' He eyed Raf. 'What are you doing here?'

'I have just returned from Avezza, looking for you and for Cecily. No one seemed to know where either of you had gone. However, I did not expect to find you together.'

'I have not seduced her.'

'I apologise for that.' Raf hesitated. 'I must apologise to you for other words as well. The ones I spoke thirteen years ago. I know you had nothing to do with Angelina's death.'

Nico looked at the man who had once been his best friend. He had changed; his face was still handsome, despite the bruises, but more chiselled, and there was a hardness that had not been there before. At this moment, Nico had no idea whether he hated him or not.

'Perhaps you will tell me what has led you to this conclusion?' Nico could not keep the bitterness from his voice.

'You loved her.'

'So did you.'

'Yes. I loved her.'

'I did not realise that until after her death. I never intended to take her from you,' Nico said.

'But she was not mine. She loved you. Just as you loved her.' Raf glanced away for a moment. 'I understand if you do not wish to accept my apology. It seems very little in comparison to what we have lost.' He started towards the door, then paused. 'You are much in Cecily's debt. She would not threaten me if she did not believe in you. I promised her I would not hurt you. But if I find out that you have hurt her in any way, I will change my mind.'

'We are in agreement. For I would have no hesitation in calling out any man who even thinks of hurting her. Including you.'

'I believe you would.' Raf left the room, closing the door quietly behind him.

Chapter Ten

Cecily rose from the edge of the bed. She held on to the bedpost for a moment while the room spun and then righted itself. She released it and took a few steps, pleased to find she could walk without swaying.

Through the open shutters she could see the brilliant blue of the sky. Although Signora Salvidori had informed her that the *signori* wished her to remain in bed for the day, Cecily had insisted on dressing. She was not about to stay in bed while there was any possibility that Raf and Nico might kill each other. Particularly after Raf learned of Mariana and Simon.

She left her room and entered the passageway outside her room. The staircase was to her left. She descended it and halted in the hall below. If she recalled, the room where she and Nico had dined was to her right. She skirted around a mound of luggage and started down the short hall. She found the room easily enough and the door was slightly ajar. She peered in and saw

Raf and Nico standing together at the other end of the room. To her great relief, she saw no signs of impending violence.

Nico saw her first. A swift frown crossed his brow. He broke away from Raf and strode towards her. She saw he was wearing a clean shirt and breeches and a coat she did not recognise. He was shaved. 'What the devil are you doing out of bed?' he demanded as he reached her side.

'I needed to speak to Raf.' She looked up into his face, now so familiar that she thought she had memorised every feature. The bruise across his cheekbone was now a dark purple. She resisted the urge to touch his face. 'Are you all right?'

'Yes,' he said shortly.

'You should be in bed as well.'

'Cecily.' His voice held a warning.

'I know. You don't like me to fuss and I remind you of your old nanny.'

A reluctant grin tugged at his lips. 'I apologise for that. You are nothing like my old nanny.' The look in his eyes suddenly made her feel shy.

She looked quickly away, only to find Raf's interested gaze upon them. For some reason, she felt even more flustered. To cover it, she said quickly, 'Raf, I must talk to you. I do not know what Ni…Severin has told you but—'

'What he did not tell me I have guessed. Nico is right, however. You should not be up.'

'But I am, so it is no use telling me I should go back to bed.'

Raf glanced at Nico over her head. 'Then come and sit down. We have things to discuss.'

She took the sofa he indicated and looked up at him. His lip was still swollen and he wore a dressing over the cut across his brow. 'You look horrid,' she said. 'In fact, both of you do.'

His smile was lopsided. 'I hope you will remember that when you hear what we have to tell you.' He glanced at Nico, who now stood next to him.

'What is it?' A knot started to form in her stomach.

Nico spoke. 'Mariana and Simon are in Venice with my mother and sister.'

'Thank God!' Relief washed over her. 'Thank you. Oh, thank you.' Her daughter was safe. Then a thought struck her. She glanced from one to the other. 'Did you know that last night?'

'Yes.' Raf spoke this time. 'I told Nico after you were in your room. I was on my way back from Avezza and saw your carriage in the road, which is how I found you here.'

She stared at him. 'And you said nothing about it last night?'

He spread out his hands. 'I apologise. I fear that seeing you with Nico drove all other thoughts from my mind.'

'If you saw them, you must know that they ran away together! And that I would be frantic with worry! Instead you must fight after hurling the most stupid accusations at him! Could you not have guessed that we were travelling together because of them? I should strangle you! Both of you, actually!' she added when she saw the faint amusement in Nico's face. 'You knew last night as well!'

The amusement fled. 'By the time I knew, you were in bed.'

'You should have wakened me. But it does not matter now.' She took a deep breath, almost dreading the answer to her next question 'Did they…they marry?'

'They started out intending to do so, but changed their minds. By then it was too late to turn back to Avezza,' Raf said. 'They spent the night at an inn and the next day travelled to Venice. Lord Ballister brought her to the Ca' Cappelletti. The Duchess knew I was in Venice and sent for me. Lord Ballister assured us his behaviour towards Mariana was honourable. I have no reason to doubt his word.'

'Is it possible, then, that they may not need to marry?'

'No, it is not possible,' Raf said gently. 'They spent the night at an inn without a proper chaperon. We could not insist they marry until you and Severin gave your consent.'

She looked at Nico, her heart sinking. He met her gaze. 'I have given my consent. We only need yours.'

She stared down at her lap and felt as if her heart was breaking. The reality she had tried to push away broke over her. Mariana would be gone, starting a new life in a faraway place where Cecily would never be welcomed. Her daughter's lovely face swam before her eyes and she already felt the pangs of missing her.

'Cecily?' Raf asked.

She looked up. 'Of course you have my consent.' She rose, her head spinning from the sudden movement. She waited until the world righted itself. 'I must beg your pardon. I believe I will take a walk.' She brushed past them before they could see how devastated she felt.

'Cecily. Wait,' Nico said.

'No.'

'Cecily. At least return to your room.' Raf had followed her across the room.

She shook her head and left them both staring after her.

'Are you going to let her walk away like that?' Nico demanded. 'She's hardly well—she looked as if she was about to swoon a moment ago.'

'I have found that it is impossible to force Cecily to do anything she does not want to do. Or stop her from doing something she has set her mind to. You did not discover that in the time you spent with her?'

Nico scowled. 'I would expect you to exert more control over her. Particularly when it comes to her health.'

Raf's brow raised a fraction. 'What would you suggest? I carry her back to bed and lock her in her room?'

'If necessary, yes.' He wanted to wipe the crooked grin from Raf's face. 'What?'

The grin on Raf's swollen lips only widened. 'I suspect your journey together was most interesting.'

'Hardly,' Nico snapped. 'I was in bed a good part of the time with an infection and she was forced to nurse me.'

'Poor Cecily. I trust you were not too difficult.'

'I was damnably difficult. Are you going to find her or not?'

'I will leave it to you to do so,' Raf said blandly. 'I

do not relish the prospect of informing Cecily I plan to lock her in her room after I carry her into the house.'

'Damn you,' Nico said and stalked out of the room before he broke his promise to Cecily and strangled Raf.

He found her sitting on a bench in the small over-grown garden on one side of the inn. He stopped and watched her for a moment. She sat on a bench in the shade of a tree. In her cream-coloured gown, her head bare and her hands clasped lightly in her lap, she looked like some sort of lovely, vulnerable creature in need of protection. His protection.

She was no longer his concern. Not with Raf here. Only a fool would fail to notice the affection and ten-derness between them, the easy way they spoke to one another. He could imagine that once Mariana was gone, she would turn to Raf for comfort. Raf would—

He jerked his thoughts away, angry with himself for caring about her. Angry that once again he was in dan-ger of wanting a woman already claimed by Raf.

He entered the garden. 'Cecily.'

She looked up at him and sniffed. He wanted to gather her into his arms and kiss away her tears. He frowned at her in an attempt to hide his traitorous thoughts. 'You should not be out here. You are far from well.'

'I am fine.' The little tremble of her lip betrayed her true state. She looked away from him as if she wanted him to leave.

'You are not. You are clearly distressed. Why? Be-cause of Mariana and Simon?'

'I…I will be quite fine. As soon as I have composed

myself I will return to the inn. Please go.' Her face was still averted.

'I meant what I told you before. Mariana will be welcomed into our family. You do not need to worry that she will not be accepted.'

'I…I know.' She half-looked at him now, her lips slightly parted.

'Then what is it? Simon? He will be a good husband and he loves her.' He was finding her soft vulnerable mouth distracting. 'You will miss her,' he finally came up with.

'Y…yes.'

'They will return to Italy probably quite often since Napoleon is gone. You can always come to England. And stay as long as you want.' He would do his best to stay away from her.

He was shocked when her mouth suddenly trembled. 'No, I…I can never return to England.' She stood. 'I…I must go to the house.'

'No.' He stood as well and caught her shoulders. 'Why can you not return to England?'

She held his gaze. 'Because I…I left in disgrace. My grandmother will not speak to me…and….'

'And?'

'There…there was a scandal when I ran away with Marco. I…I cannot let that hurt Mariana or Simon.'

'I will see to it that it will not.'

'You are very kind, but—'

'I am not kind,' he said roughly. 'But I vow I won't let anything or anyone hurt you.'

'You are kind,' she whispered. Her eyes, wide and vulnerable, and her slightly parted lips threatened his control.

'Cecily,' he said hoarsely. He bent his head towards her, but before he could possess her mouth some instinct made him look up. It was as if a fist slammed into his stomach when he saw Raf standing there. He dropped his hands from her shoulders as if he'd been burned. 'I beg your pardon.'

'Why?' Nothing in Raf's demeanour indicated he found anything amiss.

'Because—' He stopped. Confessing he was about to kiss Cecily would only make matters worse. 'We were about to return to the inn.' He sounded like a nodcock.

'Is that it? I hardly think you need beg my pardon for that. Or was it Cecily's pardon you wished to beg?'

'I've no idea.' What the devil was wrong with Raf? He was an idiot if he hadn't noticed anything amiss and damnably casual about Cecily if he had. Last night he'd been ready to kill Nico over Cecily but today he acted as if nothing had happened. 'We need to talk,' he told Raf.

'First you should greet your mother?'

'My mother?'

'The Duchess. She has just now arrived.'

He nearly reeled. 'What is my mother doing here?'

'She was at the Villa Cappelletti. I sent for her.'

'You sent for her?'

'Yes. She is understandably anxious to see you and Cecily.'

'She knows that I am here?' Cecily looked stricken.

Raf's lip twitched. 'I could hardly keep your presence a secret.'

'No, of course you could not.' She managed a wobbly smile, which made Nico want to gather her into his arms and reassure her all would be well.

Raf, damn him, should be doing exactly that. Nico intended to make certain that Raf understand exactly what his responsibilities were regarding Cecily. And that if Raf did not fulfil them, he would answer to Nico.

Chapter Eleven

The petite, dark-haired woman who caught Nico's hands looked nothing like the formidable Duchess of Cecily's imagination. She looked up into her son's face, half-smiling, half-crying. 'I should scold you terribly, only I was so worried when you disappeared and no one knew anything! Then we discovered Signora Renato was also gone, so Rafaele brought me to the villa and I was to wait there until he returned from Avezza. You cannot know how I felt when I received his message telling me that both you and Signora Renato are safe. Except now I see that you and Rafaele have fought and I will scold both of you for that.'

Nico lifted her hand and brushed a kiss over the back. 'We have called a truce, so you do not need to worry. I must apologise as well for not sending a message to you, but I expected to reach Venice long before this.'

'Next time you will do so.' She stepped back and her gaze fell on Cecily, who stood a little behind Nico and next to Raf. 'You are Signora Renato? But no one told me that you are so very young!' She went to Cecily and took her hands. 'Before I say anything, I must reassure you that Mariana is quite well for I know you must be anxious about her.'

'Thank you.' For she had not expected the Duchess to greet her with such generous warmth. 'I do not know how to thank you for caring for her, particularly under the circumstances. You are more than kind.'

'You do not need to thank me. I am only grateful that Simon thought to bring her to Venice and to us.' Her large dark eyes searched Cecily's face. 'Are you well, my dear? Your face is quite pale.'

'I am fine, only a little tired.'

'She is hardly fine,' Nico said. 'She fell and hit her head last night.'

'Then why have you allowed her out of bed?' The Duchess shot a reproving look at her son. She took Cecily's hand. 'You must sit down and after that Domenico and Rafaele will explain to me why they permitted you to hurt yourself in such a way.' Her hand on Cecily's arm, she guided her to the sofa. After Cecily sat, she turned a cool eye on the two men.

Nico glanced at Raf before he spoke. 'Cecily threw the contents of a pitcher over us. She slipped in the puddle.'

The Duchess started. 'And why did you do that, my dear?' she asked Cecily.

'They were fighting and I wanted to stop them. I feared they would kill each other.'

'I have heard it is very effective in stopping a dog-fight. Did they come to their senses after that?'

'Only after Cecily threatened us with a pistol,' Raf interjected. 'She slipped when I attempted to take it from her because she thought I intended to shoot Nico. I consider myself responsible for her fall.'

The Duchess stared at them. 'I consider both of you at fault for behaving in such an ungentlemanly and unseemly manner.' She pressed Cecily's hand. 'I think, my dear, that you have had too many things to worry you in the past few days. For now you must go to your room and rest and after that I will take you back to Ca' Cappelletti so that I can properly look after you for a few days. We will leave for Venice after that. I am certain both Domenico and Rafaele will agree.'

'Of course,' Nico said politely. He did not quite look at her, nor was his manner any more warm when she left with the Duchess to go up to her room.

Cecily sat on the bed after the Duchess left her inn room, too restless to sleep. It was as if Nico had withdrawn from her ever since Raf had come upon them in the garden. For an instant she thought he intended to kiss her, but when Raf appeared he looked stricken as if he'd been caught committing a crime. Perhaps he thought Raf would call him out, but Raf had not seemed to notice anything amiss.

She sensed it was more than that—that it had something to do with her. It was possible that he regretted his earlier words when he had said he would not let anything or anyone hurt her, that he really did not want anything to do with her. Which was for the best, for she feared that he might have the power to hurt her most of all.

They had arrived at the Villa Cappelletti in the late afternoon. The house, situated on the Brenta River, in the midst of a large park, was built in the classical style with wide shallow steps leading to the entrance with its row of columns. The Duchess had insisted that Cecily be shown straight to her room and that for tonight, she would have her dinner on a tray. Cecily had just sent the tray away when the Duchess entered her room. 'I came to see if you would object to a visitor.'

'No, of course not.' She looked up and then fought down a stab of disappointment when she saw Raf. The Duchess quietly left them as he came to her side. He pulled a chair to the bed and sat down. 'We have not had a chance to talk. How are you feeling?'

'Better. And you? Your face still looks horrible.'

He flashed her a crooked grin. 'Thank you.' He took her hand. 'But it is you that I worry about.'

'I am fine.' She hesitated. 'I am sorry about Mariana. I should have guessed that matters were more serious between them. I never thought that she…that they would run away together. I would hardly fault you if you were very angry with me.'

'I am not. Mariana and Lord Ballister both assured me that you did everything you could to stop them. In fact, Mariana seemed to worry I would hold you to blame. However, it is not Mariana's affairs I wish to discuss, but yours.'

'Mine? I have none worth discussing.'

'Not even Nico?'

'Nico? He is not one of my affairs!' She flushed. 'Not that I have any affairs…that is, not those sort of affairs.' Under Raf's interested gaze, her words seemed even more tangled.

'You mean affairs of the heart? But why not? You are still young. Now that Mariana is to be married it is time that you consider your own heart. Marco never intended that you spend the rest of your life alone and without love.'

'I am not without love,' she said, stung. 'I have Mariana and you, and Vittoria and Serefina are very fond of me. I will have Barbarina, so I will hardly be alone.'

'Barbarina is not quite what Marco intended. Or what I meant. I am speaking of a husband or perhaps a lover.'

She flushed. 'I do not want to remarry and I have always thought that a lover would be most inconvenient!'

'Even Nico?'

'Why would you say such a thing?'

'I have seen the way he looks at you,' he said gently. 'If I had not come upon you today, he would have kissed you. Nor would you have objected, I think.'

'We were together on the journey and I…I suppose it was not unnatural for some sort of bond to develop. There is nothing more.'

'Are you certain?'

'Yes, of course.' Even as she spoke, the day at the inn flashed through her mind when Nico had told her he wanted her. Heat flooded her cheeks. 'Please, Raf, I pray you will say no more about this.'

'As you wish.'

'I do wish! Can we not speak of something else?'

'Then we will. I do not wish to distress you, but there is one more thing I must ask. Nico told me you were with him the night he was stabbed. He said the man wore a cloak and mask. Can you tell me anything more?'

'Only that I felt someone was watching us when we were in the maze.'

'But you saw no one?'

'No, no one. I thought perhaps I heard something in the bushes, but I was not certain. It was so dark and quiet.' She hesitated and decided she must tell Raf the whole of it. 'Barbarina had been saying such odd things that I wondered if I was being fanciful.'

'What sort of odd things?'

'Earlier that night, when we were in the supper booth, she told Ni…the Duke that he must stay away from me because I would not be safe with him. But he was the one who was hurt.' The sudden change in his expression alarmed her. 'Raf? What is it? Do you know why she would say such peculiar things?'

The dark look disappeared. 'No, I can think of no reason. I can only think she is becoming increasingly eccentric. I am only sorry she has frightened you.'

'You think, then, that Nico's attack had nothing to do with…with Barbarina?'

He took her hand. 'What I think is that you must not worry.' He released her and stood. 'I will leave you for now. I wish to tell you, however, that I am leaving to-morrow for Vicenza. I will return to Venice in time for Mariana's wedding.'

'Must you go?'

'Yes. It is possible I will have another commission. Do not look so worried. Everything will turn out as it should.' He bent and kissed her cheek. 'Be kind to Nico.' He left.

Be kind to Nico. The words echoed in her head. How could Raf suggest that she consider Nico for a lover? But then, two days ago she had been tempted to tell Nico that was exactly what she wanted.

This was madness. She meant to keep a safe distance between herself and Nico. She could not allow herself to think of him as anything other than Simon's guardian. In time, they would undoubtedly come to regard each other in the polite manner of those distantly related by marriage. Their journey together would fade away like a half-remembered dream.

Nico glanced at the clock. What the devil was Raf doing with Cecily? He'd gone into her bedchamber over a half an hour ago. Visions of Raf leaning forward to kiss her soft, desirable mouth, her sweet shy response, assailed him. Would she be surprised? Did she suspect Raf cared about her?

Did Raf suspect how much he desired her?

'Nico.'

He whirled around. Raf stood behind him. 'How is Cecily?' he asked.

'Better. It is good she will be under your care here.'

'She is under my mother's care.'

'But of course,' Raf said in the bland way that filled Nico with the all-too-familiar desire to mow him down. He did not seem to notice, however. 'I need to talk to you.' All traces of amusement left his face.

'What about?' Nico tensed, half-expecting Raf to tell him that he and Cecily were now betrothed.

'You did not tell me that before you were attacked that night, Barbarina told you that Cecily would not be safe with you.'

'I beg your pardon?'

'Shortly before you were attacked, Cecily said that Barbarina told you Cecily would not be safe with you.'

'She did. As it turned out, she was right.'

'Barbarina said much the same thing to me before Angelina died.'

Nico stared at him, a chill creeping up his spine. 'What exactly did she say?'

'She said that because of you Angelina was in danger.'

'When did she say that?'

'Perhaps a week before Angelina died.'

'Why did you not tell me?'

'Barbarina had always assumed that I would wed Angelina, which was one reason she did not approve of you. I thought she hoped that, if she could convince me that you were a danger to Angelina, I would stop the marriage. Afterwards, I thought that…'

'That perhaps you had been right,' Nico said grimly.

'Yes. But I was wrong.'

'You were wrong about me, but Angelina is still dead. It is possible Cecily was the intended victim, not me. If so, then it seems too much of a coincidence.'

'You are suggesting that Barbarina is responsible?'

'I did not think so at first, but now…' Nico looked away for a moment, and then back at Raf. 'Yes, I am beginning to think it is possible. But why?'

'She has always been rather mad,' Raf said slowly. 'But I have never thought her capable of violence. Until we know, we must consider the possibility that Cecily is in danger. I told Cecily that I am leaving tomorrow for Vicenza. I wished to ask you to watch over Cecily while I am away.'

'I would hope that under the circumstances you would remain here.'

'What circumstances?'

'Cecily is here. She has been injured; she is worried about Mariana, and now this. After yesterday, I would think you would realise that I am the last person you should ask to watch over Cecily.'

'After yesterday, I am convinced you are exactly the right person to keep her safe.'

'Perhaps you failed to notice that I nearly kissed her.'

'It was quite obvious.'

'I came damnably close to seducing her when we were together.'

'I suspected that as well.'

'I would expect that, instead of standing there with that devilish calm expression, you would be threatening to put a bullet through me.'

'And risk Cecily's wrath for the rest of my life? I think not.'

Nico resisted the urge to throttle him. 'Are you or are you not in love with Cecily?' he demanded. 'Because if you are, I've half a mind to put a bullet through you for allowing another man to touch her.'

Raf blinked. 'In love with Cecily?' He looked truly astounded. 'Where did you get that idea?'

'From Thais Margate.'

'Thais Margate? I had heard she was in Venice, but I did not know she had met Cecily.'

'She leased a house in Avezza.'

'Has she? Then perhaps she still hopes to become a duchess, so she would naturally try to dissuade you away from Cecily. She did the same with Angelina, did she not?'

'Last time she was right. Do you love Cecily?'

'I love Cecily, but I regard her as my sister just as she regards me as her brother. So you thought I was in love with her. That explains much.'

Nico's relief only made him surlier. 'Then as her brother I would hope you would tell me to stay away from her. If you recall, I just told you I wanted to seduce her.'

'But you did not.' He regarded Nico thoughtfully. 'I think it is perhaps best that Cecily visits England until we are assured she is safe. You will watch out for her in my place. Although she is at an age where she can decide whether she wishes to remarry or take a lover, I would be most grateful if you would see to it that any man who interests her is acceptable.'

The nonchalant tone of this pronouncement made Nico curl his fists. 'I suppose you will next ask me to interview suitable candidates,' he said through gritted teeth.

Raf's expression was bland. 'If you wish.'

'You know damn well I don't wish,' Nico snapped. 'If you continue on in this vein, I might decide to call you out after all.'

Raf eyed Nico's face, a smile tugging at his lips. 'Precisely why I know Cecily will be quite safe with you. I will retire now, for I wish to leave early tomorrow. I will see you in Venice in a week at Mariana and Simon's wedding. I have no objections if you are tempted to kiss Cecily again.' He was gone before Nico could gather his wits together to form a reply.

Why the devil had he worried about coming between Raf and Cecily when it turned out Raf had done everything but thrust Cecily into his arms?

He would laugh at the irony, only the matter was too serious. Now he no longer had Raf to use as an excuse to prevent him from giving in to his desire for Cecily. To make matters worse, he knew she was not indifferent to him. He could not ask her to become his mistress—she would be too complicated and not only because of Simon and Mariana.

Hell. He was known for his cool control. There was no reason he could not keep his head around Cecily. None at all.

Chapter Twelve

The following evening Cecily stood in front of the looking glass and smoothed down the skirt of her peach gown with nervous fingers. The Duchess had invited a cousin and her family to dinner and in a few minutes Cecily would go downstairs to join them. She had been to many a dinner party so she had no reason to feel so apprehensive. Perhaps it was that ever since she had left her house that fateful morning she'd had the sense of living in a different existence. A dinner party seemed so normal that she feared she would hardly know how to go on. Which was ridiculous, of course, she still remembered the conventions of polite society.

The knock at her door startled her. She opened it. Nico stood on the other side. Her pulse quickened at his appearance. Dressed in a bottle-green coat, and snowy starched cravat, his dark hair trimmed and fashionably arranged, he looked every bit the cool, arrogant English peer. The sort of man she would never dare approach in a London drawing room.

Her cheeks coloured when she saw he was staring at her with similar appraisal. 'I am to escort you to the salon,' he finally said. 'If you are ready.'

'Yes. Yes, I am.' She started to step from the room when she realised she had forgotten her fan. 'I must get my fan first.'

She turned and went to her dressing table and found her fan. She took a deep breath. He was still the polite distant host. Raf had been quite mistaken—it was apparent Nico wanted to keep their relationship on a strictly impersonal basis. She would do the same.

He said nothing as they walked down the stairs to the next floor, the *piano nobile*, and entered the salon. The other guests were already there, a pretty, plump woman in a purple gown, a man with greying hair and a young man and woman.

The Duchess spotted them and broke away from the others. She took Cecily's hand. 'How charming you look! Do you not think, Domenico?'

'Signora Renato always looks charming,' he said.

The Duchess's eyes twinkled. 'But of course.' She took Cecily's arm. 'Come and meet Signor and Signora Parvatti and their younger daughter. Domenico once attempted to frighten Octavia away with a large toad, for she used to follow him and Rafaele about like a small puppy.'

'How gentlemanly,' was all Cecily could come up with. She glanced at Nico.

His mouth twitched. 'I was eleven and thought most females excessively annoying.'

She smiled at him and for a moment they were in perfect accord. The accord vanished as soon as she met Signor and Signora Parvatti and their daughter. Octavia was no longer an annoying young girl but an alluring young woman with great dark eyes and a curvaceous figure and, from the way Nico returned her smile, Cecily suspected he would no longer mind so much if she trailed him around.

Their son, Bernardo, was a handsome young man who proclaimed himself most delighted to make her acquaintance. He then attached himself to her until dinner was announced.

Cecily, seated between Signor Parvatti and Bernardo, was determined she would not glance in Nico's direction. Signor Parvatti was a quiet, polite man whom Cecily liked very much. Bernardo, who must be at least five years her junior, persisted in flirting with her. Despite those distractions, she could not completely ignore that Octavia was flirting with Nico almost as persistently as Bernardo was with her. A few covert glances in his direction revealed he did not seem to object at all.

Well, that should not matter to her. She turned to Bernardo and smiled at his latest ridiculous compliment.

She was glad, however, that the guests did not linger too long into the evening. Her head had begun to hurt and she felt fatigued from the effort to make conversation. As soon as the Parvattis departed, she rose. 'If you do not mind, I should like to retire.'

'But of course. I can see that the evening has tired you.' The Duchess smiled kindly at her. 'We will see you in the morning.'

Cecily turned to Nico, who had stood as well. She forced a smile to her lips. 'Goodnight, your Grace.'

'Goodnight, Signora Renato,' he said coolly.

She looked away before he saw the stab of hurt that shot through her. She walked from the room. Even with the door closed safely behind her, she refused to allow more than a tear or two to fall.

Nico unwound his cravat and tossed it on a chair in his dressing room. Instead of summoning Hobbes, he threw himself down in a chair and stretched his legs out before him. He needed to think.

He had scarcely seen Cecily at all today. He had been busy, that was true, but he had been careful to avoid being alone with her. At dinner he attempted to treat her with the polite civility he would show any guest of his mother's.

Not that she showed any particular inclination to seek his company. In fact, he suspected she wished to avoid him as well. He had told himself a cool relationship with her was for the best. Until tonight, when pure hot jealousy seared him as he watched her respond to Bernardo's blatant flirtation. Not even Octavia's smouldering glances and *double entendres* distracted him.

He realised, as he watched Cecily smile at something Bernardo said, that he did not want to let her go. He did not want Bernardo or any other man flirting with her, much less touching her. In the short time he'd spent with her, he had come to think of her as his.

He could marry her.

He needed a wife. He'd made up his mind that he would choose a wife once he returned to England. None of the possible candidates held any strong appeal. He had not expected love; merely a mutual understanding of the duties of marriage and some measure of affection.

With Cecily he would have much more.

He did not know if he loved her. He had loved Angelina with all of his being and he doubted he would ever care for a woman in that way again. But until Cecily, he had not expected to find a woman he would consider marriage to more than a mere duty.

His attraction to her was far more complex than mere lust, although her very presence made him think of nothing but taking her to his bed. He liked her, even the little things such as the way she walked, the way she tilted her head a little when she was listening, the quick flush that sprang to her cheeks when she was flustered. He needed her in some way he could not quite define.

She was not indifferent to him. He did not know if she was in love with him, but he thought she might be.

He would not allow her to refuse him.

The Duchess added more sugar to her coffee before looking across the table at Cecily. They were at breakfast the following day.

'I am glad we have had this time together before we leave for Venice, for I feel I would not have had a chance to know you so well if we had first met there. I hope that after the wedding you will consider staying with us. I know you and Eleanora will have much in common.'

'I look forward to meeting Lady Eleanora.' She was not quite so certain about staying with them, especially if it meant she would see Nico very often.

'I would also like you to consider returning to England with us. You have not been back for a number of years, I think.'

Cecily nearly dropped the cup of coffee she held. She set it down, spilling a few drops on the white table linen. 'I cannot return to England.'

'Of course you can. You need not worry about how Lady Telford will receive you, for I believe she very much wishes to see you again.'

'You know my grandmother?'

'A little. She and my husband's mother went to school together, so she knows of our connection to Avezza. When she learned we were to travel to Venice, she asked me to inquire after you. She is worried about you and I can see the breach between you distresses her.'

'I refused her invitation last year. I told her I would never return to England. It was not a very kind letter. She never accepted my marriage to Marco, nor Mariana as my stepdaughter, and although she invited me to come to England and to bring Mariana, I was still angry.' She felt ashamed thinking about it. 'I was sorry almost as soon as I sent it off.'

'Perhaps it is time for you to forgive your grandmother,' the Duchess said gently. 'Although she does not suffer from any serious malady, her health is not quite what it should be. One does not want to wait too long to forgive.' Sadness crossed her face. 'I did and it is one of the sorrows I still carry.' She glanced away and then looked back at Cecily. 'So you must promise you will consider returning with us, not only for Mariana, but for yourself and your grandmother.'

Cecily stared down at her coffee cup. She had been away so long, England had taken on an almost dream-like quality. 'I will consider it,' she finally said, looking up at the Duchess.

'I am glad.' The Duchess smiled and then her expression sobered. 'There is one more thing I wish to speak of now. I have not yet thanked you for taking such good care of my son. I have no doubt he would be much more seriously ill if you had not looked after him so well. Not only that, you saved him and Rafaele from much fool-ishness. He told me that it was because of you that he and Rafaele finally reached a truce.'

The sincere gratitude in her eyes made Cecily un-comfortable. 'I did nothing more than anyone else would do.'

'But there is a difference—I think you care for my son, do you not?'

Cecily's startled gaze met that of the Duchess. Hot colour rose to her cheeks. 'I…I cannot imagine why anyone…any woman would not.'

'Not all women see past his title and his appearance. Or into his soul.'

Cecily felt as if her own soul had been stripped

naked. She could only stare at the Duchess, who regarded her with kindly understanding. 'I do not wish to distress you, but I felt I must speak of this. For the first time since Angelina's death, he has lost a little of the hardness. He has a tenderness and a protectiveness towards you that I have not seen for a very long time.' She smiled a little. 'I can see he has tried to hide it, particularly in the past few days, for he has been too polite with you, which has made me wish to scold him. He is always like this, even as a young boy, when he does not wish to reveal his feelings. I hope you will not allow that to send you away from him.'

'I…I fear you are mistaken. We are friends, but there is nothing else between us. We have never…I do not want…' She stopped, stricken.

The Duchess reached across the table and took Cecily's hand. 'He needs you. As I suspect you need him. I only ask that you do not run away from him too quickly.'

'No.' Cecily rose. 'I…I should see to my packing. You are much too kind.' She fled the room, cheeks burning. She went to her bedchamber, where the maid had already started folding her clothes in neat piles. The walls seemed to close in on her and she knew she needed to move, walk, do anything to calm her churning emotions. She grabbed a bonnet from the bed and left the room.

Cecily tugged another weed from the stubborn ground. She had walked down a wooded path before coming upon a small building in the shape of a small temple hidden in the trees. Behind it she could see the roses and lavender and rosemary and her hands had almost itched with the need to clear the weeds around them, freeing them from the vines that entwined them like a sorcerer's spell.

First Raf, and now the Duchess. Why did they both think that she and Nico had some sort of special regard for each other? More puzzling, why were they both encouraging it? They seemed to think that Nico actually needed her, which was ridiculous. If ever a man did not need another person, it was the stubborn, self-sufficient, Duke of Severin. He certainly did not need her if his behaviour for the past two days was any indication. He had confessed to wanting her, but she could only think that had been because of the odd circumstances that had forced them together. In the ordinary world, he never would have noticed her. She would have found him impossibly arrogant.

Cecily pulled out another weed.

'We do have a gardener.'

She gasped and looked up. Nico stood on the path behind her, his expression quizzical.

'Good day, your Grace.' She rose.

'Your Grace? I thought we agreed that you would call me by my given name.'

'Under the circumstances, I do not think that would be wise.'

'What circumstances are those?'

'We are now in society, so it would be most improper for us to address each other with such familiarity. It is best if we keep a certain distance between us.'

He took a step towards her. 'I do not agree. I would prefer that there is no distance between us at all.'

The arrogant Duke had fallen away, but the intense expression in his eyes made her feel vulnerable. 'I had best return to the house. My gloves are quite dirty and I must see to my packing since we are leaving tomorrow.'

He took another step towards her. 'Don't run away.'

His mother had said almost the same thing. She looked up at him and the uncertainty in his face made her pause. 'Why shouldn't I?'

'Because I want you. Need you.'

'Nico?'

He caught her to him. His dark face hovered over hers for an instant before he lowered his head and possessed her mouth in a fierce, seeking kiss. Her knees trembled and she clung to him, returning his kisses, meeting his growing need with her own need.

But when his lips left her mouth and trailed down her neck to the top of her breast, her desire to give dissolved into an even greater need for completion. She arched into him, feeling his hardness through her skirts. She hardly noticed when they sank down on the ground and he was above her, his weight pressing her into the grass and herbs. He lifted his head, his eyes glazed with passion. 'Cecily, *cara…*'

'Don't talk. Please not now.' She threw her arms around his neck, pulling his head towards her. With a groan, his mouth sought hers in brief possession before moving down her neck in a series of fiery, mind-numbing kisses. With one hand he pushed down her bodice and shift and she felt his fingers fumble with the draw-string of her stays. He shoved the confining garment away and briefly caressed her breast before he took the erect nipple into his mouth, licking and teasing the swollen bud. Liquid heat spilled through her and when his hand stroked the silky soft flesh of her thighs, her legs parted of their own accord.

When he finally touched her intimately, she bit her lip to keep from whimpering with need. She pressed down on his hand as he stroked and caressed and when he suddenly withdrew, a little moan of protest escaped her.

'In a moment, *cara*.' He dropped a hard kiss on her lips and rose to his knees, his legs braced on either side of her. She waited, eyes closed, afraid that if she moved the spell would break. The scent of lavender and rosemary enveloped her while she waited. She finally felt his welcome weight on her and then he cupped either side of her face. 'Look at me,' he commanded.

She opened her eyes and found his face hovered over hers. The hint of gentleness mixed in with passion amazed her. 'Do you want this?' he asked roughly. 'Because if you do not…'

'I want this. I want you.' She touched his cheek.

He stiffened and then his eyes darkened. He pushed her skirts up around her knees, his gaze never leaving her face and then his weight pressed into her. He parted her thighs and lowered himself between her legs. Her body arched in response but he paused, his gaze holding hers. Then he kissed her, a kiss that was surprisingly gentle. She moaned, her body aching and swollen with desire, and when she thought she could bear no more, he entered her.

She closed her eyes and clung to him, biting her lip at the slight discomfort and then he was moving inside her and her own body was finding a rhythm to match, her need for release relentlessly growing with every stroke. When it came, she cried out as wave after wave of throbbing pleasure washed over her and an instant later Nico spilled his seed into her, and then collapsed on top of her.

They lay in silence, his heartbeat melding with hers. After a little while, he brushed the hair from her face. '*Cara*, sweetheart,' he murmured.

She opened her eyes. His face hovered over hers, his eyes still heavy with passion, but with something else as well. 'Marry me,' he said.

Her heart nearly stopped. 'Please, please do not say anything more. It is not necessary to offer me marriage because of this. I am not a young girl but a…a widow and I am—'

'I am not giving you a choice. You will marry me.'

'I will not. I…I cannot.'

He rolled off her and sat. 'I suggest we both make ourselves presentable and then we will talk.' He reached over and gently pulled down her tangled skirts. She sat up and averted her eyes as he pulled up his breeches and then fastened them.

'There is a bench we can sit on.'

He now stood and held out his hand to help her up. He led her to a stone bench near the wall. 'Sit,' he said.

'Only if you will.' She did not intend to have him hover over her while he demanded that she marry him.

He complied and pulled her down next to him. 'Why can't you marry me?' His eyes narrowed. 'Is there someone else?'

'That is ridiculous! Of course there is not!'

'Then why? From your response just now, I hardly think you are indifferent to me. Unless I forced you.'

'No! No, you did not force me. I…I am not indifferent to you but I…I do not wish to be married.' She knotted her hands together to keep them from trembling. 'I would not make you a suitable wife.'

'Why not?'

'I would make a deplorable duchess. I am not very organised and have been away from English society for so long that I would have no idea how to go on.'

'You will have my mother to guide you.' His gaze raked her face. 'I am not asking you only because of what happened today. I need a wife. I want to marry you. I made up my mind last night to ask you.'

'But why me?' she blurted out. 'You must have dozens of women falling over themselves to marry you.'

He almost smiled. 'Not quite. However, I am flattered by your perception.' He held her gaze. 'After this, you can have no doubt that I find you desirable—very desirable. But over the time we have spent together, I have come to hold you in higher esteem than any of the dozens of women you seemed to think wish to marry me. Not since Angelina have I been able to envision another woman as my wife. I can envision you.'

'I see.' Coldness crept over her—Marco had said much the same thing. *Since the death of my beloved Caterina, I had not thought I would marry again until I met you.* She forced herself to look at him. 'I am sorry, but I cannot accept your offer.'

'So, despite your passionate acceptance of my love-making, you cannot bring yourself to marry me. Precisely why did you give yourself to me? Out of pity? Another one of the many services you have performed for me?'

The slight sneer in his voice filled her with cold fury and propelled her to her feet. 'You do not need to insult me. Or yourself. If you think that, then you are beyond despicable. I would never lie with a man I did not care about!'

'You are saying you care about me?' He sounded almost stunned.

'Yes, if you must know!'

'Despite that, you do not want to marry me,' he said flatly.

'No, I…I cannot. I do not want to marry again.' She made an awkward gesture. 'I am sorry,' she repeated when he said nothing.

She was taken aback by the fleeting bleakness in his face. 'There is no need to be. You have made it clear enough that you find the thought of marriage to me repugnant.'

'Not repugnant. I…I do not wish to be married. To anyone.'

'I see. However, there is one thing I wish to make

clear. If you find yourself with child because of today, you will marry me. If necessary, I will force you to the altar. Do you understand?'

'A child is most unlikely. I was married to Marco for two years and there…there was no child.'

'You told me he became ill shortly after you married. How often did you lie together as husband and wife after that?'

'That is none of your concern!'

'Just because you did not conceive with Marco does not mean you are immune from such a possibility now.'

She looked away so he would not see he had guessed the truth. After the first few months of marriage, Marco had rarely come to her bed and eventually he did not come at all.

'If you are with child, you will tell me. Do you understand?'

'Quite.' She forced herself to meet his eyes.

'We should return to the house.' He retrieved her straw bonnet and held it out to her.

She took the bonnet and set it on her head, her hands trembling as she tied the ribbons. When she finished and looked up again, he had his coat draped over his arm. 'Ready?' he asked.

'Yes.'

She hardly remembered the walk back to the villa. They walked without touching, neither of them speaking, until they reached the edge of the garden and Nico halted. He looked down at her. 'I am taking you through the side entrance. There is a small staircase you can use to reach your bedchamber without detection.'

'Thank you.' She could imagine nothing more mortifying than to meet the Duchess in her current state.

He led her through the side garden and to a side door. He halted. 'The staircase is just inside,' he said.

'Yes.' She made herself look at him. His face was cool and set. Any words she might say died on her lips. She brushed past him into the hall.

She reached her bedchamber unseen, slipped inside and closed the door. She pulled off her bonnet and sank down in one of the chairs near the window. What had she done? No, she knew exactly what she had done. She had given herself to the Duke of Severin because he said he'd wanted her, needed her and, if she was honest with herself, she had wanted and needed him just as much.

But not so much she would marry him. How could she explain to him that she could not bear another marriage where the ghost of another love hovered between them? Nico might want her, even need her, but he still loved Angelina, just as Marco had loved Caterina. Why, why was it that she was the sort of woman men wished to marry, but did not love? Charles, Marco and now Nico. She feared that Nico, even more than the others, would tear her heart open. She could not, would not, risk that hurt again.

Chapter Thirteen

'Something is troubling you, I think.'

His mother's voice broke into Nico's thoughts. Dinner was over and they were in the salon. Minutes earlier, Cecily had gone up to bed. It had taken all his willpower to keep from running after Cecily and pulling her into his arms, demanding to know why she would not marry him, especially after their love-making. But her cool, strained manner at dinner had made it clear she would not welcome anything he had to say. He'd be damned before he forced his presence upon her again. Once they were in Venice, he would stay as far away from her as possible.

Exhaustion washed over him, a physical and mental tiredness he could not recall experiencing in an age. 'I must beg your pardon as well,' he said to his mother.

She regarded him with her clear intelligent gaze. 'But first, I must talk to you. Please, come and sit with me.' She indicated the place on the sofa that Cecily had vacated.

'If you would not object, I would rather any conversation between us take place tomorrow.' He doubted he could think clearly enough to hold a rational discussion.

'I do not wish to wait until tomorrow, for there will not be enough time before we depart for Venice.'

'Which is something I did wish to tell you before you retire for the night. I have decided to wait a few more days before travelling to Venice.'

'Because of Signora Renato?' Her worried gaze searched his face.

He hesitated, not knowing how to answer her. She placed her hand on his and continued to speak. 'I had hoped that perhaps there was an affection between you, that you would find the happiness with her that I have wished for you for so long. But I can see something is not right between you. Did you say something to distress her?'

He pulled her hand away from hers and rose. 'Apparently. I asked her to marry me. She refused.'

The shocked dismay that crossed her face made him wince. 'Why did she refuse?'

He shrugged. 'She does not wish to remarry.'

'But I am certain she cares about you. And you care about her, do you not? I have seen it in your face when you look at her. Did you tell her that?'

He could not remember for a moment, then recalled that he had told her that he held her in higher esteem than any woman he knew. And that he wanted her. 'She knows.'

Her eyes were still on him. 'Do you love her?'

'I…' He stopped. 'I have no idea. I like her more than any woman of my acquaintance. I admire and respect her. I wish to take care of her, protect her. I find her lovely. But I cannot say that I love her. Whatever that might mean.'

'I see.' She was silent for a moment. 'Perhaps it is for the best that she did not agree to marry you after all.'

He held out his hands, frustrated. 'Why? Why does it matter if I say that I love her? I have not found any other woman since Angelina that I've the least interest in marrying. I have offered to her everything that I have.'

'Not everything.' She rose. 'Angelina still holds your heart. You do not have that to give. Because of that, you have the power to greatly hurt any woman who might care for you. Including Cecily.'

When he said nothing, she pressed a kiss to his hand. 'Goodnight, my love. Think a little about what I have said.'

'Yes,' he said and watched her go.

Cecily tried to tell herself she was relieved that Nico had decided to delay his journey to Venice and, although he said something about estate business, she had no doubt it was because of her. The Duchess said nothing, however, on their carriage journey to Mestre.

Once in Mestre they left the carriage and stepped into the covered gondola, which would take them across the lagoon to Venice. Although the city was but two days' journey from Avezza, Cecily had never visited Venice. She would never forget her first glimpse of the city, with its turrets and domes shining in the sun that appeared to float on the water as if enchanted.

Her awe did not dissipate as they reached the city and entered the Grand Canal. She had seen paintings depicting various scenes, but none of them prepared her for the sheer wonder of gliding through the water past palazzo after palazzo with their exotic arches, graceful columns and elaborate balconies. Or the domed churches whose steps seem to rise up from the water.

The Duchess touched her arm. 'See, there is the Palazzo Cappelletti although we say Ca' Cappelletti for we consider the Doges Palace the only true palace in Venice.' The Duchess had explained as well that both her family's villa as well as their Venetian palazzo bore the family name of Cappelletti.

Cecily did not realise how nervous she was about meeting Mariana and Simon until she saw the façade of the Ca' Cappelletti. Three floors high, it was an imposing building with its row of arched windows separated by columns of white stone. Balconies of the same stone ran the length of the first and second floors above the canal level.

A servant appeared as soon as the gondola reached the stone steps in front of the water gate. He helped the Duchess and then Cecily from the craft. Cecily followed the footman and the Duchess across the patterned stone floor of the long *androne* to a staircase leading to the *piano nobile*. At the end of the *androne*, just before they started up the steps, Cecily caught a glimpse of an open courtyard.

They were shown to a spacious salon, which Cecily barely had time to notice before Mariana flew up from a sofa at one end of the room.

'Mama!' Mariana flung her arms around Cecily's neck. Cecily pulled her close, revelling in the feel of her slender, warm body.

Mariana finally pulled away. 'Oh! You do not know how worried I was about you! When no one knew where you were, only that you had left very suddenly and you were not to be found, I was so terribly frightened!'

'Just as I was frightened when you went away.' She touched Mariana's cheek, wanting to take the sting from her words.

'I am so very sorry. I did not think,' Mariana whispered.

Cecily glanced up and saw Simon had come to stand behind them. His expression was wary as he moved protectively towards Mariana. Cecily drew away from Mariana and held out her hand. They would marry and no purpose would be served by scolding him. She would not forget how her grandmother had looked at Marco with such cold disdain before informing them that they were never to see her again. She would not do the same thing to Mariana. 'Thank you for keeping Mariana safe.'

He took her hand after a moment. 'I would do anything for her,' he said quietly. 'I am only sorry that…'

She met his gaze. 'You do not need to say more. I will welcome you as my son-in-law.'

His eyes met hers. 'Thank you.'

He dropped her hand just as a young woman entered the room. 'Mama? You are here at last?' She was dark and pretty and Cecily had no doubt she was Nico's sister. She eyed Cecily with an almost haughty gaze that quickly turned to astonishment. 'You are Mariana's mama? Why, you cannot be much older than me! I quite expected you to be—' She stopped. 'I beg your pardon. You must think I am insufferably rude.'

'Eleanora!' the Duchess said with a reproving glance at her daughter.

'I do apologise. It was only that I expected you to be quite different.' Her appraising gaze travelled over Cecily and then she smiled and held out her hand. 'Welcome to Venice.'

'Thank you.' Cecily returned her smile. 'And thank you as well for looking after Mariana.'

'We are already quite fond of her.' She released Cecily's hand. 'But where is Nico? Was he not to travel with you?' she asked the Duchess.

'He has decided to stay at the villa for another day or two.' Nothing in the Duchess's voice indicated she found that odd. 'I have no doubt Signora Renato is quite fatigued. She must go to her room and rest.'

'I have given her the room next to Mariana's.' Eleanora smiled quickly at Cecily. 'I thought you would wish to be next to her.'

'Yes, thank you.' Cecily was touched by Eleanora's thoughtfulness.

Eleanora said she would show Cecily to her room and Mariana insisted on accompanying them. The bedchamber was located on the floor above the *piano nobile* and, like the floor below, consisted of a large main saloon flanked by a series of smaller rooms on either side. Cecily was shown to one of these, a pleasant room with an old-fashioned bed in a small alcove. 'I will send my maid in to help you unpack and change,' Eleanora said. 'I will allow you to be private with Mariana. I am certain you have much to discuss.' She left the room.

Cecily found Mariana watching her, her dark eyes filled with concern. 'Is something wrong, Mama?'

'No, nothing is wrong.' She squeezed Mariana's hand. 'How can it be, now that I can see for myself that you are safe?'

'But you looked so sad.'

'It is only that I am rather tired.' She smiled at her daughter. 'I did not sleep well last night. I never do the night before I am to leave on a journey.' She sat down on the bed and patted the spot next to her. 'Come and sit. You must tell me what you have done this week while you have been in Venice.'

Mariana obligingly sat down and after a question or two, chatted quite eagerly about the many interesting things she had seen. As Cecily listened to her, she vowed to put Nico from her mind. Now that she was in Venice and reunited with Mariana she must keep her thoughts on the upcoming wedding. She could not allow her own affairs to interfere with Mariana's happiness.

Two nights later, Mariana entered Cecily's bedchamber and then stopped, her eyes widening when she saw Cecily. 'Mama! I have never seen you in such a gown before! I did not know you could look so...so beautiful!'

Cecily smiled, flushing a little at her daughter's mixed compliment. 'I have not worn such a gown before. And you!' Her heart caught a little at her daughter's appearance. 'Oh, Mariana, you look so pretty. And so grownup.' For, in her blue silk shot with gold, she no longer looked like a child at all but a young lady.

'It is a wonderful gown, is it not?' Mariana twirled in front of the looking glass. 'I am so glad you permitted me to wear a real colour. I do not think I will ever want to wear pale blue or that horrid shade of pink again!'

Cecily could not disagree, for the pastels deemed appropriate for young English ladies, which so well complimented many of their soft delicate complexions, only dulled Mariana's lovely olive skin.

'What necklace will you wear?' Mariana peered into Cecily's jewellery box. 'This one, I think.' She held up a garnet. 'The colours will looked splendid with the colour of your gown.'

She was right, of course. Mariana's instinct for such things was flawless. She helped Cecily fasten the necklace and then led her to the looking glass. 'See how perfect it is! And how beautiful you are!'

Cecily peered at herself. The gown and the necklace might have been made for each other. But as for the other, she hardly recognised herself. Eleanora had insisted on loaning her a gown for tonight—they had been invited to a *conversazione*. It was to be Mariana and Simon's first formal appearance as a betrothed couple. The gown was indeed lovely and certainly cast even her best gown in the shade.

Now that she was about to appear in company, she was beginning to wish she had insisted on wearing one of her own gowns after all. The bodice seemed to reveal too much of her arms and back and far too much soft rounded breast. Her hair was braided in a circle behind her head, a style Eleanora assured her was all the thing. She had no idea if she was as beautiful as Mariana said, for she looked so unlike herself she could not make a judgement at all.

She turned away. 'I certainly look different,' she said doubtfully.

'Beautiful,' Mariana corrected. 'If the Duke was to see you I am certain he would say the same thing,' she added with a teasing smile.

Cecily nearly dropped her fan. 'The Duke? Why would you speak of him?'

'I rather thought he liked you. Even Simon said so.'

'Indeed.' She prayed Mariana would not notice her suddenly flushed cheeks. 'We had best go downstairs. I dare say they are waiting for us.'

By the time they had been in Signora Fiori's elegant crowded salon for three-quarters of an hour, Cecily was certain she and Mariana had met at least half of Venice. Despite her absence of thirteen years, the Duchess seemed to be acquainted with everyone. They even met Mrs Hoppner, the English consul's wife, who greeted both her and Mariana very kindly.

Now Mariana stood with one of Eleanora's cousins, a pretty girl who was Mariana's age. Eleanora had just suggested that they take a turn around the room when someone said Cecily's name. Thais stood there in a pale yellow gown, smiling. 'I could not believe my eyes when I saw you! I thought you were in Padua. And Lady Eleanora! I had no idea that you and Cecily were acquainted.'

'Cecily is staying with us in Venice,' Eleanora said politely. She did not look particularly pleased to see Thais.

Thais looked momentarily surprised. Then she gave a little laugh. 'Indeed. How did that come about? I was quite certain you would be with Mariana in Padua.'

'Mariana is also here,' Cecily said.

'Mariana? Is she also staying with you?' Thais asked Eleanora.

'Yes. Perhaps you have not yet heard, but Signorina Renato and my cousin are betrothed.'

An odd expression crossed Thais' face. 'How delightful!' she finally said. 'Although I am certain it will be difficult for Cecily to have Mariana so far away.'

'We hope Cecily will return to England with us for a visit,' Eleanora said. 'Signora Abruzzi has arrived. You have not yet made her acquaintance, have you, Cecily? Then you must excuse us, Lady Margate.'

'I had hoped to speak to Cecily for a little while before you take her away. You do not mind, do you?'

Eleanora glanced at Cecily. 'No, but you cannot have her for too long.' She gave Thais a little smile before walking off.

Thais watched her for a moment. 'She is pretty enough, but has such odd manners. But I do not wish to speak of Lady Eleanora, but of you. Let us go into one of the smaller rooms. And Mariana, of course. However did you managed to persuade Severin to allow the match? And Rafaele Vianoli? I presume he must have given his approval?'

'Of course. Both families are quite delighted.' Cecily bit back her annoyance at Thais' offhand dismissal of Eleanora.

'I am so pleased, as I am certain you must be.' Thais appeared genuinely pleased. 'So you will return to England? It would be very odd to return after so long, I would think.'

'I have not made up my mind.'

'I quite understand.' She looked over Cecily's shoulder, then placed a hand on her arm. 'Whatever you do, do not smile at the man who is approaching us. He has the most shocking reputation.'

Before Cecily could say anything, a man appeared next to them. He was heavyset and expensively dressed. 'Good evening, Lady Margate. You have decided to end your rustication and once again grace Venice with your charming presence?' He spoke English with an accent Cecily recognised as Austrian.

'For a little while. I will own I did not expect to find you here either. I have heard rumours that you bought a villa on the Brenta.'

'I did. It has been badly neglected, but the restoration is nearly complete and I will soon hold a little party in celebration.' He turned his clear, almost colourless gaze upon Cecily. 'But we are most inconsiderate to talk of these things when I have not yet been introduced to your lovely companion.'

'Then, Signora Renato, you must allow me to present the Baron Eberhart,' Thais said.

Eberhart took Cecily's hand. 'Enchanted, *signora*.' He raised her hand slowly to his lips, his eyes never leaving her face in a way Cecily found disconcerting. 'But you are not Italian?'

'I am English, sir.'

He finally released her hand. 'An English rose,' he murmured.

Thais tapped his arm with her fan. 'I have already warned her of your reputation, so you must not try to flirt with her. She is, as well, related to Rafaele Vianoli by marriage.'

'Indeed.' The Baron looked at Cecily even more closely. 'He is very talented. I had hoped he would be available to oversee the repairs to my villa, but alas he was not.'

'He has been very busy.' His praise of Raf softened her a little towards him. 'I must find my companions so I beg your pardon.'

'You are not with Lady Margate?' the Baron asked. 'For I had hoped to persuade you to stay to talk with me a little longer.'

'I am sorry, but I cannot.' She started to move away, only to find the Baron's hand on her arm.

'I am quite harmless, no matter what Lady Margate has told you,' he said.

She gave him a polite smile. 'I really must go.'

'But I must insist you stay.'

'And I must insist you release Signora Renato.'

Thais gasped and Cecily froze. Nico? The Baron dropped his hand away from her. 'Good evening, Severin. I assure you, I intended only conversation with the *signora*.'

'Against her will?' Nico regarded the Baron with cold eyes.

'I am beginning to think that perhaps I should be insulted.'

'Really, Severin!' Thais said.

Cecily forced herself to smile at Nico. 'I am quite certain the Baron did not intend to detain me, so there is no harm done. Perhaps you would not object to escorting me back to the salon. I wish to find Mariana. Have you yet spoken to her or Lord Ballister?'

'Not yet. My sister sent me to find you almost as soon as I stepped into the salon.'

'Then we most certainly need to go.'

'Yes.' His gaze fell on the other two. '*Buonanotte*, Eberhart. Lady Margate.' He held out his arm to Cecily. 'Signora Renato?'

His brusque cold tone made her heart sink. 'Yes, your Grace.' She placed her hand on his coat sleeve. 'Goodnight, Thais. Goodnight, Baron Eberhart.'

Nico barely gave them time to respond before whisking her from the room to the salon. He did not pause until they were near a table with a large vase of flowers. He stopped, and she pulled her hand from his arm. 'I would like to find Mariana, if you please.'

He scowled down at her. 'Stay away from Eberhart. He's dangerous.'

'Really? He seemed quite congenial.' She did not particularly care for the Baron, but she was even more irritated at Nico.

'He's a rake of the worst sort.'

'Are there better sorts of rakes than others?'

His mouth tightened. 'Yes. Where did you get that gown?'

'I suppose, your Grace, you intend to tell me you dislike it?' She met his gaze, her own defiant.

'I like it too much. Don't wear it in public again.'

'You've no right to dictate what I can or cannot wear.' She wanted to throw something at him. Or cry. Or both. 'If I wish to wear nothing, then I will do that as well!'

'Not unless you are with me, my sweet.'

She stared at him. 'That will never happen,' she said coldly and walked away from him.

Nico stared after her. What the hell had come over him? He'd planned to treat her with cool indifference, not quarrel with her in the middle of a *conversazione*. He'd arrived in Venice a short time ago, and, after changing from his travel clothes, had left for the Fiori palazzo. The first person he found was Eleanora, who wasted no time in informing him that Cecily needed to be rescued from Baron Eberhart.

As soon as he saw her in the damnable dress, beautiful and desirable and obviously not pining away for him, he'd lost all rational thought. Nor did it help that he saw his own feelings reflected in the Baron's gaze. He'd made a fool of himself over the dress because what he really wanted to do was pull her into his arms and kiss her into submission. Until she knew she had no choice but to marry him.

He thought of his mother's words after he said he did not know if he loved Cecily. *Then perhaps it is for the best that she did not agree to marry you after all.* Her words made no sense, for he could not see why it mattered whether he loved her or not. Cecily had not spoken of love at all—surely if she were in love with him, she would have accepted his offer. Perhaps that was why she refused his offer. She did not love him.

Which should make no difference at all to him.

But it did.

Chapter Fourteen

Mariana and Simon were married a week after Nico returned to Venice. The ceremony itself was quiet, with only family present, but the banquet held afterwards at the Ca' Cappelletti was a much more elaborate affair. After the lavish meal, a trio of musicians entertained the guests in the *piano nobile*.

To her surprise, Raf had managed to persuade Barbarina to attend. He had brought her from Avezza two days ago to stay with her cousin, Signora Gamba, although she insisted that Raf was to take her back to Avezza the day after the wedding. Now she was sitting alone on a sofa in an alcove of the salon in her customary black, an odd little figure among the colourful gowns of the other guests. As soon as she could politely do so, Cecily excused herself from the Contessa Alberti, the older sister of the Duchess, and made her way to Barbarina's side. She sat down next to her. 'I wanted to tell you how grateful I am that you are here. And that you have accepted Mariana's marriage to Lord Ballister.' She had been fearful that Barbarina would make some sort of fuss, but she had not.

Barbarina turned and fixed Cecily with her small dark eyes. 'It is done, so what could I do? At least he is not a poor man, so she will not suffer in that way.'

'He loves her and she loves him. Is that not important as well?'

'Only if both love equally, otherwise it is worse than no love at all. You learned that, as I did.'

'Mariana and Simon will be happy.' She would not allow Barbarina to tell her otherwise. 'Would you like something? A lemonade? Or wine?'

'When will you return to Avezza?'

'I do not know. The Duchess has invited me to stay until Simon and Mariana return from their wedding journey. They are going to Lake Garda.' She had not made up her mind to do so. As much as she wanted to be here when Mariana and Simon returned, she did not think she could bear to stay under the same roof as Nico once they were gone. With the preparations for the wedding and the dinners given in honour of the forthcoming nuptials, she and Nico had managed to avoid each other. But with Mariana gone and the strain between them, she could not imagine staying on any longer.

'You have quarrelled with the Duke, no? So why do you wish to remain in Venice? It is foolish to hope he will love you as he did Angelina. It will be just as it was with Marco. You will love him and he will not love you.'

Cecily rose before she said something to Barbarina she would regret. 'Would you like something to drink?'

'A small glass of wine.'

Across the room in the corner she saw Thais with Nico. She managed to find a waiter and procured the wine and started towards Barbarina, careful to avoid Thais and Nico. Thais, however, met her before she could reach Barbarina. 'I have not yet had a chance to speak with you, Cecily. How beautiful and happy Mariana looks! You must be so pleased, but perhaps a little sad as well.'

'Yes, a little.' If she thought of Mariana's going away too much, she would probably burst into tears.

'Then I have the most splendid idea. You must come and stay with me after Mariana and Lord Ballister leave on their wedding journey. You do not need to give me an answer now, but please consider it.'

'You are very kind,' Cecily said, taken aback by the invitation.

'But I am not. I sometimes become quite lonely in my little palazzo, so I would quite enjoy your company. So you would be doing me a great favour.'

'I will consider it, then.' Cecily saw that Barbarina was now staring at them. What if she suddenly decided to join them and say some peculiar thing to Thais? 'I must take this wine to Barbarina now.'

'Most certainly. Poor creature, but she is so fortunate to have you to look after her.'

'What did she want?' Barbarina asked as soon as Cecily returned.

'Nothing in particular. I hope you will like this.' She handed Barbarina the glass.

'She is wicked beneath her smiles and rich clothes. You must not forget that.'

Oh, dear. She hated to think what Barbarina would say if she discovered Thais had invited Cecily to stay with her. Or worse, what she would say if Cecily accepted.

Nico glanced across the salon to where Cecily now stood with Bernardo. It was apparent from the way Bernardo Parvatti hung on to every word that he was besotted. No matter that she was five years his senior. He found himself crossing the room.

'Good evening, Signora Renato. Bernardo.'

The smile faded from Cecily's face. 'Good evening, your Grace.' She spoke as if they were complete strangers, as if they had never been together as lovers. She turned to Bernardo with a charmingly sweet smile. 'I will leave you so that you and your cousin may converse. I hope we will have the opportunity to meet again.'

Bernardo looked as if he'd been offered a fortune. 'I…I would like that, *signora*.'

Nico reined in his temper. 'Actually, I want to talk to Signora Renato.'

'Ah, yes. I beg your pardon.' Bernardo executed a slight bow and then backed away, almost running into an elderly lady behind him.

Nico looked down at her. 'Are you certain it is sporting to give him false hopes?'

'What sort of false hopes would that be, your Grace? If you have come here to scold me about that, then you are wasting your breath, for I intend to walk away from you.' She spoke in a low angry voice and it occurred to him that she possibly hated him.

He felt completely out of control. Then he saw the distress in her eyes. Hell. 'We can go to the library. I promise I will behave as a gentleman. My mother and my sister will have my head if they think I've overset you. Especially today.'

The almost-smile that touched her lips made his heart thud. He wanted to kiss her. 'Will you come with me?'

'Very well.' She made a few polite comments as they left the salon, undoubtedly for the benefit of anyone who might be watching.

The library was shrouded in shadows; the only light provided by the full moon, spilling through the tall arched windows and across the marble floor. 'What is it?' she asked.

What did he want to say to her? His mind was blank; he could only think of how the moonlight shone across her hair and how much he wanted to take her into his arms.

'Your Grace?'

'I wanted to tell you that I plan to accompany Simon and Mariana as far as Mestre. To ensure that their carriage is ready and they are properly prepared for their journey.'

'Thank you. You are most kind. Shall we return to the salon?'

'I wish to apologise for my ungentlemanly behaviour after the *conversazione*.'

'We were both angry.'

'Yes.' He drew in a breath. 'Damn it, Cecily, why did you refuse my offer?'

She looked up at him, her face pale in the moonlight. 'Because you still love Angelina, just as Marco still loved Caterina. Her ghost would always be hovering between us. I have lived with one ghost; I cannot live with another.'

He did not know if he understood. 'I cannot help loving her.'

'I would not expect you to stop. But I would always be in her shadow. You would look at me and I would see that you regret that I am not Angelina. No woman ever will be, you know.' She sounded almost wistful.

'I hardly would expect you to be. For one thing, you look nothing alike.' The words did not come out as light as he had intended.

Her face clouded for a moment. 'No, I do not suppose we do. Everyone said she was beautiful.'

He had insulted her. 'But so are you. In a different way, of course. Is that it? You think I would compare your beauty to Angelina's?'

She moved a little away from him. 'No. Marco did not compare me to Caterina, at least not like that. But he had loved her since childhood. He adored her, worshipped her, and to him she was the embodiment of all that a woman should be.' She turned her clear gaze on him. 'But I was not.'

'He told you that?'

'No, he was too kind. But I could sense it. I could not

be all that Caterina was. I cannot be all that Angelina was either.'

No response sprang to his lips. For the truth of what she said hit him with blinding force—he held all other women up against Angelina and found them wanting. Even Cecily.

She watched him for a moment. 'We had best return to the others,' she finally said.

'There is one more thing.' He did not move. 'Is there any chance you are with child?'

She shook her head. 'No. I…I knew that a few days after our…our encounter.'

'We were fortunate, then.' Instead of relief, he felt a sense of loss.

'Yes, we were.' She did not quite look at him. 'I must return to the salon. We must before someone notices we are gone.'

'Cecily…' he began and then stopped. Nothing he said would be of much use now.

Cecily waited until after Simon, Mariana and Nico left before telling the Duchess she planned to accept Thais' invitation to stay with her. 'Please do not think that I have been unhappy here, for that is not it at all. I—'

'You do not need to say anything more—I quite understand. My son told me that he asked you to marry him, but you did not accept his offer. You worry that it will be awkward for both of you if you stay.' She took Cecily's hand. 'He told me the night before we left for Venice and only because I asked him,' she said gently.

'I am sorry. It is not because—'

'You do not need to explain. I only wished to assure you that you will always be welcome under our roof whether we are in Italy or England.'

'You are much too generous.'

'No, I am only sorry that I will not have you for a daughter-in-law, but you are still part of our family, no?'

She looked at the Duchess's lovely, familiar face. 'I will miss you and Lady Eleanora very much. You have been so kind.'

'And we will miss you.' She leaned forward and kissed Cecily's cheek. 'If you decide that Lady Margate does not suit you, then you will come back to us. You must promise me that.'

'I will.' Cecily was quite certain she would not set foot in this house again.

A week later Cecily sat next to Thais in a carriage that was taking them to Baron Eberhart's villa. The Baron had invited Thais and her as well as a number of others to his newly renovated villa for a few days. Despite the clear blue skies and pleasing scenery, Cecily felt more than a little trepidation about actually staying under the Baron's roof.

During the week she had been with Thais, the Baron seemed always underfoot, escorting them one night to his box at Le Fenice, accompanying them to a dinner given by the Austrian governor another. He had even gone on a shopping trip with them and afterwards had insisted on taking Cecily and Thais to a small café for a light repast. He had always been courteous to Cecily, but she found the speculative way he sometimes looked at her unnerving.

'Georg looks forward to showing you the improvements he has made,' Thais suddenly said. 'You will be most impressed.'

'I am certain it is lovely,' Cecily said politely.

'Dear Cecily, you must guess that Georg is quite taken with you. I hope you like him a little?'

'I hardly know him well enough to form an opinion.' Cecily could think of no polite way to tell Thais she did not really like the Baron despite his impeccable manners and amusing conversation. She certainly did not like the way he persisted in referring to her as a 'delicate English rose' even after she had told him she did not like roses.

'Now you have a perfect opportunity to know him better,' Thais said. 'My dear, he is not so much a rogue that he will force you into anything. A little flirtation will do you good. You are still young and very pretty and, now that Mariana is married, you cannot hide yourself away with Signora Zanetti in that dull little town. Georg may be exactly what you need to take your thoughts from Severin.'

'I have no idea what you mean.'

'It is quite apparent that you have developed a *tendre* for him.' Her large blue eyes rested on Cecily's face.

'You are quite mistaken.'

'I do not think so, for I know the signs.' Her smile was not unsympathetic. 'It is quite natural for you to do so, particularly when he has not exactly been indifferent to you. You are quite the opposite of many of the women he meets, so it is not surprising he finds you rather intriguing.'

'He…he looks upon me as a relation. Which is exactly what I consider him. Nothing more.' Cecily spoke firmly and prayed the colour in her cheeks would not give her away.

'I hope not. He does feel quite protective towards you now that you are related by marriage, for he told me so. It would be easy for one to mistake his protective instincts for a warmer, more personal regard.'

'I quite suppose it would.' Cecily bit back a stab of hurt that he would discuss her with Thais. She glanced out of the window. Through the trees she caught a glimpse of a large square house with a classical portico. 'Is that Barbarigo?' she asked brightly.

'Yes.' Thais touched Cecily's hand. 'I did not mean to overset you, but I do not want you to be hurt as I was.' Her smile had vanished and she looked at Cecily with wide unhappy eyes. 'You see, I too was in love with Severin. I had hoped that we would marry, but he was to marry Angelina instead.'

Nico looked down at the letter the groom had just handed him. 'My lord, the Lady Eleanora says I must tell you that it is a matter most urgent,' the man added with an anxious look, as if he feared Nico intended to lay it aside. 'I am to tell you also that the Duchess is in the best of health.'

'I am relieved to hear that.' He glanced at the man, who still waited. 'I will open it while you go to the stables and see to your horse.'

'Thank you, my lord.' He bowed and backed out of the study.

Nico frowned for a moment, wondering what the devil was of such urgency that Eleanora must send a groom all the way to the Villa Cappelletti. Particularly when he was to return to Venice in the next few days. He broke the seal, quickly perused the contents and then swore.

If Eleanora was correct, then Cecily and Thais were, at this very moment, guests under Eberhart's roof. More disturbing, Eleanora reported that ever since Cecily had gone to stay with Thais, the Baron had been seen everywhere with them and it was rumoured a bet had been placed on how long it would take Eberhart to seduce Cecily.

He could not imagine Cecily a willing participant in any such scheme, but then why the hell had she agreed to attend this house party? And when he told her to stay away from Eberhart, she had replied that she found him 'congenial'. Cecily might not want him, but he'd abduct Cecily before he'd allow Eberhart to touch her.

If he left within the next hour, he would reach Eberhart's villa in time for dinner.

Chapter Fifteen

Cecily picked up her fan and wondered if Eberhart would suspect she was avoiding him if she pleaded a headache tonight and stayed in her room instead of going down to dinner. She had no real desire to see Thais either—the conversation in the carriage had disturbed her greatly.

Thais had been in love with Nico and expected to marry him? Had there actually been some sort of formal promise between them? Or had Thais only hoped there would be? She must have been in love with Nico that summer, but had anyone noticed? Perhaps not— Viola had described Thais as the sort of pale girl no one seemed to see. Despite living under Thais' roof for a week, Cecily did not feel she knew Thais much better than she had in Avezza, almost as if the pale unremarkable girl still lurked beneath her charming smiles and blonde loveliness.

Even the few confidences she had shared with Cecily did not, in retrospect, reveal much about her. She knew that Thais had been widowed twice, but Cecily had no idea if Thais had regarded either of her husbands with any sort of affection. She had numerous acquaintances, but none of them seemed to be a friend, at least not in the sense that Cecily considered Viola and, if circumstances were different, Lady Eleanora.

Certainly Thais had been hospitable and the week had passed in a whirlwind of social affairs, visitors and shopping, which had left Cecily in a sort of daze. She had scarcely a moment to herself except when she tumbled into bed at night and she was so tired she fell asleep with hardly a thought for Mariana and Simon. Or Nico. She felt as if she had left the Ca' Cappelletti a year instead of a week ago, for although they were in the same city, the only time she had glimpsed Eleanora and the Duchess was when the Baron had escorted them to the theatre. Thais had pointed out their box and Cecily had been taken aback by the jolt of longing that pierced her when she saw their familiar figures.

She was puzzled and a little hurt that neither the Duchess nor Eleanora had made any effort to visit her as they had promised they would. She thought that perhaps she had insulted them after all by leaving in the way she had.

Nothing seemed right. She walked to the window. Below were the formal gardens. Everything looked serene under the clear blue sky of an Italian afternoon. None the less, she felt on edge, as if she expected something unpleasant to happen. She would avoid Eberhart as much as possible but surely Thais was right and he would not do anything she did not want. She had worn one of her less becoming gowns tonight, a pale lavender silk, hoping he would consider her less of an English rose and more of an English thistle.

Someone rapped lightly at her door. She crossed the room, opened it and found Thais on the other side. She was dressed in a gown of delicate pink silk that emphasised her porcelain skin. Around her neck was a stunning necklace of diamonds. 'Dear Cecily, it is time to go down…' She stopped. 'Why are you not wearing the cerulean gown we had decided upon?'

'I found it had a stain.' The lie sprang quite easily to her lips.

'But this gown is so…so dull. Everyone will think you are someone's companion! And that necklace! It is so ordinary!' She pressed her lips together, dismay written all over her face. 'It is too late to do anything now. Perhaps if the bodice was arranged a little lower.'

'No! That is, I was feeling a trifle cold. I should hate to catch a chill.'

'It is too late for you to change, for we must go down. Tomorrow I will insist on supervising your dress.'

Cecily refused to feel guilty over deceiving Thais. She would have worn sackcloth and ashes if she thought that would help her escape Eberhart's attention.

Cecily followed Thais into the richly decorated salon where the guests gathered before dinner. Her hopes for an unobtrusive entry were dashed when the Baron's cousin and hostess, the Countess von Essen, spotted them and crossed the marble floor to their sides. Her cool grey eyes swept over them. 'A most charming gown, Lady Margate.' She turned to Cecily, a hint of surprise crossing her thin features. 'You are in mourning?'

'No, Countess.'

She looked a trifle puzzled. 'Come, my cousin most particularly wishes to greet you and Lady Margate.'

Cecily did not dare look at Thais as they followed the Countess across the room. She had the unpleasant sensation that several of the guests stared and whispered as they passed.

Eberhart stood with a heavyset man Cecily did not recognise. In fact, she realised she recognised none of the fashionably dressed guests she glimpsed as they crossed the room. The Countess excused herself, leaving Thais and Cecily with the men.

'Thais, my dear,' Eberhart said as he took her hand. 'As usual, you are the pinnacle of health and beauty. Another new gown, perhaps?'

'Will you scold me if it is?'

'Only if it did not become you.' He dropped her hand and turned to Cecily.

'Signora Renato,' he murmured. He possessed himself of her hand and brushed a brief kiss across the back of it. He impaled her with his strange colourless eyes. 'Welcome to my villa. I have anticipated your arrival since I learned you were coming.'

She forced her lips into a diffident smile and wondered how long he intended to go on holding her hand. 'Thank you.'

He finally dropped her hand as they were presented to his companion, Herr Schuler, who proclaimed himself in a heavy German accent delighted to meet such beautiful ladies. He too held Cecily's hand a trifle too long, his gaze a trifle too bold, before turning to Eberhart and speaking in rapid German. The Baron smiled and Cecily had the uneasy sense the Baron's comment concerned her.

The Baron started to speak just as a footman appeared at his side. He spoke to Eberhart in a low voice and the Baron frowned. 'You must excuse me, my dear ladies. An unexpected guest has arrived.' He left them with Schuler.

Schuler cleared his throat. 'I am most pleased to once again find myself in your splendid city.' His Italian was laboured as if he read from a schoolroom book.

Thais started to speak and then her attention riveted to something over Cecily's shoulder. 'Good heavens!' Pure dismay crossed her fact. She turned to Cecily and spoke in English. 'Dear Cecily, I fear I must warn you that Severin has just arrived.'

Nico? Cecily nearly dropped her fan. She slowly turned. Nico stood in the doorway. He seemed not to notice his approaching host as his gaze swept the room. Then his eyes fell on her with an intensity that was almost physical and she knew he was here because of her. She turned away and realised she was shaking.

She had no idea whether it was from anticipation, fear or relief. Or something else altogether.

* * *

Nico glanced down the table at Cecily. She was seated between Schuler and an elderly gentleman he did not recognise. Her profile was turned away from him as she listened to her dinner partner, her soft brown hair gleaming with bits of gold from the candlelight. Among the fashionable dress and glittering jewels of the others she looked like a poor relation in her drab gown, but that only rendered her more vulnerable.

His gaze shifted to the Baron, who laughed at a joke before gulping his wine. Although Eberhart was attentive to the lady seated at his side, his gaze frequently fell on Cecily with a speculative interest that raised Nico's hackles. He could not tell whether Cecily was aware of his interest, for she steadily avoided looking at the Baron. As she had steadily avoided looking at him since they had sat down to dinner.

'Are you certain it wise to stare at Cecily so often? Some might decide you are here because of her.'

He forced his attention back to Thais. She wore a little smile, but there was an edge to her voice he did not often hear.

'They would not be wrong.' He was in no mood to dissemble.

Slight colour stained her cheek. She stared at him and gave a little laugh. 'Whatever for? Really, I would think you must know by now that she finds you rather…well, intimidating. If you persist in this sort of thing, you will quite scare her.'

'I had not noticed that she finds me particularly intimidating.'

'Of course you do not! Men always assume that a woman who blushes and looks away from them is merely shy, but it is most often because they find the man too over-whelming. Contrary to what most men wish to believe, women do not in general like men who overwhelm them.'

He felt irked. 'You are speaking of women in general, or of Cecily?'

Her smile held a touch of pity. 'Have you not real-ised that Cecily wants nothing to do with you? Why else did she leave your house and come to stay with me?'

In that moment, he realised how much he disliked Thais. 'Perhaps, but what interests me is why you were so conveniently at hand to invite her to stay with you? More than that, my dear, I am quite curious as to why you brought her here, a place where most of the guests are no more respectable than their host?'

Her blue eyes widened. 'Dear Severin, I have no idea what you mean.'

'I think you do.' He held her gaze, his own hard. 'What game are you playing?'

Cold anger flickered across her face and then she gave a little laugh. 'Games? Why, none!' She looked away and picked up her wine glass.

What the hell was she up to? She knew exactly what she was doing when she brought Cecily here. He had no idea whether she deliberately intended to hurt Cecily or if Cecily was merely a pawn for some other nefari-ous purpose.

It did not matter—he intended to remove Cecily from this place as soon as possible.

* * *

The dinner was followed by a tedious tour of the Baron's collection of antiquities, which included two nude male statues. Eberhart chortled. 'I did not wish to offend the sensibilities of the ladies. Or make them dissatisfied with their current pleasures. Rather magnificent, are they not?'

A few crude comments followed, which only served to increase Nico's impatience.

Nico dallied, intending to allow the others to go ahead so he might fall behind and steal away to the salon. Eberhart usurped his plans by suddenly announcing they must join the ladies. He fell into step beside Nico.

'I am quite curious to know exactly why you decided to join my little party.' He glanced at Nico. 'Shall I guess? A certain lady, perhaps?'

'Yes.'

'I would hope you are referring to the delightful Lady Margate.'

'I am referring to Signora Renato.'

There was silence. Then Eberhart turned to look at him. 'I must ask you to turn your attention elsewhere. Perhaps you do not realise that I have an interest in the lady myself.'

'I have heard rumours to that effect. However, I have a prior claim.'

'Then I must ask you to relinquish it.'

'I am going to wed Signora Renato.'

Eberhart momentarily lost his bland expression. 'How very interesting, particularly since I had the impression from Lady Margate that the lovely *signora* had all but run from you.' He stopped in front of a painting. 'What do you think of my most recent acquisition? A present from an unfortunate Frenchman just before he was compelled to leave Italy.'

Nico looked up at the painting. 'Very nice. Which noble family did the Frenchman rob?'

'You are far too cynical, my dear Severin. If you insist on continuing in this vein, I might suspect you of harbouring radical sympathies.'

'My only interest is in Cecily Renato.'

The Baron began to walk again. 'Of course. I am curious if you have yet informed your intended bride she is to wed you.' He cast Nico a sly look. 'Because if you have not, then I still consider the lady fair game.'

'I suggest you rid yourself of that notion. Unless you want a bullet through you.'

'I would take offence, but since you are caught up in the throes of passion I will overlook your lack of gratitude for my hospitality. You would be wise to keep in mind, however, you are here only because I have allowed it.' They had reached the salon. Eberhart paused. 'We will make a little wager. I will give you until noon tomorrow to convince the *signora* to marry you. If she does not agree, then I will continue my pursuit of her without your interference. However, there is one more condition.'

'And that is?'

'If she agrees, we will announce it to the rest of the guests. To ensure that your intentions are honourable.'

'As yours are, no doubt.'

Eberhart smiled. 'Perhaps I am also in need of a wife.'

'You had best look elsewhere.'

'She is lovely, is she not, with an air of innocence despite her widowhood. One wonders if she has ever been brought to the height of passion. I have no doubt that, if properly tutored, she will be a most pleasurable bedmate. I am not certain if I wish to relinquish that task to you after all.'

Nico nearly lost his tight control then. 'The choice belongs to the lady,' he said coolly.

'Naturally. You will understand if I do not wish you success in your pursuit.'

'I do not intend to lose.' He stepped into the room.

Cecily was nowhere in sight.

Cecily had been glad to escape from the salon to the quiet of the bedchamber. But after the maid finished helping her into her nightclothes and left, an unexpected surge of homesickness washed over Cecily. Not for her house in Avezza, but for England. This room, with its silent marble floors and dark bed coverings, seemed huge and strange and she suddenly longed for the cheerful simplicity of her childhood room. For the first time in an age, she missed her grandmother. Lady Telford had been stiff and demanding and not very physically demonstrative, but when Cecily had been truly overset her grandmother would sit with her.

'You may cry for a while, but then you must dry your eyes and decide what you must do next,' Lady Telford told her many times.

After that she would gather Cecily into her arms, rather stiffly, and Cecily had known she was loved. Now, she felt an aching need for someone to hold her.

'Cecily.'

Her heart leapt to her throat. Nico?

'Cecily. It is Nico. Open the door.' His voice held a note of impatience. 'Now.' She did not think he would go away if she ignored him. She padded to the door.

She turned the key and opened the door a crack. 'I was about to go to bed.'

'Let me in before any of the guests find me shouting through the door.'

'Oh.' She stepped back. He brushed past her, closed the door behind him and turned the key.

She stared at the key and then at him. 'Whatever are you doing?' Her voice was a trifle too high.

'Locking the door. So our host doesn't disturb us.'

'Us?' Her voice squeaked.

'Yes. Us. We need to talk.'

'Could we not do it some other time?'

'No.' He folded his arms and leaned against the door, his eyes on her face. 'I told Eberhart I plan to marry you,' he said coolly.

Her heart thudded. 'Why did you do that?'

'So he would cease his pursuit of you.'

'You know of that?' How utterly humiliating.

'Yes, as do a good many others.'

'I see. You are most kind, but it was not necessary to tell him that—'

He stopped her. 'It was. I promised Raf I'd look after

you. I'm not about to let you end up as Eberhart's mistress,' he said roughly. 'Or have your reputation ruined.'

'I am certain Raf did not expect you to go around telling people untruths in order to protect me,' she said coldly. So that was why he was here—to keep some sort of stupid promise to Raf.

'It is not an untruth. We are about to become betrothed.' His expression was grim. 'Eberhart will not touch you if you are under my protection. Furthermore, our betrothal will quell any rumours linking your name with Eberhart. There is one more thing. If Raf returns and discovers you have been compromised in any way, he will come after Eberhart. I doubt you would like to see Raf imprisoned or worse for killing an Austrian baron.'

'No, of course not, although I would hope he would be more reasonable.'

'Not where his family is concerned.' He moved away from the door. 'So you see, by agreeing to a betrothal, you will possibly spare Raf's life.'

'Surely things are not quite that dire!'

'They are.' He had come to stand in front of her and she resisted the urge to back up. 'Why did you leave my house in the first place? Was it because of me?'

'Only because I thought it would be awkward under the circumstances if I stayed.'

'Not because you are afraid of me?' He seemed to really want to know.

She gave a strangled laugh at this sudden change in topic. 'No, although when you stare at me in the grim way you are doing now I quite fear you are about to scold me or attempt to ride roughshod over me. But, no, I am not afraid of you.'

'I am glad.' Some of the harshness faded from his expression.

The air suddenly crackled with tension. She clutched her dressing gown more tightly about her. 'I think you should go. It is late…and…'

'I am spending the night with you.'

She took a step back, her pulse beating wildly. 'Spending the night with me? Whatever for?'

'To protect you from Eberhart. He has an unfortunate habit of roaming during the night. I should not want him to wander into your bedchamber and find you unprotected.' His voice was cool and matter of fact.

'But the door has a lock!'

'I doubt that will stop him. If he thinks we are spending the night engaged in passionate lovemaking, he is unlikely to stray into your room. Or question the veracity of our betrothal. He would like, I think, to discover I am only bluffing.'

'Oh.' She took another step back, crossing her hands over her breasts.

'I am not planning a seduction, if that worries you. I intend to sleep here.' He had crossed the room to one of the chairs near the mantelpiece.

'Th…there is a cot in the dressing room. It might be more comfortable.'

'I would prefer to be in the same room with you. In case, our host decides to investigate.' He had started to shrug out of his coat.

'Surely he would not do that! And if he did, he would think it equally odd if you are in the chair.'

He finished removing his coat. His hands stilled on his waistcoat. 'You are right, my dear. Then perhaps I should share the bed with you.'

She swallowed. Her eyes met his and even in the dim light of the room, she could not mistake the blatant desire in his eyes. The knowledge he still wanted her sparked the aching need for him she had tried to ignore. The strangeness of the day…everything whirled around her, everything but him.

Her gaze did not waver from his face. 'I think, yes, that would be the best thing to do.'

He stared at her. 'I beg your pardon.'

'I think we should share the bed.'

He looked incredulous and then gave a short laugh. 'My sweet Cecily, I was hardly serious. Sharing a bed with you would be disastrous.' He fumbled with the button of his waistcoat.

He was right. Even if his bluntness hurt. She sat on the edge of the bed and wondered how she was ever to sleep. Worse, the lost feeling had returned in full force. Having him in the room only intensified it. She sniffed, praying she would not start to cry like some missish creature.

'Cecily.'

Her head jerked up. He stood in front of her dressed only in his loose shirt and breeches. 'What is wrong?'

'Nothing is wrong.' She looked away. 'We…we should go to bed.'

He did not move. 'Do you really want me to share your bed?'

'N-not really. It…it would be st-stupid.' To her chagrin, her voice shook.

'Stupid. Dangerous. Disastrous. All of those.' He took her hands and drew her to her feet. 'Do you know why? Because I would want to make love to you. Over and over. All night.'

'Would you?' she whispered. She hardly seemed to be breathing.

'Yes.' He moved closer to her, imprisoning her between the bed and his body. She could feel the hard planes of his body against hers, feel the beat of his heart. His mouth was inches from hers and she could almost taste him. She reached up and tangled her hands in his hair and pulled his head towards her. Her mouth found his. He did not move while she explored his mouth. Her hands moved down from his head to his shoulders to the hard muscles of his back. He still stood motionless. She finally lifted her head. 'You do not like this?'

'Not like it?' His voice was ragged. 'My sweet, I can think of nothing more pleasurable than having you touch me. And if you continue, I will lose every vestige of control I possess.'

'What if I want you to?' She touched his cheek.

'Are you attempting to seduce me?'

'I…I think so.' She pressed closer to him.

He stilled. 'Are you certain you want this?'

'Yes. Will you kiss me?' She was beyond caring whether she made a fool of herself or not.

An odd light sprang to his eyes. 'Anything to oblige you.' And then his arms were around her, his mouth crushing hers in a kiss that sent her senses spinning. She clung to him; when he finally lifted his head, her legs nearly buckled.

'What else will please you, my lady?' His voice was husky with desire.

She managed to speak. 'Your shirt. I want it off.' Impatient, she fumbled with the buttons and then started to lift it over his head.

'Allow me.' He finished the task and stood before her. She had seen him partially unclothed before, but not like this, standing before her as a lover. She took him in, the broad shoulders and chest, the muscles, the dark hair on his chest, his narrow hips. He waited under her perusal, his eyes on her face. 'What else, sweetheart?' he asked softly.

She wanted to touch him everywhere. She swallowed and ran her tongue over her dry lips. 'I don't know.'

'It is my turn to make a request. Your shift must go.'

She thought she would explode when he undid the ribbon and then helped her from the garment. Then she stood naked before him. The heat in his gaze rendered her self-conscious for the first time and she crossed her hands over her breasts.

'Don't,' he said softly. He gently removed her hands and held them to her sides. His gaze seemed to burn through her as his eyes took in her breasts, her hips, the juncture of her thighs and her legs. He did not need to tell her he found her desirable; his sudden intake of breath was enough. 'Turn around,' he said hoarsely.

She did and then his arms circled her waist, pulling her back against him. He caressed the back of her neck with his mouth. He cupped her breast with his free hand and then moved down to her stomach, stroking the soft roundness in lazy circles. A whimper of pleasure and need escaped her and when his hand moved to the mound between her thighs, she shuddered.

He removed his hand. 'Come, we will continue this in the chair,' he said thickly.

'The chair?'

He took her hand and led her to the wing chair. He sat and pulled her down on his lap so she was facing him. He looked up at her, his eyes dark and sensuous. 'Kiss me, Cecily.'

She leaned forward, her hands bracing against his shoulders, and found his mouth. She kissed him, tentatively exploring his mouth, tasting him. He responded, his own kiss unhurried. The feel of the bare flesh of her thighs against the rough cloth of his breeches was unexpectedly sensuous and she found herself leaning forward and pressing into him. Her breasts fell forward and he cupped them. When he drew one nipple into his mouth, she thought she would die. She leaned into his caress, wanting more and then his hard length pressed into the sensitive nub between her legs. She shuddered with pure, hot desire.

He pulled his mouth away from hers. 'What next, my lady?' he whispered.

'I…' She was too far gone to think of propriety. 'Your breeches.'

He laughed softly. 'Of course. But we will need to stand for a moment.'

He rose, his arm around her. Her legs nearly buckled when she stood. In fascination, she watched as he undid the fastening of his breeches and then stepped out of them. But when he started to remove his small clothes, she averted her eyes. Whatever was she doing?

But he was drawing her to him. 'No need to be shy, *cara*.' He tilted her chin and kissed her mouth. 'Come and sit back down. This time properly. Or most improperly, as you wish.' He sat again, slightly sprawled, and she could not look anywhere but at his face.

A slight smile touched his mouth. 'Come and kiss me again. Just like before.' He held out his hand.

She took it and again was on his lap. She leaned forward to kiss him and this time he met her mouth with a hard, possessive opened-mouth kiss. Her head spun as his hand cupped her buttocks, lifting her slightly and then he was parting her thighs. She gasped as he slipped two fingers in her swollen opening. She clung to him as he explored, stroking and caressing the most sensitive places in her body until she was completely at his mercy. Her breath came in shallow gasps and when he finally withdrew, she thought she would explode. She opened her eyes. 'Please…' she begged.

'Lift your hips.'

She complied and then drew in a sharp breath when

his hard length filled her. 'Lean forward and ride me,' he whispered.

She nodded and braced her hands on his shoulders and began to rock. Her body seemed to know what to do, moving and adjusting to seek the most pleasure possible. Her body was swollen and full, the movements only increasing her desire for release. He moved under her, matching her rhythm. She climaxed, wave after wave of sensuous pleasure crashing over her. His own climax followed and she collapsed against him, as her breathing slowed.

And sanity returned. She was sitting on the Duke of Severin's most private part after begging him to take her to bed. Except they hadn't even made it to the bed.

His hand brushed her cheek. 'Regrets already, my sweet?'

She opened her eyes. He watched her with a lazy, sensuous expression, but she felt as if he could read her soul. 'No. I…I don't know. I have never been like this.'

'Like what?'

'So…so…brazen.'

Slight amusement lifted his mouth. 'I feel more than complimented.'

'I suppose women often throw themselves at you.'

'But rarely with so much passion.'

She had no doubt this sort of lovemaking was nothing out of the ordinary for him. If his cool, slightly amused manner was anything to go by, he had not felt the same loss of control she had. 'Thank you for…indulging me.' She started to move backwards, only to find his arm trapping her against him.

'But I have not finished indulging you.'

'I really do not expect you to do any more.'

'Don't you? Then perhaps you will indulge me.'

'What do you mean?'

His smile held a hint of wickedness. 'This time I will tell you what I want.'

Her body was already tensing in anticipation. 'What sort of things do you…want?'

'This to start with.' He rose with her and pulled her to him for another raw kiss. He was already hard, his erection pressing against her flesh. He lifted his head. 'I think now we can go to bed.' He took her hand.

The pleasurable warmth of the body cradled against his slowly penetrated his sleep-fogged consciousness. She lay under his arm, her back to him, the soft round-ness of her buttocks pressed against his stomach, one leg under his. He kissed the back of her neck and then pulled away. For the first time in an age, he was reluc-tant to leave a woman's bed. If he did not, however, they would be here for the rest of the day.

He half-turned, easing out from under her and bit back a groan as he moved his stiff arm. He managed to sit on the edge of the bed. His gaze was drawn to Ce-cily, to the curve of her cheek. One slender arm was flung over the covers. She looked vulnerable and soft, and innocent. Unexpected protectiveness surged through him—something he had not expected after a night of such wild passion.

As much as he'd wanted her, he had not expected to

lose himself in her so completely that he no longer knew where he ended and she began. The pleasure had been nearly unbearable and, for the first time since his youth, he had lost control.

He'd never had such satisfying sex in his life.

He rose and found his shirt on the floor. He slipped it over his head, wincing a little. His breeches were flung over the chair where they had first coupled. The sudden hardness in his groin made him curse. He pulled up his breeches. When he looked up he saw Cecily was sitting, holding the bedcover up around her chest. Soft colour tinted her cheeks when she met his eyes and she looked away.

He walked over to her. Her hair was tousled about her bare shoulders and her mouth was soft. He wanted nothing more than to pull her back into his arms and entangle his hands in her hair, pulling the cover to reveal her breasts and make love until he lost himself in her. 'Once again, *cara*, we must talk.' He forced his voice to remain calm.

'I would like my shift first,' she said quietly. She did not meet his eyes.

'Of course.' He retrieved the garment from the floor and handed it to her. Then he walked to the window although the curtains were still drawn in order to give her privacy.

He waited until he heard her soft footsteps on the floor before he turned to face her. She stood at the foot of the bed, properly covered in the voluminous white gown, which did not render her any less desirable. But he was no longer a youth who could not control his desires. No matter what had happened last night.

'Sit down. Please,' he said.

She took a chair, not the one they'd made in love in. He had no idea whether she intended to avoid it or not. 'I hope you are not planning to beg my forgiveness for seducing me,' she said. 'In fact, I should beg your pardon for seducing you.' Her voice was calm, but the way she twisted her hands together told him she was not.

'Why? Because you regret it or you think I do?'

'I do not know.' She finally looked at him. 'You were here to do me a kindness and instead I…I took advantage of you.'

'My sweet girl, if I had not wanted to be taken advantage of, then there is nothing you could have done to, er…persuade me.' The conversation was not the one he had anticipated. He had never had a woman apologise for having her way with him. 'Will it ease your conscience if I tell you I have never been so enjoyably ravished in my life?'

She flushed. 'Oh.'

'Once we are married, we can repeat the experience any time you desire,' he said carelessly.

'Married? I thought…'

'You thought what?'

'That we were only to be betrothed. You said nothing about marriage.'

'I believe, my sweet, that in general marriage follows a betrothal. After last night, you do not have much choice. I've no doubt Eberhart knows we spent the night together and it is likely the others will suspect as well. Particularly after we announce our engagement today.'

'Today? Must we do it so soon?'

'Yes.' He scowled at her. 'Damn it, Cecily, marriage to me won't be that bad. I won't beat you.'

'I know,' she said quietly.

'Then why do you look as if you've just been sentenced to death?' He demanded.

'I…' She looked at him rather helplessly.

A cold fist slammed through him. She did not want to marry him despite the passion they had shared. It was possible Thais had been right after all, that for some reason Cecily feared him.

'Then we will consider the betrothal temporary. After a suitable length of time you may jilt me. For now, I had best leave your room and allow you to dress.'

'Yes.'

He tucked his shirt into his breeches and picked up his coat, then realised he'd forgotten to put on his stockings and shoes. He collected his shoes and stockings and sat down.

He finished and looked up. She stood near the window and he sensed it mattered not at all that the curtains were drawn, for her eyes seemed to be focused on something far away. Her shoulders drooped as if her thoughts gave her no pleasure. He rose and moved to stand behind her. 'Cecily.'

She turned, her expression rather confused as if she'd almost forgotten his presence. The forlorn look in her eyes tugged at his heart and he reached out to touch her cheek. She flinched and he dropped his hand. 'I am leaving now,' he said.

'Leaving?'

He supposed he should be gratified at the dismay in her face. 'Just the room. Not this villa. I would not leave you here.'

'No, of course not.'

'We will make the announcement before noon. After that we will leave.'

'Together?'

'Together, my sweet. Furthermore, you will return to my house. I will not allow you to go to Lady Margate so do not waste your breath in futile argument.' He did not wait for an answer. He turned and left the room before he could see her undoubtedly horrified expression.

Chapter Sixteen

Cecily rose from the bench. She could not spend the entire day in the villa's lush garden, as tempting as it was. She must return to the house and face the rest of the party. And Nico.

She had been beyond foolish to allow Thais to convince her to come here. The thought had never entered her mind that Nico would find out, much less come after her. Or that he felt such a…a stupid sense of honour that he would offer marriage to protect her.

Before they had made such passionate love.

Her whole body heated even thinking about it. Last night had been far different from the first time. Then, he had needed her and she had responded, but his love-making had held a certain desperation.

Last night had been something entirely different. He had made love to her, not out of need but out of desire. He had wanted her and she had wanted him back with a physical desire that had shocked her. Always slightly embarrassed by her unclothed body, she had stood naked before him, revelling in the knowledge he found her nude body beautiful.

She had run her hands over his body with an abandon she had never shown with Marco, fascinated with the strong male hardness of his muscles, enjoying the feminine power she felt as he lay still beneath her hands, his breath coming harder and harder until she finished her exploration. And then…

No. She must put last night aside before she did something rash such as seduce him again. She must be completely depraved. Women, at least well-bred women, were not supposed to be thinking about such things. As much as she had enjoyed Marco's considerate lovemaking, it had never occurred to her to indicate she desired him.

She started up the path towards the house. She must face the others, including Thais. She only hoped Nico was wrong and no one would know they had been together last night.

She had nearly reached the lawn directly behind the house when she saw Nico coming around the side of the house. He paused for a moment and then he saw her. He strode towards her and there was no mistaking his black expression.

He halted in front of her. 'Where were you?' he demanded. 'No one could find you.'

'I was in the garden,' she said coolly. It was quite apparent he was not thinking about last night.

'Alone? What if Eberhart was to come upon you?'

'Well, he did not.' She must have truly lost her mind to think she would ever want to seduce this arrogant man. 'I am going back to the house. Are you coming, your Grace? Or were you about to visit the gardens yourself?'

To her great satisfaction, he looked as if he were about to explode. He did not. 'We are going back to the house where we will announce our betrothal,' he said through gritted teeth.

'Very well, your Grace.' She started to walk away, only to have him catch her arm.

She stopped and looked up at him. 'Is there something else you wished to say to me?'

'Yes.' He dropped her arm. His eyes still held an angry glint, but there was another emotion as well. 'This.'

He grasped her shoulders and pulled her into his arms. She was too startled to protest as his mouth covered hers. Her feeble attempts at resistance were swept away by his leisurely, seductive kiss and she melted into him, her mouth soft and pliable beneath his.

He lifted his head. 'We can go in now that you look well kissed. We would not want Eberhart to suspect we were quarrelling.' A little smile played about his mouth.

'And you do not appear to have been affected at all,' she said tartly, hoping to cover up her confusion. If he could look so calm and collected after ravaging her senses, then she would pretend the same.

A sardonic light leapt to his eye. 'In that, my sweet Cecily, you are quite wrong.'

* * *

Thais was the first person they met when they entered the house. 'Severin! Thank goodness you found her!' She grasped Cecily's hands. 'I was so worried you were not in your room and then no one knew where you had gone to!'

'I only wished to walk in the garden. I did not think anyone would worry.' Nothing in Thais' face indicated she guessed Cecily had been in Nico's arms a short time ago.

'You should have asked me to come with you. I adore walking in gardens. We can walk together tomorrow.' She smiled at Nico. 'I am certain you will not object if I steal Cecily away?'

'Actually, I do object.'

Thais stared at him, then gave a little laugh. 'Well, really! Then I will ask Cecily instead. I hope you will not go against her wishes!'

'Ah, so Signora Renato has not run away after all.' Eberhart had come up silently behind them.

'Of course she would not,' Thais said. 'But Severin refuses to let her out of his sight. I hope you will convince him he is being quite selfish!'

Eberhart's gaze raked over Cecily in a way that made her think that he guessed exactly how she'd spent her night. Her face heated, which brought a knowing smile to the Baron's full lips. 'You have pleasing news, I see.'

She glanced at Nico. His eyes were on Eberhart. 'You may congratulate us.'

'Most certainly.' Eberhart turned to Cecily. 'My dear,

I must wish you all happiness.' He took her hand and brought it to his lips, his mouth lingering an instant too long, before releasing it. Nico's expression did not change, but he shifted closer to Cecily.

Eberhart turned to Thais. 'Lady Margate, do you not intend to congratulate the Duke and Signora Renato on their upcoming nuptials?' he asked blandly.

Thais had gone very still. For a moment, Cecily did not think she would answer. Then a strained smile crossed her face. 'Of course. I was just rather surprised, but I should have suspected something when Severin appeared last night.' She took Cecily's hand and kissed her cheek. 'I hope you will be happy, but it was very sly of you not to say a thing. In fact, I rather thought you did not care much for Severin at all.' She spoke in her light, teasing way.

'Thank you.' Why did Thais now say she thought Cecily did not care for Nico when yesterday she had accused Cecily of being in love with him?

'There is only a quarter of an hour left until noon, so I suggest we make the announcement without delay. Unless, Severin, you wish to postpone it,' Eberhart said.

'I would prefer—' Cecily began. Everything was happening too fast.

Nico's hand closed around hers. 'We will make the announcement now.'

Eberhart smiled. 'Then let us proceed to the salon.'

Thais insisted on accompanying Cecily to her bed-chamber so she could help Cecily pack. 'Although I think it is very bad of Severin to insist that you must stay with his family instead of me—I would have liked to have held a little party for you,' Thais said as they entered the room. Once inside, however, she closed the door and faced Cecily, the smile gone from her face.

'Perhaps I should not say anything, but as your friend I cannot remain silent.' She hesitated. 'Dear Cecily, are you certain you wish to marry Severin? I only ask because you do not seem happy. I worry that he has somehow forced you into accepting him.'

'Of course he has not.'

'Are you certain? He can be very overwhelming when he wants something. Particularly if he wants a woman. And it has been quite apparent from the very first that he has wanted you.' Her large eyes were filled with concern. 'Just as he wanted Angelina. Poor thing— he pursued her even though she found him quite intimidating. Everyone knew that she and Rafaele were to marry some day, but Severin did not care for that. He only wanted Angelina and would not allow her to refuse him. Sometimes I have wondered if her death was no accident, that perhaps she deliberately threw herself from the path rather than marry him.'

'That is a horrible thing to say.'

'Not if it is the truth.' Thais walked to the door. 'Do not make the same mistake Angelina did.'

Five days later, Raf was shown into the salon of the Ca' Cappelletti where Cecily and Eleanora were seated in front of the long windows facing the Grand Canal.

Cecily looked up from the book she had been attempting to read, her pleasure at seeing him tinged with apprehension. 'Raf! What brings you to Venice? I thought you were in Vicenza!'

He smiled. 'You, of course.' He looked over at Eleanora, who had thrust the sketch she was working on under a paper. The smile left his face. '*Buongiorno*, Lady Eleanora.'

'*Buongiorno*, Signor Vianoli,' Eleanora said curtly. She stood, clutching the sketchpad to her chest. 'I am certain you wish to speak to Cecily in private, so I will leave you.' She brushed past him.

Cecily glanced at Raf, who regarded Eleanora's retreating back with a slight frown. She had no idea why Eleanora did not seem to like Raf.

Raf said nothing about her when he turned to Cecily. 'A few days ago I met an acquaintance who informed me that a certain Austrian baron has been pursuing you. He also mentioned you were staying with Thais Margate. When I called there today, I was told you were no longer with Lady Margate but were now here.' He regarded her, his face serious. 'Is any of this true?'

'As you can see, I am here.' She had hardly expected such news to reach him.

'I was referring to the rest,' Raf said.

She hesitated for a moment. No purpose would be served by dissembling. He would learn the truth soon enough.

'Cecily?'

'Yes. I went to stay with Lady Margate. I did not wish

to stay here after Simon and Mariana left. It was too awkward.'

'Because of Nico?'

She flushed a little.' Yes. I met Lady Margate a few days before they departed and she suggested that I stay with her. I accepted.'

'Nico allowed you to go?'

'He did not know. He accompanied Simon and Mariana as far as Mestre and then went on to the Villa Cappelletti.'

'I see. What of Eberhart? Is this true as well?'

'Yes. He…he had an interest in me.'

He swore softly and she put her hand on his arm. 'But no longer. He invited Lady Margate and me as guests at a house party at his villa. Just before dinner Nico arrived.' She took a steadying breath. 'He told the Baron that we are to be married. But only to protect me,' she quickly added.

A peculiar gleam shone in his eye and then his lips curved. 'Of course. I should have known that Nico would not allow such a thing.' He took her hand. 'May I offer you my felicitations for your future happiness. I must call on him, however, since he did not ask my permission, although he can be forgiven under the circumstances.'

She gathered her wits together. 'We are not really to be married. The betrothal is only temporary.'

'Has it been made public?'

'I suppose, yes. The Baron announced it at the house party.'

'And did Nico object?'

'No, he quite wished the Baron to do so.'

'He means to marry you. He will not publicly humiliate you by breaking off the betrothal.'

'But he does not mean to marry me!'

'Then he is only trifling with your affections?'

'Raf!' She realised he was only teasing her, but she was uncomfortable none the less. 'No, of course not. I do not want to marry him, either.'

'So you intend to humiliate him?'

'No!' She took a deep breath before she lost her temper. 'I would never do such a thing. We mutually agreed that, after a suitable period of time, we would break off the betrothal. There will be no marriage.'

His mouth curved in a most wicked grin. 'But I have decided otherwise.' He brushed a brief kiss across the back of her hand 'It is time that I speak with your *fidanzato*.'

'Raf!'

But he was gone. She suspected he meant to tease her but she was not completely certain. Not that she was certain about anything to do with Nico. Since their return to Venice she had seen him twice. Both times in company and both times he had treated her with all the solicitousness of a devoted fiancé. Nothing in his manner indicated they had spent a night in each other's arms. She prayed nothing in her manner indicated how his impersonal touch sent her pulse racing and made her knees tremble. She would die if he guessed how much she wanted to throw herself in his arms again.

She feared she was very much in danger of falling in love with him.

Nico looked up from the letter he was attempting to write. He started when he saw Raf. 'What the devil are you doing here?'

Raf strode into the study. 'I heard rumours that Eberhart had been pursuing Cecily. She informed me that you had already dealt with the situation in a most admirable fashion.'

'Her words, I imagine,' he said drily.

Raf grinned. 'Of course. You have my blessing.'

'She does not want to marry me.'

'Do you wish to marry her?'

He stood. 'I have asked her twice. She has turned me down the same number of times.'

'Has she? I wonder why. She cares for you.'

He shrugged. 'Not enough to marry me.' He could not quite keep the bitterness out of his voice. She had given no indication since they had returned to Venice that she had been affected by their night together. When all he could think about was having her beneath him, while he made love to her again and again.

'Do you want to marry her? Or are you only doing what is honourable?'

'I need a wife.'

Raf merely looked at him. Nico folded his arms. 'Well?'

'You are in love with her, are you not?'

Nico stared at him. 'Why the hell would you say that?'

'I cannot fathom why you would put yourself to so much trouble if you were not. But it is more than that. Your face softens when you speak of her. You look at her the way a man looks at a woman he loves. You frown now and swear because you wish to cover your hurt that she has refused you.'

He wanted to shout and call Raf a fool, but the words died on his lips. 'I loved Angelina.'

'As did I. But she has been dead for over thirteen years. You cannot bury yourself with her.'

'I've hardly done that.'

'No?'

'No, damn you.' He eyed Raf coolly. 'I could fling the same accusation at you. For I do not see any indication you have fallen in love again.'

'Perhaps I have not met the right woman.'

Nico said nothing.

'Cecily is not Angelina. But then you are not the same youth who fell so wildly in love with her. I wonder—if you were to meet her now for the first time, would you still want her? Or if you would discover it was Cecily you wanted after all?'

He turned and left Nico.

Nico did not move. He should have cursed Raf. Mowed him down. Finished the mill they started at the inn that night.

For what? Suggesting he might not want Angelina at

all? That he would choose Cecily instead? He should have thrown Raf's words after him, but he had not.

He had no idea why.

The letter arrived the next day. It was written in a thin, uneven hand that Nico did not recognise.

Cecily Renato will come to great harm if you do not end your betrothal. You must stay away from her.

He stared at it, his initial anger followed by a prick of fear. Barbarina. Of that he had no doubt, for the wording of the note bore too much resemblance to Barbarina's other dire warnings. How the devil had she found out about their engagement? The notice of their betrothal had been published only yesterday and few people had known beforehand. Except the guests who were present. Of those, only Thais knew Barbarina.

He frowned. He could think of no reason why Thais would take it upon herself to inform Barbarina. It made no sense.

He dismissed Thais; his greater concern was Barbarina. He had not thought much about Barbarina or the fête until now. Or the discussion with Raf and the possibility Barbarina had tried to harm Cecily.

Hell. Why had it slipped his mind? He stared down at the note, his expression grim. He had promised to look after Cecily and he'd failed when she had gone to stay with Thais. He would not make the same mistake again.

Chapter Seventeen

Eleanora turned to Cecily. 'Would you mind very much if we stop at one more shop? It is not very far from here. If you are not too fatigued, that is. I fear I can go on wandering for ever and never tire while my companions have nearly collapsed. I promise we will not get lost again.' They stood outside a small milliner's shop in one of the many narrow, fascinating streets winding through Venice.

Cecily smiled. 'Even if we did, I would not mind because it is such an interesting place in which to lose oneself.'

Eleanora smiled back at her. 'Oh, Cecily! I am so glad we are to be sisters! Have you tired of hearing that yet?'

'No, for I feel exactly the same.' She would not think about Eleanora's disappointment when she learned Cecily would not be her sister after all. For since her return to Venice nearly a week ago, she was more and more convinced marriage to Nico would lead to nothing but unhappiness for both of them. She shook off her uneasy thoughts—she did not want to worry Eleanora. 'Let us find your shop.'

Eleanora tucked her arm through Cecily's as they started off, Giacomo, the footman, trailing after them. The small streets between the tall narrow buildings fascinated Cecily. As did coming upon the quiet canals where one must cross a bridge in order to reach the next *calle*.

The small shop was located in a tiny *campo*. Several women were gathered around the cistern in its centre to procure buckets of water. A few children and a dog chased after a hoop. They crossed the square towards one of the little shops. The sign proclaimed one could procure papers, paints and brushes.

Cecily turned to Eleanora. 'You are interested in art, then?'

'A little,' Eleanora said carelessly. 'I sometimes like to sketch or attempt a watercolour. We do not need to go in if you would rather not.'

She was not certain why Eleanora suddenly seemed so hesitant. 'I will look for a present for Mariana as she also enjoys drawing.' She stepped into the shop and after a moment Eleanora followed.

No one was in the shop. Eleanora looked around and then went to the display of paints. Cecily looked about her. 'It is exactly the sort of place Raf would like.'

'Raf?' Eleanora started. 'Of course. He is an artist, is he not?'

'Yes, although he does not paint much any more.'

'Oh.' She turned back. After a few moments, she

chose a box of watercolours. 'This is all I want. Have you found something for Mariana?'

'Perhaps some paper and a new set of pencils. What would you recommend?'

Eleanora was soon engrossed in helping Cecily; by the time she stepped up to the counter to pay for the purchases, she was convinced Eleanora was more than an amateur artist, for she sounded exactly like Raf when Cecily had accompanied him to such a shop. Why then did Eleanora seem so reluctant to admit it? She held back her questions, not wanting to pry into Eleanora's affairs.

By the time they left the shop, Eleanora had reverted to her usual cheerful self. 'We can go over the Rialto,' Eleanora said as they crossed the *campo*. 'There is a little place where we can have an ice. It is not as grand as Florian's, but I must admit I like their ices better.'

Cecily was amazed how well Eleanora managed to find her way through the narrow maze of streets. Soon they were on the bridge that spanned the Grand Canal.

They slowly made their way up the shallow steps of the bridge through the crowds, stopping here and there to peer into one of the shops that lined the bridge. As they started down the other side of the bridge Eleanora's attention was caught by a display of books. 'I promise I will look at nothing else after this,' she told Cecily with a sheepish smile.

Cecily laughed. 'Should you promise that? There are certain to be more shops before we are home.'

'Yes, well.' Eleanora crossed to the display and

picked up one of the books. 'Come and look, Cecily. Is this not an odd illustration?'

Cecily was about to move to Eleanora's side when she heard a shout. She looked up and froze in horror, for a small cart was careening down the steps towards her. Just in time she jumped away. Her foot caught on the edge of the step and then she was falling.

'Cecily!' Eleanora cried. She dropped beside Cecily. 'Thank God! I thought the cart was going to hit you.'

Cecily attempted to sit up and her head spun for a moment. She saw the cart lying on its side a few steps below her.

'*Signora!*' Giacomo suddenly appeared. Soon a crowd of fascinated, horrified onlookers surrounded them.

Giacomo helped her to her feet and to the inside of the nearest shop where someone procured a chair and insisted she sit. Her entire body hurt, she had torn her glove on one hand and, to her chagrin, she felt tears prick her eyelids.

Eleanora knelt next to her, her face worried. 'I have sent Giacomo for Nico. You cannot possibly walk home.'

Oh, dear. 'I am fine, really. Just rather shaken. It is not very far. I am certain I will be able to walk.'

'Well, I am not about to let you. Nico would strangle me.' Eleanora rose as a burly man, who appeared to be the proprietor, approached them. With him was a man wearing the uniform of an Austrian officer.

The officer introduced himself as Captain Guttman. He had seen the disturbance and had come to make certain the *signora* had not been badly hurt and to offer his assistance. After Cecily reassured him she had sustained no serious injuries, he offered to see them home.

'It is kind of you to offer, but I have sent for my brother, the Duke of Severin,' Eleanora told him.

'I will wait with you until he arrives,' Guttman said. He had a pleasant face and manner and Cecily had recovered enough to notice the admiration in his eyes when he looked at Eleanora.

Shortly after that, the proprietor announced the *signora*'s cousin had arrived. Expecting to see Nico, Cecily was stunned to see Raf instead.

She half-rose and then winced. 'Raf? Why are you here?'

He strode to her side. 'I was just leaving the Ca' Cappelletti when Giacomo arrived and said you were hurt. Nico was not home, so I came. Are you all right?'

'Yes, of course. Just a little bruised.'

Raf looked at Eleanora. 'What happened?'

'She was almost knocked down by a cart. She fell down the steps when she tried to get away.'

Raf's mouth tightened. 'Whose cart was it?'

'I do not know,' Eleanora said.

Guttman spoke. 'I would like to speak to you for a moment, *signor*.'

Raf turned to him. 'Captain Guttman offered to stay with us until Nico…or you arrived,' Eleanora said quickly. 'Signor Vianoli is a relation of Signora Renato,' she told Guttman. 'Oh, dear, I should have made a more formal introduction.'

'Under the circumstances this will suffice,' Raf said. 'You had something you wanted to tell me, Captain?'

'Yes. If you will step outside with me.'

Raf followed him out and they returned a few minutes later. Raf's mouth was set in a hard line, although his expression relaxed a little when he informed Eleanora and Cecily he would take them home now.

Guttman took his leave, bowing over Eleanora's hand a trifle too long.

It did not escape Raf's notice. 'You have an admirer,' he said.

'Hardly,' Eleanora snapped. She picked up her reticule and then Cecily's. 'Did you bring a gondola?'

'It is waiting near the bridge.' Raf looked down at Cecily. 'I will carry you.'

'I can walk perfectly well.' She rose, albeit rather stiffly. 'Shall we go?'

Raf did not argue, although she suspected he wanted to. The thought crossed her mind that Nico would have swept her up into his arms no matter what she said. Which was one reason she should be glad he was not here.

However, he was on the small dock outside the palazzo with its black-and-white striped poles. He helped Eleanora step from the gondola to the landing and then held his hand out for Cecily. Raf helped her to her feet and she grasped Nico's hand. She stumbled a little, her balance shaky, and then she was on solid ground, his arm supporting her.

'Thank you.' She drew away from him and managed a step before she swayed again.

He was at her side. 'I am carrying you to your room.'

She looked up into his cool, arrogant face. 'I suppose if I said I was perfectly capable of walking, you would completely override my wishes.'

'You are correct in your supposition.'

A strangled giggle escaped her. 'Then I will not argue.'

'Good.' He swept her up, his arms strong and safe around her. He looked down at her, and she saw the worry in his eyes. He was overbearing, but it was because he wanted to take care of her.

She closed her eyes before he could read the truth in her face.

She had fallen in love with him.

Raf whirled around when Nico entered the salon. 'How is Cecily?'

'She is bruised, but nothing more serious, thank God.' Nico met Raf's eyes. 'Thank you for bringing her home.' He'd arrived at the palazzo minutes after Raf had left. Only his mother's calm reassurance that Eleanora was with Cecily and Raf would see her safely home kept him from going after her.

'I am only glad that I was still here when Giacomo arrived,' Raf said. 'It was not an accident.'

'How do you know?'

'An Austrian captain was waiting with Eleanora and Cecily when I arrived at the shop. He took me outside and told me that several witnesses claimed someone deliberately pushed the cart towards Cecily. A person in a black cloak and possibly wearing a mask.'

Nico's blood ran cold. 'I received a letter today. An anonymous letter. The writer said that if I did not end my betrothal to Cecily she would come to harm.'

'Do you still have the letter?'

'It is in my room.'

'I would like to see it.'

'Then come with me.'

Raf followed him to his room. He retrieved the letter from his writing desk and handed it to Raf. Raf read it and looked up his expression, grim.

'Do you recognise the handwriting?' Nico asked.

'I cannot say for certain.'

'Is it possible that Barbarina has returned to Venice?'

'I will call on Signora Gamba and see if Barbarina has returned to her. If she is not there, then I will leave for Avezza tomorrow—we need to know for certain if she has left Avezza and when.'

'And if she has not?'

'Then we will consider other possibilities. For now we must keep Cecily safe.'

'I will not allow her to leave the house unless I am with her. Or Giacomo. Once he understands what we want, he will guard her well.'

'How much do you want to tell your mother and sister? Or Cecily?'

'Not much until we discover Barbarina's whereabouts. I do not want to alarm them or Cecily unduly.'

'Very well. I will call on Signora Gamba now and let you know as soon as possible what I have discovered.

I will show myself out.' Raf looked at Nico. 'I know you will keep her safe.'

'Yes.' He would. He had failed Angelina, he would not fail Cecily.

'You still have not decided what you wish to wear? Perhaps go as Brighella? A shepherdess? Or,' Eleanora said with a teasing smile, 'should we ask Nico?'

'Nico?' Cecily jerked her thoughts back to the topic at hand. 'Ask him what?'

'What you should wear to the masquerade. I do not suppose he has mentioned to you what he plans to wear.'

'No, he hasn't said a thing. I am certain I can think of something. For myself, that is, not Nico. I can always wear a domino and a mask.' She could only imagine what he would say if she attempted to choose a costume for him.

Eleanora made a face. 'You are as bad as he is! That is exactly what he always wears to a masquerade. I had hoped you might persuade him to actually wear a costume. I have a splendid idea. We can go out today and find masks. There is a little shop near San Marco that has the most interesting ones that I have seen. We can find one for Nico as well.'

'Find what for me?' Nico asked.

Cecily started and looked up, her heart pounding much more than it should. He stood in the doorway of the small salon.

'A mask. Cecily and I are planning to visit a shop today to find masks for the masquerade. I suggested we find one for you since you seem too busy to go yourself.'

'Are you certain Cecily is well enough for such an excursion?' He did not look at all pleased by the idea.

'Of course I am,' Cecily said, annoyed that he did not directly address her.

'I will go with you,' he said abruptly. 'When do you wish to leave?'

Eleanora and Cecily both stared at him. 'Well?' he asked impatiently.

Eleanora recovered first. 'As soon as Cecily and I are ready. Before you change your mind.'

Chapter Eighteen

It was not Nico who changed his mind, however, but Eleanora. An hour and a half later, Cecily entered the salon and found Nico there with the Duchess. 'Eleanora is not well, but wants you and Nico to go without her. She would like both of you to choose a mask for her,' the Duchess said.

Cecily glanced at Nico, whose polite expression conveyed no enthusiasm for the idea. 'I do not mind waiting until Eleanora is better. I am certain the Duke has other business to attend to.'

A gleam appeared in his eye. 'On the contrary, I am at your service.'

The Duchess smiled. 'Good. He can take you to Florian's for an ice for you have not yet been there. In fact, Cecily has not even seen San Marco, although it is not at all the same since Napoleon. He was a criminal, no better than the *banditti*.' She spoke with an angry passion that Cecily had not witnessed before. She quickly collected herself. 'But it is still beautiful, he could not destroy that. So Domenico will take you and you will enjoy yourselves and not think of these things today.'

By the time they reached the Piazza San Marco, Cecily wondered why he had agreed to accompany her—he had said very little on the journey through the canals. Once or twice, when they had accidentally touched, he had jerked away as if burned. Not that she had fared much better, for her pulse jumped every time he came close to brushing against her. She wished she had thought of developing a headache.

The shop was located in a narrow L-shaped *calle* several streets behind the Piazza San Marco. Nico pushed opened the door and Cecily stepped inside. It was a tiny shop and masks of every description covered the shelves and counters. A white-haired man emerged from a room behind the counter. Through the curtain Cecily could see half-finished masks spread across a worktable. 'May I be of assistance?'

'We are interested in your masks,' Nico said.

'For the lady or yourself or both?'

'For both of us,' Cecily said before Nico could answer. Eleanora had wanted him to get a mask so she would make certain he did.

'Very good, *signora*.' He came around the side of the counter. 'Do you wish to find a mask for the *signor* first?'

'For the *signora* first,' Nico said.

'Allow me to show you what I have.'

In a few minutes he had set out a bewildering assortment of masks. Some were plain white ovals; others were lavishly decorated with feathers or sequins. There were full masks and half-masks and Cecily hardly knew where to start. She finally picked up a purple one, all too aware of Nico hovering near her shoulder. 'We must choose one for Eleanora first.' She set down the mask and forced herself to concentrate on them instead of Nico. She finally found a silk half-mask in blue and gold. 'What do you think?' she asked Nico.

'I have no doubt she will like it.'

He certainly was no help. 'I will take this,' she told the proprietor. She turned back to the selection, finding she had very little enthusiasm for choosing one for herself. She picked up one of the plain white masks. 'This will do.'

'No.' Nico removed the mask from her hand. 'This one.' He picked up a mask. It was of green silk and exquisitely decorated with small jewels. He stepped back. 'I want to see it on you.'

She stared at it. 'It is very beautiful, but…'

'Turn around. I will tie the ribbons.'

She obeyed and he stepped close to her, his body almost touching hers. His hands brushed her hair as he tied the strings. He moved his hands to her shoulders and she had the sudden desire to lean back into his arms as she had that night at the Villa Barbarigo. Oh, lord, what was wrong with her?

'Let me see you.' His hands fell from her shoulders.

She slowly turned around and faced him, grateful the mask would hide her embarrassing desire. His gaze travelled over her in a way that brought heat to her face. 'I will buy this.' His voice was husky.

'The *signora* is beautiful, no? It is a very fine mask, made by my son.'

Cecily untied the strings. 'I cannot accept this,' she told him in English. 'It is not proper.'

'You are my fiancée, so it is quite proper. Don't argue. I am buying it for you and you will wear it.'

'Indeed. Then it is only fair that I choose one for you that you will wear.'

'I have a mask.'

'But I did not choose it,' she said with a tight smile.

An odd glint appeared in his eye. 'Very well, my dear. Find something for me.'

She turned to the shopkeeper. 'I wish to look at masks for the *signor*.'

'Of course.' He pulled several from a shelf and spread them out before her. While she examined them, he brought out more.

She finally found what she was looking for. 'This one,' she told him. 'I want you to try it on.'

'Only if you will tie the strings for me,' he said softly. He suddenly looked quite dangerous and she wished she had not made the offer. But it was too late and she refused to back down.

'Turn around. You will need to bend a little.'

As soon as her hands touched his thick, dark hair she knew she had made a mistake. Not only by her own pounding heart and trembling fingers, but by the way he suddenly stilled under her hands. She finished tying the strings and stepped back, her mouth dry.

'It suits the *signor*.'

The shopkeeper's voice startled her out of her trance. She glanced at Nico. 'Yes. Yes, it does. He will take it.' She hardly knew what she was saying. To her relief, Nico removed the mask himself. She pretended interest in a display of masks while the shopkeeper wrapped their purchases, every nerve in her body on edge.

Nico finally turned. 'Shall we go?'

She jumped. 'Yes.'

She followed him out the door, careful to avoid touching him. Outside the shop, she paused. 'Perhaps we should return to the Ca' Cappelletti. I am certain your sister is eager to see our purchases.' She started to walk away.

He caught her arm. 'You are going the wrong way.'

'Oh.' She looked up at him and her heart pounded at the expression in his eyes. 'Then I had best turn around.'

'Damn it, Cecily, this is impossible.'

'What is?' She could barely form the words.

'This,' he murmured. He stepped towards her and then his mouth was on hers. Her eyes fluttered shut and she gave herself over to his kiss, hardly noticing when the package slid to the ground. He pressed her to him and her arms circled his neck, her hands finally tangling in his silky hair. His mouth was hard and demanding and she met him kiss for kiss.

A sense that someone watched them broke into her consciousness. She pulled away and he lifted his head, his eyes heavy with desire. He saw her face. 'What is it?'

She looked around. The street was deserted. 'I thought someone was here…watching us. I am being fanciful again.' She shivered. The high walls of the buildings seemed to close in on them.

'You were not fanciful last time. Come, we need to leave this place.' He retrieved the fallen package and then took her hand.

The grim set to his jaw alarmed her as he led her through the narrow street, around the corner and through the short passage to the streets that would take them back to San Marco. The crowded street was reassuring and when they finally entered the piazza, her uneasiness dissipated.

He dropped her hand. 'We can stop at Florian's before we return home.'

'Yes.' He led her across the piazza to the colonnaded row of shops. They sat down and she looked across at him. His face still looked grim. 'What is wrong?' she asked. 'Do you really think there was someone there?'

He looked over at her. 'I do not know…'

'Why such sober faces? I hope you are not quarrelling already!'

They both looked up. Thais stood next to them, a quizzical expression in her blue eyes. She was very prettily dressed in a canary yellow pelisse and matching bonnet.

Nico rose. 'Good day, Lady Margate.'

'Lady Margate? When have you become so formal?' She turned a smile on Cecily. 'How are you, dear Cecily? It has been quite dull without you. You cannot imagine how I have missed our little chats.'

'Perhaps you would join us,' Cecily said.

'If Severin would not object to sharing you. I suspect him of wanting to keep you solely for himself.' She cast a droll look in his direction.

'I do,' he said coolly.

'He is only teasing,' Cecily said hastily. 'Please sit down.'

'Thank you.' Thais took the chair opposite Cecily. After a moment, Nico sat down next to her. 'You have been shopping,' Thais said. 'What have you purchased?'

'Masks,' Nico said briefly. It was quite apparent he did not welcome Thais' company.

'Masks? For the Weston masquerade? How delightful! Where did you go?'

'In a little shop nearby which Lady Eleanora recommended.'

'I shall have to visit it myself for I have not yet purchased anything!' She looked up at the waiter who had returned to take her order and asked him for a coffee. After he left she smiled at Nico. 'I cannot help but think of Angelina whenever I visit the piazza. She so loved St Mark's. Do you remember how devastated she was when Napoleon removed the horses?'

Nico's face tightened. 'Yes.'

'I can only imagine the pleasure she would have felt upon their return!' She turned to Cecily. 'She was such a sweet girl, rather like your own Mariana. When I first saw your daughter I was quite reminded of Angelina. It is a pity you did not meet her, for I am certain you would have adored her, do you not think, Severin?'

A sick feeling rose in Cecily's throat at his bleak expression. She turned to Thais. 'I know I would have liked her very much.' She looked up and saw the waiter carrying a tray towards them. 'Our refreshments are here, thank goodness. I am starving.' She prayed Thais would be distracted by the cakes and coffee.

The waiter put the tray down on an adjoining table and set the plates and cups in front of them. After the waiter left, Thais took a sip of her coffee before speaking. 'Angelina always had a lemon ice when we were here. I quite forgot until now. Does this not remind you of the time the three of us came here? Except you are now betrothed to Cecily instead of Angelina.' She picked up her fork and calmly took a bite of her cake.

The thought darted through Cecily's mind that Thais meant to hurt Nico. She must stop her from saying anything more about Angelina. 'Have you yet decided on a costume for the masquerade? We have talked of nothing else.' She began to chatter about the various ideas Eleanora had suggested and when she had exhausted that topic began describing the plot of a novel she had just read in minute detail. Thais had no chance to do more than say a word before Cecily prattled over her. She was quite aware that Nico stared at her as if she had gone mad, but at least he had lost that horrible stricken look.

As soon as the bill had been paid, she rose. 'How nice to see you, Thais. But we really must return home.'

'I quite understand.' Her smile was guileless. She turned to Nico. 'I hope we will have the chance to speak of Angelina again. I miss her just as I know you do.' She walked off before he could reply.

Cecily touched his arm. 'We must go.'

He looked down at her as if he'd forgotten she was there. 'Yes. We must.'

He said little on the tedious journey home and Cecily had no idea if he even noticed her presence.

At the top of the staircase, outside the doors to the salon, he stopped. 'I will see you at dinner.'

'Yes. Thank you, your Grace.' She turned and left him. He had shut her out and she knew there was nothing she could say to help him.

Chapter Nineteen

Nico looked up just as Cecily appeared in the doorway of the small salon. He caught his breath. Ready for the masquerade, she was dressed as a lady from the preceding century. Her gown of embroidered cream-and-green silk emphasised her small waist and the soft curves of her breast. She wore a white wig, which was unexpectedly erotic, and he felt his groin tighten in response. For a moment she stared at him and he thought he glimpsed a similar awareness until her face closed. 'Good evening, your Grace. You wished to see me, I believe.'

He did not like the impersonal politeness in her voice. The same politeness that had been there since the day at San Marco. He had no idea how to bridge the gulf between them. He kept his own voice cool. 'I do. I have something to give you.'

'To give me?' She entered the room and stood a few feet from him.

He forced his eyes away from her lovely mouth and

pulled the small packet from his waistcoat pocket. 'A ring.' He unwrapped it. 'Hold out your hand.'

She looked at the ring and then quickly up at him, dismay clearly written all over her face. 'But that is the ring the duchess wears.'

'It is traditionally presented by the Dukes of Severin to their intended brides upon their betrothal. My mother wished you to have it now.'

'It is lovely, but I cannot wear it,' she said quietly.

'Why?' He felt angry and frustrated. 'We are betrothed, are we not?'

'Yes.' She drew in a breath. 'It is only temporary.'

'Then you will wear the ring until we put a halt to it. It will look damnably odd if you do not. Hold out your hand.'

She did so. He took her slender hand in his own and slipped the ring on to her finger. He stared down at her hand now wearing the symbol of his family. He hadn't expected to feel anything, but the surge of possessive desire startled him.

She pulled her hand away. 'It is very lovely. I will take good care of it, your Grace.'

'Don't do that.'

She looked up at him. 'Don't do what?'

'Act as if we are strangers. No, worse, as if you can hardly stand to be in the same room with me.'

She lifted her chin. 'That is not true!'

'No? Ever since we have returned to Venice you have treated me with nothing but cold disdain.'

'I could accuse you of the same thing. You barely

speak to me except when necessary and after that day we bought the masks you have hardly been around!'

'Only because you have made it clear you do not want me around.'

'This conversation is pointless. You do not want me around and I do not want you around. It appears neither one of us is particularly fond of the other. I really think, your Grace, that perhaps we should end this betrothal now.' She started to tug the ring from her finger.

'If you do not want to marry me, then perhaps you will consider becoming my mistress.' He regretted the words as soon as they left his mouth.

Her head jerked up, the colour draining from her face. Her chin inched up a notch and she met his eyes. 'I would be most honoured to become your mistress.'

This time he was the one who started. 'You are bluffing, my sweet Cecily.'

'Only if you were bluffing when you asked me.' The little cool smile on her face did nothing to improve his temper.

'Not at all. I am leaving for the villa tomorrow. When I return we will negotiate the terms.' He had no idea what he was saying.

'You are leaving?' For a moment, her gaze faltered and then she recovered. 'I will look forward to discussing your terms.'

'Then let us seal our bargain. Properly.' He did not give her a chance to reply, instead he swept her into his arms and found her mouth. He finally lifted his head and released her. Her cheeks were flushed, her lips swollen, her breathing hard.

He stepped back, angry at his loss of control. 'You may slap me now if you'd like.'

'No. I do not think that will be necessary. The others are waiting for us. You are going to the masquerade, are you not?'

'Cecily.'

She swept from the room, leaving him staring after her.

He could no longer deny that he was falling in love with her.

Cecily stood with Bernardo and Eleanora in the salon of the huge palazzo leased by Sir Thomas and Lady Weston. Festoons of flowers and vines decorated the room and Chinese lanterns lent an exotic eastern aura.

'The musicians should arrive soon,' Eleanora remarked. She looked beautiful and quite intriguing in a flowing gown of dark blue silk.

'Then we should go to the *androne* now so we might have the best view.' The highlight of the evening was to be a barge of musicians arriving in front of the palazzo at midnight. Bernardo, dressed as Pantalone, held out one arm to Eleanora and the other to Cecily. Cecily smiled at him, determined she would not think about Nico. She had no idea where he was for Octavia had spirited him away shortly after they arrived.

Their parting before the masquerade had dashed any hopes she might have secretly entertained that something was possible between them. He'd asked her to become his mistress in anger and she had accepted in equal anger. She knew he regretted his words, the instant she saw his face after he'd kissed her. She was too numb to care, so when Bernardo appeared, a handsome troubadour, she found she had no trouble engaging in a mild flirtation with him. Perhaps her heart would not break after all.

Where was Cecily? Nico had lost sight of her among the crowd of masked guests. He finally spotted her with Bernardo and Eleanora heading towards the small hall that led to the stairs. He wanted to go after her, but he would hardly blame her if she refused to talk to him. Not after he'd insulted her. He felt a flicker of despair every time he thought of her face after he'd offered *carte blanche*.

'Severin, I must speak with you. In private.'

He turned and found a woman in a black half-mask and domino at his side. For a moment he thought he was staring at Barbarina Zanetti, then just as quickly recognised Thais Margate despite the black wig covering her curls. 'This hardly seems the time for a private conversation.'

'Please, I must talk to you before it is too late.'

She had an almost desperate note in her voice he had never heard before. 'What is it?'

'Not here. There is a room off the salon where we can go.' She placed her hand on his arm, her grip firm as if she had no intention of allowing him to get away.

Torn between curiosity and unease, he followed her across the crowded room and into one of the smaller rooms. Surprisingly enough, it was empty. She turned to face him, and even through the slits of her mask he felt the intensity of her gaze.

'What is wrong?' he asked.

'You cannot marry Cecily Renato. It is all wrong.'

'Why is it wrong?' he asked carefully.

'Because I love you. I always have.'

'Thais…' Shocked, he took a step back as she came towards him. He found himself backed up against a sofa.

'You must care for me at least a little.' She stood so close she was almost touching him.

Was she drunk? He caught her hand. 'Do not say anything more that you will later regret.'

She gave a peculiar little laugh. 'I only regret I did not tell you this when you were so determined to marry Angelina. Would it have changed your mind?'

He released her hand. 'I loved Angelina.'

'You could not have. Just as you do not love Cecily.'

'You are wrong. I love Cecily. I am going to marry her.'

She stared at him. 'I will never let that happen.' She spoke in a cold, controlled voice.

'What do you mean?'

'I mean that you will never marry her.' She whirled away from him and before he could stop her had run from the room. He dashed after her, but she slipped past a trio of harlequins. A feeling of dread washed over him and he knew he must find Cecily.

He started through the crowd. Many of the guests were gathered in front of the tall windows facing the grand canal. Others were leaving the salon and starting down the stairs to the *androne*. The barge of musicians must be coming. He vaguely remembered Eleanora mentioning they would watch the barge from the *androne*. He crossed the salon and out of the corner of his eye saw a short dark figure in a black cloak. The hair on the back of his neck prickled. He pushed his way through the crowd, ignoring the indignant mutters at his rudeness, and reached the stairs. For a moment, he could see nothing and then saw the black-cloak figure was already in the *androne*.

He ran down them, shoving past a quartet of youths who were idling on the stairs. He had nearly reached the bottom when he saw Eleanora and Bernardo. They were nearly at the gates leading from the palazzo to the dock on the canal. At first he did not see Cecily and then he caught a glimpse of her green mask. He heard someone call his name, but he paid no heed.

He jumped down the last step and began to run across the marble floor through the crowd.

Cecily stood next to Bernardo on the small dock in front of the palazzo. Sounds of a Vivaldi concerto drifting out over the water heralded the approach of the floating concert.

The crowd pushed forward, hoping to glimpse the barge. A large nun jostled her way in front of Cecily, who stumbled a little. She righted herself and found Bernardo was no longer next to her. The mass of guests seemed to close around her and a sliver of panic shot through her.

A hand closed around her arm. She attempted to draw her arm away and found herself looking at a dark shrouded figure. A prickle of fear shot down her back, for there was something sinister and familiar about the figure. 'I think, sir, that you have mistaken me for someone else.'

'Good evening, Cecily.'

She nearly sagged with relief. 'Thais. You frightened me.'

Her grip tightened around Cecily's wrist and she pulled something from the folds of her garment. 'You cannot marry him, you know.' With sick shock Cecily saw a flash of silver and realised she held a dagger. Thais raised it just as the musicians reached the palazzo, the strains of the concerto echoing all round.

'No!' Cecily pulled away with all of her strength and stumbled. At the same time another dark figure burst through the crowd and leaped towards Thais. They both tumbled into Cecily and all three of them fell into the cold, dark water.

She went under for a moment and then clawed her way up, gasping and terrified. Her heavy skirts wrapped around her legs and she fought to keep from slipping into the chilly depths. There was a splash next to her. Strong arms grasped her. She flailed out, fearing it was Thais who meant to drown her.

'Cecily.'

Nico. She had no idea how he came to be there. 'Thais, she…she tried to stab me.'

'Don't talk, sweetheart. I need to get you out.'

He helped her to the edge of the dock. He half-lifted

her as a man reached down and pulled her out. Her knees shook so hard she could barely stand and she was hardly aware of the voices and music around her. Someone draped a long cape over her shoulders. 'Come, *signora*, you must go inside.' She looked up and saw a man standing next to her.

'No. The…the others.' She realised Nico had not followed her out and in the dim light of the torches she thought she saw him swimming towards a black shape.

'Cecily. Thank God.'

Raf was suddenly at her side. 'Where is Nico?'

'In…in the water.'

He ran towards the dock just as Bernardo and Eleanora appeared. 'Cecily. Oh, dear lord, it was you.' Eleanora's face was pale. 'We must get you inside.'

'No. Wait.' For Raf had stooped to help another woman from the water. A woman whose hair was long and dark instead of blonde. He laid her on the dock and knelt beside her. Cecily ran towards her.

Cecily dropped down next to Raf. 'Barbarina!' Barbarina's eyes were closed, but she was breathing, thank God. She gripped Barbarina's hand. 'Barbarina, it is Cecily.'

Barbarina's eyes opened for a moment. 'You are safe. I tried to stop her…tried to warn you…warn him that she is wicked.'

'You must not talk.' She squeezed her hand and then quickly slipped the cape from her shoulders and covered Barbarina. 'She…she saved my life, Raf. We must take her inside. It is too cold.'

'I know.' He looked up and Cecily saw Nico standing next to them. Water dripped down his forehead and he was breathing heavily. 'How is she?'

'Alive,' Raf said. 'But barely. The other?'

'I could do nothing.'

Raf bent towards Barbarina. 'Barbarina. I will carry you inside.'

Her eyes fluttered open. 'No.' She looked past him to Nico. 'Must tell him…the Duke…' Her breathing was heavy. She closed her eyes.

'Nico?' Alarmed, Cecily looked up at him.

Nico dropped to the ground beside her. 'Signora Zanetti. Barbarina.'

With a great effort, she opened them. 'I saw her that day, when Angelina…'

'When Angelina what?'

'When she went to meet you. She followed… Angelina.' She paused, struggling for breath. 'She killed Angelina. I…I saw it in her eyes. At the fête, she…tried to kill Cecily. Because of you.' Her eyes closed and she drew in one last shuddering breath.

Horrified, Cecily stared at Barbarina and then at the others. 'Nico?' she whispered. He looked as if he'd turned to stone.

Chapter Twenty

Cecily set her book aside on the bench and waited for Nico to cross the *androne* to the courtyard where she sat. Two days had passed since Barbarina's funeral; nearly a week since the nightmarish masquerade. Her heart sank a little when she saw his face—he still wore the remote expression of a man who was utterly unreachable, buried away in his grief.

'I wanted to tell you that I am leaving Venice for a while,' he said.

'When will you go?'

'Today. In a few hours.'

She would not let him see her dismay. 'Where will you go?'

'To a small villa near Vicenza.'

She stood. He was polite, none of the arrogance she so associated with him present. If only he would attempt to ride roughshod over her. Or scold her. But he'd done nothing but shut himself away since that night. 'I am sorry.' She could think of nothing else.

If anything, his expression only shuttered more. 'Why? You almost lost your life because of me.'

'You are wrong. I almost lost my life because of Thais. You saved my life. You and Barbarina.'

He said nothing. A sort of angry despair washed over her. 'Thais deceived all of us, even me,' Cecily said. 'I do not want to spend the rest of my life thinking that you blame yourself for what happened to me. I could not bear it. So for my sake, I pray you will not.' She picked up her book. 'I will say goodbye to you now. As always, I wish you happiness.' She waited for him to speak and when he did not, she left him. She did not look back.

Raf called just before Nico was about to step into the gondola. 'What do you think you are doing?' he asked Nico without preamble.

'I am leaving Venice.'

'Why? Because you blame yourself for Angelina? For Cecily?'

'I am about to leave. I would prefer to continue this discussion later.' Or not at all.

'Damn you, Domenico. We will have this discussion now.'

Nico had rarely seen Raf so angry. He suspected that, if he were to step into the gondola, Raf would follow. 'We cannot talk here. Come into one of the offices.'

Inside the office, Raf glared at him. 'What is it? You

wish to take the guilt for Angelina's death upon yourself? You were not the one who pushed her that day.'

'No, but Barbarina spoke the truth; because of me Thais killed Angelina and tried to kill Cecily. I should have seen, should have known, what she was capable of doing.'

'None of us did. Do you think I have not blamed myself for the very same things? Thais did everything possible to convince me that Angelina was not happy with you—that Angelina loved me. I had some idea that Thais was jealous of Angelina, but it never occurred to me she would harm her. What of Barbarina? She suspected, but yet said nothing.'

'Thais did not have an obsession with you.'

'So that makes Angelina's death your fault? Did you encourage Thais?'

For the first time since that night, Nico felt a stirring of anger. 'No, damn it, but I should have made it clear I wanted nothing to do with her.'

'Do you think it would have mattered? She was not right; she was undoubtedly mad.' He looked at Nico. 'What of Cecily? You will leave her here by herself?'

'She is with my family. She has you if you are ever around.'

'She is betrothed to you, or perhaps you have forgotten that.'

'It is only temporary.'

'She loves you.'

He looked at Raf. 'Then she is a fool.'

Raf's fist balled. 'I should call you out for that,' he said softly.

'Choose your weapon.'

Raf stared at him for a moment. 'I am beginning to believe she is better off without you. She needs a man who will treasure her love, not trample it underfoot.' He strode to the door and then paused. 'Angelina is dead. And you have buried yourself with her.' He was gone.

Cecily looked around the bedchamber. The dressing table was bare; her fans and gloves neatly packed away in her bandbox. In another half an hour she would be leaving with Raf. She had decided she must return to Avezza. She had left a note for Nico with instructions it was to be given to him upon his return. She had left the ring with the Duchess.

'My dear, are you certain you want to leave us?' the Duchess asked. Cecily had not heard her enter the room. 'I do not like the thought of you returning to your home alone like this. You have been through a great deal in the past few weeks.'

'I will not be completely alone. Raf promised he will stay in Avezza for a few days.'

'Domenico needs you.'

She looked up at the Duchess. 'If anything, he has made it quite clear he does not. He would not allow me to give him anything. Not sympathy, not kindness. When I told him I was sorry he told me I did not need to be.' Just as Marco had refused to accept her comfort.

'My dear.'

'I can do nothing to help him,' Cecily whispered.

The Duchess was silent for a moment before speaking. 'He has not allowed any of us to help him, just as he did not before. In some way, for him, it is almost as if Angelina has died again. He blamed himself, you see, thirteen years ago, and I can only imagine how he must feel now. Not only about Angelina, but also about you. I have no doubt he feels he failed to protect you from Thaïs.'

'He is wrong. He did everything he could.'

'For him that was not enough,' she said gently. She took Cecily's hands. 'I cannot fault you for wanting to go, for you can do nothing for him unless he allows it. I only pray that he will open his heart before it is too late.' She bent forward and pressed a kiss on Cecily's cheek. 'It is time for you to go down.'

He had gone to the villa in the hills above Vicenza for a few days, but the solitude had brought him no relief. Instead his dreams had been restless and filled with imagies of Cecily and Angelina. He had given up and left for Treviso, the town where Angelina was buried.

Her grave was in the small cemetery near the villa that once belonged to her family. He found the marker easily enough, under the spreading shade of an old tree.

He thought of her dark laughing eyes set in an oval face, which she considered too long and which he found adorable, and her beautiful, curving body. She had enchanted him; he had wondered how any creature so exquisite and alive could adore him the way she had. He'd always had a sense she was not quite real; even their kisses tasted of magic, and he sometimes feared he would open his eyes and find she'd vanished like some enchanted creature.

In the end, she had vanished, leaving him bereft and empty-handed and wondering if his very attempts to capture her had somehow destroyed her.

In the end she had been destroyed because of him.

As Cecily had almost been.

Raf did not blame him. Nor did Cecily. He would never forget the look of despair on her face when she walked away from him, as if by holding himself responsible he was somehow hurting her as well.

Raf said Cecily loved him. He wondered if that was still true.

Raf was correct; he was not the same youth who fell in love with Angelina. *I wonder—if you were to meet her now for the first time, would you still want her? Or if you would discover it was Cecily you wanted after all?*

For despite the hours he and Angelina had spent together, talking and laughing, and flirting, he could not recall one time when he had told her anything of substance. He had not spoken to her of the sorrow he felt over his father's ailing health. Or the apprehension he felt at the prospect of becoming the next Duke and finding himself responsible for his family's vast holdings and wealth and all those, family and employees, who would be dependent upon his goodwill and judgement. The few times he had brought such things up, she would tease him for his seriousness. 'You will become dull, Nico, if you continue to speak of such solemn matters!'

He could imagine telling Cecily those things. Just as

he could imagine coming to her now when he needed her quiet understanding. Raf had asked him, if he met Angelina for the first time now, would he want her?

He had no idea if she would even want him, for he had changed just as Raf had said. He was no longer the young raffish marquis she had adored. He had a reputation for a cynical coolness she would undoubtedly find appalling and he spent more time on his estates than he did in London.

With cold clarity he suspected, if they met now, they might feel nothing more than a passing attraction for each other. If Cecily was with him, he doubted he would look at Angelina at all.

The realisation brought him no comfort. Tears sprang to his eyes. He bowed his head and for the first time since Angelina's death he was finally able to weep for her.

And allow her to rest in peace at last.

He decided to return to Venice that day. He must see Cecily. He had hurt her, trampled over her heart, just as Raf said he had. He had thought only of his own needs when he'd offered for her. He wanted her, but on his terms. He had not been prepared to give her all of himself, but he wanted all of her. He had not understood why, if she cared for him, she would refuse him.

He understood now. He would offer himself to her and pray she might forgive him.

Nico found his mother in the library. She was sitting on the sofa, a book open on her lap. She tore her gaze away at his approach. A warm smile lit her face when she saw him. 'Domenico. You are finally back.'

She set her book down on the sofa and rose. She held out her hands and searched his face. 'I think that you are better.'

'I am better. Much better.'

'I am glad.'

'So am I.' He pressed her hands. 'Where is Cecily?'

'She is not in Venice. She left for Avezza with Rafaele.'

He felt a stab of fear and then anger. 'Why? With Raf?'

She hesitated. 'She sent a note that she wished given to you when you returned.'

'Where is the note?'

'In your bedchamber.'

He released her hands. 'Then you will forgive me if I go to retrieve it now.'

'Of course.'

He found the note on the bureau. He broke the seal and quickly scanned the brief missive.

To His Grace the Duke of Severin,

I am most deeply grateful for your kindness in offering me the protection of your name so that I might be safe from the attentions of a man whom I find most repugnant. Under the circumstances I feel it is best that I return to Avezza and that we do not meet again.

As always, I wish you all happiness,
Cecily Renato

He cursed. What the devil did she mean by saying she felt it best they never meet again? He had intended to beg her for forgiveness and then insist she marry him. And why the hell was she with Raf? Common sense told him it was quite natural for Raf to escort her, but he remembered Raf's parting words—what if Raf had changed his mind and decided he wanted Cecily after all?

At the very least she could tell him face to face that she never wanted to see him again.

He went down the stairs and met his mother in the hall. 'I am leaving for Avezza,' he told her.

'What will you say to her?'

He stopped. 'I intend to ask her exactly why she found it necessary to leave Venice before I returned. I will also inform her that if she wishes to end our betrothal she must do it in person.'

'Perhaps she thinks it is you who wishes to end the betrothal.'

His brow snapped down. 'Why the devil would she think that?'

'What did you tell her when you left Venice?'

'I told her I was leaving for a few days. What else was I to tell her?'

'I do not suppose you told her that you love her?'

He could feel an unfamiliar heat rising to his cheeks. 'No.'

'Then I think you must.' She gave him a gentle smile. 'Go, then. I will inform Eleanora you needed to leave straight away. I have no doubt she will understand.'

* * *

Cecily found the leather-bound book under a pile of old shawls in Barbarina's room. She picked it up and saw it was a journal. How odd, for Barbarina did not seem the sort of person who would write down her innermost thoughts. She carefully opened it and saw the delicate, neat writing did not resemble Barbarina's spidery scrawl at all. The first page was dated 1 January 1803.

She rose and sat on the chair near Barbarina's bed. She turned to the last page: 15 August 1803. *I am going to meet Nico…*

Nearly an hour later, she slowly closed the book, tears streaming down her cheeks. Angelina had not believed Thais' lies; she had loved Nico up until the very end. She wanted to meet him that day, not to call off their betrothal, but to tell him she would marry him.

Barbarina must have read this as well; why had she allowed Nico to believe Angelina no longer wanted to marry him? But then Barbarina had done nothing to stop Thais; she had known about Thais' lies and had used them herself to attempt to drive a wedge between Nico and Angelina.

Because she hoped Angelina would marry Raf if Nico was gone. It was only after Angelina died that Barbarina realised how truly wicked Thais was.

She stood. Perhaps Nico wanted nothing from her, but she had one last thing she would give him before he returned to England. She had no doubt he would marry

soon; most likely a proper English girl who would provide him with beautiful dark-eyed children…

How ridiculous. She could not think of such things.
She would miss him. Terribly. She was grateful to him
for so much. She had finally broken out of her self-im-
posed exile. She had written a letter to her grandmother
and, for the first time in years, the burden of the anger
she had carried towards her grandmother was now gone.
She had even begun to think of visiting England.

She had loved again and, although he had not returned her love, it had not destroyed her.

Perhaps knowing that Angelina had loved him to the
end would ease some of the pain he carried. She would
give this to him, but it was not her gift…it was Angelina's.

Raf did not look surprised when she told him she
planned to leave for Venice the next day or when she explained why. 'I will, of course, accompany you.'

'You do not need to.'

'It is what I wish. For you, for Nico and for Angelina.'

Chapter Twenty-One

They stopped at an inn the late afternoon of the following day. Cecily stepped down from her carriage and waited while Raf spoke with Figaro.

She started towards the inn and then her heart lurched when she saw the crest on one of the carriages standing near by.

It could not be. No, that was quite impossible. Perhaps she could inquire if an Englishman was staying at the inn. Then determine if he was dark and spoke fluent Italian and was a duke. If so, she would…

'Good evening, Cecily.'

She spun around, her hand going to her breast. The blood rushed to her head and for a dreadful moment she thought she would swoon.

He stood behind her, arms folded. He was hatless, the sun slanting through the trees onto his hair.

'I…I had no idea you were here,' she stammered.

'And if you had, you would have jumped back into

your carriage and driven away as quickly as possible?'

'I do not know.'

He smiled, although it was not pleasant. She knew, then, he had received her note. He was angry.

Part of her was relieved. If he could feel angry, then perhaps there was hope after all. His gaze fell on something behind her and then his brow snapped down. 'Vianoli. What the devil is he doing here?'

'He is escorting me to Venice.'

'The hell he is.' He strode past her to Raf.

'Nico! Stop!' He looked as if he planned to knock Raf down. She hurried after him and caught his sleeve just as he stopped in front of Raf.

'What are you doing with my fiancée?' he demanded.

Raf's brow shot up. 'Is she? I was under the impression that your betrothal was of a temporary nature.'

'You are wrong. At least until she tells me to my face that she will not marry me.'

Raf glanced at Cecily. 'Do you wish to tell him that?'

'I…' She took a deep breath. 'This is ridiculous. We cannot stand out here and discuss this.'

'Then we will go inside,' Nico said. He took her arm. 'Coming, Vianoli?'

'Of course.' If anything, Raf looked slightly amused.

She glanced up at Nico. 'You can release my arm. I do not plan to run away.'

'I beg your pardon.' He dropped his hand away. They went inside to one of the vacant public rooms.

'Where are you travelling to?' Raf asked politely.

'Avezza.'

'Ah.'

'And why are you and Cecily going to Venice?'

'That is for Cecily to tell you.'

Nico turned to her. 'Why?' he demanded.

In an inn with Nico glaring at both her and Raf was not how she'd envisioned telling him about the journal. She wondered why she had ever felt sorry for him, for he was in the stupid arrogant duke role that she detested. Why was it any of his business what she was doing with Raf? 'I would prefer to tell you at a time when you are not in such a disagreeable mood, your Grace. And when you speak to me in civil tones. For now I wish to go to my room.'

He stepped in front of her. 'At least tell me if you are in love with Raf.'

Her mouth fell open. She looked up into his dark eyes and the hard set of his jaw. 'At the moment, I do not think I am in love with anyone. Or ever want to be. Good evening, your Grace.' She swept past him with a feeling of satisfaction.

Nico turned on Raf as soon as she had left the room. 'Do you plan to let her walk away like that?'

'Do you?'

'She has made it clear she wants nothing to do with me.'

Raf merely looked at him. 'So why are you going to Avezza?'

'To see Cecily. To beg her to marry me. If it is not too late.' His gaze hardened a little. 'I will not let you have her without a fight if you have changed your mind about wanting her.'

'She is not in love with me. Nor am I in love with her. However, that does not mean I intend to let you have her. Not until I am assured that you will not walk all over her heart.'

'I love her,' he said quietly.

Raf eyed him for a moment. 'Then I suggest you tell her that.'

'If she will listen.'

'I will talk to her and ask her to dine with you. However, if she does not wish to hear you, I cannot force her.'

Hope was beginning to rise in his chest. 'I would not expect you to.' Not that he intended to allow her to refuse.

Raf smiled a little. 'One more thing—I would suggest you actually ask Cecily to marry you rather than telling her she will do so.'

Cecily gazed around the room. It was small but at least the bed linens appeared fresh and there were no unpleasant smells that would indicate a general lack of cleanliness. She sat down on the single chair in the room. She had no idea whether to laugh or to cry. Was it possible Nico was acting so oddly because he thought she was in love with Raf? That she and Raf were travelling together for some clandestine purpose? Just as Raf had accused her and Nico of the same thing?

They could be, at this very moment, fighting in the

public room downstairs for all she knew. Not that she particularly cared. Perhaps they would knock some sort of rational sense into each other. At any rate, she was quite weary of feeling responsible for everyone else.

She bent down and was about to unlace her half-boots when someone knocked on the door. She straightened, feeling slight trepidation. *'Sì?'* She prayed it was not Nico.

It was Raf. She walked to the door and opened it. 'I would like to speak to you for a moment,' he said.

'Come in.' She stepped aside and allowed him to pass her into the room. 'You have no bruises,' she told him.

'What?'

'It is nothing. What do you wish to say to me?'

'Nico would like you to dine with him tonight. In private.'

She frowned at him. 'I really do not feel inclined to do so.'

He sighed. 'I am rather weary of playing matchmaker for both of you. He cares for you. You care for him.'

She shook her head. 'He asked me why, if I cared for him, I could not marry him. I told him I could not live with another ghost.'

'Caterina.'

'I never made Marco really happy. He always mourned her.'

'Barbarina told you that, no? She did not want you taking Caterina's place, but more than that, because her husband did not love her, she did not want Marco to love you.'

'It was not just Barbarina. I saw it when he looked at me.'

He took her hand. 'Listen to me, Cecily. He mourned her, it is true, but he loved you as well. He knew he was ill almost as soon as he brought you to Italy, but he did not know how to tell you. He worried about you and did not want to burden you with the knowledge he would not live very long.'

Tears sprang to her eyes. 'I…I did not know. He never said anything to me.'

'It was not always easy for Marco to speak of his feelings. Nico is much like him in that regard.' He looked at her for a moment. 'I think you should at least hear what Nico has to say to you. You did wish to give him the journal, no?'

'You could give it to him.'

'It will mean more if you do.' He closed her hand over her palm. 'At this moment, you hold his happiness here, in your hand. It is only right that you let him know what you have decided.'

'What if I do not know?' she whispered.

He brushed a kiss across her knuckles. 'I think you do.'

Cecily stood in the doorway of the small salon for a moment. Nico stood near the window and turned immediately. He stared at her for a moment as if she was an apparition. 'You came,' he finally said.

'Yes. Raf said you wanted to see me.'

He moved towards her. 'Come in.'

She stepped into the room.

'You are only here because of Raf?' he asked.

Certainly he did not look as if she held his happiness or fate or whatever nonsense Raf had said in her hand. 'Is there something you wished to say to me?'

'Why are you travelling to Venice with Raf? Particularly since you so recently left it.'

'I was coming to see you. Raf insisted on escorting me.'

Surprise flickered across his features. 'Indeed. I rather thought from your polite note that you had no wish to see me again. Except in the capacity of a relation. So were you coming to see me as a relation?'

'I have something to give you.'

'Indeed. Then it is most convenient that we met here. You will not need to travel all the way to Venice after all. What is it you wished to give me? It cannot be the ring—you left it in Venice.'

He was still angry. Because she had hurt his pride? She was suddenly very tired.

She held out the journal. 'I found this among Barbarina's possessions. I wanted you to have it.'

He took it from her and then opened the book. He stared down at the page for a moment, then slowly looked up at her. 'It is Angelina's journal.'

'Yes.'

'Why did you bring it to me?'

'Because you loved her. And because, if you read her last entries, you will see that she loved you. She never had any intention of breaking off your betrothal.'

He looked back down at the book. She waited for a moment and then silently left the salon.

She had just reached the door of her room when she heard footsteps behind her. 'Cecily,' Nico said.

'What is it you want?'

He hesitated for a moment. 'I was going to Avezza to find you.'

She looked up. 'Why? To take me to task over the note I wrote? Or the ring? Perhaps I should have waited until you returned, but you were so distant and so cold that I did not think it mattered whether I was there or not. At any rate, I think we have said all that needs to be said between us.' She inserted the key into the lock, only to find his hand over hers.

'We haven't said all that needs to be said. At least, I have not,' he said quietly. 'Would you grant me a few moments at least? I vow I will not approach you again unless it is your wish.'

The arrogant duke had fallen away. Instead he looked almost desperate. 'Very well.'

'In your room or downstairs? I promise I want nothing more than to talk to you.'

Downstairs would be more circumspect, but she was too tired to think of going back down. 'My room, if you please.'

She managed to open the door despite her trembling hands and stepped into the room. He followed her and she moved as far away from him as she could. He shut the door and leaned against it. He had Angelina's journal in his hand.

She tried to keep her voice calm. 'What do you want to say to me?'

'When I read your note, I was angry. But more than that, I was afraid.' His dark eyes were fixed on her face. 'Afraid I would not see you again. Afraid you would never agree to marry me.'

'I thought we had agreed we were not going to marry.' She clasped her hands together to keep them from trembling.

'I've changed my mind. I want you to marry me.'

'I have no idea why.'

'I love you.'

Her head spun for a moment. 'You cannot,' she whispered.

'But I do. I came to ask you to forgive me for hurting you. For wanting all of you without offering you the same in return.' He took a step towards her and set the journal down on the dresser. 'I am offering you myself. All of me. With no ghosts between us.'

'Nico…'

He took another step towards her, his eyes never leaving her face. 'You said you cared for me. Is there any chance you still do?'

'Yes. I—'

'Good.' He moved towards her and she found herself backed up against the dresser. 'Because I intend to make you fall in love with me.' A touch of his usual arrogance had returned.

She drew in a shaky breath. 'You do not need to make me fall in love with you.'

His body was nearly touching hers. 'Yes, I do. I intend to begin now.'

'You…you said you only wanted to talk.'

'I have changed my mind about that as well.' The determined look in his eye made her legs tremble.

'Nico…wait, there is something I must tell you.'

'Later.' He caught her into his arms and pulled her against him. His mouth sought hers. She resisted for a moment, and then her body melded into his as she gave herself completely to him.

Nico opened his eyes. The soft, warm body against his filled him with a lazy, peaceful contentment. He shifted a little, moving his arm out from under her so that he could turn and pull her more fully against him. He felt the stirrings of arousal, but he would control his urge at least for now.

He could not keep from nuzzling her neck, however, revelling in her clean, sweet taste and the faint scent of lovemaking that clung to her. She had responded with the same passion as before. She would succumb soon enough. Before they returned to Venice he intended to first take her to the small villa he owned in the hills above Vicenza where he would thoroughly and enjoyably compromise her.

She stirred. His groin tightened and he could not resist planting another kiss on the back of her soft neck. She half-turned, her breast brushing his hand and he nearly groaned. Her eyes fluttered open. 'You are still here,' she whispered. 'I was not dreaming.'

'No, *cara*.' He brushed the hair from her forehead.

'Nor were you dreaming when I told you that you are going to marry me.'

A half-smile touched her lips. 'You could ask me, you know.'

'You might say no. I would rather you had no choice.'

'I might say yes.'

His pulse quickened. 'Would you?'

'Yes. Yes, I think I would.'

'Only think? I want you to be certain.'

'But are you?'

He saw the doubt in her eyes. His first impulse was to kiss all her reservations away, but something in her expression stopped him. 'Why would you think I am not?'

She sat up. 'Where did you go after you left Venice?

He sat up as well, the cover falling from his chest. 'I needed to tell Angelina goodbye.' He looked away for a moment. 'For the first time since her death I felt she was finally at peace. I knew she was finally gone.' He glanced down at Cecily. 'I left that day to return to you. I wanted to see you, beg your forgiveness. But you were gone.'

She caught his hand. 'I am so sorry. I did not think you needed me. Or wanted me. So I…I left. But then Raf came. He insisted that I return to you because you needed me. And because he needed a happy ending.'

'Raf is very wise.' He drew her against his chest. 'Promise me you will not run away again.'

'No. Yes, I promise I will not.'

He drew her against him. 'So, if I ask you to marry me, will you say "yes"?'

'Yes.'

His arm tightened around her. 'Will you marry me, Cecily?'

'Yes.'

'As soon as I procure the licence.'

'In the family chapel?'

He laughed and dropped a kiss on her forehead. 'No. Here. First, I've no intention of giving you time to change your mind. We can have a second ceremony when we return to England. We will spend as much time in Italy as you wish.'

'I think I would like to become reacquainted with England. I finally wrote to my grandmother.'

'Good. We will invite her to our wedding.' Although he was not paying much attention. The quilt had fallen away to reveal one pink-tipped breast and he could think of nothing but loving her again. He slid down and pulled her on top of him. 'But for now, I have other business to attend to. Such as making you fall in love with me.'

His hand cupped one of her rounded breasts, his finger and thumb tracing leisurely circles around the sensitive, hardened nipple.

Her little moan made him smile. 'In fact, I am considering holding you prisoner until you do.'

'Nico…' She gasped as his hand drifted down her stomach to the juncture of her thighs. 'Please…wait. I must tell you something.'

'Not now.' He had no intention of allowing her to change her mind. His mouth found hers, stifling any protest.

* * *

A fortnight later Cecily and Nico stood in the garden of the Villa. Their wedding had taken place that morning, a quiet ceremony that was attended only by their families. Raf had come as he promised, although he did not stay long. After the ceremony and the breakfast, Nico brought her outside to the garden.

He took her hand and she glanced at him, her heart swelling with tenderness and love. His face, which had always seemed so harsh, was now familiar, the hardness no longer quite so visible, particularly when he turned to smile at her as he did now. He looked happy and she was still amazed that she had that effect on him. She returned his smile and then took a breath.

'I have something I have wanted to say to you since we met at the inn.' For some odd reason, her hand was shaking.

His smile faded and he dropped her hand. 'It is rather late if you have suddenly changed your mind about wedding me.'

'Oh, no.' She caught his hand to hold it again. 'It is not that at all. I wanted to tell you that I…I love you.'

He looked rather stunned. 'You love me?'

'I tried to tell you at the inn. That you did not need to make me fall in love with you because I was already in love with you. You would not give me a chance to tell you.'

His laugh was shaky. 'I promise from now on I will give you as many chances as you want. I cannot think of a better wedding gift from you.'

She wrapped her arms around his neck and drew him to her. Their kiss was tender and unhurried, a kiss full of promise and, most of all, a kiss full of hope.

* * * * *

The Gambler's Heart

by

Gayle Wilson

Gayle Wilson taught English and world history before turning to writing full time. A winner of a number of prestigious writing awards, she is also the author of over ten contemporary romantic suspense novels. Gayle Wilson is married, with one son, and lives in Alabama, USA.

Prologue

December 1815

The inn teemed with stranded travelers, its entrance hall redolent of their wet woolens, now drying in the welcoming heat provided by the enormous fireplace. A representative sample from every class in England was companionably gathered around its fire. The freezing rain, which had finally turned into blinding snow, had leveled the social standings of the inn's occupants far more effectively than the late Revolution in France had ever managed.

With a reluctant anxiety that centered more on the welfare of the struggling horses than on any concern for herself or for her late stepfather's retainers, Lady Madelyn Fairchild had finally given in to the necessities of the situation and called a halt to her own journey.

She stood now in the smoky entry hall of the country public house where she had been forced to take shelter, well aware that she was the focus of every masculine eye. Since she was, it seemed, the only female who had been foolish, or desperate, enough to continue to travel on a day that clearly foretold its intentions, she turned expectantly to the host and raised a pair of beautifully shaped brows. Familiar with the ways of Quality, he knew immediately what she was asking with those aristocratic arches.

"Not a closet, my lady. I couldn't bed down a mouse. Not if she was my own grandmother. I've been full up since last night."

"I'm sure, for a lady traveling alone…" she suggested in her low contralto. Although in her Season she had been an acknowledged diamond, there were many who claimed Madelyn Fairchild's voice was her best feature.

Its pleasantly persuasive quality had no effect now.

"It's ladies I've got. Too old and sick or too young and green to be left either below or on the road. And with a prior claim."

"I see," Maddy said simply.

But he knew that tone, also. It was another trick of the ton he was very familiar with. He'd not run a hostelry on the Plymouth road for twenty years and learned nothing. She was about to suggest that surely he was mistaken. *Surely* he could wave a magic wand and there would be another room simply because she wanted one.

"But surely—" she began, and he interrupted to save her the trouble.

"Doubled up, sleeping stacked to the ceiling as it is. There ain't nothing, my lady. And I can't be making you a room. It ain't to be had."

Her slim hands in dove gray kid gloves lifted to remove the darker gray hood of her redingote. The cloth had rested without disarranging a strand of the smoothly shining coils into which her silver-gilt hair had been arranged. She looked as if she had just stepped out of her hairdresser's hands. She certainly did not look as if she had been traveling in a poorly sprung, aged coach since dawn.

Her brows and long, thick lashes were a pale brown that framed beautiful violet-blue eyes. Her cheeks were still touched with pink from the bitter cold she had just left. They were the only sign that she, like the other patrons of his establishment, had been a victim of the elements. She looked as if she might be paying a call at one of the elegant London town houses he imagined she frequented.

"Then I suppose I'll have to make do with a private parlor. Would you bring tea? And whatever else you have already prepared. We didn't stop for luncheon, hoping to outrun the storm."

Maddy had already begun to turn to give instructions to the hovering groom when she registered the negative movement of the host's head.

She looked back and allowed the full force of the violet gaze to consider the landlord's suddenly flushed features.

"No?" she asked softly, the delicate brows arching again, and her patent disbelief at his refusal coloring her voice. "Old or sick?" she suggested with just a trace of amused patience.

"Well, no, my lady," the host admitted, faltering now.

There was no reason at all to favor the present occupant's claim to his parlor over the needs of this benighted gentlewoman—except for the fact that the gentleman ensconced there had demonstrated a generous hand in scattering gold coins on the inn's delighted staff since his arrival. He had wanted warmth and privacy and was more than willing to pay handsomely for both. English Quality the likes of this lady were, on the other hand, apt to make demands and expect one to rush about for a brusque "Thank you, my good man." The landlord found that he preferred the color of the Frenchman's gold to the color of her ladyship's eyes, remarkable though they were.

"Then perhaps you might persuade whoever..."

"Most determined on having the parlor. I don't believe—"

"Then we shall simply have to share. Surely if you impress upon the ladies my situation—" She halted suddenly at the arrested expression in his eyes.

"Well, um, you see, my lady..." he began to stammer.

"A gentleman?" she asked, softly enough, but he could hear the steel.

"A foreign gentleman," he acknowledged. Maybe that in itself would discourage whatever idea he could see growing behind those lovely eyes.

"And you would let an Englishwoman, a fellow country-woman, spend the night in your public room while a foreigner occupies your best parlor?"

"He was most insistent. Quiet and private. That's what he wanted. And considering…" The host's voice faded as he realized what he had been about to say. He hoped he wasn't the kind who would hold something like that against a man. But he certainly could understand his guest's desire to avoid the curious gaze of the public.

"Then given your obvious reluctance, I suppose I shall have to persuade him myself," Lady Fairchild said and watched the host struggle between his obligations to English womanhood and his greed. "If you'll be so good as to direct me?"

"My lady," he began to protest, but his eyes flicked, as she had known they would, to the closed door across from the crowded public room with its smoke and noise and babble of masculine voices. The sounds emanating from the room were already taking on the relaxed tones of men who find themselves suddenly among strangers who have heard none of their wittiest stories and who do not care if they have imbibed too freely while telling them.

"Thank you," she said, smiling in genuine amusement at having outwitted him.

Now, if the foreign gentleman in the adjoining room were only half so easily managed, she thought, making her graceful way across the entry hall.

Maddy was surprised to find the parlor dark when, after a perfunctory knock, she opened the door. The fire that flickered on the hearth was the only light, and she was forced to wait while her eyes adjusted to its wavering glow.

The man who was standing before the fireplace might have turned at her entrance. If so, his glance toward the opened door had been brief. Unaccustomed to the darkness after the cheerful blaze of the hall's candles, she was forced to allow her eyes time to adjust. The image that eventually emerged from the darkened room resolved itself into the tall figure of a man, standing slightly to the side of the flames that danced behind the andirons. His right arm was stretched along the mantel, the fingers of that hand wrapped loosely around a glass whose contents glinted amber in the firelight. A booted foot was propped casually on the fender, and he was leaning, elegantly at ease, against the massive stones of the fireplace.

He pretended to be unaware of her presence, contemplating instead the liquid in the crystal he held, and as she watched, he tilted the glass slightly so the brandy swirled enticingly under the movement of his long fingers. His head was in profile, the right side shadowed and blending into the darkness of its background; the left was backlighted by the fire and seemed, therefore, to stand out from the somber colors of the room, sharp as the profile on a Roman coin.

The purity of line revealed in the features silhouetted by his stance literally made her catch her breath. She had never before associated the word *beautiful* with any masculine visage. Indeed, she was not an admirer of men. But as people stood before a Renaissance masterpiece and, moved by the skill of the creator, were held silent and awed, she stood on the outer edge of the domain he might, quite rightfully, consider to be his, and mutely admired.

"A rare woman—one who can hold her tongue," he complimented finally at her continued and unthinking silence, "but in this instance, I think some explanation is appropriate. Unless you're a gift. From my host. He has certainly been accommodating, but I must admit, I never expected you."

She should have been prepared for the accent. She had been told he was foreign, but his English, tinged as it was with French inflections, had caught her off guard. As had his very masculine beauty. It took a moment before what he had just suggested penetrated her still-dazed senses.

What's the matter with me? Maddy thought distractedly. She was not a woman who was often at a loss, and certainly not because of the shape of a man's nose, the spare line of his cheekbone. Or the strong angle of his chin, she mused. Or the height of his brow disappearing into disordered dark curls that fell casually over his forehead. She knew well enough the dangers of judging anything or anyone by outward appearances.

"How dare you," she said icily, although she had found that men generally dared anything they thought they might get away with. "I assure you, I am no one's gift."

"Probably not," he returned regretfully, and laughter lurked annoyingly in his response. "I'd wager you'd be a delightful Noel present. But if that's not the case, may I then ask what the hell you're doing in my parlor?"

Enjoying the scenery, she almost said, and fought to conquer whatever fantasies those perfect features were causing to stir uneasily in her breast. She had thought, given her experiences, that such fanciful nonsense would have disappeared, even from her imagination. She was more than a little surprised to find images of dark and brooding Byronic heroes emerging unbidden from what she had, until tonight, considered to be a very practical nature.

Despite her addiction to the romantic literature of the day, all her dreams revolving around the presence of such a man in her *own* life had long ago been gutted. And finding the epitome of those dreams standing before her in this remote rural establishment didn't mean that she could again begin to live with the idea that there was anything to be gained by indulging such fancies.

"Obviously, I've been stranded by the storm. Or have you been enjoying the warmth of your fire so long that you missed the change in the weather?" she gathered her wits to ask.

Not conciliatory enough. Not by half. Not if you want the parlor, Maddy thought, disgusted by her lack of control. She eased a deep breath and fought to rein in whatever he was doing to her composure.

Plague take him, she thought bitterly. Why couldn't he have been some fat country squire who would consider it an honor to give up his room to a lady, instead of…instead of what he was? The image of all she had once dreamed of possessing. And of being possessed by.

"I stopped two hours ago," he said. "As soon as I realized what the conditions of the road were likely to become. And while there were accommodations still to be had. As I take it, there now no longer are. Do you intend to charm me out of my room? If so, might I suggest…''

He paused and even in the low light she was aware that the one visible corner of his well-shaped lips had quirked upward. He still had not turned to face her, watching instead the slow swirl of his brandy under the restless direction of those long fingers.

Maddy found herself thinking about the color of his eyes. Brown, no doubt, with that midnight hair. In her imagination they had always been the clear blue of the black Irish. But no, he was French, so of course… Brown, she had decided finally when he spoke again.

''Obviously not charm. Do you get better results from leaving your victims in suspense? Whatever your method, I warn you that it won't work on me. I have paid for the room, and I intend to make use of its comforts, such as they are. Attempt whatever it is you're attempting with some other traveler. Here, you're destined for failure.''

''How unflattering,'' she said, turning her mind again to the task at hand. ''You must enjoy remarkable success with the ladies of your acquaintance with *that* sense of gallantry. But perhaps the 'ladies' of your acquaintance,'' she suggested with a careful touch of sarcasm, ''enjoy that domineering lack of chivalry. However, the gentlemen I know—''

''Ah,'' he interrupted softly. ''That's the problem. You are operating under the impression that I am a gentleman. May I disabuse you of that notion.''

It was said politely enough, but its effect on her plan was profound, especially because she believed him. How was she to get him to give her the room if, as he willingly asserted, he made no pretensions to having the qualities she had intended to utilize to insure her own comfort at the expense of his?

''But surely…'' she said to him as she had to the host, unable to believe that he was not in the least moved by her plight.

''No,'' he said, the corner of his mouth controlled, but she had seen the reflexive twitch that his amusement had caused. "Nothing is sure except death. And if you've reached your age without knowing that, then you're far less intelligent that I'm giving you credit for."

"My age," she gasped. "What possible..." She paused, angry at her automatic reaction to that provocation. Control, she urged, watching that mobile corner of his lips for some clue to what he was thinking. "I only wanted a place to enjoy a cup of tea and a light supper. We didn't stop for luncheon, and I've been traveling since dawn without any—"

"So because you were so foolish as to travel on a day like this without making proper provisions, you are now proposing to invite yourself to share my parlor and perhaps even my supper."

"No," she denied, and then realized that was exactly what she had just proposed. "That is... You see, there's been a death in my family. Unexpected. And I have to get to London, and there was no time for preparations. Think me as foolish as you wish, but surely you can't send me out to eat in the public room with those..." She paused, trying to think of a word that wouldn't be offensive to this man who had openly admitted that he was no more a gentleman than most of the members of that group gathered by the fire.

"I assure you I could cheerfully send you to perdition," he ruthlessly answered her appeal. "This is my room. I intend to have supper and then stretch out in the largest and most comfortable chair it affords. And I don't intend to share it with you. Unless, of course, you're offering to remain here after we've eaten. For entertainment. I really don't believe that any of the furniture is large enough to accommodate that arrangement, but I'm not opposed to sharing the floor. As the 'ladies of my acquaintance' would certainly tell you, I am very adaptable. But somehow you don't appear to be the type who would suggest that sort of intimacy. I'll be delighted if I was mistaken in my assessment of your intentions."

"You..." she began, and then couldn't think of any epithet worthy of the outrageous suggestion he had just made.

"Take your pick," he advised graciously. "I've been called most of them."

"How dare you!" she finally got out.

"You said that before," he reminded her gently. "It's no challenge to quarrel with someone who's forced to repeat. Do try for a little originality, or, despite your beauty, I'm going to quickly tire of this diversion—even if we are in the country and lacking for real entertainment."

"*You* are an unfeeling monster," Maddy said softly, too tired and disappointed to deal wisely with his mockery. She couldn't know that she had unwittingly chosen the perfect weapon for her target.

Had she not been angry, she might have been aware of the sudden tension in the fingers that held the brandy. The relaxed and almost hypnotic swirl of the liquid stopped suddenly as the tips of his fingers whitened against the glass. He set it down with careful deliberation on the mantel and picked up a long fireplace match, which he ignited from the heart of the fire.

She watched as he turned away from her to light the tapers in the candelabra standing on the small table behind him. Their soft glow gradually filled the chamber, chasing shadows back into the farthest corner.

Get out, her brain advised, and had been advising for the last few seconds. But for some reason, she was unable to retreat, in spite of the danger she sensed. She was locked in place by the sight of those broad shoulders moving under the dark coat. She watched the play of muscle in his back as his hands brought light into the room, light that illuminated also strong, well-shaped legs displayed to advantage in tight doeskins tucked into gleaming Hessian boots.

She knew she was still standing here, watching a dangerous man she had just insulted, because she wanted to see his face. Somewhere in the back of her mind floated still the image of that girlhood fantasy that he seemed to match so completely. Only the full face and the color of his eyes remained unrevealed. And she wanted...

"A candlelight supper, perhaps. Am I to assume that's all,

then, that you desire of my hospitality? If so, madam, how can I, gentleman that I should be, refuse? Would you join the monster for supper, my dear?''

His voice had changed, no longer full of the gentle derision with which he had greeted her attempt to procure the room for herself. There was something different, some quality she couldn't identify; however, he was apparently offering part of what she had come here to accomplish. But after all that had been said between them, surely he didn't expect to sit down to supper as if nothing had happened. What was he doing? she wondered desperately, and then saw that he was lifting the candelabra from the table.

He turned suddenly and advanced, carrying it, across the room. As he stalked nearer, his anger revealed now in every taut line of his body, the blaze of the candles he held fell on the side of his face that had not before been revealed. And on the ruin of the perfection of features that was so evident in the other profile.

It was only in seeing that contrast that the devastation could be completely understood. There, and in the comparison to the image of Maddy's perfect hero she had, unknown even to herself, cherished for so many years.

The right side of his face was mottled by severe burns. The eye was hidden by a black patch, and she found herself imagining what lay beneath that piece of velvet, considering the damage to the burned skin that surrounded it, and then blocking that vision as too painful to consider. What would fire do to the delicate tissues of the human eye?

Hazel, she realized suddenly. His eyes were hazel. Eye, she amended, remembering even in the midst of her shock what she had fantasized before about their color. Even the corner of those beautiful lips was slightly twisted by the damage. His arrogant nose was untouched, its perfection almost a mockery in that ruined face. The nostrils were now flared with anger as he held in one lean brown hand, unwavering, the candles that were exposing, in graphic detail, what he had hidden before.

The textured discoloration disappeared under the high collar of the snow-white shirt he wore beneath the intricately tied cravat, and she wondered how extensively the scars covered the underlying shoulder and chest. So different from the perfection of her dreams. So painfully marked by whatever had happened to him.

"An intimate candlelight dinner, madam? Was that your intent? Or perhaps you now prefer, as I do, the dark?"

Maddy could not have spoken through the thickness in her throat had she known words to express the emotions that churned in her brain. How tragic that this should have happened to someone who must have been…

Why did the unmarred beauty of the opposing side make the scarred countenance more affecting? She tried to imagine his face whole and unblemished, but her eyes sought again the cruel brutality of the scars he would bear forever.

Despite the number of times the Frenchman had seen that appalled reaction, he found that his stomach muscles had tightened, and it was surprisingly difficult to force the next measured and steady breath. He had watched as her pupils had slowly dilated, so that the rim of violet that surrounded them had all but disappeared, and her cheeks had drained of any color, leaving them white as the snow that continued to fall outside.

"No?" he suggested an answer to his own question, knowing that she was incapable of speech. The bitterly mocking tone was the one he always employed in response to whatever reaction the scars evoked.

Her continued stillness infuriated him. She had not turned away, the usual initial response of a sensitive woman. Instead, she seemed unable to look away, unable to even meet the assumed mockery of his gaze. She was still tracing the disfigurement with eyes that suddenly glazed with unshed tears. She blinked, and the spell that had held her motionless was broken.

Her eyes met his. The unaffected corner of his mouth lifted in cynical response to that telltale moisture.

"Then I take it you've decided against joining me. They tell me, in time, one can grow accustomed to my face. Perhaps in exchange for the warmth and hospitality of the parlor, you would care to put that observation to the test?'' he suggested, feigning the trace of humor.

And he waited, angered anew by her silence. He knew he had deliberately forced this confrontation. Deliberately thrust the grotesqueness of his face into her sight, highlighted from the darkness by the flame of the candles he held. But in spite of what he had said, he had never before been confronted with someone who didn't seem to be able to deal with the sight. God knows, he understood the horror better than anyone. But the continuing shock that he believed so profound as to hold this woman speechless broke open something cold and hard within him. She stood staring at him, her own undeniable beauty intact and undamaged, as if he had crawled from under some rock. So repelled by his ugliness that she was crying.

''I thought…'' Maddy whispered, remembering her impression on entering the room that the fantasy lover of so long ago had finally taken flesh and had come to find her, to carry her away from the travesty of love that was all she had ever known. But she couldn't tell him that. He must think she was a fool, standing here with the tears welling. She tried again, forcing the words past the constriction of her throat.

''I thought you were so beautiful,'' she said, wanting him to know what she had felt before. Wanting to explain why she was crying. Her discovery of her long-forgotten dream standing before her had been emotional shock enough. And then to find that its perfection had truly existed and was now forever destroyed, so brutally hurt that in the place of the hero she had always imagined, was this caustic, snarling stranger. Like the child the fantasy of his perfection had made her feel, she had unthinkingly spoken aloud her own distress.

Of all the things she might have said, it was, given the fact that he still remembered the way women had once looked at him, perhaps the worst. The unforgivable mockery. His instinctive reluctance to expose the scars had made her think that he was still a handsome man and not the horror he had become.

She saw the impact of what she had said briefly on his features before he answered with a twisted smile.

"And discovered you were wrong," he said, unable to completely mask the bitterness. "Perhaps some other time," he suggested, setting down the branch of candles, which had served its purpose, to totter dangerously on a nearby table.

Her puzzlement showed in the depths of her eyes, and she shook her head slightly.

"I don't understand."

"Some other time for our candlelight supper. Some other occasion. I believe you owe me that," he suggested softly and watched the color sweep back into the pale cheeks.

She couldn't believe what she had done. She must not allow him to think that she had been so affected merely by the scars. It was only because he was what she had dreamed. Or at least, he had, at one time, been the epitome of that dream. Only, she couldn't tell him that.

"You don't understand," Maddy said, knowing that excuse wasn't enough.

"Believe me," he answered, "I understand. Better than you can imagine."

"No," she began. What could she say that would make him feel what she had felt? But what did that matter? She'd never see him again. As soon as she could leave this room, it would be over. She'd sleep in the coach. Or sit up all night by the public room fire. Nothing mattered anymore but getting out. And telling him some of the truth, some of what she had thought as the light he held had revealed the damage to her dream.

"You don't understand," she tried again. "It's not the scars."

He laughed suddenly, and she thought she had never heard any sound that contained less amusement.

"Of course," he said softly. "The cut of my coat. Or my accent. Or perhaps the fact that I am not a gentleman. But then, about that I never deceived you."

"It's not..." she whispered, looking up to meet the half smile with which he had rejected her denial. At the sight of that unmoving, scarred corner, she lost whatever thought she had been attempting to articulate.

She can't even look at me and finish a sentence, he thought bitterly. He could taste the bile of his self-disgust. A monster to frighten women and children. He had known it, of course, but few people made it as obvious as she had. Damn you, he thought, damn you for not even turning away. At least then I don't have to see what you're thinking. I don't have to watch the loathing in your eyes.

Her eyes that were, he became aware suddenly, still fastened on his face.

Fury flooded his body. He caught her head between the strength of his lean hands and pulled her ruthlessly toward him. She struggled briefly to free herself, her palms pressed futilely against the fine material of his coat that covered the hard muscles underneath. Muscles that would not be denied their revenge. Relentlessly he brought his scarred mouth down over hers, which trembled and gasped beneath his. Not a kiss, but a punishment. Not only for what she had allowed him to see, but for all the women who had turned away rather than reveal their shock. And even for those who had smilingly pretended not to notice the damage, chatting desperately while their shocked gaze slid back and forth between the unmatching dichotomy that was now his face. Damn you all. And especially you.

It's not the scars, she had whispered. And he ground his lips against the ones that had spoken that lie. His tongue had pushed into her mouth, sweet and hot beneath his. He thought for a long, breathless moment that hers moved to answer his demand, her hands relaxing against the wall of his chest.

He felt her shudder. The shivering force of it moved through her entire body. And then again. He released her suddenly, sickened by what he was doing. As sickened as she apparently was by his touch.

She swayed slightly with the removal of his hands, and her eyes opened to find his face.

He watched her fingers, still covered by the smooth, supple

kid, reach up to touch the trembling lips his mouth had just caressed.

He laughed at the thought of her wiping his kiss away, as if his ugliness might contaminate her own perfection.

"You may have the room," he said, his voice tight and hard with a pain he didn't acknowledge, even to himself. "I find I prefer sleeping with the horses. They, at least, don't mind the way I look. You've won, madam, by defeating the monster. Try to appear a little more pleased with your victory."

He turned before he could be tempted to spew any more of the venom he usually controlled and moved through the door that was open behind her. She found that the room was empty—warm, private and nothing now that she wanted. The only remaining evidence of his presence was the glass that rested, half-full on the oak mantel.

Almost in a dream, she walked with shaking knees across the floor and stood staring at the tumbler a long time. Finally she touched it with fingertips that continued to tremble in reaction. She ran her thumb along the rim where she knew his mouth had been and thought again about the seductive movement of his hard lips against her own. She had been kissed before by only one man, and it had been nothing like the sure domination of the Frenchman's mouth on hers.

Just as she had always imagined it would feel to be kissed. Just as it should feel. All that a kiss should be. Nothing like the other. Nothing...

Maddy's eyes filled again with tears, and this time she allowed the moisture to gather and overflow. Everything had gone wrong, and it had been her fault. He had been here. She had found him, and then she had driven him away. And she would never see him again.

Perhaps... She suddenly turned and walked quickly, then almost ran, through the parlor door and across the hall until she could see into the public room. But he wasn't there. Maybe he meant what he'd said about the stables. If so, she could try to explain. You'll only make a fool of yourself, her common sense cautioned.

And if you don't try? questioned the romantic nature that she had believed long dead. Will you regret, for the rest of your life, that you didn't try?

The host reappeared from the kitchens, a steaming container of mulled wine making his destination obvious.

She put her hand on his arm, and he stopped, wondering at her agitation. Whatever had happened between those two had affected them both. He had just listened to the foreign gentleman's assessment of his failures as a publican given in scathing terms while his horse had been brought around. Although he had tried, he had been unable to change the mind of his former guest. The Frenchman had ridden off into the gathering dusk as if the snow were not continuing to blanket the countryside. And now this lady was standing in his entry hall looking as shattered as he had felt under the blistering wrath of that caustic tongue. Perhaps she, too, had felt the force of his anger.

"The gentleman who had hired the parlor?" she asked. "Do you know where…?"

"Gone. Like the hounds of hell were after him. He didn't insult you, did he, my lady?" the host asked.

"No," she said, shaking her head. And since there appeared nothing else to do, she began, with something of her normal composure, to direct him as to what she would need to assure that her night's stay should be comfortable.

When her host had finally delivered all her requirements and had left her alone, she drank the contents of the glass he hadn't noticed on the mantel. It was the last trace of the former occupant of this room, and after she had drained it, she rubbed the glass's smoothness against the matching texture of her cheek. Then she carefully replaced it.

It was over. And if she had missed the opportunity to turn the direction of her life from the path others had chosen for her, then she acknowledged that she had no one else to blame. The failure was only her own. As with everything else that had been given to her to bear, she would eventually learn to accept that burden, too.

Chapter One

London
March 1817

The shock of the sudden spill of diamonds on the surface of the gaming table held the watchers motionless as the Viscount Mannering had, of course, intended. The shimmering reds, greens and blues reflected in the brilliance of the stones exerted a fascination over the occupants of the last table remaining in play in the elegant gambling den.

It was well after four, and soon dawn would introduce the demands of a new day. None of the men gathered to watch this contest, however, entertained thoughts of retiring. The play was too deep, the stakes growing steadily since the wagering between these two had begun early the previous evening.

The tension was palpable, the tang of sweat-kissed starch in wilting cravats mingling with the aroma of fine cigars and brandy. It was a masculine environment that enjoyed its exclusivity—an environment that had only one purpose: to introduce into these jaded lives the excitement of risking vast sums of money on the roll of a die or the turn of a card.

The man who provided that opportunity was the only one who now seemed unmoved by the glittering offering lying on his table. The fall of priceless lace against the black coat was as crisp as when he had come downstairs; his fingers, moving with an almost hypnotic grace over the cards, as steady. Only by the lift of one strong, dark hand, which briefly touched the black velvet patch covering his right eye, did he reveal any trace of tension.

"Quit fingering that bloody patch," Mannering demanded, his own tension blatantly evident in the sharpness of his tone. "Every time you touch it, I find myself looking at your face. It throws me off my game. Damn, if I don't believe you do that deliberately."

The soft slur had become more marked in the past two hours. But then the viscount, noted for the hardness of his head and the firmness of his nerves, had been drinking steadily all night. And the more he had drunk, the higher the stakes had climbed.

"No, my lord," the man across the table said simply.

"What the hell do you mean? The diamonds more than cover the wager. What the hell do you mean no? You'll take the—"

"No," the quiet voice interrupted to reiterate the refusal.

"Look at them, Gavereau. Look at them," the viscount demanded again. He suddenly ran the soft, white fingers of his hand under the stones and their gold settings and the chain that connected the massive necklace. "The Mannering diamonds, and you say no as if you were turning down a beggar in the street. Have you ever seen anything like them?" he asked softly, allowing the stones to run flashing through his trembling fingers back to the table below.

The hazel gaze seemed for a moment to be drawn to the sparkling display, but it lifted quickly to meet the bloodshot eyes of the waiting aristocrat.

"No," he said again. "I'm not qualified to judge their worth. I'm not a jeweler. And the rules were table stakes."

"You arrogant French..." Mannering stopped the insult with great effort. "You'd deny a king's ransom in gems because of some stupid rule. Everyone knows the Mannering diamonds. Been in my family for a hundred years. If you knew anything—''

"If you want to cover the bet, then do so." The voice was utterly calm, as unmoved, seemingly, by the insults as he had been by the magnificence of the stones. The French accent echoed through his speech like a tread of gold in a tapestry— faint, but the glimmer adding color to its richness.

"You'll take my marker," the viscount suggested arrogantly. It was ground they had already covered, but he was unused to being told no. And unwilling to accept it.

"I have your markers," the gambler said without raising his voice, but the depth of his anger was allowed to show for the first time. His long fingers closed around an untidy pile of chits lying beside him on the table, and crushing them in his fist, he deposited them in front of the cards that lay face-down before him. "More than I shall probably ever be able to collect. No more. I told you the limit I was willing to hold, and you've surpassed it. If you have nothing else…" he said, and waited, one brow slightly raised in that nearly satanic face—Lucifer, the beautiful, touched by the fires of his own kingdom.

"The diamonds," the viscount said again, pushing the necklace toward the middle of the table. "They'll all tell you. Everyone knows them."

He lifted a sweating hand to move in a arc to include the watchers and then closed it into a fist to hide the trembling. Nerves, alcohol or anger. No one was certain, considering the temper the viscount was noted for. The Mannering diamonds and the murderous Mannering rages were equally famous.

Several heads began to nod before they became aware that the single hazel eye of the Frenchman had not followed the inclusive gesture. It was locked, instead, on the blue eyes of the man who believed so earnestly that he was holding the hand that would begin the rebuilding of all that his family had lost. Who obviously believed that this was his opportunity. That his luck had finally changed.

"Or is this refusal simply your coward's way of escaping the outcome of this game?" the Englishman taunted softly.

If the silence had been heavy before, it now pressed upon the watchers strongly enough that none of them dared even to breathe. The Frenchman's features had not reacted at all to the word. The fingers of his right hand, which rested on the table behind the pile of crumpled markers he had thrust forward, had moved slightly and were as quickly controlled.

But the challenge was ignored.

"And if the diamonds are not…" the soft, accented voice began.

"You have my word. The word of an English gentleman. If *you* can possibly understand what that means," the viscount sneered.

The hazel eye considered the flushed and sweating features for a long time, and then, at whatever he saw revealed in the unwavering focus of the nobleman's eyes, he reached finally and pushed the necklace into the center pile of coins and notes.

The smile that grew on the viscount's handsome features should have made the gambler regret the move. Once again the pale face revealed his satisfaction that he had gotten his own way. Mannering didn't like to be denied. Especially by someone whom he naturally considered beneath contempt.

The viscount quickly flipped the first of the cards that lay under his waiting hand to reveal its suit and value. The rest followed, the hand he had just bet his remaining worldly goods upon, finally exposed. There was a soft sigh of satisfaction from one of the watchers at the significance of that revelation.

Mannering's smile was now triumphant and clearly hostile as he lifted his gaze to his opponent's face. For good measure, he allowed his eyes to drift over the marred cheek before returning to meet the gambler's steady stare.

At something in that cold hazel gleam, a constrictive trembling shook Mannering's hand, which still rested on the table. Only one combination of cards could beat the hand that he had just turned up. And the odds of two such hands occurring were…

But in the sudden uncontrollable lift of the unmarked corner of that bastard's mouth, they all knew. The viscount didn't need to watch the dark fingers slowly reveal his defeat. Whatever the odds, the Frenchman had beaten them. And him.

The gambler's long fingers swept the centered pile into the velvet bag that had appeared from somewhere. And then they moved back to caress, almost with a lover's touch, the brilliant diamonds that were all that remained. Finally they lifted the heavy piece of jewelry, hefting its weight as if by feel alone they might accurately evaluate its worth.

Mannering didn't raise his head from his contemplation of the empty table. The Frenchman rose and waited a moment, looking down on the beautiful blond curls of the lowered head of his victim.

"Gentlemen, the house is closed. I bid you all good-night."

He turned and made his way across the rich Oriental carpets, through the cloud of lingering cigar smoke that hovered several feet above the floor, and disappeared into the darkness beyond.

The servants moved to bring hats and sticks to the departing patrons. Finally someone put a kindly hand under the viscount's arm, and with guidance, he, too, was persuaded to leave. After all, there was nothing to keep him here. It was over. He had lost, defeated by a man he would not have considered worthy to be his valet.

The familiar afternoon babble of White's should have been comforting to Harry Mannering. Here he was surrounded and protected by rights guaranteed from his birth. Here the emptiness of his pockets was not a topic for discussion. There had been more than a few in this room who had, at some time in the past, been in a similar predicament. And they had survived. Survival had become his dominant thought since the cold air of dawn and the growing realization of the seriousness of his situation had broken through the viscount's cocoon of arrogance and alcohol. He possessed almost nothing, now, that was not written down on one of those markers the Frenchman had treated with such disdain.

Harry Mannering was not an introspective man, but he was

looking on the ruins of life as he had always known it. And that was enough to sober even the most profligate bounder. Which was, of course, in many people's opinion, a perfect description of the young man sitting so dejectedly in the midst of a group containing the most notable bloods London could boast. If they suspected the true state of his affairs—the long slide to bankruptcy his father had so nobly begun, the state of decay of each and every piece of property he had inherited, the size of the mortgages each bore...

Mannering heaved a sigh and couldn't resist lowering his aching head into his two slightly unsteady hands.

"Foxed," Ned Stapleton said as he watched his boyhood friend. "I knew you were foxed. Damme, if I didn't think he was going to kill you when you told him to quit fingering that patch. I thought you must be the bravest man of my acquaintance, considering the Frenchman's reputation, but all you were was foxed."

"Shut up, Ned," Mannering said softly.

"Don't blame me," his friend protested, smiling. "I tried to get you to leave. I never should have let you talk me into fetching those stones. Maddy, bless her heart, tried to stop me. You'd best be glad your father's dead and doesn't know what's become of his great-grandmama's diamonds. He'd disown you."

"The diamonds are mine. And you saw my hand. There's no way... He must have cheated. He couldn't..."

"If I were you, Harry," Stapleton warned, "I wouldn't say that outside this room. And I wouldn't say it too loudly here. The last man who called him a cheat almost didn't come back from the elms. I'd hate to lose a friend as entertaining as you to that bastard's bullet."

"Shut up," the viscount said again, an almost automatic response to his friend's advice. "How can I think with you yammering at me all the time? My head's bad enough without..."

He became aware suddenly of the commotion that was occurring. Almost as soon he raised his aching head, he realized the cause of that disturbance. The unthinkable was happening.

Something that was certainly not supposed to occur at White's, where the outside world of tradesmen, bootmakers and tailors was never allowed to intrude on a gentleman's society. Even if those importunate creatures were justified in dunning a member of the club for overdue bills, it was certainly not done in White's. White's was sacrosanct. Or it had been until today.

The arrogant figure who moved with an almost feline smoothness of motion and grace through these sedate rooms could not have been more out of place. It wasn't the cut of his garments nor their price. Indeed, his clothing was as tastefully elegant and as expensive as that which had been worn by Brummel's set. It was, rather, an aura that emanated from that tall, muscled figure and the dark, marred face. Something alien and foreign—like a stalking jungle cat sauntering through a group of sleek, well-fed tabbies. He carried the air of danger with him even here in the gentle snobbery of White's.

Here, where someone like him should never be. He should never have been let in. And to judge by the trailing entourage of outraged staff, someone had finally realized the error.

The Frenchman ignored the breathless procession behind him and the fascinated stares of those who were awakening from their postluncheon lethargy. He stopped before the table where Lord Mannering and his friend were watching his approach, slack-jawed.

"'The word of an English gentleman,'" Jean-Luc Gavereau said softly. "I believe that's the phrase you used. And you implied that *I* couldn't possibly know what that meant."

He paused, waiting for some reaction in the blue eyes of the man seated before him. And was disappointed. The reaction might be read as surprise, bewilderment, disbelief. But not guilt. The guilt he had expected was, surprisingly, absent.

His fury too fresh to allow him to question that discovery, Jean-Luc reached into his pocket and tossed the Mannering "diamonds" onto the gleaming wood of the table as one might toss a bone to a waiting dog. The diamonds slid, glittering, across the polished surface, stopped only by the reflexive movement of the viscount's hand to prevent their over-shooting the edge and landing in his lap.

"'The word of an English gentleman,'" the gambler repeated with even more contempt than before.

"Are you giving them back?" the Englishman questioned in bewilderment, trying to find an explanation for the bizarre behavior. "Then you're admitting you cheated. I knew—"

The words were cut off abruptly as lean fingers locked into the cravat Mannering's valet had spent more than twenty minutes tying. The viscount found himself lifted off the comfortable chair he had occupied most of the afternoon, held dangling like a rat caught by a terrier.

"Paste," the scarred man whispered, yet the sound carried clearly to the far corners of the club. His fist trembled slightly, but no one watching believed that it was due to the strain of holding his victim suspended. He seemed to be accomplishing that with an unwavering ease. "The damned stones are worthless. I'm not the one who cheated, *monsieur,*" he said softly. "But then, I don't claim to be a gentleman."

"You lying bastard—"

"Paste. You may see the jeweler's evaluation. And your friends, if they're interested. And I want to know how you intend to deal with your debt to me."

"You substituted—"

"In less than eight hours? Do you really think anyone is going to believe that? That anyone in London could make an exact duplicate of that necklace with that setting in eight hours?"

He threw the nobleman back into his chair with the completion of that last sarcastic question.

As if to prove his point, he manipulated one of the larger stones so that it lay, still attached to the magnificent gold chain, but isolated from its fellows. Before anyone realized his intent, the Frenchman took a bottle of burgundy off a nearby credenza, and using the strength of the bottle's design, brought the bottom rim down on the fiery beauty of the gem like a mortar in a pestle. The "diamond" dissolved into a white powder.

The gasps were audible. No one was attempting now to oust the gambler. And as the truth was realized, the eyes of the gentlemen gathered in the elegant smoking room moved from the figure of this scarred Nemesis to that of Harry Mannering, whose mind was frantically trying to find an explanation for the unfathomable.

Paste. There could be no mistake. But how? And when? And by whom? The dark suspicion began to grow within the viscount's brain that his family's fortunes would have long ago taken a more desperate path had it not been for the diamonds, obviously used, perhaps by his own father, to retire debts now long forgotten. But he had done exactly the same— used his heritage to fuel his own pleasures, and his children, when they arrived, be damned. He had never expected that from his father, but he couldn't really pretend to be surprised. At the least, he might have been told.

His inward contemplation of his father's betrayal faded as he finally became aware of the heavy silence. He could hear for the first time in his memory the ticking of the gilt-and-marble clock on the mantel. He'd always hated that clock with its stupid naked Cupids. Too pretty for a gentlemen's club.

They were waiting for some explanation. Denial, perhaps. But it was there for all of them to see. What was the use of denying it? And he had nothing else to offer the Frenchman. Nothing to his name. He was ruined. Not just the lack of funds. The disgrace. A debt of honor that he couldn't hope to pay. That he had, albeit unknowingly, tried to pay with counterfeit coin. Never again would he take his place here at White's. His table. His chair. Or any of the other haunts that were the sum of his existence.

He was aware that they were still waiting. Especially the bastard who had done this to him.

Mannering rose on legs that trembled. He steadied himself against the table with one sweating palm. He felt physically ill and knew it was not the aftereffects of the alcohol he'd drunk last night. It was the ruin of his life.

He raised bloodshot eyes to the steady gaze of the man waiting for his explanation.

"I'll call on you tomorrow with the money," the viscount said. He was aware that Ned's brows rose sharply at the promise, but he said nothing. No one spoke as Harry brushed past the Frenchman and walked unsteadily to the opened front door. He didn't bother to collect his beaver and stick. Nothing mattered but getting away from the watching eyes. Nothing. There was nothing left, and he had just promised to hand over, from that nothing, seventy thousand pounds on the morrow.

The gambler retrieved the damaged necklace he had so cavalierly thrown on the table. He raised his head only when the front door had closed behind Mannering and met the cold stares that surrounded him. The unmarred corner of his mouth twitched in sudden amusement, and in the deep, slightly accented voice, reminding them all of his alienness to this environment, he politely bid them good day.

His walk across the echoing chamber displayed none of the unsteadiness of his victim. It was, if possible, more arrogant than the stalk with which he had entered. No one spoke until he, too, had exited, and the massive doors had closed behind him.

The sudden upsurge of sound that swept through those rooms would have surprised neither of the men who had just departed. The difference was that one cared nothing for what was being said behind his back and to the other it was, literally, a matter of his life or his death.

Only one patron of the most exclusive of London's clubs took no part in the general uproar of speculation. But then the mind behind the remarkable silver eyes was too busy analyzing the situation to care what those around him were saying. He had recognized the voice that had made those accusations. A voice he had heard last almost two years ago. In a situation he would never forget.

The Duke of Avon waited until the fascinated buzz of gossip and horrified outrage had faded to whispers, and then he made his exit as unobtrusively as his own notoriety would allow. But he wouldn't forget the scene. He had a strong premonition that before this particular game was played out, he would be called upon to take a hand. Avon had learned to trust his instincts where his forebodings were concerned. It was a lesson he had learned painfully, but very well. And one he would not forget.

"No, Harry," Madelyn Fairchild said furiously. "Not again. Not ever again. And there's *nothing,* this time, that you can do to make me. That's a lesson I learned from your father."

"Then you're willing to see our name trampled in the mud?"

"If preventing it depends on my marrying again to please you, then yes. More than willing. I won't do it, Harry. And I swear to you, there's nothing—"

"Damn it, Maddy," her half brother interrupted furiously, grabbing her shoulders and shaking her as he spoke. "Do you realize what our life will be if I can't pay that scarred bastard tomorrow? How you'll be treated? How you'll be forced to live?"

At Maddy's sudden stillness, such a contrast to her violent agitation of a few seconds ago, Lord Mannering began to hope that his arguments had suddenly broken through the stubborn resistance with which his half sister had met his quite logical suggestion. After all, what else did he have to offer the gambler? And it wasn't as if Maddy had anything else to look forward to. It was surely not such a sacrifice as to cause this outrage. She'd married Fairchild, and that was a far greater—

"Scarred?" she repeated softly.

In memory, Harry's fingers involuntarily touched his own soft cheek, as clear and unblemished as an infant's. They traced an area corresponding to the marks the gambler bore, and then he realized what he was doing.

"Harry?" his sister questioned.

"A burn or something," Harry muttered, almost certain what had caused those distinctive scars.

"A burn," Maddy repeated, visualizing the marks on the cheek of the tall stranger at the inn. Was it possible, after all this time…?

"God, Maddy, it's not so bad. It's hardly noticeable…"

Harry's voice faded. Somehow, accomplished liar that he was, Maddy would know he wasn't telling the truth. She had always known.

"Is that all?" she asked calmly, waiting for the answer that would confirm or deny whether that man, who had represented every fantasy she had ever held in the last empty years, might again have come near enough to her existence to give her another chance.

"His eye," Harry said. "There's something wrong with his eye." The violet eyes of his sister closed, the long lashes dropping as if in prayer over the sudden flame of hope. "It must have been damaged in the same... He covers it with a patch. I don't know..." Again her brother's voice stopped.

Madelyn Fairchild opened her eyes then, knowing that if she were not very careful, she would give it all away. Harry wasn't stupid, no matter how big a fool he might be. And he knew her very well.

"Who is he?" she asked.

"I don't know. A gambler. A bloody, arrogant French gambler," Harry said, and she felt the small quick flutter in her stomach. She knew she was right. French, he'd said. And if ever "arrogant" fit a man...

And then her brother continued, interrupting that spurt of joy. "He opened a gambling den here more than a year ago. No one knows anything about him beyond the fact that he's very lucky and very good with a pistol. Gavereau is the name he's using, but somehow— Damn it, Maddy, it doesn't matter who he is. Don't you realize what's going to happen? If I sell literally everything we own, I could raise part of the money, maybe enough to hold him off, but as a result, we'll be out on the streets. Then everyone else we owe will smell blood and move in. I'll end up in Newgate, and you'll be back in Cornwall. Is that what you want? My God, Maddy, do you want to go back to that hole?"

"That hole that your father drove me to?" she asked bitterly.

"You're not going to hold what my father did against me? I had no hand in that. I'm sorry that—"

"And if I do what you ask?" she interrupted his self-serving denial.

"Then I promise, I'll get you out. A year. No more. I'll have recouped my losses, and you can get a divorce. A lot of people nowadays—"

"A divorce?" she said incredulously, almost laughing at his offering that horror as an inducement. Trust Harry to be willing to sacrifice her reputation for his wants. And besides, if she were supposed to be the payment for their debts, it didn't seem logical that the gambler would then be willing to divorce her. "Do you think that he'll agree to that? Do you think—"

"He won't have any choice. I promise, Maddy, I'll arrange it all. Just do this for me. For both of us."

Her smile was bitter, but he couldn't know that she had long ago stopped trusting anything her half brother said. She knew that Harry would do exactly what pleased himself and be damned to anyone else. He'd have forgotten all these promises a fortnight after her marriage. But Harry's promises were unimportant because in this situation, to do what Harry wanted was also to do what she wanted. Incredible as it seemed, fate had apparently given her another chance. And she didn't intend to let anything stand in her way.

Only one small doubt intruded.

"But, Harry," she said, "what makes you believe he'll be willing to accept me instead of the money? What if he refuses?" Her brother had not told her the amount, but she imagined, knowing too well his habits, that he hadn't played for small stakes.

Harry's quick, disbelieving laugh was reassuring. He caught her slim shoulders, this time not in anger, and turned her so that she faced the huge mirror surrounded by its heavy gilt frame. Reflected there was still the beauty that had made Madelyn Fairchild the reigning toast throughout her Season, the beauty that had lured the old man to whom her stepfather had sold her—the beauty that was such a shocking contrast to the disfigurement that was all the Viscount Mannering had seen in the French gambler to whom she had given her soul in a country inn so many months before.

"He'll take you. No man's ever been able to resist you. And he... Well, Maddy, my love, I'm afraid the only way this man will ever have a woman like you is to buy her. He'll want you, my dear. That's never been in question. All you have to do is offer. And I'll make it up to you, Maddy. I promise. You won't be sorry," Harry vowed softly.

No, I won't be sorry, she thought. *But it won't be because of you. You'll forget me as soon as you have what you want. And that's just what I'm counting on. And I hope you're right. My supposed beauty has always been my curse, but if only this once... Oh, God, Harry, I hope this once you're right about something.*

Chapter Two

Maddy had stood in the shadows behind the door, patiently waiting through the long hours, her eyes focused, through the uncurtained window, on the street below. There had been no trace of nervousness in the composed face or in the steady hands that were clasped serenely before her. Hers was a hard-learned tranquillity, but it had stood her in good stead tonight.

Only with the sound of slow footsteps ascending the narrow stair did her body betray the calmness that had surrounded her since she had made her decision. Now it was difficult to breathe, and the fluttering near-sickness of anticipation moved through her stomach. She closed one hand hard upon the other to ease the sudden trembling and pressed her lips more tightly together. Please, God, she thought. And then the door opened.

Jean-Luc didn't notice the still figure waiting in the darkness. He walked to his desk and stood looking down at the spread of papers that needed his attention. But he was too tired to think about business tonight. He lowered his head and rolled it from side to side, trying to ease the tightness in his neck. Too little sleep. Too much anger. He could still hear that arrogant voice.

The word of an English gentleman. If you can possibly understand what that means.

Apparently, that you lie and cheat, he thought, fighting down the building anger. The viscount had promised the money tomorrow. Today, he amended, remembering how late it was. And he knew that Harry Mannering had nothing to bring and no way to raise any additional funds. He owned Mannering's markers and, therefore, he owned Harry. If it hadn't been for the sneering superiority of tone when he had spoken that phrase...

Jean-Luc Gavereau wasn't a vindictive man and had he not so bitterly disliked this Englishman, he would have forgiven the debt, as large as it was. He had no wish to see a man lose everything because of a mistake. He had realized, on further reflection, that the viscount had not known the diamonds were paste. Given the reputation of the old man, it was not surprising that he had played such a trick on his heir. If it were anyone else in London, he thought. But not Mannering. Not that arrogant bastard. He could almost feel the viscount's eyes mockingly tracing over the scars.

"We have an engagement, I think."

The low contralto that he had heard once before spoke from the darkness behind him.

She had waited for him to notice her, carefully controlling the emotions that the sight of those broad shoulders had caused. She wanted him to turn around. She wanted...

But when he did, she found that in her imagination she had softened the memory of his face. She had pretended, because she wanted it not to matter, that it was not so cruelly marred. But her eyes were drawn again to the contrast between the perfection of the left profile and the other.

"An engagement?" he said softly, watching the slow movement of her eyes over his features, so different, somehow, from the mocking cruelty of the Viscount Mannering's gaze.

"A candlelight supper. Or don't you remember?" She smiled at him, knowing that he would.

"I remember," he answered, but the damaged mouth that she knew was quickly mobile in amusement was almost stern now. She took a deep breath and waited.

"What are you doing here?" he asked finally. She couldn't tell what he was thinking from the disciplined features. He was controlled, a professional gambler. He was probably very experienced at reading emotions, but she was not so skilled.

"I suppose..." Maddy began, and then paused, unsure, when before she had been so certain. She had only to offer. Harry had promised her that was true, and because she had wanted to believe him, she had come. But now it didn't seem so simple. What if it were only *her* dream? He looked as if...

"I suppose," she tried again, "that this time I *am* a gift."

The silence stretched as he waited.

"A gift?" he repeated finally.

And she told him. What she had planned to say. What she had been sent to say.

"I'm Harry Mannering's sister."

His shock was sudden and then swiftly hidden. Again the features were set and still.

"Mannering forced you to come here?"

"No," she whispered. "I came because I thought you might..."

He was going make her to say it. To put into words what she had hoped he would understand.

Suddenly he laughed.

"Seventy thousand pounds?" he suggested mockingly. "Really, *mademoiselle*," he began and shook his head gently. The one-sided smile traced upward as the color flamed in her cheeks.

"No," she whispered. "You don't understand."

He waited, and recognizing the pain in that whisper, the unscarred corner of his lips was once again carefully governed.

She had thought he might make it easier for her. Because she again knew with certainty that he, too, had felt something of what she had known that night. In spite of his anger, she had felt his kiss become, not a punishment, but something else. Cherishing against her trembling lips. So she told him the truth.

"There's nothing left. You have everything. Harry can't raise the money. You must know that."

"And so he sent you here to...?" His inflection rose, indicating his question. An unanswerable question. "Forgive me, but I'm not sure why he sent you here, if not for…for what you just denied. To ask for more time? To beg the forgiveness of the debt?"

"You could give him a hundred years, and he couldn't put together that much money. And as for forgiveness…" She paused, thinking that perhaps it wasn't forgiveness for *Harry* she was seeking.

"Your brother's an arrogant bastard," he said softly.

"Of course. They all are. All the young bloods. It's bred into them in the cradle. But they'll reject Harry's arrogance now. Although they think there's no reason to pay the money they owe a merchant or tradesman, they believe there's honor in meeting gambling debts."

"The vagaries of the aristocracy," he agreed cynically. "But my dislike of your brother isn't based on a dislike of his class."

"And your dislike of me?" she asked.

"I don't like pity," he said and watched the violet eyes widen.

"Pity?" she echoed.

"The kindest word, perhaps, for what you felt that night."

Her laugh was soft, but its bitterness at his misreading of her emotions was clear.

"Not pity," she contradicted, smiling.

The tenderness of her smile was unexpected. He felt his body, almost against his will, respond to the trembling curve of that soft mouth. He could even remember what her lips felt like beneath his own. He had remembered them far too many nights, even nights when he had sought and found release for the tensions her memory had produced. But none of those women had had violet eyes. And none of them had cried because of the ruin that was his face.

He didn't understand how the thought of those hated tears, shed so many months before, could cause the wave of desire, strong and fierce, that was surging through his loins.

"Why are you here?" he asked again.

"I thought…" Maddy began, and the soft voice faltered

over the unspeakable. "I thought that you might accept me. Instead of what Harry owes you. He can't pay you. You know that. I'll marry you. If you…" She stopped suddenly, unable to go on, watching the derision grow over the hard features.

"You value yourself very highly. I doubt seventy thousand pounds is the going rate for whores. Even in London."

"I'm not a whore."

"A woman who sells her body for money? What else are you pretending this is? It's a business transaction and nothing more. Are you even a virgin?" he asked bluntly.

She flinched against the question.

"No," she whispered.

"Not even a virgin. Tell your brother—"

"I'm a widow," she interrupted whatever jeering message he wanted her to deliver.

"Married for how long?"

"For five years," she told him, but he couldn't know the horror of those years.

"A well-used widow," he said cruelly, fighting against his growing need to hold her, to kiss away whatever had caused the distress that was clearly associated with those years. Not grief. She wasn't grieving over the bastard, whoever he was. Whoever had enjoyed that slim, elegant body for five years. He fought, too, against the mental image of gilt hair loosened and tangling over his shoulders while he supplanted with his lovemaking whatever remembrances of her marriage had caused that look. Something was wrong here.

He steeled himself against the pull of her suffering. It had caught him before. He hadn't understood what he had seen in her eyes that night, but he had never forgotten it. It had haunted him. Loss, betrayal, the death of dreams. And it was back. Violet eyes that told him that he could change whatever had been done to her. That it lay within his power and that, unbelievably, she wanted him to.

"I'm sorry," she said, speaking into his confused emotions. "I won't keep you any longer. It's late and you must be very tired."

She walked to the door, and his voice stopped her.

"Did you know? Before you came?" he asked, his tone as soft now as hers had been.

She turned back, the question clearly in her eyes. But they were again composed, serene and unfathomable, as if what he had seen there had never existed.

At her hesitation, he explained his question. "That I was the man your brother owed?"

She smiled at him, its gentleness again catching him unprepared.

"Of course," she said simply. "I came *only* because you were that man. Why else do you think I would come?"

And then she waited.

"The word of an Englishman. Does that mean anything to you? Or are you like your brother?" he said.

"I don't understand," she whispered, but a breath of warmth burned softly where there had been only the coldness of despair.

"I don't want a marriage of convenience. A platonic relationship. If you're my wife, then you will *be* my wife. In every sense of the word. I want you to have no doubts about that."

Unable to speak, she nodded, but her eyes didn't quail before the demand in his. She understood the damaged pride that had made that challenge. He would never ask her again. This was part of the game. Table stakes and no reneging when the hands had been dealt.

She swallowed the thickness that blocked her throat and wondered what it had cost him to seek that assurance.

Whether *you* had wanted that or not, my love, Maddy thought, *I* intended it. And a faint smile trembled again over her full lips.

"Of course," she said finally into the silence. His eye fell before the concern she hadn't been wise enough to hide.

Damn your pity, he thought again. But when he looked up to tell her that he had been wrong, that it wasn't an exchange he was willing to accept, she was gone. The dark corner where she had stood was empty, bathed once more in shadows and moonlight. He wondered briefly if he had imagined it all. As he had imagined meeting her again through so many long, dark nights. He took a deep breath and the scent of her perfume floated to him. No dream. Not any longer.

His fingers lifted to touch the dark patch that hid the blind, clouded horror that was all that remained of his right eye. They traced downward, feeling the roughness of the scarred flesh. He knew the softness of her skin touching his face would be an abomination.

Just another whore, he told himself. You've paid a few of them. What else is left for what you are? She's only more expensive than the ones you've had before.

Somehow there was no comfort in the icy bitterness of that thought. So he repeated it, engraving it on his mind, which wanted her to be far more. Dreamed in its darkest recesses of making her more. And knew with cold logic that someone like her could never be to someone like him what he wanted. My wife, the thought came unbidden. And he mocked himself for that romanticism.

Just another whore. After all, why else would she have come? Why else would she seek out what he was? The only difference is the price, he reminded himself, and the fact that you want her.

Knowing he wouldn't sleep, he walked behind the desk and sat down. His long, dark fingers found the papers that were most urgent, but the memory of whatever had been in her eyes intruded again and again between his usually disciplined mind and the work that he had laid out for himself.

Finally he reached and turned down the lamp and sat for a long time in the darkness. He knew that in the decision he had made tonight, his life had taken a turn. Whatever the outcome of the agreement he had just made, nothing would ever be the same.

Maddy's hand, cold and trembling, had rested in his as the vows were spoken. Jean-Luc had not seen her since the night she had come to his office with her offer. Not until this morning when she had stepped out of a hackney coach before the small church where she had agreed to meet him. Their correspondence had been brief and to the point. A date, a time and this place.

He had wondered if her brother would have the nerve to come. Mannering's influence had been used to allow this marriage to proceed with such unseemly and illegal haste. He knew the story of Harry's losses and the fake diamonds was still making the rounds at the clubs. To add even more spice to the tale, the fact that he and Mannering's sister had been married by special license would soon be public knowledge.

But it appeared that the viscount had at least had the sense not to show up as his sister sold her body for his good name. Sold herself, he supposed, with the intent of keeping Harry out of Newgate.

Jean-Luc didn't allow himself to think about his own motives. That question had been one he had found no answer to in the preceding days. No answer except his desire. And the reality of that he no longer bothered to deny.

He had not been prepared for her beauty. He had seen her only in the semidarkness of the inn's parlor and his office, and now, in the clear light of the spring afternoon, the perfection of her features emphasized the mockery of his possession of her.

The gown she wore was old ivory, well made, its satin rich and heavy, but the cut, obvious at least to him, was several years out of mode.

He had not answered the tentative smile she had given him as he stepped forward out of the shadowed recesses of the doorway to meet her. She had placed her hand willingly on his arm and allowed him to lead her to the waiting clergyman. Her fingers were shaking enough that he had felt their movement through the rich material of the elegant coat he wore.

He wondered again, as he had in the long nights after she had made her offer, what hold Harry had over his sister that could compel her to marry a man who was not only so far beneath her social standing, but as hideously scarred as he thought himself to be. Perhaps that was what he had seen in her eyes. A desire to escape whatever hold her brother had and not what he had thought he read.

He repeated the ancient words of the marriage ceremony without being conscious of their import. He was far more aware of the woman whose beautiful low voice never hesitated as she committed herself into his keeping.

In sickness and in health. For richer, for poorer. Forsaking all others...so long as you both shall live. In spite of the sincerity of her tone, this was a travesty, surely, he believed, of all those words intended.

Maddy allowed herself to think briefly of the first time she had made these pledges. She had been defeated, lost and brutally broken of any defiance. She had been compelled to marry by her stepfather's cruelty, and she had obeyed. But this time... Unbidden, her eyes lifted to the face of the stranger into whose hands she was committing her future, her body, her very life.

This time *I* have chosen. You didn't know, Harry. You couldn't know. But this time...

She realized that the vicar had finished speaking and was waiting. It was not until her husband turned to her that she remembered what she was supposed to do. She looked up, and then closed her eyes as the Frenchman leaned down and placed the expected wedding kiss against the corner of her mouth.

She smiled at the thought of his nervousness, clearly revealed by the tentative touch of those cold lips. She hadn't considered how he might feel about today. But she had seen the shock in the eyes of the clergyman when he had first glimpsed the groom's face. And the quick look of pity he had sent in her direction. She realized that this wedding was probably far more an ordeal for her husband, who was still watching her with that quiet aura of waiting.

Suddenly she smiled at him and stood on tiptoe to twine her arms around his neck. She put her slightly opened mouth against his, allowing her tongue to push against the barrier of his lips. They softened and then parted, welcoming her, perhaps out of sheer surprise. And then he straightened, removing his mouth from the temptation of hers.

He took her elbow and almost propelled her to the door of

the church. There was no one at all in the shadowed pews. No member of the ton had watched the exchange of their vows. But she knew, as he had, that this marriage would be the talk of London. No one who discussed it would really understand. No one would know why she was here, beside this tall, dark stranger who was now her husband.

"I have something for you," Maddy said quietly. The carriage he had helped her into was far more elegant than anything she was accustomed to. Because of its newness, there was no creaking symphony of aged parts to soften the silence that had existed between them since they had left the church. She could see only the unmarred side of her husband's face, and, had she still wished, she might successfully have pretended that she had married the handsome hero she had pictured throughout her girlhood. But somehow, fascination with the reality of the man who was sitting beside her was beginning to replace the dream image that she had lived with for so long.

He turned slightly now, at what she had said, but he didn't speak.

"I know that it's not much. But you must be aware that I no longer have… There's not anything material that I can give you. Except for this. And it's mine. Not Harry's or my stepfather's. I would never—"

She stopped the outpouring of explanation. There was nothing she could explain in her relationship to those men. Not now. No one would believe…

She took a deep breath, searching for control and began removing the long gloves she had worn. She had placed her father's heavy gold signet ring on her thumb this morning and then put on the glove to hold it in place. It was all that remained of the man she could barely remember. But it was hers, and not tainted by the Mannerings.

"It was my father's. It's all I have of his. And I thought…"

She was aware of his surprise, but his hazel gaze revealed nothing of what he was thinking. She slipped the ring off her finger and waited until his hand moved to take it. He hesitated, as if considering the wisdom of accepting such a gift, and finally the long dark fingers slipped it on the third finger of his left hand. It was then that she noticed for the first time the faint scars that marred the backs of both hands, visible only in the strong light.

"And this," she said, forcing her eyes away. From her reticule, she took the stained and tattered deed she had treasured so long. "I know that legally it's already yours, so I suppose this is only symbolic. But I wanted to give it to you."

"What is it?" he asked, the first time he had spoken since the ordeal of the vows.

"A deed. A piece of land in Cornwall. My grandmother left it to me. There's very little there but a house. A cottage. But I've used it as a hiding place, a retreat. And because I—"

"No," he said softly. "It may be—"

"But that's why. Why I want you to have it. I don't want a place to run. I won't ever need one again. I have you now."

"And if it's from me you want to run?" There was some nuance of tone in the quiet question that made her know he was teasing her, that he believed, as she did, that she would never leave.

She laughed, and Jean-Luc felt again that uncontrollable surge of desire. God, he wondered suddenly, how can she do that to me. Make me want to take her here in the carriage. To burn away the memory of everything she's been forced to flee. Of every other man who's ever touched her. To make her mine.

"No," she whispered, her seriousness now a contrast to her laughter. She wanted him to understand. "Don't you know? Don't you understand, even yet? It's *to* you that I've run."

She felt the deep breath he took, but he turned away to look out the window of the coach, and she waited. Finally he took the paper she held and, folding it once, put it in the inside pocket of his coat.

Unable to resist, she dropped her ungloved hand on top of his, which rested motionless on the muscled thigh that had once or twice brushed hers with the swaying movement of the coach.

His fingers closed around her smaller ones, and he held them until they reached their destination.

"I know this is nothing like what you're accustomed to," he said, after he had opened the door to the bedroom they would share above the casino.

She had scarcely glanced around the furnishings of the room and was only vaguely aware of dark massive pieces, including the high bed. She loosened the new ivory ribbons she'd carefully sewn on her old bonnet and removed it, careless of her hair, and laid it on the top of the chest beside the door. Its feminine daintiness was patently out of place in the heavy masculine atmosphere of his room.

"It doesn't matter. If you could see that cottage in Cornwall, you'd know. I know what's important in a home. And it isn't its elegance."

He watched as her fingers touched the top of the chest and ran smoothly along its edge, tracing the intricate design. She moved farther into the room, lightly tracing, too, the footboard of the bed and then the counterpane. She was aware suddenly that she had entered the room alone. Her husband still stood in the doorway, watching, as he had all afternoon, with that quiet intensity. She turned and smiled at him again. Jean-Luc, she thought, remembering her pleasure at the rightness of the name he had spoken in answer to the clergyman's soft questions.

"I have some business. Forgive me. I won't be long. Ling will bring up your trunks."

"Of course," she whispered, knowing that his business had probably been fabricated to allow his escape.

"You're safe here," he said softly. "In my home. You know that, don't you?"

"Of course," she said again, wondering what he was thinking. Wondering what had made him think she needed that reassurance. Whatever else she might feel in his presence, it would not be fear. Even the angry stranger of the inn had never frightened her. The opposite, in fact. And with that thought she realized that he had known that. His question had implied that knowledge. But how could he know? she wondered.

"Then I'll let you rest. Until later..." He held her eyes with his as if there were other things he wanted to say, but finally he turned and retreated down the stairs, the clatter of his boots against the wooden risers more pleasant than she would have believed that simple sound could be. She turned back to the room he had apologized for and found that it, too, was more appealing than she had expected. She leaned against the tall post of his bed and knew that if she allowed herself, she would soon be lost in the romantic daydreams that had persisted in haunting her waking moments since Harry had made his outrageous suggestion.

Oh, Harry, if you only knew what you've done, she thought, smiling. There was something deliciously appealing in the idea of having made Harry think that she'd given in to his demands, when in reality...

When in reality, for once in her adult life she had done exactly what *she* had wanted. And now had, as a result, the one thing she had ever desired.

Maddy had waited through the long hours, tamping down the impatience that she would never be foolish enough to let him see. Listening through the growing twilight. Into the lengthening shadows of darkness and the soft stillness of the night. She refused to light the lamps, but finally lay down on the vast bed, whose cool sheets she had turned back hours before. Soft and inviting. And still he didn't come.

It was nearly midnight before she heard footfalls on the uncarpeted stairs. She lay, holding her breath, waiting for the turning handle and the slender shaft of light that would announce that, finally, he had chosen to join her. But instead, the softly echoing steps had gone past the door and across the hall to his office where once before she had waited for him, trembling in the darkness.

The long minutes stretched, and she knew he wasn't coming. He had chosen to leave her waiting. Her eyes that had strained in the blackness, imagining his form moving silently to join her, closed against the prick of tears.

And then she took a deep breath, denying that disappointment. She remembered the pitying eyes of the man who had married them and her husband's forced air of calmness. He, too, had waited in the shadowed doorway of the small chapel, alone and perhaps as unsure as she was tonight. If the first move in this union must be hers, then she would make it. There was no way he could know, could understand why she was really here. No way that he could guess that she had been waiting so long for his touch.

Maddy stood and straightened the crushed gown as well as she could. Ling, his Chinese servant, had silently brought up her trunk, but she hadn't changed. She was still wearing the cream-colored gown from her trousseau. She could almost hear the laughing chatter of the modiste who had made it so long ago, assuming her to be the happy bride she'd expected to fit.

The light from his office was like a beacon in the dark hall. She could see his tall form, bent over something on his desk. With his attention on whatever he was doing, he was completely unaware of her presence.

He was whispering in French, too softly for her to understand the soothing sibilants. She took another step into the room and the flooring betrayed her, creaking ominously under her slender foot.

Jean-Luc turned suddenly, and his shock at finding her standing almost at his elbow was evident.

"What is it?" she asked. "What's wrong? You look…"

He straightened, the movement allowing her a glimpse of the small white kitten he had been ministering to. The dirty, bedraggled fur was matted with blood, which he had been attempting to clean off with a cloth dipped in a nearby bowl of warm water.

Her involuntary sound of distress preceded the movement of her gentle hands by only a fraction of a second. Her examination was quickly, yet thoroughly, made. A torn ear. But she could find no other wounds. Surely not enough to explain all the blood. No creature so small could afford to lose that much blood.

"I can't find any other wound than this," she said, her troubled violet eyes finding her husband's face. "But there's so much blood."

The one-sided smile flicked upward quickly, and she knew that the kitten wasn't seriously injured. Had it been, she was sure, and didn't know why she was so certain of that knowledge, he would not have smiled.

"Actually," he began and then hesitated. "Actually," he repeated finally, "I think most of that's mine."

"Yours," she whispered. "But…"

And then she noticed the bloody handkerchief that bound his right hand.

"My God…" she breathed.

"It's nothing. But it wouldn't stop bleeding. And he was frightened, so I had to hold him. However, you're right. There doesn't seem to be anything damaged, other than the ear."

"What happened?"

"Dogs. Strays. He would have been an easy supper—"

"But for you. And you were bitten."

He smiled again and shook his head slightly. "They didn't see the need to give up their prize without a struggle. One, hungrier than the rest, I suppose, resisted my attempt at rescue. And I *had* promised Ling a kitchen cat."

Maddy hid her smile at the thought of this minute creature handling the rodents that were the bane of every kitchen. She believed he'd fabricated that promise to hide what she was beginning to suspect was a very soft heart, at least where the defenseless were concerned. She wondered suddenly if he had married her because he had been told something of her past. And then, knowing the impossibility of that, she banished the thought in more practical considerations.

"You'd better let me clean that," she suggested, her capable fingers reaching for the stained cloth that he'd used to bind the wound.

"It's nothing," he said again, moving his hand behind his back like a small boy about to be caned.

The smile caused by that image tugged at her lips, and she looked up into the dark face of this surprising man who rescued kittens.

"I won't hurt you. I promise I'll be very gentle," she teased softly, and waited for the quirk of his lips. Finally she was rewarded for her patience.

"And our friend?" he asked, nodding in the direction of the handful of matted fur.

"He seems to be occupied at the moment," she said, and they watched as the tiny pink tongue began to cleanse the night's damage from paws and whiskers. A too-vigorous attempt at reaching a distant spot resulted in an awkward sprawl. Trying not to look embarrassed at his own ineptitude, the kitten righted himself and returned to his grooming, pretending, in the time-honored way of cats, that the indignity had never happened.

Her husband's soft laugh drew her attention from the cat. She thought she had never heard a more pleasant sound and acknowledged to herself that she would do almost anything to ensure that that was a sound she could enjoy frequently. What kind of spell, she wondered, has he cast...?

"It's all right," he said, not understanding the look in her eyes. "I'll clean it. Go to bed, and..."

She reached again for his hand, and this time he didn't pull away, but allowed her to untie the clumsily knotted cloth.

The punctures were still welling blood. She dabbed at them ineffectually, his hand unmoving and relaxed in hers, in spite of the fact that she knew she must be hurting him.

"You'll have to come back to the bedroom. There's water in the pitcher. I wish I had something with which to make a poultice, but at least we can clean it."

"I'll have Ling look at it downstairs. He's something of a healer. He attends to all our minor cuts and bruises, and this is very minor," he assured her, smiling.

Finally she nodded and, removing her own small handkerchief from her sleeve, she tied the delicate cotton-and-lace square around the hard, very masculine hand. Its feminine whiteness seemed out of place over the dark skin, marred with the old burns that were still visible above the makeshift bandage that hid the newer wound.

Without thinking, she brushed her fingertips over the scars that marked the back of the strong hand that rested in hers. And felt him flinch. She had watched him exert a force of will that had held his hand absolutely still while she'd examined the deep bite. Yet, the touch of her fingers on the old scars caused that involuntary reaction.

He removed his hand from hers, and her eyes lifted to his face.

He smiled at her again and said softly, "Thank you. And now I think I need to take care of our friend."

She had almost forgotten the cat in the muddled emotions of the last minutes. She turned back to the desk and found the kitten was curled up, asleep, its small ribs, clearly visible with his thinness, moving up and down with its gentle breathing.

"Apparently, he knows he's safe," she said, and smiled up at the man who had guaranteed that safety, in spite of what it had cost him.

He was watching her with the same strange intensity she had felt at the church.

"I hope so," he said softly.

The silence stretched between them.

"Come to bed," she invited softly, daringly. And waited.

For a long time Jean-Luc studied the beautiful face raised invitingly to his. And then with the bandaged hand, he touched her cheek, running his forefinger gently down the satin smoothness and then under her chin. He lifted her face to meet his descending mouth that touched as delicately as had his hard finger. Touched and caressed her lips so briefly. Too briefly and then drew away.

"You'll sleep better tonight without me. I'm afraid that—" He stopped, unwilling to explain how he knew he wouldn't sleep. Another night of remembered violence.

''Then let me stay here,'' she whispered and watched his smile.

''Tomorrow night,'' he said softly, and they both understood what he was promising.

Exactly as he had touched her, her own fingers rose to caress the rough, discolored scar tissue of his right cheek, and he controlled his reaction, as he had been unable to do earlier at the sight of her slim, perfect fingers smoothing over the old marks on the back of his hand.

But at the sudden obvious rigidity of his body, her fingers fell, and she moved around him into the darkness of the hall.

He closed his eye and allowed the long shuddering breath he had been holding to finally rasp out. And then, again controlled, his fingers reached to gently caress the soft fur of the sleeping kitten, a poor substitute, he acknowledged, for the silken skin of his wife's body.

Chapter Three

"Good morning."

Her husband's deep voice intruded pleasantly into Maddy's consciousness.

She had been drifting, totally relaxed, enjoying the sensation of being utterly at peace, protected and cocooned by the warmth of the big bed and the piled comforters. Tomorrow, he had promised. And then he'd kissed her. She had been dreaming about his lips, moving gently over hers.

But that accented, slightly amused voice was not part of the dream. It had been night, not morning...

Suddenly she struggled upright, blinking in the flood of late-morning sunshine. Jean-Luc was standing at the foot of the bed, darkly elegant in a coat of blue superfine and cream pantaloons, his cravat as intricately tied as any of the dandies her brother tried so hard to emulate. But her husband didn't look as though he were trying to emulate anyone. He looked...

She felt a sudden skip in the slightly accelerated rhythm of her heartbeat. He looked handsome, she thought with surprise. Different, of course, but very appealing. He'd always been appealing to her, but she had thought that was because he had looked like the fantasy lover of her daydreams. At least, before whatever had happened to him.

"I'm sorry, but I wasn't sure what you preferred, so I asked

Ling to fix chocolate. If you'd rather have tea…'' His voice
trailed off with the question. He didn't understand why she
was staring at him like that. Almost as if she'd never seen
him before.

The light, he thought suddenly. Perhaps in the strong morning light she was really seeing him for the first time. He
fought the urge to turn away, to hide the damage from those
wide violet eyes.

And then she smiled. He felt what he had felt last night,
whatever incredible emotion had suggested that she had
wanted him to kiss her. To touch her. Apparently his instinct
had not been wrong then.

"Chocolate's wonderful. I don't usually sleep all morning," she began to explain, embarrassed that he might think
she was accustomed to being waited on.

"Here," he said, deliberately reminding her of her changed
circumstances, "we work at night and sleep most of the day.
You were up very late."

He walked to the side of the bed and held out the fine
porcelain cup and saucer, the fragrant chocolate still steaming
in the cool room.

The clumsy bandage she'd contrived with her handkerchief
last night had been replaced with a very professional-looking
strip, rivaling his shirtfront in its gleaming whiteness.

She reached automatically for the cup he held out, and the
fingers of her left hand lifted also to touch the bandage. He
allowed his hand to rest under hers a moment and then
straightened away.

"That looks as if it's been more competently cared for than
my efforts last night."

"Ling poulticed it with something he swears will cure anything and then rebandaged it."

"Is it better?"

"It's fine," he said, flexing the long fingers to demonstrate
a lack of pain and swelling.

"I don't think I was very effective…."

"Effective or not, I found I much preferred your ministra-
tions."

"Why?" she invited, softly.

His lips lifted in self-derision at an admission he had not intended to make. But he told her—what she had wanted to hear.

"There were additional benefits to your treatment that Ling, thankfully, didn't provide." He waited a heartbeat for her to think about that, and then he added, his tone totally emotionless, "I brought your friend to say good morning. He seems to have benefited far more than I from Ling's care."

He moved his left hand from behind his back, presenting the small white kitten, now clean and looking very contented with his new condition in life. Someone had adorned him with a blue ribbon that almost matched the wide, inquisitive eyes.

Jean-Luc released him onto the piled quilts of the high bed, and the kitten stepped gingerly, his small paws sinking into the softness as if he were walking through snowdrifts. He explored daringly, another new environment, until he reached Maddy's caressing fingers. His purr vibrated, its sound far too big for his size.

Enjoying the picture they presented, Jean-Luc thought again how incredibly lovely she was. Even in the unfashionable garments that were all he'd seen her in. He wanted to dress her as she should be dressed. He knew she'd be more enchanting than any other woman in London. Her face and the figure were ideally suited for the classical styles the Empress Josephine had made so popular all over Europe.

"I hope you'll forgive the presumption, but I've made an appointment with a modiste I know. I thought—"

"A modiste?" she said, her tone more sharp than she realized. It had been so long since she had had new clothes, but somehow the thought of his arranging that was both embarrassing and unpleasant.

His face was again carefully controlled. As was his voice when he said softly, "Ling said there was only one trunk. So I—"

"No," she said.

I don't want your pity, she thought, embarrassed. I may not have anything to bring to this marriage, but I'm not some poor relation you have to dress before she can be seen in public.

Aloud she said, "Thank you, but I really don't need anything. I have…"

His eyes never left her flushed face while she spoke, but his fingers had unconsciously found the soft neck of the kitten and gently massaged the area below each ear. The cat stretched to allow him greater access to that delightful spot.

"I think, my dear," he said, his voice still soft and without any hint that he had taken offense at her words, "that you must allow me some leeway in that decision. It would be my greatest pleasure to dress you as you deserve, as you should be dressed. And I know just the dressmaker who can accomplish that."

She watched the caressing fingers of that scarred hand against the soft whiteness of the kitten's fur. He heard her sharp, almost rasping inhalation, and then her eyes lifted, wide and haunted, to meet his.

"Of course," she whispered, the violet gaze dark and shadowed. "Of course," she said again. "Whatever you want me to do."

"I want you to be happy," he said truthfully, and the unmarked corner of his mouth lifted slightly at that unexpected confession. She blinked, and what had been in her eyes was gone, as suddenly as the chill that had settled over the room with her whispered agreement.

Her smile was too tentative, unsure as he had never seen it before. Something was wrong. He felt that unpleasant surety again. Felt it strongly with that gambler's sixth sense that had never let him down. Something had happened that he didn't understand, but then the look, whatever it had meant, was gone.

"I'll wait for you downstairs," he suggested, at a loss, and saw her surprise.

"You're going with me?"

"How else will I be sure that what Madame Darnet chooses will do you justice?" he said, smiling.

"I've never shopped with…" She paused.

He waited, but she didn't complete the thought.

"Then it will be a new experience," he suggested. "Perhaps one of many."

His smile had appeared briefly again with his last comment, but he had turned away before she had had time to realize the full implication of that statement.

"Jean-Luc," she said.

He turned back, his raised brow questioning. He hadn't realized how much he would enjoy hearing her husky voice employ that slightly Anglicized version of his name.

"Would you take the kitten? Downstairs, please. Back to Ling."

He hesitated, trying to read her tone, her eyes. But there was nothing there now, no hidden messages.

"I thought you liked cats."

"I do," she said, her fingers carefully clasped together before her on the sheet. "But there's no sense in spoiling him."

Her gaze had dropped to the kitten who was again engaged in the endless ritual of bathing.

"And *I* think he's had too little of that," her husband said softly. He was smiling when she glanced up, surprised at the seriousness of his tone. She hadn't seen the puzzled look with which he had assessed her unexpected request. But he scooped the cat off the counterpane in one large hand without any further comment. He nuzzled the tiny creature against the scarred profile, unconscious of what he was doing.

As he carried the kitten out of the room, she could hear him whispering to it softly in French.

Ghosts, she thought, when even his voice and footsteps had faded. Nothing is the same. Nothing will be the same unless I allow those ghosts to spoil it. He's *not* my stepfather.

She leaned back against the banked pillows and closed her eyes, forcing the picture of the kitten's white fur contentedly resting against her husband's cheek to block out the other images.

"But, my lord…" the viscount's man of business protested.

"I've signed your damned papers and given you your instructions. I am engaged for lunch. Pay what you can and put off the rest. And for God's sake, man, quit bothering me over every importunate tradesman who presents a bill. What am I employing you for?''

"But, my lord, the estate will bear no more. I've tried to tell you…''

"*Ad infinitum. Ad nauseam.* I should think you would give up by now. I've told you that I have things well under way for a restoration of my fortunes. The creditors will simply have to be patient. To convince them of that is your job. Surely we've not reached a point in this country where a peer can be hounded because his accounts are slightly in arrears.''

"Slightly!'' Mr. Pennington gasped the interruption, and then blushed furiously at his indiscretion.

"No more than my father. Even you must admit that,'' Harry argued.

"Well, no, my lord, perhaps not. But some of these creditors have been waiting since your father's death and they—''

"If they've waited that long, then their needs must not be very great. They can wait a while longer.''

Since his sister had successfully rescued him from the threat of Newgate, the viscount had been feeling unusually optimistic. That had been so easily arranged. He had wondered, briefly, at Maddy's cooperation. But too self-centered to worry about anyone else's emotions for very long, he had soon lost that puzzlement in anticipation of his changing luck.

"The tide of my fortune is about to turn. I've made a new investment, Pennington, that even you would approve of.''

"I should be very interested to hear what that is,'' his man of business said, no trace of the disbelief he felt allowed into his careful tone.

"Destiny,'' Harry announced with a distinct touch of self-satisfaction.

"I beg your pardon, my lord.''

"Destiny. Bloodlines that trace back to Eclipse. The sweetest goer—''

"A horse,'' Pennington interrupted again, incredulously.

"You've invested in a racehorse." His already florid complexion had taken on a decidedly dangerous hue.

"A sure thing. I have it on the best authority. He'll run in the Derby, and then we'll be on the road to prosperity. By this time next week, we'll be turning down poor relations seeking a handout. You mark my word, man. By this time next week, the duns you've shown me this morning will be merely an unpleasant memory."

"Indeed, my lord," his adviser said faintly. "I trust you are right. However—"

"Oh, damn you, not today. Don't waste any more of my time. Take another mortgage. Sell something. Do what-ever's necessary. But for God's sake, don't pester me with the business," Harry said.

"Indeed, my lord," Pennington said more grimly, his despair over the affairs of the Mannerings driving him to a desperate courage. "If there were anything left to sell or to mortgage, believe me, I should have done so without pestering you."

"Good," said Harry absently, the meaning of that declaration lost on him entirely. He was idly leafing through the stack of communications that had been urged to his attention. Suddenly he paused, his eyes rescanning one of the letters. Straightening the flimsy page, covered with the crabbed hand of an overworked scribe, he started again at the top, slowly and carefully reading now every word.

"Good God," he said softly. His eyes left the closely penned lines to stare into the air before him as if calculating or considering the meaning of what he'd just read.

"Pennington," he said suddenly, turning to face his startled man of business. "Do you know what this says?"

Settling his spectacles more solidly on his nose, Mr. Pennington glanced at the sheet the viscount was holding out demandingly for his inspection.

"It's from your agent in Cornwall. I believe I wrote you about that, my lord. Twice, if memory serves. Once last month and then again on the third. However, receiving no reply..."

"Damme, man, do you actually think I read that drivel you send me? Of all the fool—"

"Forgive me, my lord, but I did try—"

"Well, trying isn't good enough. Don't you know what's happening now in the market?"

"Indeed, my lord. If you'll remember, I suggested in my letter of the third that you might…"

"How could I remember what I never read? You fool, this is the answer to all my problems. And you're writing me letters about it while I'm racking my brain to find a solution to the setbacks that have lately occurred. Why, don't you see? All I have to do is to arrange for the sale of this…"

Suddenly the triumphant voice faded as the speaker realized the impossibility of that sale.

"Damn you, Pennington. Damn you for the bungling idiot you are. You and your damned letters. You've had this more than a month, and you never brought it to my attention. I ought to kill you. I ought to strangle you with my bare hands and throw your worthless carcass out the window. My God, I believe I could do it."

"My lord, I beg you—"

"You ought to beg. The thought of your causing this opportunity to slip through my fingers like… I swear I could kill you!"

"My lord, I'm sure I don't know what you mean. You must realize that nothing prevents your selling the property now. The market is still very strong and looks to be growing. Indeed it is so strong and offers so much possibility, however, that as your agent I should advise you to hold on to—"

"You ass! Thanks to you, I no longer have the opportunity to hold or to sell. Thanks to your sniveling, idiotic letters, it's gone. Gone, you fool. Do you understand?"

"But, my lord, if it's not been sold, and I assume I should have been asked to handle that transaction, then how can it be gone?" Pennington asked in his confusion.

But Harry's mind had already moved from the realization that the solution to all his problems was out of his reach to the contemplation of how he could get it back.

"I wonder how that bastard knew," he said softly, bitterness and fury added to the cold hatred that already lodged deeply within him.

"My lord?" Pennington's voice intruded faintly into Harry's consciousness.

"Two hands you've won," the Viscount Mannering said softly, and still without the least understanding of the situation, Mr. Pennington shivered at the quiet vindictiveness of the whisper, "but the game isn't ended. Not by far. And there are a few trumps that you can't possibly know I hold."

The faint smile that lifted the aristocrat's thin lips was as frightening to the man who was watching as the whisper had been. He waited silently, unwilling to draw attention to himself again, as the viscount dropped the sheaf of papers he had been holding back onto the desk. Except for the one that had caused so much excitement. That one he carefully folded and placed in his coat pocket. He didn't say good day to his man of business. After he was gone, Pennington spent a long moment collecting his scattered wits and wiping the perspiration off his brow. He was very glad that it seemed he was no longer the bastard the Viscount Mannering was blaming for this last disastrous piece of bad luck. Very glad indeed.

Jean-Luc and Maddy were greeted with genuine enthusiasm by Madame Darnet, the tall, beautiful modiste. Jean-Luc was obviously an old and valued acquaintance. Their initial conversation was in rapid French, but Maddy's husband quickly apologized for their rudeness. He had introduced her with something that looked almost like wariness, but he seemed relieved by the dressmaker's delighted and spontaneous welcome.

"But she is charming," Madame Darnet said, smiling up at him. "However did you convince her to marry you, *mon ami?*"

Madelyn glanced at her husband's face, wondering at the closeness of friendship that would allow this woman to question their marriage. She felt a defensive spurt of anger at the unthinking cruelty of that remark.

But her husband's lips were already moving into that slow half smile that marked his amusement.

"I don't know," he said honestly, considering with the modiste the perfection of his wife's features. "Perhaps you'd better ask her. I've been afraid to question my good fortune."

"Good fortune that you deserve," Madame Darnet said softly. Her smile was warm with shared memories, but the understanding in their eyes when they met did not include the Englishwoman who was intruding, she suddenly felt, on the reunion of two very old friends.

"And I want you to create a wardrobe as beautiful as she is," Jean-Luc said softly. "I don't really believe that's possible, but I know that if anyone in London is capable of doing that, it's you."

"With her coloring…" the modiste began, and then in the contemplation of the challenge he had just given her, she forgot to finish the thread of the thought she had begun. She walked around Madelyn's tall, slim figure and even, unthinkingly, touched the silver-gilt hair. The Englishwoman reacted to that invasion, moving instinctively closer to the strength of her husband's body. She saw, but didn't understand the sudden lift of the dressmaker's lips, a smile that was quickly hidden.

"And you're here to supervise?" Madame Darnet asked lightly, turning to face Jean-Luc.

"Of course," he said, smiling.

"You don't trust me?" she questioned in amusement.

"Implicitly, or we should never have come, but this is…" He hesitated suddenly.

"This is something very special to you, and you value your own taste more than mine," she suggested, laughing.

"When it comes to my wife," he answered, and was aware of how pleasant that word sounded.

Madame Darnet smiled again with perfect understanding. She had meant what she said. It was only what Jean-Luc deserved. She could think of no one whose happiness would give her more pleasure. And it was obvious that he was happy.

She extended a capable hand, indicating the dressing room at the back of the shop.

"If you would, madame," she urged softly. "I'll join you in a moment."

Madelyn nodded, still feeling very much the outsider, and walked gracefully across the room to disappear behind the velvet curtain that separated the outer salon from the dressing rooms.

Silence stretched briefly between the old friends she'd left behind.

"She's very beautiful," the Frenchwoman said again, studying Jean-Luc's marred countenance.

"Too beautiful for the likes of this," he said, lightly touching with his long, dark fingers the scars her eyes were still considering. "*You*, at least, should say what you're thinking."

"All right, I will. I'm wondering if she's good enough for you, my dear."

His laugh was sudden and brutally short.

"What you're really wondering is how I tricked her into marrying me," he suggested harshly.

"No," she denied, shaking her head, her eyes never wavering from the gentle contemplation of his stiff features. "I'm really wondering if she knows how much in love with her you are."

He didn't answer her because he couldn't deny the accusation. She waited a long time, and then she touched his hand that had reached, as if by habit, to be sure that the black patch was in its accustomed position.

"Don't," she advised, and they both knew it was not that unthinking gesture she was questioning. "You'll lose her if you dwell on your imperfections."

"I don't 'dwell' on them," he repeated sarcastically. "I just wonder what will happen when *she* begins to."

The modiste shook her head again, knowing there was nothing else she could say to assuage that doubt. Turning to the small room where his wife waited, she left him alone in the salon.

* * *

"It fair gives me the creeps just looking at him. Like some kind of monster, he is, with all them scars."

The whispering voice floated into the small dressing room where Maddy waited for Madame Darnet to take the careful measurements necessary to ensure the exact fit of the new dresses. The vulgarly common tone was out of place in the elegant gentility of the Frenchwoman's shop.

"How she can stand to be in the same room with him when he takes off them fancy clothes is what I'd like to know. Imagine having to touch whatever's under 'em," the hateful voice continued as Madame Darnet swept aside the curtain.

Its echoing ugliness lingered in the sudden stillness. Madelyn could see the dressmaker's shock give way very quickly to anger.

She strode to the door that led to the workroom, a door that had, apparently, been left slightly open.

Her voice, commanding and clearly furious, quickly set the seamstresses back to their neglected tasks, all conversation silenced by the force of her anger.

She turned back to the white face of the woman who waited, concerned only that *he* hadn't heard the cruel discussion of his disfigurement and the speculation about their marriage.

"I'm sorry," Madame Darnet said finally, accurately reading her reaction. "They're fools..." she began, and stopped as Maddy shook her head.

"They're like my brother. They only see the scars, the outside."

"And you?" the Frenchwoman asked curiously. "What do you see?"

"What's inside," she answered softly.

Madame Darnet stood a moment, studying the woman before her. And then she smiled. "I was afraid that you didn't know," she whispered.

"I know. Just as I know..." she began, and then shook her head again. She knew how sensitive he was about the scars, in spite of his pretense of immunity to the stares. But saying that aloud was, of course, in itself a betrayal of his courage in facing this artificial world that always judged by outward appearances.

"I'm going to make you more beautiful than you've ever been before," Madame Darnet promised softly. "For him. Because he deserves that. And so, when you're with him, perhaps no one will ever say those things again. They will only wonder what there is about him that has attracted the most beautiful woman in London. Will you let me make you that woman?"

Maddy wondered briefly what, beyond friendship, might have been between this Frenchwoman and her husband. But the sincerity of that offer and the conspiracy to protect him showed clearly in the modiste's eyes, so that she knew that whatever the tie, it was no longer anything she need fear.

"Of course," she agreed. "Whatever he wants. Whatever you think will protect him from people like that."

"Nothing can really protect him, but you can teach him that it doesn't matter."

When the measurements were taken and Maddy and the dressmaker returned to the salon, Madame Darnet and Jean-Luc had eventually lapsed into French, discussing, as if Maddy weren't there, the colors and styles that would best become her. The display of materials seemed endless, and she lost track of the number of dresses that her husband had ordered, far more than she should ever need.

"And this," Madame Darnet said finally, spreading the shot silk to drape across the Englishwoman's slender shoulder and spill onto the floor. Almost in wonder Maddy's fingers touched the violet iridescence. She had never seen anything like it—the color or the texture. Fine enough to pull through the proverbial ring.

"For evening," the modiste's voice suggested, watching the widening of the violet eyes that so nearly matched the material.

"But…" Maddy whispered, forcing herself to be reasonable. Years of hoarding every shilling intruded. He'd already spent so much, and there would, of course, be nowhere to wear this. The great town houses of the ton where wearing a dress made from this material would be appropriate were for-ever closed to her. Even those old friends who had tried to include her in the events of the Season when she'd first re-turned to London had finally given up. She'd refused to be-come an object of pity, attending dinners and parties in the same bedraggled, outdated gowns. And so she had cut the ties to that life. Even those who had accepted her then because of their genuine friendship would certainly not accept her hus-band. The realization of the finality of her exile from that world into which she'd been born struck painfully as her trem-bling fingers caressed the silk.

"It's perfect," Jean-Luc said. "And I think, made up like this…" he suggested, pointing out one of the illustrations they had considered earlier in the latest edition of *La Belle Assem-blée*.

"No," Maddy said sharply, and they both turned in sur-prise. She had let them decide everything else and now, when this was so obviously perfect, her objection was almost shock-ing.

"No," she said, controlling her voice, so that it was only slightly above a whisper. "I won't need anything for eve-ning."

"Why not?" Jean-Luc questioned, smiling at her.

"Because there's nowhere I can go now to wear…" She stopped, appalled at the effect of what she'd just said.

Her husband's smile had disappeared, wiped out by the quiet bitterness of her declaration.

"Make it up," he ordered Madame Darnet. His gaze never left his wife's face and it was to her that he said, without inflection, "Whether you ever wear it or not is your deci-sion."

He held out his left wrist, the polite coldness of the gesture apparent to both women. Since she had no choice, Maddy put her fingers on his arm, the firm muscles under their tips as steady as they had always been.

When they were outside the shop, she knew that she needed to explain, to apologize. Her bitter avowal of her banishment had spoiled his pleasure in the afternoon.

I'm as selfish as Harry, she thought in disgust. What did it matter what the very people she had so often inveighed against thought of the man at her side, and, of course, of herself for marrying him?

"I didn't mean..." she began, and at the look he shot her, the lie froze in her throat.

"I am aware of what our marriage means to your position, but after all, my dear, *you* proposed this arrangement. Or was I right the first time? Did Mannering force you to make that sacrifice?"

"No," she denied hotly. "I told you—"

"I know what you told me," he said harshly. "But surely you must have thought about what becoming my wife would mean. Or has it just become clear to you that you've given up your birthright? A little late for regrets, Madame Gavereau," he mocked.

"No regrets," she said, catching his chin and turning his face so that he was forced to meet her furious gaze. "Except that I'm going to have the most beautiful gown in London and nowhere to wear it. That's the only regret I meant to express. Whatever you're imagining..."

She stopped suddenly as the corner of his mouth quirked upward in amusement at her anger.

Unsheathing claws as harmless as the kitten's, he thought, his own anger forgotten. Because, after all, he wanted very much to believe what she had just declared.

"No regrets?" he asked again, allowing his rich voice to caress.

Her breath caught, remembering his promise last night.

"No regrets," she whispered. She slipped her hand into his and felt it close tightly around hers. He raised her fingers to his lips that lightly traced across their knuckles.

"One night you can wear it for me," he said, smiling, and her answering smile was a mixture of anticipation and of gratitude for his forgiveness. He enjoyed the shock in those beautiful violet eyes even more than her smile as she realized what he meant when he finished the suggestion.

"But probably not for long."

Chapter Four

Jean-Luc escorted her home, handing her out of the carriage at the side entrance that opened on stairs leading to the living quarters above the gambling salon. She unconsciously turned her face away from the street, carefully shielding her identity from any curious passerby. Ashamed of that reflexive response, she glanced up to find her husband's mocking smile. He was well aware of the impulse she had just yielded to. Angry at herself, she stepped inside, and only then realized that he was giving another order to the waiting coachman.

"Jean-Luc?" she said questioningly.

"I have an errand. Before the casino opens." He offered the explanation with his back to the doorway where she stood.

"Of course," she said softly.

She watched until he had climbed back into the coach, and then she retreated into the dimness of the small hallway, hearing the muffled sounds of the carriage wheels moving against the cobbled street.

"Idiot," she chided herself under her breath.

"Says your brother to see you." Ling appeared out of the shadows that led into the public rooms. "Says he wait. No speak to boss. Speak to lady."

"My brother?" she repeated, trying to make sense of the broken English. "Harry?" she asked incredulously.

"In salon," Ling assured over his shoulder and melted silently back into the shadows from which he'd emerged.

She wondered if she were supposed to follow him. And if she did so, if she would be likely to encounter any of her husband's patrons. Of which her half brother was certainly one, she thought in sudden self-derision. She was finding it very difficult to throw off the familiar restraints society had placed on where and with whom a woman of her class might properly go. Shrugging her shoulders, she went in the direction the servant had taken and found him waiting for her at the turning.

He indicated a room and disappeared again into the unlighted hall.

She found Harry seated at a small, elegant table, a fan of cards spread across its surface.

"Pick one," he invited, glancing up at her entrance.

"What do you want, Harry?" she asked instead.

"Can't I come to visit my sister? What are you so suspicious about? Purely a social call, my dear. I wanted to find out how you're enjoying the married state."

She held his eyes a moment, but then that innocent, baby blue gaze fell back to the cards.

"Pick one. Let's see if your luck's in," he urged again.

"No," she said simply. At something in her tone, he looked up.

"Then it would appear that you aren't happy with your bargain. Our bargain. I'm sorry, especially now that—"

"Why did you come to my house, Harry? I don't want you here."

"Your house," he mocked in surprise, looking pointedly at the scattered tables. "I could have sworn—"

"I did what you wanted, Harry. And it's finished. Whatever you want now, the answer is no."

"What makes you think I want anything?"

"Because I know you. And I know all your tricks."

"I simply wanted to wish you happy. My only sister, you know. Sorry I missed the ceremony. Hardly a crowd, I should imagine," he suggested, smiling.

"No," she agreed. Harry's taunts had long since lost their ability to hurt.

"And your husband. How is our friend, the elegant gambler? They say that the French are very skilled in…" Harry paused, looking at her with a suggestive smirk.

"My husband is fine. And the weather is lovely. And I hear that the Regent's health is improving. Are there any other topics of polite conversation we should cover?" she asked calmly. Eventually, Harry would get tired of playing cat and mouse and get to the point. He always did.

"So he *doesn't* know anything exotic enough to make you forget his face. And perhaps even his body. Someone said that the scarring underneath all that expensive Parisian tailoring is even more…" Again he paused delicately.

"And how would *someone* know?" she asked sardonically, determined not to make him aware that he was succeeding in angering her.

His eyebrows raised at that, and he said with a scintilla of feigned hurt, "I'm only repeating what I've heard. You, I should think, would be in a position to know better than I the truth of that statement."

She didn't answer him, but her lips involuntarily tightened in disgust, and Harry, recognizing that she was reaching the end of her patience, decided he'd annoyed her enough that she might be willing to do what he wanted just to get rid of him.

"I met an acquaintance of yours today." He paused, but she made no response, knowing that this was all leading to something. "Lady Rutledge. And her husband."

She waited, silent and patient.

"Can you imagine, Maddy? Such old friends, and they cut me dead. Pretended I wasn't there. Suddenly, for them, Harry Mannering didn't exist. And do you know why?"

"No, but I'm certain that you intend to tell me," she said indifferently. But she was trying to formulate some explanation for Harry's almost visible aura of excitement. Something was going on in that ever-scheming brain. Something that probably boded no good for her.

"Because your husband brought his filthy accusations from the gutter that's his life into *my* club."

"His accusations?" she questioned.

"About the necklace. That I'd cheated him."

"Harry, the necklace was paste. It was worthless. You told me that. What did you expect him to do? You owed him seventy thousand pounds."

"I didn't know the damn thing was paste. It wasn't my fault. He could have come to me privately, like any gentleman...."

The word hung in the air between them, and they were both aware that the Frenchman made no pretense of being bound by those restrictions.

"I don't know what you want me to do," she said finally.

"But don't you see? It's all for naught. It's all been in vain. Your marriage. Clearing the debt. None of it made the slightest difference in the face of that accusation. And I can never regain what we've lost."

"I'm sorry, but I really don't—"

"I can never get you out of this marriage, Maddy. Not if everyone's turned against me. Not if I'm an outcast to my own class. Don't you understand."

"Harry," she began, and then knew that she couldn't tell him the truth. That she had never believed he would recoup his family's fortunes. That she knew he would never be in a financial position to arrange for the divorce he had promised her. And especially the truth that she had never wanted that divorce. The knowledge of her genuine feelings for her husband was not a weapon she would give him. He might not be her stepfather, but he shared the same blood and the same cold-blooded self-interest. She had learned that lesson all too well. Never let the Mannerings know what you value, what you care about. Never give them something they can use against you.

"Maddy?" Harry said softly, watching her face. She blinked, realizing that she was being very foolish. He must never suspect. Never.

"What do you think I can do?" she asked, and this time he didn't deny the purpose of his visit.

"Make him take it back. What he said."

"But it was true. You told me it was true. And that he showed them. At White's. How can he now—"

"He can come to the club and make a formal apology. Tell them that he was wrong. That *he* switched the diamonds. That *he* was the one...."

She laughed suddenly, shaking her head. "Can you really imagine him doing that?" she asked, incredulous that he could even suggest that ridiculous scenario.

"He will if you ask him to."

"No," she said softly, shaking her head again. "You know that's not true, Harry. You know how...arrogant he is," she said, using his own description of her husband.

"If you ask him," Harry repeated doggedly. "You could make him."

"How? How do you imagine that I can compel him to lie, to admit publicly to a dishonorable act he didn't commit?"

"Dishonorable?" Harry laughed. "God, Maddy, he's a gambler. He has no honor to lose. *I'm* the one who's lost here. *I'm* the one who's the outcast. And you can remedy that. It seems a simple choice to me. Your brother's honor, clearing your family's name, in exchange for a gambler's lie. And you can make him. Withhold your favors. I would imagine, now that he's tasted that lovely body of yours, he'd be more than willing—"

His words were arrested by the involuntary downsweep of her lashes over the violet eyes and the sudden blush. At her reaction, whose significance Harry all too easily recognized, he laughed.

"Do you mean...? Ah, Maddy, I'm surprised at you. You haven't been able to bring yourself to share his bed, my love? Have you lost your courage? I can't say that I blame you, but you know it's inevitable. Whatever you're using as an excuse, he won't accept for long."

He smiled again at the slow blush that she couldn't control at his knowing comments.

"Make it a condition. If you do it at the right moment, he won't be able to refuse. No man would. I told you—you're a very beautiful woman, my dear. He'll agree. If you ask him nicely."

Harry's smug surety that she would use her body that way made her slightly ill.

"No," she said again, as she had at the beginning.

"And I wonder why not?" he said softly. "There is, I hate to admit, a certain dark sensuality about him. You aren't beginning to be attracted to all that French *sangfroid,* are you?"

He isn't stupid, she reminded herself silently. Don't mistake his selfishness for stupidity. Don't ever let him suspect....

"Don't be ridiculous," she said, forcing herself to meet his eyes.

He studied hers, calm and indifferent, as they rested on his face. "You were remarkably easy to persuade into this marriage, my dear. And I'm beginning to wonder why you were so willing to fall in with my plans? I know you, Maddy—"

"And you also know Cornwall. I decided *anything* was better than Cornwall." The lie was an inspiration. She knew how much Harry despised the country.

He laughed suddenly at her confession.

"I *do* know Cornwall," he admitted, still smiling, "so I guess I shouldn't have been surprised. And, of course, you hadn't seen our gambler friend when you agreed. I'm *not* surprised, however, that you're having a hard time keeping up your end of that bargain. Still think anything's better than Cornwall?"

She forced an answering smile, shaking her head. "I'm not sure anymore," she lied again.

"He won't wait forever, Maddy. Ask him. For me. And ultimately for yourself. For the divorce. Let's put this whole unpleasant incident behind us as quickly as we can and get back to our lives. I know you can do it. A public apology is all I'm asking."

"I'll try," she promised softly. She was caught. She couldn't let Harry suspect that she had wanted this marriage. That she had never intended to seek the divorce he'd prom-

ised. And most of all, she could never let him know that she
cared about the man to whom she was married. Because she
knew very well what happened to the things she cared about.

The afternoon stretched long and lonely. As much as she
regretted the morning's mistakes, her unthinking words about
the dress and her too-obvious embarrassment over entering
what was now her home, it appeared that she was not to be
given an opportunity to make amends for them. Apparently
this was to be another night that she would spend alone in
the bed that was her husband's, a bed he now wanted only to
avoid.

Maddy's fingers paused over the split seam she was restitching in one of his elegant evening shirts. She had been
driven at last by her sense of failure to investigate the contents
of the chest, and she had spent the last hour repairing the few
signs of wear she had found in his wardrobe. She let the
completed sewing rest in her lap, and unconsciously breathed
a sigh, her lips tightening in frustration.

"What are you doing?" Jean-Luc asked softly from the
doorway.

"Trying to pretend that I know something about housewif-
ery," she answered truthfully, glancing up. She tied off the
completed stitches and clipped the thread, offering her handiwork for his inspection.

The familiar movement of the corner of his mouth began
but was quickly controlled. He looked down, attempting to
hide his amusement at the thought of her assuming those
wifely duties.

"That's not why I married you. To repair my wardrobe.
Ling generally takes care of that. I'll speak to him."

"I really don't know why you need a wife," she said,
watching the hazel eye rise to lock suddenly on her face.
"After all, you already have the ever-efficient Ling," she finished, smiling.

His face relaxed at her slightly challenging tone.

"But, my dear," he said very softly, and she was relieved
to hear that the teasing note was back, "there are some things

that Ling, however capable…'' He let the sentence fade, and knew from the faint color that had stolen into her throat that she knew exactly what he was suggesting.

''Thank goodness,'' she whispered, her eyes modestly lowered, but her own lips lifted slightly at the daring answer to his remark, and she was rewarded by his laughter.

It was so long before he spoke again that the silence finally compelled her gaze to lift to his face, its expression free now of the humor he had used to bridge the awkwardness between them. An awkwardness that her unthinking cruelty had caused.

''I'm sorry,'' she whispered, knowing that he would realize exactly what she was apologizing for.

''I had thought that in this marriage I was offering you an escape,'' he said. ''Not a prison. But of course, in some ways, that's exactly what this is. You only pointed that out to me.''

''An escape?'' she repeated, questioning.

''From whatever Mannering used to make you agree to come to me. I'd met you. I knew you weren't a woman who'd marry because you were ordered to. I knew there was more to your decision, something that would explain—''

''I told you why I married you,'' she denied, hoping he'd never learn the truth about the reasons for her first marriage. He was crediting her with a courage she didn't possess.

His lips tightened, but he didn't continue whatever line of thought she'd interrupted.

''I suppose it really doesn't matter anymore,'' he said. ''Whatever your reasons, you *are* now my wife. And there's nothing you can ever do to change that.''

''But I don't want—''

''I have something for you,'' he interrupted her denial, almost as if he didn't want to hear her make it. He brought the dressmaker's box from behind his back, much as he had presented the kitten for her inspection this morning. ''Thankfully, Genevieve was able to provide exactly what I required.''

The box, when opened, revealed a dark rose domino and matching half mask. Maddy hesitantly unfolded the hooded cloak whose rich folds reached to the floor. She raised her eyes to find her husband watching with that enigmatic half smile she found so intriguing.

"I thought that you might give me the opportunity to prove that our marriage may also represent a freedom you've never before enjoyed."

"I don't understand."

"Have you ever seen a firework display at Vauxhall Gardens?" he suggested, smiling.

"Of course not," she denied, scandalized at the thought of attending that less-than-genteel pleasure ground. Ten years ago the ton had made the gardens fashionable, but now they were widely recognized as the province of the underclass.

"Of course not," he echoed mockingly, but his dark brow rose in gentle derision. "Even if our marriage is in some ways a prison, remember that you have now been liberated from all the old rules. And there should be something very appealing in having the freedom to do exactly what you wish— if you are courageous enough to grasp that freedom. The gardens are very beautiful in the moonlight. Quite romantic, or so I've been told."

"You, of course," she said, smiling back at him, "having never been there."

"Perhaps. On occasion. But never with the most beautiful woman in London. Never with my wife."

The word that she was not yet accustomed to brought again that slight rush of color to the translucent skin, and she lowered her eyes at the intimacy of his tone.

"Or are you not romantic enough to be tempted by moonlight and fireworks?" he asked softly. "Will you go with me tonight, my lady wife? Let me show you something of my world?"

"Yes," she whispered, raising her eyes to the dark, scarred face of her husband. "I should very much like to be shown your world."

But when, much later, he carefully handed her into the carriage, he seemed almost a stranger. The formal evening dress he wore was hidden under a black domino. Although the mask he had chosen for her, exactly matching the rose of her cloak, was small and heavily jeweled, covering only the area around her eyes, the black mask he had donned covered, by design, his entire face. Only his chin and the beautifully shaped mouth were fully revealed by its arching cut, and she knew that he had deliberately hidden his visage from the stares of the curious. She wondered if this were the reason he found an evening in the gardens so pleasant, the night and the ridotto offering the opportunity to escape, if only for a few hours, the disfigurement that the world found so abhorrent.

With that thought, she slipped her hand into the lean one of the man who sat beside her. He lifted her fingers, and she felt his lips caress them, unhurriedly and without self-consciousness, bestowing a lingering kiss on each one.

"Nervous?" he asked, and she heard again his amusement.

"No, not with you beside me."

"There's really nothing to be frightened of. *I'm* the undesirable element your mother was afraid you'd be exposed to at Vauxhall. And since you and I have already met..." His teasing voice trailed off suggestively, and he was rewarded with her soft laugh.

"Then I think I'll enjoy the evening very much."

She was surprised at how true that prophecy proved to be. He was the perfect guide, his familiarity with one of London's most notoriously romantic locations obvious. She wondered briefly how many women he had brought here, and then blocked that question from her mind.

He treated her with charming courtesy, as if she were very fragile and perhaps seventeen years old. The tomboyish hoyden she had been at that age might not have appreciated the formality of his manners, but the woman who had married him found herself relaxing into his sophisticated chivalry. Just as she found herself enjoying his wit and his open appreciation of this newly discovered world that teemed around them.

"Look," he said softly, turning her chin with one long finger so that she found an elderly gentleman bestowing a tender kiss on the cheek of the buxom and rather grandmotherly lady he was accompanying. The old lady's blushing response might also have better been made at seventeen, but Maddy's smile as she watched then was as tender as the kiss had been.

"Shockingly vulgar," her husband said sternly, but below the darkness of the mask he wore, she could see the slant of his smile.

"You're jealous," she teased. "No such lovely lady on your arm."

"The lady on my arm would surely object to such a public avowal of the affections of her beau," he agreed. He turned away from the scene and continued to guide her on to a spot that he'd promised offered a better vantage from which to view the fireworks.

She made no verbal response to his disappointing reply to her half-veiled suggestion, but she tucked her hand into his arm and felt his other hand warmly cover hers. Arm in arm they strolled to the spot he'd suggested, away from the milling throng.

They were almost alone, silhouetted against the backdrop of the trees as they awaited the beginning of the evening's spectacular. She shivered suddenly in the light breeze and felt him move behind her. His arms brought the dark folds of his domino around them both, shielding her from the coolness of the night air. She was pulled against the hard heat of his tall body, his warm fingers gently holding her upper arms. She could feel his breath stir against her hair. Unconsciously, she leaned back into his strength, incredibly comforted by his arms around her.

Sometime in the course of the display that spangled the darkness of the sky over the vast park, she became aware that her husband was thinking of something other than fireworks. Finally, in embarrassment, she eased away from his growing response to the slender body he held so closely against his, and without protest he released her. They stood, not speaking, until the last trembling shimmer of light had faded from the sky.

"It was so beautiful, I didn't want it to end," she confessed.

"There will be other nights," he said, offering his arm. "Besides, only if we hurry do we have time enough for the remaining conventions of this unconventional site."

"And what are those?" she asked, smiling up at him. He had again placed her on his left, and she now realized, given the loss of sight in his right eye, that her position there was a necessity.

"The lovers' maze. And its fountain," he said.

"A real maze?"

"The most challenging in London. And in the center..." He paused enticingly.

"And in the center?" she repeated obligingly, a more-than-willing participant in whatever else this evening held. The entire night had been an adventure for her after the long, drear years of exile. Even those months after she'd returned to London had represented an exile of sorts.

"Lovers meet at midnight and share a kiss."

"And if they're still hopelessly lost in the maze at midnight?" she asked, laughing.

"Then they never, ever admit to having failed the rendezvous. How are you at mazes, lady wife?"

"I don't know. I've never—"

She stopped as his forearm fell away beneath her fingers. He turned suddenly, the black domino swirling around his figure, its movement deliberately dramatic, in the style of the most heinous Drury Lane villain. And then he was gone.

The echo of her laughter hadn't faded from the high, dense walls of the hedges that surrounded her when she realized that she was really alone and that he had already led her, unaware of his intent, into the maze. She supposed she'd been too fascinated by the promise of midnight kisses to pay proper attention to where he was carrying her. Too trusting. And why not? He had given her no reason not to trust him. Of all the men she had known...

That unbidden thought was banished, its dark memories not allowed to disturb the pleasure of this night. All she had to do was to reach the center of the maze, and she would find him waiting for her. She had no doubt about his instructions, cryptic though they had been.

She turned back to face the path they had taken, trying to get her bearings. She need only to move a few feet in that direction, she decided, to retrace their steps and to be once again in the gardens. Perhaps it might be wise to do that, to begin from outside the maze, she reasoned. She had never been lost, even in the frenzy of a hunt. Her sense of direction was too keen to allow...

Her breath eased through the suddenly constricted muscles of her throat. She had not thought of riding in years. Had not allowed herself to remember the pounding excitement of her Thoroughbred moving in perfect unison of motion beneath her. Freedom. He had promised her that, and she wondered if it might finally really be so.

She shook her head, still smiling, and moved to where she knew the entrance to be. And found herself blocked by another wall of foliage. Turning, she tried to find the spot where he had deserted her and found instead a branching that she didn't recognize.

"Jean-Luc," she whispered, wondering if he would really leave her alone. But there was no answer from the darkness. She thought she had read that in a maze, most of which were concentric, one should choose a direction and follow that choice at each turning. And so taking a deep breath, she walked without hesitation to the right. Because I have chosen right, she thought, aware of the sheer childishness of her reasoning. And because the left is always the sinister, she finished the thought. *Bar sinister* slipped into her brain. The bastard branch. And then she forgot that foolish conceit as she put her intelligence and her strongly developed sense of direction to solving the puzzle he had set for her.

Several times she came close enough to hear the fountain that she realized must occupy the center. Once she gave in to her uncertainty, allowing herself to again call his name, hoping that he might hear her from where she was sure he waited, already secure in the dark heart of the maze. There was no answer but the tantalizing murmur of the waters, which soon faded as, in her attempt to reach them, she instead moved farther away from their promise.

It was only by accident that she finally stumbled across the entrance to the heart of the maze and saw before her the sparkling cascade that shimmered in the moonlight, just as the fireworks had cast their glittering colors against the dark velvet of the sky. And standing beside the fountain, as if contemplating the water's unceasing return to its source, was the tall figure in the black domino.

She thought he was still unaware of her presence. Her slippers made no sound on the damp grass as she tiptoed until she was directly behind him. Smiling, she lifted her fingers to place them lightly on the broad shoulders, the only part of his body not hidden by the fall of the cloak. At her touch he turned, catching the slim fingers of her right hand in his and bringing them to his lips. She gasped when she realized that the unmasked stranger had carried her hand to a mouth that was as finely shaped as her husband's, but unlike his, its movement unhindered by damaged nerves and muscles. In her shock, she allowed the prolonged kiss that he was ardently pressing against the back of her hand.

"I don't believe we've been introduced, but I certainly have no objections to that impropriety," he said, smiling at her. "If you don't."

"How dare you?" she breathed, trying to pull her hand from his.

"But you, my dear, accosted me. It seems hardly fair that I should be accused—"

"I thought you were my husband," she explained breathlessly. "He said he'd be waiting at the fountain...." She paused, wondering suddenly if she had been mistaken about his intent. Perhaps he had meant her to follow him out of the maze and was now standing impatiently outside the green prison that held her.

"Your husband," the stranger in the black domino mockingly repeated her declaration, smiling in disbelieving amusement. "Pardon me, my dear, if I find that very difficult to believe. Not that I should like to doubt the word of so charming a…''

The brief pause was very telling of his opinion of her, but even if he had completed the thought, Maddy would have been unfamiliar with half of the choices London's lexicon offered for what he believed her to be.

''Even the most understanding husband seldom accompanies his *own* wife to Vauxhall, my dear. And if yours were waiting in the lovers' maze, he would be unusual indeed.''

''How dare you,'' she said again, still trying to secure the release of her hand.

''You said that before,'' the slightly accented voice of her husband chided from behind her, echoing the admonition he'd expressed on the night they'd met.

At the sound of the rich timbre and intriguing cadence that were uniquely his, her relief was so great that her knees lost their strength, trembling suddenly, and she even forgot to struggle with the stranger. But somehow, miraculously, her fingers were once more her own.

''There seems to have been some mistake, *monsieur*,'' Jean-Luc said reasonably. ''Please forgive my wife's inadvertent error. I had told her that I'd be waiting here, and seeing your costume, she rather naturally assumed—''

''Of course,'' the interloper agreed.

''I implore your forgiveness, *mademoiselle*,'' he said to Maddy, easily recognizing her husband's nationality, despite the few words he had heard.

''*Madame*,'' Jean-Luc corrected softly.

''Of course,'' the stranger said, the amused disbelief obvious. ''Forgive me, *madame*,'' he said derisively. They watched as he effected a low and sweeping bow and then disappeared through one of the entrances behind the fountain.

Maddy turned in relief to find her husband smiling at her.

''I thought you'd be waiting. And when I found him here…''

''Did you really believe that I'd leave you in the maze alone?''

''But—''

"I was behind you the entire time. I would *never* leave you alone here. Surely you must have known that. But you didn't seem to be frightened...."

"So you didn't answer when I called."

"Forgive me. I had thought that you were enjoying the challenge. And you did very well. Once you'd decided that the left turnings were the correct ones."

"But—" suddenly she laughed "—I never did. I had thought the right, and then, when that didn't work out, I simply wandered. You were giving me far too much credit. I remembered that the left is always the sinister. I'm afraid that I'm really not very good at mazes."

"However, we've still managed to reach the fountain," he reminded her quietly.

"But it must be well after midnight," she said, wondering if he intended what he'd suggested. Wondering if it would be the brief, insubstantial touch of his lips that she'd felt last night, or if it might be instead like the kiss at the inn. "Surely too late for a kiss."

"Perhaps, but some rules cry to be broken. And I have never had the respect for them you seem to possess. That should be obvious by our marriage."

"Which is against the rules?" she asked, smiling.

"All of them," he assured her.

"Then perhaps I'm not so fond of obedience to society's dictates as you believe me to be. After all, I did marry you."

"And I'm still attempting to discover why."

Her eyes dropped before his continuing questioning of her motives. She didn't know what she could do to convince him that she had married him because she wanted to. Apparently there would always be that doubt in his mind. She would always fight the belief that loyalty or fear of Harry had governed her consent, instead of her own desire.

She realized suddenly that, his steps hidden by the gurgle of the fountain behind her, he'd moved so that he now stood before her. He touched her chin, forcing her eyes up to meet his too-serious contemplation.

"Tell me," he urged. "What hold does Mannering have over you to force you into this marriage?"

"I've told you," she said. "I don't understand why you won't believe me. I married you because I wanted to. I told you. Because at the inn..."

She paused, realizing where her anger had led. *Because I thought you were the dark and beautiful lover I had always waited for.* She could never tell him that. He would think, as he had that night, that she was mocking what he now had become. Not knowing how to answer for emotions that she still didn't fully understand, she turned slightly, hiding her expression from his relentless pursuit of the truth.

She heard the deep breath he took before he spoke.

"Because at the inn?" he reiterated patiently, waiting for her explanation.

"You kissed me."

"And because I kissed you," he asked, remembering only the angry punishment he had thought he was inflicting. He was not aware that she was remembering something very different, something that had changed, that had grown out of his initial intent.

"I knew that I wanted you. And when Harry asked me to marry you, it seemed an answer to prayer."

He was very still, the murmur of the fountain the only sound in their isolation. He had ceased even to breathe as he examined her response.

She knew that without the addition of any of the other reasons she was afraid to give, without the recitation of the dream she had thought he matched as he stood outlined against the gleaming firelight, he would never believe her. The candles he had used that night to show her the scarring had pitilessly revealed that he was not the handsome lover she had imagined, but his kiss had made him something else, something far more real and tangible than those fantasies had been.

"'An answer to prayer,'" he repeated finally, sardonically, denying that her words could mean what he wanted them to.

She turned to face him, her fingers finding the ribbons that held in place the small, slanting mask that covered her eyes.

She fumbled a little to untie it and then finally succeeding, she lowered it, allowing the trailing ribbons to dangle in fingers that trembled.

"We could pretend that it's midnight," she whispered, inviting.

And despite whatever doubts he still held, his body responded to that soft invitation.

The dark mask lowered slowly. His lips touched beside hers and felt them part. But instead of answering that unconscious appeal, his mouth lifted to caress her eyes that closed under his gentleness. And then her temple. His lips' progress across her skin was feather light, like the velvet of flower petals. But she knew that the gliding softness was not what she wanted.

She lifted her hands to the back of his head to find the ribbon that secured the mask he wore, but his hard fingers caught hers and prevented that intent.

"Don't," he ordered softly, and then his mouth covered hers. The sure authority with which he had kissed her in the inn was overlain now by a tenderness that had been missing that night. Then he had begun in anger, but now there was nothing of that in the movement of his mouth. There was the heat of desire, the firmness of possession, but no anger. Whatever his command about the mask had intended, it was not a reprimand.

The ravishment of her senses went on a long time. At some point during that gentle assault, she had relaxed into his arms that held her with the same security she had treasured as they had watched the fireworks. He seemed to instinctively know how she wanted to be touched. And there was no awkwardness in his possession. Instead, he brought to their embrace an assurance that she found relaxing, so that she was allowed to concentrate only on the demands his tongue was making. She had known he was strong, but the demonstration of his hard body's power over her slender frame was the most comforting force she could remember in the turbulence of her troubled life. Never before had she enjoyed a man's embrace. Always before she had endured.

At last, his lips lifted from hers so that she could feel the coolness of the night air over the moisture they had left. Her mouth felt hot and swollen, like a bruise. And she wanted again the warm pressure he had just removed, but her mind was incapable of formulating any coherent expression of that thought. She lay in his arms and met the dark intensity of his eye. She thought that perhaps he must know something of what she was feeling.

Her fingers lifted, compelled by some emotion she didn't bother to identify, and touched the full underlip that had just deserted hers.

"Why don't you believe me?" she asked softly.

He held her questioning gaze a long time, but he didn't answer. Finally he shook his head, allowing his arms to release her.

She straightened, suddenly embarrassed by her too-willing surrender to his dark mastery.

"Would you join me for a midnight supper, my beautiful wife?" he suggested instead of replying to her soft question.

She hesitated, not because she didn't want to share with him the quiet privacy offered by the scattered booths that could be reserved for an intimate late supper, but because she wanted to resolve the doubts that remained between them. The firm line of his lips denied that she would have that opportunity, and finally she nodded, placing her fingers again on the wrist he formally presented.

He led her out of the maze, and by the time they had returned to the lighted environs of the gardens, he had again assumed the smiling ease of manner. And again she willingly allowed herself to relax into the cradle of his care. There would be time enough to assure him that she had not, as he apparently believed, been forced into this marriage. That instead she had grasped at Harry's offer as she had so often wished she had grasped at fate's overture in that small country inn so many months before.

Chapter Five

She had never before tasted champagne, and at her involuntary start of reaction to the tingling bubbles, she was aware of the slight, upward movement of her husband's lips. He had courteously refrained from teasing, refilling her glass without comment when she'd drained the sparkling wine too quickly. Much later, sheltered by the booth's dimness and replete with his carefully selected supper and far too much wine, she had practiced her French on him, while her fingers had unconsciously played with the lace of his cuff that fell over the bandage on the back on his hand.

He had smilingly corrected her slightly slurred pronunciation, knowing that it would be wise to begin the homeward journey before he would have to carry her through the park. He could imagine what the wagging tongues of London would make of that spectacle.

"And where did you learn to speak English?" she asked. She dipped one finger into her wine and daringly ran the moisture along her husband's bottom lip. Finally in the quiet privacy of the booth, he had removed the black mask.

His mouth lifted into the slanting smile, and he touched with his tongue the liquid her finger had left. She found herself suddenly unable to breathe at the sight of his tongue tracing her finger's path. He was aware of her eyes following the deliberately seductive movement.

"I would imagine the same way you learned French," he answered.

She laughed at the image dredged from her childhood. "I doubt it. I find it hard to imagine you with a governess."

"Then, no," he agreed, smiling. "Perhaps not in exactly the same way. But in my profession, an acquaintance with a variety of languages is necessary."

"But you have more than an 'acquaintance' with English."

"And you, my dear, ask far too many questions," he said, pouring the last of the champagne into her glass.

"Forbidden and mysterious," she suggested, smiling. The violet eyes challenged him over the rim of her wineglass.

"The champagne?" he asked blandly.

"The past," she said.

"And why not? The past is dead and better forgotten."

Suddenly it was there again, hauntingly reflected in the beautiful eyes. The expression that had bothered him before. The expression with which she had watched his hand caress the white fur of the kitten.

"Not forgotten," she denied, the ghosts all crowding into the pleasant spell he had woven.

"But I'm going to make you forget," he promised softly. At the surety in his whisper, she glanced up into his face, not even aware that, for the first time, she had failed to contrast the beauty of the unblemished profile to the other. "Eventually," he finished.

"Yes," she said. "That's exactly what I want you to do."

The casino was dark and silent when at last he brought her home, the aristocratic gamblers who had played tonight under the supervision of his able staff having long since returned to their own beds. During the coach ride, his wife's head had rested against his chest. He had smilingly helped her out of the carriage, aware, by the unsteady movements, which were such a contrast to her usual serene gracefulness, that she was rather charmingly inebriated.

The long stairs had proven the turning point. She had

laughingly attempted to negotiate them with his help and had found that they had an alarming tendency to swirl beneath her feet. More than once she had been forced to clutch her husband's sleeve until he had taken their progress into his own hands. Suddenly she was in his arms, being carried, without any apparent effort, up the flight.

She was vaguely aware of standing, swaying and holding to the tall post of the bed for support, as he threw back the counterpane and the linens. She remembered when he turned to her because of the sensation that moved through her stomach at what was in that dark face.

Tonight, she thought. Her fingers rose to release the rose domino. It fell to the floor, surrounding her like the circle of petals surrounds the heart of a flower. She stood there, the shimmering straightness of the ivory gown almost glowing in the soft light of the lamp. Her arms lifted to the buttons down the back, but her fingers were so unsteady that she knew she'd never be able to accomplish what she intended. Instead, she turned her back to the watching figure of her husband and waited.

Finally she felt his hands against her shoulders and then the brush of his lips over the nape of her neck. She shivered into his touch. At that involuntary movement, his mouth hesitated. And he began to divest her of the gown. It, too, eventually joined the rose circle on the carpet, and she turned to face him.

His features were almost hidden by the dimness and by the downturned position of his face.

"Jean-Luc," she whispered, and he lifted his head.

"I think…" she began, and found her mouth was dry with anticipation. She wished she hadn't drunk so much of the champagne. He, in contrast, had partaken of only a single glass. He had assured her, in smiling response to her question, that gamblers had a professional obligation to remain sober at all times.

The images of the gardens floated in and out of her head like dreams. The fireworks and the music. The maze and the booth. She remembered touching him, her fingers caressing his hands and the gleaming midnight of his hair that curled softly at the back of his head, so dark against the whiteness of his collar.

She raised her arms to clasp around his neck, and then he was again lifting her, carrying her, finally, to the high bed where she had slept alone. He placed her in the center and then stood up to remove his clothing.

Her eyes closed involuntarily, the long lashes drooping to fan against flushed cheeks. When she felt the weight of his body beside her, they lifted, the lavender gaze unfocused. His mouth trailed over the white shoulder, pushing the ribboned strap of her chemise out of the way. She murmured something, her breath moving with sweet warmth against his face. He raised his head in response to that whisper and saw that her lips were slightly parted, relaxed, and she was... unconscious.

The damaged mouth lifted in self-mockery as he contemplated the sleeping beauty of his wife. He wanted to release the coiled hair, to ease the delicate undergarment off her body, but he allowed himself none of those satisfactions.

Instead, he placed one soft kiss on the blue-veined temple. Her hand reached sleepily to touch his face and then fell, relaxed, back onto the counterpane. He finally pulled the coverlet over her shoulders, and as dawn was lighting the sky, he left her again to sleep alone.

Maddy slept through the morning and awoke in the afternoon with a pounding headache. Ling had brought a milky potion with her breakfast and insisted that she drink it first. By the time she had finished her meal, the headache had disappeared.

In the absence of her husband, who, Ling explained when she'd questioned, had been "called on business," the hours again stretched endlessly before her.

Later, Ling brought her dinner up from the casino's kitchens and laid it on a small table under the window. He seated her and waited on her during the meal. It had been too long since she'd had servants to feel really comfortable with his silent stance behind her chair, and she found herself nervously picking at the meal. The remembrance of Harry's demand and the implications of not yet having done as he'd asked disturbed her peace of mind, however, far more than the presence of Jean-Luc's unusual servant.

Finally she rose and waited by the window for him to clear the table.

"Does my husband take his meals up here?" she asked idly.

"Boss downstairs. Eat kitchen," Ling said, shaking his head. "You ask him, eat here."

Her smile in response to that suggestion was hidden by turning her head to again contemplate the street below.

"Something else, lady?" Ling asked from the doorway.

"Would you ask them to bring up some water, please, from the kitchens?"

"Water there," he said, indicating the pitcher he'd left on the table.

"Not for drinking. Hot water. For bathing," she explained, and saw him nod.

But there had obviously been a lack of communication. Ling's return trip included six huge buckets, carried up through his efforts and those of two of the kitchen boys who eyed her with open curiosity. Ling supervised the filling of the slipper-shaped copper tub that had been stored in one of the bedroom's long wall cupboards. When the task was finished, the boys sent back downstairs, Ling paused to test the water.

"I didn't mean..." Maddy had begun, but the steaming water looked too inviting. And they had accomplished the task with speed and apparently no great effort. "Thank you, Ling," she finished instead.

"Much washing. All time boss wash. All time clean linen. Now lady."

Maddy again controlled her amusement at the very accurate description of the effects Brummell's obsession with cleanliness had had on the ton. She had never before thought about the extra trouble those strictures, unknown a generation before, had meant for the servant class. The Beau's followers even sent their linens out to be dried in the sun on the neighboring village greens so as to emulate their god. She was sure her husband wasn't that foolish, but remembering the pleasantly clean smell of his body, she could well believe Ling's words. When the door had closed behind the servant, she glanced again to the small tub and pictured her husband's long form trying to fit into that confined space. He probably bathed standing up, with Ling nearby to pour water over his body when necessary for soaping or rinsing.

However, the tub certainly looked large enough to accommodate her. Although all she had intended to suggest by her request was enough hot water to ensure personal cleanliness, this was surely more inviting.

She was well used to dressing and undressing without the services of an abigail, so it was only a few minutes until she was stepping into the still-steaming water. The soap she'd found on the washstand was French and, she had thought, unscented, until she'd lathered it. The cleanly masculine, faint sandalwood aroma that she associated with her husband filled the room.

She allowed her head to rest against the back of the small tub and lifted her hands to her face, still holding the bar, savoring the pleasantness of the fragrance. And, of course, thinking of him. Her eyes closed, she was remembering last night, wondering if he'd come now.

"I hope I'm not intruding," Jean-Luc said softly.

She jumped, the soap falling with a slight plop into the water. She swallowed convulsively, watching the careful control exerted over that corner of his lips that had a tendency to lift in mockery—whether at himself or at others.

"But I've always found it helpful to have someone to wash my back. It's so awkward otherwise," he continued.

She couldn't imagine him in any awkward situation. He always moved with an innate grace that seemed to have nothing to do with his obvious strength and masculinity. Again the image of that tall body standing naked, streaming with the gleam of water that highlighted the sleek curve of muscle and the tightness of tendon and bone flashed into her head. She lowered her eyes and took a deep breath.

He watched her breasts lift with that inhalation, the rose areola surrounding her darker nipples briefly visible beneath the water's lap. Tendrils of gilt hair clung damply to her neck. He couldn't tell whether the soft color under the translucent pearl of her skin was caused by his presence or was simply the result of the temperature of the bath.

"Unless you'd rather I go?" he asked, and waited.

"No," she said softly, and again he watched the lift of her breasts against the water's edge. "And I haven't washed my back."

This time the control was relaxed and the crooked half smile touched upward. She felt the slight ease in a tension she had not even been aware of. Too concerned with her own shyness, she hadn't realized that he had really been waiting, unsure of her answer.

"Then," he began and paused. "I think you'd better find the soap. Unless, of course…"

Her own lips lifted, but she shook her head slightly at that suggestion and, after a few abortive efforts, she located the small bar and held it out to him. She didn't notice that the water streaming down her uplifted arm was reentering the bath by coursing over the rounded globe of her left breast, now almost completely above the level of the water.

He moved finally, just as she thought he must not have intended his offer to be taken seriously. He stripped off his coat and threw it on the bed. His lace cuffs followed, and then he was turning back the sleeves of the lawn shirt. His gaze had never left her face. He walked to the tub and took the soap from her outstretched fingers, but he didn't move to complete his suggestion.

Conscious suddenly of her nudity, she pulled her arm back into the water and allowed her body to slide an inch or two deeper into the tub. She glanced up to find his gaze resting on the gentle lap that hovered now on the beginning swell of her breasts.

The white strip of Ling's bandage was a contrast to the

darkness of his hand and exposed forearm, so that she suddenly remembered the injuries.

"Your hand," she reminded him.

Whatever expression had been in his face cleared, and he glanced down at the bandage as if he'd never seen it before. He unconsciously flexed his fingers, watching the slow movement.

"You probably don't want to get that wet," she suggested.

"Ling says soaking is good for the swelling," he said, slowly flexing it again. "It's still swollen. And a dealer with a stiff hand…" He didn't complete the thought.

"Is that why you came up tonight? Because your hand was too painful to deal the cards?"

"I thought we had an appointment," he answered softly.

"After last night… I thought you must have decided not to keep it. I'd never had champagne before. I didn't realize…"

He studied her face a moment, and then shook his head. "Whatever happened last night was my fault. I should have realized that you would be unaccustomed to champagne. But when Ling began bringing up your bathwater, I thought you might be sufficiently recovered.…" He paused, allowing the suggestion to lie between them.

She dropped her eyes, but he could see the slight smile.

"You didn't have to leave," she said softly. "Last night. I didn't mean to drive you away. I'm your wife. And we agreed—"

"When you truly *become* my wife," he said, interrupting her hesitant invitation, "I intend that you're fully aware of what's happening between us."

At the quiet intensity of his tone, she felt a fluttering anxiety somewhere deep inside because she knew exactly what the word *wife* implied. She had wanted the romance of his interest, but when she remembered, when she finally allowed herself to picture the infrequent joinings of her first marriage, there was also an unexpected frisson of fear and revulsion. Nothing she'd read or heard had prepared her for the events of her marriage bed. Even Harry had called her marriage a perversion, considering the vast difference in age between her husband and herself.

She was pulled back from those memories with the touch of Jean-Luc's lips against her shoulder. She realized he was kneeling behind her. His lips were so soft that she held her breath, wondering at their tenderness. Until he had married her, she had never been touched with sexual gentleness, and she was finding its deliberate use to arouse very disconcerting.

Jean-Luc's tongue flicked upward to catch a drop that was slipping down the slim column of her neck into the hollow of her collarbone. He pushed a small kiss into that pulsing softness and felt the faint vibration of reaction in her shoulder. With his teeth he caught a strand of the damp hair that touched her neck and pulled. Her head followed that slight tug, so that she found her face leaning against his hair. Its midnight softness felt like silk against her overheated cheek, and she breathed in again the scent of sandalwood that surrounded them.

His right hand cupped her shoulder, the strip of bandage over his palm roughly caressing down the slope of her upper arm and then back up. His mouth was tasting the left side of her throat, nuzzling the slightly soap-slick texture of her skin. She lifted her left arm and touched the back of his head. The water streaming from her elbow followed the line of her arm and ran under his face as it rested against her shoulder. She felt his smile against her neck.

"Are you by any chance trying to drown me?" he asked.

Her fingers threaded into the silken darkness of his hair that curled over her hand as if alive, and she shook her head, unable to find words to answer him.

She felt him shift position behind her and then his lips were caressing lower, and she lifted her chin to allow him fuller access to her body. His left hand slipped into the water, under her raised arm. She felt the fingers glide against the underside of her breast, raising it slightly so that the nipple rode above the line of clouded water. His thumb caressed downward, pushing the peak below the warm liquid and then upward into the cooling air. Again and again, until the gentle demand caused a taut swelling of the small bud to grow under that relentless stroke.

"Look," he commanded softly, and she obeyed. Her eyes dropped to find the darkness of his hand against the blue-veined whiteness of her breast. They both were aware of her breathing, its shuddering intensity stirring the waters. In response to that emotion, he dropped a kiss on the fragile bones of her shoulder. She realized that his right hand had left her upper arm and was moving under the water, slowly tracing down the small ridges of ribs and then caressing across the slight rise of her belly. She thought that she should move, should protest, but the mesmerizing quality of his stroking thumb against her nipple held her motionless. And then his fingers touched beneath the water the most secluded area of her womanhood. She moved then, her body responding to that invasion with an inward curl, automatically protecting, and away from his hands.

She sat trembling in the cooling water, her head lowered and her arms crossed over her breasts, hands locked on her upper arms, aware, again, of her nudity.

She felt his hands cover hers as they gripped the opposing shoulders.

"What's wrong?" he asked softly.

She couldn't think of a reasonable answer. He was her husband, and she had no right to refuse him anything. He could do with her as he pleased. And because she certainly had cause to know what that might entail, she was, for the first time, afraid.

She shivered suddenly, the movement coursing through her slenderness.

"I thought you wanted me here," he whispered. His lips found the nape of her neck.

"You haven't washed my back," she answered, irrelevantly.

"To hell with your back."

"You said—"

"I lied. Tell me what's wrong. Don't you like me to touch you? You seemed to. Before."

There was something very relaxing about the movement of his lips, about the softly accented words. He didn't appear to be angry. But rather, as if he really wanted to know. And so she told him, whispering.

"Not there."

She felt the hesitation of his fingers that had been massaging the tension out of her upper arms.

"But the other?" he asked, running his thumb along the top of her shoulder and up the side of her throat. "You liked the other," he said, and it wasn't a question.

"Yes," she whispered, unconsciously turning her head to allow his caress to trace along the softness under her jawline.

He hesitated, and she wondered what he was thinking. He was so still, and yet there had been no anger in his tone at her denial.

"Then I won't touch you there. Until you ask me. Until you want me to."

"And you think I will?" she asked, realizing what he'd just implied.

"Yes," he answered softly, a promise. "Eventually."

He stood suddenly and, reaching down into the water, lifted her. She had been unprepared, but her arms were around his neck, holding as he took her toward the bed. Their position around his shoulders at least allowed her some coverage, some protection for her nakedness against his hard chest. He didn't seem conscious of that, however, as he carried her.

"You're ruining your shirt," she said softly, the damp material rubbing erotically against her breasts.

"To hell with my shirt," he answered in exactly the tone he had used before.

He laid her on the bed, the moisture from her body instantly marking the counterpane.

"And to hell with the bed," he said softly, before she could protest.

"But Ling will think…" she began and realized how stupid that was.

He laughed suddenly.

"I imagine he will," he said softly. "And I imagine he'll be right."

His hand reached for the lamp on the small table and then the room was in darkness.

He was still sleeping when Maddy woke. They hadn't pulled the draperies across the window above the small table where she'd eaten her lonely supper last night. The morning sun had finally moved into that rectangle, dimly lighting the dark chamber.

The old man had never stayed with her, not even after his occasional successes. But Jean-Luc had held her last night, held her after his long, shuddering release. And she thought that, beyond the pleasant strength of his arms around her, that might be important.

His face was turned toward her now in the growing light, its spare planes relaxed and almost vulnerable with sleep. The shadow of his beard darkened the beautiful undamaged side, and the long lashes rested against the faint lines under his eye. The low light softened somewhat the scarred landscape of the other profile, the dark patch slightly twisted against his cheek. She resisted the impulse to straighten the cloth, remembering his long fingers habitually lifting to assure that it covered whatever it was intended to hide. The ribbon that held the velvet in place disappeared into the darkness of the fall of hair that brushed over his high forehead.

The white collar of the lawn shirt touched against the dark growth of beard. He had never removed his shirt. She had waited in the darkness after he had turned down the lamp, listening to him undress, waiting for him to join her in the bed they still shared. She hadn't realized at first that he wasn't completely undressed because he had spent a long time simply caressing her with those dark, skillful gambler's hands before he had lain down beside her, allowing her to feel the stiffness of the starched cloth against her breasts. By then, she had been unable and, of course, unwilling to interrupt what had been happening between them to ask. She had wanted the texture of his skin against her softness, its warmth and smoothness, rather than the abrasive quality of the lawn. But he had made even the roughness of the shirt sensual, so that she had eventually forgotten that she'd anticipated the hard muscles of his chest moving over her body. Somehow, in the dark hours of the night they had shared, she had forgotten almost everything. Except his hands. And his lips. And finally…

After he had made love to her, his arms had enclosed her body a long time, his fingers soothing against her shivering skin. But sometime in the night, she had moved out of the circling heat of his arms. Moved to the cool spread of the empty half of the bed. Her half, she thought in wonder. Her bed, too, now.

He stirred slightly, still asleep, turning to find a more comfortable position against the curve of her hip and thigh. His hand moved to lie loosely curled over her stomach, its darkness highlighted by the gathering light against the alabaster skin of her body. She had not known strength could be so delicate, hardness so sweet. Not until he had shown her.

He had begun with her breasts because, perhaps, she had told him she enjoyed his touch there. He had been endlessly patient. As if he had all the time in the world. It had felt as if he did. Relaxed and unhurried, the touch of his hands and his mouth. And then the gentleness had grown into something that hadn't been relaxing. Something that had caused her to catch her breath, unable to identify the sensations that were twisting through her body. Sensations that made her want to move, to touch him in return, so that she was forced to hold her body rigidly still against that need, a need she didn't understand.

She hadn't protested when he'd placed one of the pillows beneath her hips. She had been beyond questioning. Biting her lips to control the shivering urge to move. But she had whimpered when he'd entered her. Despite the painstaking care. Despite her own growing hunger that she didn't know he could relieve. Despite his experience, it had been too long since anyone had touched her. And somehow, underlying her desire for his touch, had been the old fears. There had been nothing in his lovemaking to remind her of the old man's rutting and, too often, futile attempts. But her muscles and bones had remembered what her mind had buried, so her body itself had betrayed her, had fought him, unconsciously condemning her to the discomfort.

She had felt that unpleasant soreness each time she'd moved during the night. She shifted her long legs experimentally, feeling again the ache between them. Her toes brushed the hair-roughened length of his calf, and then she turned into the warmth of his body, comforted again by his presence. Reassured that he was still here. He must not have disliked her body, despite its shivering need to move under him that she'd successfully conquered only with such determined effort. She hadn't interfered with his fulfillment. And so she thought he would probably return to touch her again. She'd enjoyed that. Almost too much, she thought smiling. She closed her eyes against the invading light of dawn and drifted back into sleep.

Jean-Luc woke much later, used to sleeping through the early light of morning, unbothered by the sun's touch on the bed. Sometime in the midst of what they had shared, the heavy silver-gold of her hair had loosened from the careful chignon, and its spread across the pillow caught the light that drifted across the room from the unshaded window.

He touched a strand of it, which lay curled over the small, perfect curve of her breast. He remembered how the rose nipples had lifted to meet his lips in the darkness. Hard and responsive to the flick of his tongue. So damned responsive.

And that was what he didn't understand. He had held her, patiently waiting, a long time after the soft outcry that had marked his entry. Allowing her to become accustomed to the fullness of his possession. He'd held her, whispering softly against the sweat-dampened rigidity of her throat. Whispering finally in English when he'd remembered. He'd felt her relax gradually, the pain behind them, and he'd tried with all the considerable skill he possessed to make her forget that pain. He didn't know the memories that fought against his success.

Eventually he had been forced to admit that he'd failed. If only she'd let him touch her. Prepare her. But he'd promised, so sure, so arrogantly certain that he could arouse her enough without that. She told him she'd been married for five years, but the inflexible denial of her body told him things about those years that she hadn't admitted, hadn't shared.

Finally he'd reluctantly allowed his own release, fearing that he would only defeat his purpose by prolonging his attempt to help her to join him. His arms had encircled her, the bitterness of his failure gnawing his soul. She'd never moved beneath him, never lifted her body in that automatic response to passion that would bring them both to fulfillment. He had wondered briefly if she were one of those women who couldn't enjoy the pleasures of the body. But the memory of her responses in the bath negated that thought. And those later, under his fingers and his lips. So he had held her and wondered, until she had slipped into sleep, relaxed finally, her breath flowing with a gentle rhythm across his cheek.

She wasn't afraid of him. He had known that from that peaceful rise and fall of her breasts against the fabric of his shirt. He had wanted their softness against his skin, but he closed his mind to that impossibility. He wondered suddenly if that could be the answer. Despite what she had told him. Despite any seeming lack of revulsion when he'd touched her. Perhaps in spite of the shirt he'd never removed, while he had made love to her, she'd been imagining what his body looked like. And he knew that whatever she'd imagined, no matter how repulsive, it couldn't match the reality.

She awoke again when the porcelain cup Ling held touched against the glass of the bedside lamp. Her panicked response to the servant's presence was to grasp for the covers that had been thrown to the foot of the bed sometime during the dark hours her husband had spent with her. She was relieved to find the sheet and even the counterpane carefully tucked around her shoulders. Ling had already glided silently out the door by the time she'd made that discovery. She sat up carefully, clutching the sheet against her bare breasts. The chocolate was fragrantly steaming, its aroma enticing, the steam reminding her suddenly of last night's bath. The copper tub was still standing in front of the fireplace, the water cold and gray in the morning light.

She pushed the pillows into a more comfortable arrangement behind her shoulders and sipped the chocolate and remembered. Her husband would have been unaccountably comforted had he seen the small smile that played over her lips. But he was already downstairs, seeing to the business that he had so willingly deserted last night. And in the course of the day that wouldn't end until several hours after midnight, his thoughts strayed too often to the dark bedroom where he'd made love to his wife. She couldn't know how many times he, too, thought about last night and wondered what she was feeling today.

Chapter Six

The altercation had begun innocently enough. The patrons of these exclusive rooms were always as carefully screened as Jean-Luc's instincts and experience could guarantee. But occasionally a valued customer brought a less-desirable companion, and then, of course, the decision had to be made whether to accept the friend or to alienate a profitable client.

But he had not even been aware of the group of elegant young bucks. There had been no sixth sense of danger. On later reflection, he admitted that his mind had been on something other than his clientele, and he knew well enough what that distraction was.

Throughout the evening he had also been forced to ignore several discreetly speculative glances. He realized that the ton was now aware of his marriage to a woman of their own class. More than one pair of noble eyes considered the marks on his cheek and traced their disappearance into the high collar of his evening shirt. He had schooled his face to calmness and had fought to control his anger as he identified the thoughts forming behind those veiled glances.

He hadn't heard the beginnings of the man's muttering discontent. Whatever he had said had been quickly covered by the group of young bloods who were sharing his table. Jean-Luc had been standing in the doorway of the room, wondering if it might be safe to leave the supervision of the few remaining die-hard players to his capable staff. And he had been remembering, as he had all evening, the slim, beautiful body of the woman that he had left sleeping this afternoon, when he finally became aware of the tension.

"I don't care if the bastard does hear me...."

He deliberately turned his head from the quickly suppressed voice, allowing his gaze to focus on another table. He watched the play there for a moment until the same voice rose again out of the subdued noises of the almost empty salon.

"Harry deserves to be drawn and quartered. Selling his sister like..." The rest of that sentence was also quickly shushed into silence by the efforts of the handsome Corinthian seated beside the speaker. One of the gentlemen, wiser than the rest, began the eventually successful operation of getting the drunk to his feet, and the procession started toward the front door.

Jean-Luc's fury was enough to cause him to react in a way foreign to his usual cool avoidance of trouble. He remained obstinately in the doorway leading to the foyer as the speaker and his escorts approached, all the unspoken insults of the evening crystallized now on this drunken aristocrat. He allowed the disdain of that single glittering eye to meet and hold the gaze of the man who had spoken.

"You bastard."

The drunk's words accompanied the unexpected lunge which carried him away from the reaching hands of his friends and into an unintimidated confrontation with the gambler.

"Maddy Carlton has more courage than her brother. A thoroughbred, as much as her horses. But they sold her. First to the old man. And then to you. She was too good for Fairchild, and she's certainly too good for the likes of you."

The name had taken him unaware. It was so unfamiliar that he didn't connect it to his wife for the few vital seconds that might have made a difference. His surprised silence was, perhaps, the catalyst for the ridiculous attack that followed. They all watched in stunned horror as the nobleman snatched a bottle from the sideboard. Left-handed, he smashed it viciously against the frame of the door. He swung the broken half like an avenger's sword. Jean-Luc had already begun the twisting evasion when the jagged edge sliced into his right side.

He felt the glancing blow, but there was no pain. Not yet. The pain would come later. And even as he was thinking that, his left fist connected with the exposed chin of the drunk who fell as if he'd been poleaxed. When it was over, Jean-Luc wasn't even breathing hard. But he kept his elbow pressed tightly against the gash that had been opened in his side.

"God's teeth, Ned," one of the elegant gentlemen said in disgust. "You bloody idiot."

Several of them stooped over the still body, but the Marquis of Ainsley, the man who had spoken, whose guest was now stretched like a side of beef at his feet, remained standing.

"My apologies," he said quietly to his host. "Stapleton's attack was unforgivable. But we all knew Maddy. She…"

The aristocratic voice was suddenly cut off at whatever was in the hazel gaze that had lifted—at the unthinking use of Madelyn's childhood name—to meet his. But finally, being an extremely courageous young man, he continued.

"If you want satisfaction, I assure you Stapleton will meet you."

"A meeting which would restore the damage this melodrama has done to my wife's reputation, I suppose," Jean-Luc asked sarcastically.

"No," Ainsley agreed, thinking of the gossip a duel would arouse. "I simply thought—"

"Get him out of here," the gambler ordered quietly. He pressed his arm more tightly against the pain that was beginning to burn in his side, an involuntary grimace tightening his lips.

"Are you all right?" the marquis asked, noticing the sudden pallor in that dark complexion. "Ned didn't manage to…"

At the challenging amusement in the gambler's steady gaze, the English nobleman realized that Stapleton's wild lunge had had some success.

"Nor would that particular piece of information staunch the

gossips. The less said, the better," Jean-Luc suggested quietly. "If you are Maddy's friend."

"Of course," said Ainsley quietly. "Is there anything that I—"

"Get out. All of you. Just get out."

Surprisingly, the marquis obeyed, efficiently taking charge of the group's exit.

The shocked silence of the patrons who remained after their departure reminded Jean-Luc that his wife's good name, whatever shreds were left of her reputation after her marriage to him, was at stake here. He signaled the hovering servants to refill the glasses, and eventually the soft flow of cultured masculine voices replaced the quietness that the sudden and unexpected violence had produced. The shattered glass and the spilled liquor were swiftly and unobtrusively cleaned up. It was not until the salon had returned to some semblance of normality, that Jean-Luc allowed himself to move out of the doorway against which he had been leaning since the attack.

He had felt for several minutes the warm blood trickling down his side, and at the first step, its quick, hot gush down his thigh. He pressed his elbow more tightly against the gash, thankful again for the concealing blackness of evening dress. The stairs seemed endless, the pain growing more demanding at every step, but at least the upper story was away from the eyes of the men who drank his wine and smoked his cigars. He hoped someone on his staff would have sense enough to send for Ling. He climbed slowly into the dark at the top of the stairs. Finally, reaching that sanctuary, he leaned, exhausted, against the wall.

"Jean-Luc?"

He closed his eye in response to the whispered question that floated at him from out of the doorway of his bedroom. And then he forced himself to open it again. The soft light of the lamp behind her outlined her slender shape, silhouetted through the thin cotton of her nightgown.

So damn beautiful, he thought. The light shimmered around her figure, dancing suddenly with spots that hurt his head. He only wanted to lie down. But if he went into the bedroom, then he'd be forced to reveal what had happened below. She'd contrast that sordidness, the violence which was a rare but ever-present danger in his profession, to the life she'd left behind. And again she'd have cause to regret the decision she'd made. Been forced to make, he amended mentally, remembering Stapleton's words, a reinforcement of all he'd believed from the first about her reasons for agreeing to this marriage.

"Go back to bed," he said, and even to his own ears his voice sounded too harsh, demanding.

"Last night…" she began, and her voice quivered a little on the words. The pause lengthened, and then she began again. "I hope that…"

He straightened from his position against the wall, unable to listen now to whatever reproaches she wanted to make about last night. He knew he'd hurt her. But that had never been his intent. He had intended something far different. And he had failed. But there was nothing he could do now to erase that failure. No words he could formulate to convince her that it wouldn't always be like that between them. That promise was something else he'd made in the clear light of morning as he'd watched her sleep.

"Go back to bed," he ordered again, instead of trying to explain anything. Nothing of his intentions. Nothing of what had happened tonight. Certainly nothing of the blood that continued to flow unpleasantly from the burning wound in his side. He gathered his remaining reserves of strength and took a staggering step across the top of the stairs and was forced to lean against the banister on the other side.

"You're foxed," she said, and he heard the shocked accusation in the quiet whisper.

A spurt of ironic laughter escaped him, as much occasioned by her use of the cant phrase as by her conclusion. It was as good an explanation as any, he supposed. One more mark against whatever he had hoped for in this marriage. God, what a fool he'd been.

"Drunk as a lord," he agreed mockingly, and using the banister rail as support, he began the seemingly endless journey to the sanctuary of his office. There, at least, he could sit down, away from the violet eyes of the woman who was watching in condemnation as he proved himself guilty of all of the vices she had probably already attributed to him.

Suddenly she was beside him, slipping her body beneath the left arm he had been using to prop himself against the railing.

"You're going the wrong way," she said, smiling at the surprise on his ashen face. "The bedroom's on the other side of the hall."

She tried to turn him, but unbelievably, he staggered again, and then his arm was pulled to drape over the support of her shoulders. Unable to find the strength to resist, he let himself be guided into the bedroom where the welcoming lamp burned, and he tried not to imagine what she would think when she saw the blood.

"Maddy," he whispered, unconsciously repeating what the young aristocrats had called her, an effort now even to form any words. "I need Ling. Go down the back stairs, the kitchen stairs."

"I can help you undress. It's all right," she said softly, smiling. "I thought gamblers never drank. I thought you needed to be sober and clearheaded. I thought that's why Harry lost so often."

"Harry loses," he said, as he felt her beginning to ease the coat off his shoulders, "because he is very arrogant and therefore very reckless. He doesn't believe anyone would have gall enough to beat him."

She moved the elbow he had been pressing hard into his side instinctively maintaining pressure over the wound. He heard her soft laugh at his accurate portrayal of her half brother, and then her fingers were suddenly still, the coat allowed to fall unheeded to the floor.

He heard the small shocked intake of breath, and he looked down to find her hand held out into the lamplight before their bodies and covered in his blood. He watched the sudden tremor of those fingers, and then she began to guide him again to the bed. She helped him ease down on the high mattress, and he almost fell into the comforting softness.

He became aware finally that he was alone. He supposed she'd left him, too disgusted by the vulgarity of the life she was now expected to lead. He wanted to tell her that this was almost as unusual to his existence as to hers. He wondered if he'd ever have the opportunity to tell her anything at all. He closed his eye in regret because he suddenly remembered that there had been so many things he had wanted to say to her. And now it was too late.

He was jerked back into consciousness with the sting of Ling's needle. He flinched against that new pain, unconsciously contrasting it to that of the gash itself.

"Be still," she advised softly. "Ling says you only need a few stitches to close the cut. It really isn't very deep."

He relaxed slightly in response to the calmness of her voice. She sounded as if she watched her husband being sewn up every night. She was holding his hand, and she squeezed it gently in response to the shuddering breath he took when Ling set the next stitch.

He struggled for control and was relieved when he allowed no outward reaction to the next invasion of the needle. He found himself focused instead on the perfection of his wife's features. Her eyes were too wide and her paleness the result, he supposed, of shock. Her hair was braided into a single long plait that lay over her left breast. He thought, again, that he had never seen anything more beautiful. She was watching Ling's careful movements, unaware of that single hazel eye whose gaze clung to her face.

Suddenly, as if she felt its intensity, her eyes met his. She smiled at him, and his hand, in involuntary response, tightened over her cold fingers.

"It's almost over," she whispered. "Only a few more."

He nodded, allowing his eye to close. He used a technique he had learned in dealing with the endless agony of the burns. He returned to last night, to the memory of the scented steam of the bath and to how her body had felt in his arms as he'd carried her to this bed. He forced himself to feel again her arms around his neck, trusting herself to his strength. The pain of what Ling was doing began to fade, to drift away in the remembrance of that body, much later, beneath the caress of his lips. And then under the driving force...

"What happened?" she asked softly, seeing the relaxation in those rigidly controlled muscles around his mouth. She thought he was slipping once more into unconsciousness, and she was unaccountably afraid that if he did, he might not, this time, wake up. There had been so much blood. She glanced down at the stains that marred the maidenly whiteness of her cotton rail. So much blood.

"A drunk," he whispered. And no other details.

"Fight about woman," Ling said, setting another stitch.

"No," Jean-Luc denied, but the hazel eye opened in time to witness the shocked response in his wife's face.

"Woman named Carlton," Ling added softly.

It seemed there was nothing that was not going to be revealed to her about the events of the night. He had hoped to protect her from the knowledge that she had now become a topic for discussion in the hells the ton frequented. He had failed her there, too. He had allowed himself to accept what she had offered because he had wanted her. God alone knew how much. He'd never thought beyond his possession of her. And now she was his, and he'd made her name and her reputation the grist for the gossip mills of that society in which she'd grown up, whose ranks were now, because of her marriage to him, forever closed to her.

Nothing else was said as Ling completed the unpleasant business of sewing up the slash—a slash made by a broken bottle in the hands of a drunk who had shouted his wife's name in a place in which a good woman should never be mentioned. And Jean-Luc knew it was all his fault.

She was too good for Fairchild, and she's certainly too good for the likes of you. He had always known that was true, but until tonight he had not fully recognized the implications of what he had done to her.

* * *

"Sit up," Maddy said softly, slipping her arm under his shoulders.

He struggled to obey, feeling the tightness of the bandage Ling had wrapped around his stomach and the pull against the stitches. So many damned stitches. He knew he had drifted out again some time after Ling's revelation. He vaguely remembered them undressing him, cutting away the blood-soaked shirt despite his angry and futile protests. And then the bandaging, but not much else. The room was empty now, the servant gone and the lamp trimmed lower than before.

She slipped behind him, between his upper body and the head of the bed. Her hands guided his shoulders to lean back against the softness of her breasts, and she held him a moment, her arms encircling his chest from behind.

She reached finally to the cup waiting on the table by the bed and placed its rim against his lips. He could feel her cheek against his as she leaned forward to carefully position the lip against his mouth.

"Drink it," she whispered. "Ling says its good for the fever. And the pain."

Incapable of the energy it would take to deny the command, he drank, feeling the warmth of the bitter tea against his tongue. She coaxed him until the cup was empty, and he heard her replace it on the table.

She leaned her head against his, her hands caressing the marred skin above the bandage she'd help Ling affix.

"My mother used to hold me like this when I was sick," she said softly, her breath stirring the softness of his hair. "I always thought—" Her voice stopped, but her lips nuzzled soothingly over his temple.

"What?" he managed, feeling whatever Ling had added to the tea begin to sap the little self-control he had left.

"That it was the safest place in the world," she whispered, smiling.

He could feel the movement of her lips now against the scarring on his cheek. He nodded, but the effort it required was massive, and his eye drifted closed even on the thought of his unfamiliarity with that kind of childhood.

"Who was he?" she asked after a long time, and he couldn't think what she meant until she explained. "The man who stabbed you?"

"Stapleton," he whispered, the last coherent thought he would have that night in the forced cocoon of Ling's drugs.

It was only what she'd expected. A flashing memory of a laughing boy and a race. She'd beaten him on Heart's Fire. Beaten the best his father's vast stables had had to offer. One of Harry's friends. Somehow she had known, but she'd hoped that she was wrong. It had started all over. She tightened her arms protectively around the strong body that she held. Her husband was, of course, unaware of the deep breath that she took as she tried to think what she could do to change the outcome.

Because she knew that this time she couldn't afford to let the Mannerings win.

With the drug, Jean-Luc slept through the morning and well into the afternoon. She had sat beside the bed watching him sleep and thinking about what her brother had asked her to do. Last night had certainly been a warning. Harry didn't like to be denied, but she wondered how he had managed to convince Ned Stapleton to be a party to that attack. It would have been arranged to appear as if it had nothing to do with the diamonds, but she knew too well how Harry's mind worked to doubt that this had been his reminder to her that she hadn't done what he'd wanted.

She became aware that her husband was awake and watching her, his head turned slightly on the pillow.

"How do you feel?" she asked, smiling at him. She touched his forehead lightly with the back of her hand, testing for the fever she had feared might develop, despite Ling's warranty of his medications.

"Like I've been asleep for days," he said, turning his head away so that her fingers no longer made contact with the reassuringly moist warmth of his skin.

"Only hours," she answered, the smile forced now in reaction to his rejection.

"Have you slept?" he asked.

"A little."

"In that chair?"

"It doesn't matter. I can sleep later. I wanted to be sure that you were all right."

The silence stretched a moment, and then he closed his eye. Despite his reassurance and the lack of fever, the gray tinge that underlay his complexion reminded her of the bloody clothing she'd had Ling carry downstairs to burn. So much blood, she thought again.

"I thought you had a fitting with Genevieve this afternoon," he said.

"A fitting?" she repeated, momentarily at a loss. That was so removed from the direction her own thoughts had taken since she had found him on the stairs last night.

"For the new dresses."

"I'd forgotten. I'm sure she can rearrange it. It really doesn't matter if—"

"I'll send someone with you. You'll be late, but you should still have time."

"If you think that I'm going to go to the dressmaker's while you're—"

"I don't need a mother. I didn't marry you for *that,* either," he said. "Go get the damn dresses fitted. I'm tired of you looking like someone's poor relation. Tell her I said to finish something today. I don't really care which one."

"I'm not trying to be your mother," she said angrily. "You don't need a wife. You don't want a mother. I'm not to mend your clothes or worry about you when you're hurt. I'm beginning to wonder why you bothered to marry me at all."

The pause was only a heartbeat.

"So am I," he whispered, again turning his head away.

She couldn't believe how badly those few words had hurt. What had happened to the smiling cavalier who had escorted her to Vauxhall? To the tender lover who had carried her from the bath and had...

Suddenly she realized that must be the answer. In spite of the fact that he'd not left her that night, he had been disappointed. He had married her only because he'd desired her body. Even Harry had said that and, apparently, now...

"I'm sorry," she said bitterly, fighting the effects of the loss of the dream that had sustained her so long, but something of her anguish must have been revealed in the low whisper.

"Go try on the dresses, Maddy," he said, hearing the pain in her strained voice and hating what he was doing to her. He could think of no other way to get her out of this room, away from the casino, so he could accomplish what he knew he had to do. "Wear something pretty for me tonight," he added, unable to prevent the concern he, at least, could hear clearly in his own voice.

"I don't understand you," she whispered, wondering what that meant. He'd called her Maddy last night. In exactly that same caressing tone.

"Go on," he ordered softly. She raised her eyes and found that he was watching her again. But before she could identify whatever was in that look, he had allowed the dark lashes to fall, hiding his feelings as effectively as he had hidden them from the beginning.

She didn't even bother to change her dress before she obeyed. She found Ling in the kitchens and asked him to make the arrangements, expecting he would be the one sent to accompany her. But her tall, silent escort was no one she'd ever seen before. One of her husband's dealers Ling explained.

She was vaguely surprised when her escort handed Madame Darnet a note, and she was aware of the modiste's quick glance at her set features after she'd read whatever instructions her husband had sent. After all, it didn't really matter what the note contained. She had certainly been given her own mandate before she'd left. *Wear something pretty for me tonight.* As if she were on display. As if she were not his wife, but rather his whore.

And why not? she acknowledged, mocking herself. That, of course, *was* the reason he had married her.

She took a deep breath, fighting the bitterness. He wasn't

responsible for her foolish hopes. Why should she be angry if he didn't conform to the fantasy she'd been creating about him since the night they had met?

Dear Lord, she thought, I've been such an idiot, a romantic child. But it had seemed… She shook her head, blocking those images. Today had been the reality, not whatever she had been imagining before.

The dressmaker was as kind as she had been on the first visit, and although the fittings seemed more interminable than any she'd endured in the past, she had to admit that nothing she'd ever worn had been as becoming as the sea green walking dress in which she left the shop.

When she stepped out into the street, she was surprised to find that it was well after dark. She wondered if Jean-Luc would be worried about her, and then smiled at what she now knew was wishful thinking, remembering his response to her bitter speculation. She should have known better. All her fantasies of the dark and tender lover were only that. She was a grown woman. Too old to indulge in the futility of dreams, she thought, ridiculing herself.

She slowly climbed the narrow stairs to the bedroom, dreading the meeting with Jean-Luc. She had done what he'd asked, but there was no pleasure in the new gown. There was no pleasure in any of it anymore. Such a child, she thought again.

The high bed was empty. As was his office across the hall. Her panic grew as she'd hurried down the back stairs that led to the kitchens. Perhaps he had come down to eat supper, but surely Ling wouldn't have allowed that dangerous attempt.

Ling was serving her escort his delayed meal. Their eyes lifted at her entry, but there was no surprise in either pair.

"Where is he?" she asked. Their glances met briefly in some masculine conspiracy, but Ling shrugged his shoulders, feigning ignorance.

She turned to the dealer her husband had sent with her today and repeated her question. His hesitation was so prolonged she thought, that like Ling, he intended to deny knowledge of his employer's whereabouts.

"Jean-Luc's in the salon," he said finally.

"But... You know he's in no condition to be out of bed," she said, turning angrily to Ling. "Why would you let him come downstairs? What if the bleeding starts again?"

"You think I stop boss if he want? You don't stop him."

"I?" she asked unbelievingly. "I wasn't here. I couldn't..."

Suddenly she realized that he had deliberately sent her away this afternoon so she couldn't attempt to prevent him.

"But why? Surely whatever's happening in there tonight isn't important enough to risk his life?"

Again the meeting of two pairs of eyes in perfect understanding. And again no answer.

"Then I think, gentlemen," she said, turning to the door that led to the public rooms, "that I shall have to tell my husband exactly how I feel about this—"

She stopped as the dealer's hand caught her arm.

"Don't," he said softly. "If you go in there, you'll destroy what he hopes to accomplish."

She waited for him to finish the explanation, but he politely removed his fingers from her forearm and stepped back, apparently having said all he intended.

"And what does he hope to accomplish by this idiotic display of masculine bravado?" she asked finally.

Again the pause was so long that she thought he intended to let the question go unanswered, but finally he said quietly, "Half the people who came to gamble tonight have heard about what happened here. A lot of them came *because* of what they'd heard. If Jean-Luc doesn't show up, then their speculation, and the gossip about the incident last evening, will increase tenfold. So he's dealing tonight. And acting as if *nothing* happened except a slight altercation with a drunk. Hopefully, some of them will even believe the act."

The kitchen was very still, even the chattering boys silenced by the fascinating presence of the boss's elegant lady in their domain. The violet eyes considered the face of the man who had given her the reason for her husband's behavior this afternoon. He had to get rid of her so he could, by his presence, put an end to the gossip about the fight.

"Because of me," she said softly, and it was not a question.

"Of course," the dealer said. "You don't believe he cares what *they* think about *him?*"

She could hear his mockery of her world in the simple question. The opinion of the ton, the approval of those self-important fops and dandies that Harry cared so much about, didn't matter a jot to this man. Nor to her husband. But because he knew it still mattered to her, because she had so foolishly made him think she cared, he had sent her away so that he could carry out this dangerous charade.

She shook her head, an unnecessary answer to his rhetorical question, and turning, made her way through the heavy silence to the bedroom upstairs.

She had long ago taken off the new dress. She had waited in the chair she had occupied last night and this morning, clothed now in one of her old and threadbare rails. It was several hours after midnight before she'd heard his slow steps climbing the uncarpeted stairs. She'd forced herself not to move, not to go rushing out to help, even when the sound faltered, even when she knew he'd been forced to stop and rest. Finally his tall form blocked the open doorway. Even in the low lamplight she could read the shock when he saw her. He had apparently expected her to have long since gone to bed, sleeping soundly while he played cards below for her sake. *You don't believe he cares what* they *think about him,* the dealer had asked. And she knew he didn't.

"I took off the dress. I didn't want to ruin it while I waited for you," she said. And then defiantly, the hours she had spent worrying about him coloring her voice, "I'll wear 'something pretty' tomorrow. Tonight, you'll have to be satisfied with the poor relation again."

He didn't move from the doorway. He could hear the anger threaded in her voice and, after what he'd said today, he didn't blame her for her bitterness. But he'd faced too many openly mocking stares tonight, heard too many whispered conversations die at his approach. And his side hurt like hell. He was in no condition to deal with the humiliation he had deliberately inflicted.

"I thought you'd be asleep," he said finally.

"While you played cards with my friends?"

"I wasn't aware…" he began, and then realized that saying that no one he had encountered tonight had seemed to be her friend would be hurtful. He shook his head, too tired to think what he might say that would change the situation between them.

He began to loosen the intricate folds of the heavily starched cravat and found that his hands were almost numb with fatigue. He finally managed to remove the lace-edged cloth, but in his tiredness, it fell from his trembling fingers to lie mockingly on the carpet. He knew he couldn't bend down to retrieve it.

"Sit down," she said. Whatever emotion was in her voice now was too subtle to identify, but a change, at least, from the anger.

She drew him to the chair in which she'd waited through the long hours, and he obeyed because he had no choice. Unless he wanted to fall at her feet. He had managed this long only out of sheer, bloody-minded determination, but he was forced to acknowledge, to himself at least, that his strength was at an end.

Before she allowed him to sit, she gently removed the black coat. She helped him down into the chair, hearing the soft grunt of pain when the movement pulled against the stitches. She knelt before him and slipped off the evening slippers. He was too tired to do more than watch her kneeling beside him, too tired to understand what she intended. Finally she stood and began the painful process of divesting him of his shirt. When she had succeeded, her fingers touched Ling's bandage, running lightly around the startling whiteness that was such a contrast to the fire-mottled skin of his broad chest that stretched above it. Surprisingly, she bent to drop a slow, lingering kiss on the damaged shoulder. And then she stepped back away from him while he was trying to understand what that unexpected action might mean.

"Stand up," she ordered softly, putting her hand under his arm.

"I'm not sure I can," he admitted truthfully, but he used her support and the tall post of the bed to accomplish what she wanted.

When she began to unfasten the flap at the front of the formal trousers, she heard, above her head, his soft laughter.

"Maddy, my love," he asked, "have you no shame?"

She glanced up at that dark, scarred face, smiling at her as he had in the gardens.

"Apparently not," she agreed, as she began pulling the fitted trousers down the long length of muscled leg. "At least, not where you're concerned."

She helped him ease back onto the bed and began to remove the fine silk stockings. She didn't even try to resist the impulse that forced her hand to caress down the long length of one shapely, hair-roughened calf and over the strong, very masculine foot. She looked up finally to find him watching her.

"And the rest?" he asked, the damaged mouth sternly controlled, but she could hear the teasing challenge in his question.

"Those you can sleep in," she said, ignoring the provocation as she reached to turn down the lamp.

"And are you going to sleep in that damned chair again?" he whispered in the darkness.

"After the way I let you trick me this afternoon, after the gullible simpleton I was today, I doubt you still want me in your bed. But if you do..." she offered, and waited.

"I'll always want you in my bed," he said softly. "I don't know how I ever managed to convince you of anything else. Come to bed, my beautiful Maddy," he invited.

She slipped under the covers beside him and felt the warmth of his arms enclose her. He wouldn't be able to make love to her tonight, but it was enough. He wanted her, even as foolishly as she had reacted today to his ruse. And slowly, dream by dream, she allowed the familiar fantasies she'd spent the long afternoon destroying to reoccupy all the empty corners of her heart.

Chapter Seven

Jean-Luc awoke to the glide of her fingers against the scars on his upper chest. She was sitting beside him, cross-legged, the thin cotton of her nightgown carelessly bunched around her slender thighs. He studied the seriousness of her expression a moment, trying to read what was in her face, to understand what she was thinking. And finally, alerted by the change in his breathing that he was awake, she glanced up into his face.

"I can't imagine..." she began and hesitated.

"Then don't," he whispered. "Don't even try. I never intended that you'd...be exposed to them."

"Exposed." She repeated his word choice unbelievingly, and smiling, she shook her head. "And how did you intend to ensure that I should never see these? Did you intend to sleep in your clothes the rest of our lives?"

He examined the incredible promise of that phrase. *The rest of our lives.* He took a breath before he answered.

"If necessary."

"But it's not."

"Not?" he questioned softly.

"Necessary," she whispered, leaning down to touch with her lips the thick ridges that marred the misshapen shoulder. She could feel the shuddering breath he took against her caress. She wondered if, after all this time, the scars could still be that sensitive, if she could possibly be hurting him with the softness of her mouth.

But it wasn't any pain she was causing that had evoked that shivering intake. He was, instead, momentarily reliving the agony that had caused the scarring. With the concealment of clothing, only the marks on his face were a visible reminder of what had happened. And, God knows, those were enough, he thought. But every day he, at least, was reminded of the hideousness of the rest of his body.

But now she was kissing his shoulder as if she weren't bothered by the ugliness. Just as she no longer seemed to notice the discolored texture of his cheek. Or the patch that covered the damaged eye. As if she no longer even saw them, he realized in wonder.

In response to that thought, he threaded his fingers into the fall of loosened silver blond hair. At his touch, she lifted her head and smiled at him again. He pulled her down, wondering at whatever was in those eyes. It wasn't pity and it certainly wasn't revulsion. Or any of the other things he'd always expected a woman to feel when exposed to what his body now looked like. Instead…

And admitting finally what had been in her eyes, he used his hand against her scalp to guide her mouth over his and felt it open again to his tongue, welcoming as she had done before. He put into his kiss all the thankfulness that he felt because she had just removed the need for any barriers between them. He didn't have to hide from her. She had given him freedom, too. A freedom he had never expected.

Out of this marriage, which, according to the standards of the world they occupied, was such a *mésalliance,* had come an opening of prison doors that no one else would ever understand or condone.

Her mouth turned to fit more securely against the heat of his. He could feel her body melting into his hold, unconsciously seeking to strengthen the bond that was flowing between them, that had been between them since the inn. He put his other hand behind her back and pressed her breasts into the hard muscles of his chest.

Her fingers hesitated briefly over the scars, wanting to cup naturally around his shoulder, but unsure after his reaction to her previous touch if that were allowed. He caught her hand and, holding it captive under the strong warmth of his, moved it down his body. Gliding over the swell of muscle under the small, hard nub of his nipple. Skimming along the rib cage. Across the bandage and over the protrusion of his hip.

The thin, knitted drawers she had declined to remove last night offered little concealment of the strength of his desire. He drew her fingertips gently along the rigid length of his arousal that tautened the overlying cloth, and allowed their brief struggle against his hold before he released her.

"Surely you're not shy, Maddy. After all, you did undress me last night," he teased gently as she quickly sat up, too far away from his suddenly aching body.

His hand found hers, entwined as they rested in her lap. He held both of them in his, the brown of his skin a contrast to her twisting fingers and the pristine whiteness of her rail.

Finally she raised her eyes to meet his.

"But last night you weren't…"

"No, regrettably, I wasn't," he agreed, smiling. "Are you afraid of me? Because that night… After I took you out of the bath…" He paused, wondering how to explain. "I didn't intend to hurt you. I intended something very different. I thought, because you'd been married, that…"

He stopped, seeing the delicate vibration of the breath she took. His hand tightened over hers.

"Don't," he said softly. "Don't remember. Just tell me. Is that why you're afraid?"

She sat still, head again lowered, and when she answered, she never looked up from her contemplation of their joined hands.

"I'm not afraid. Not of you. It's not that. I don't know what you want me to do. I knew what he wanted, but it doesn't seem the same."

The whispered confession faltered as the gentle pressure of those long dark fingers again communicated his strength to hear whatever she needed to tell him.

"I want you to do whatever you want to do," he said. "Whatever you feel."

He didn't ask what Fairchild had wanted her to do. He didn't want the memory of that to be between them, to make the old man a spectator to their lovemaking. He had thought from the beginning that was one ghost he could exorcise, whatever the bastard had done to his Maddy. *His Maddy.* He took a deep breath, acknowledging how true that had become. His to care for and to protect. Even from her memories.

"I wanted to move," she said softly. Her eyes lifted finally to his face, and he smiled at her.

"I wanted you to," he said.

"He told me—"

"Don't," he interrupted harshly, so that he regretted her quick start of reaction. He deliberately fought to keep the anger out of his voice, to caress her with the sound of it again. "Don't tell me what he wanted. Just concentrate on what I want. And I want you to do and say whatever you feel. I'll never know what you enjoy unless you tell me."

"Like…touching my breasts?"

"Yes," he whispered.

"I liked that," she said.

"I know."

"How did you know?"

"Because I watched them grow hard and tight, and they lifted to my lips. They wanted to be kissed. They wanted to be in my mouth."

"Don't," she said, shocked that he would talk about the intimate things he had done to her body. The faint rose stained her cheeks and neck. "You shouldn't say such things."

"I can do them, you're willing to enjoy my doing them, but I can't talk about them?" he asked, smiling.

Realizing the ridiculousness of her restrictions and of her shock, she shook her head. "When you said that," she said, "it made me feel…"

"As if you wanted my lips over them again," he suggested, and watched the violet eyes widen slightly.

"Yes," she whispered finally.

His fingers lifted obligingly to the ribbons that secured the front of her gown. She watched as he expertly unfastened the barrier between them. His hands guided the thin cotton off her shoulders, so that her upper body was revealed, but the sleeves still covered her lower arms, caught by her bent elbows. She had not moved as he undressed her.

He paused, and she heard the quick breath he took. He marveled again at the delicate curve of pale perfection, the shell-pink tips lifting with each soft breath.

"You are so beautiful," he said softly. His fingers touched against one small nipple, and together they watched it tighten with reaction.

"I thought you were going to..." she began softly, and then was too embarrassed to finish the request.

"You'll have to help me, Maddy. Unless you want me to undo all of Ling's handiwork."

Although it would certainly have been painful, he knew he could sit up enough to touch her with his lips, but he wanted her to come to him. To choose to participate in their lovemaking.

"What do you want me to do?"

"Put your breast in my mouth," he suggested and watched her swallow, the slender column of her throat moving beneath the renewed rush of color.

She hesitated so long he thought she was going to refuse, but at last she freed her hands from the constraint of the long sleeves. As she leaned slowly toward him, he found he was holding his breath. Finally unable to wait any longer, the throbbing engorgement of his groin making him wonder why he was doing this to himself, he placed the tips of his fingers against the swelling curve at the side of her breast that had stopped, an inch above his waiting lips.

She swallowed again at the sensation of his hands on her body. As they had been two nights ago. Her reaction to that memory was so strong, he could feel it vibrating through the pads of his fingers. And then the delicate bud of her nipple was lowered to the damaged lips that opened and closed tightly around it.

He pulled, and the suction caused another shiver of reaction to rake her entire body. He caught her shoulders in his hands and steadied her, holding her securely so she was left to concentrate on nothing but the pleasure of what he was doing. He couldn't see her face, and he silently damned the inconvenience of his blind eye, but he could feel her heartbeat and the almost continual shimmering tremor of the slight shoulders he held as his teeth and tongue teased the sensitive tissue she'd offered him. And finally he was rewarded with the gasping moan of desire that he had waited for so long the night he had made love to the silent body that had lain rigidly beneath his own.

At that sound, he released the pressure and touched a gentle kiss against the side of the wet, distended nipple. With that, he expected her to sit up, to react in some way to what had just happened. Instead, her fingers guided the other breast against his lips. She never saw the smile that he briefly allowed before his mouth enclosed the dry warmth of that nipple and began again those cherishing movements.

And after a long time, she writhed slightly, her body twisting unconsciously, and she whispered, "Jean-Luc, please. Please."

Knowing that for some days he wouldn't be able to answer that whispered request with any hope of accomplishing what he intended the next time he made love to her, especially given the restrictions she had imposed, he opened his lips. Using his grip on her shoulders, he reluctantly pushed her upright. Removing temptation, he thought grimly.

He could make love to her, but given the painful stiffness of his injury and the very real possibility that, in attempting to treat her as she deserved, despite his limited mobility, he would reopen the wound, he decided that the torture he was inflicting on them both had gone far enough.

"Soon," he whispered. He released his hold on her arms to touch with his thumb the sheen of moisture covering the darkened nipple he'd just released.

She jumped in response, and her eyes opened to find his face.

"Tell me," he said softly.

"I don't know how."

"What you feel."

"Like the champagne," she suggested, and her beautiful lips curved slightly in remembrance. "Giddy and floating. Anchored only by your mouth. Held to earth only by its pull." She paused as her tongue touched against the dryness of her bottom lip. "And aching," she finished.

"Here?" he asked, moving his thumb to drag against the darkened, sensitized skin he was touching.

"Yes," she whispered. He allowed another stroke, backward, his nail against the hardness of the rose tip, and then she said the rest.

"But you satisfy that ache. It's the other... Inside," she admitted softly. "Between..."

He allowed the pause to lengthen, hoping she'd find the courage to finish that confession.

"That's because you want my mouth there, too," he said finally.

He watched the shock in her eyes at that suggestion.

"No," she denied, but he could see the images flickering behind the wide violet gaze.

"Yes," he said, smiling at her.

"But that's..."

"Very beautiful," he insisted softly.

She shook her head slightly, more embarrassed by the idea of allowing him that intimacy than she had been by the hard invasion of his body the night he had made love to her. It had been dark then, and she had known to expect that painful entry. But this... The very idea of what he was suggesting her body sought was so foreign to anything she had imagined. Too intimate to contemplate.

"Anything between a husband and wife... Anything that gives them both pleasure," he amended, "is right."

She glanced up at the quiet surety of that statement.

"And I will give you so much pleasure," he whispered, his eye searching the lovely oval of her face. "I have so much I want to show you about how I feel."

Again the dark, patient lover of her fantasies was there. And it didn't matter if the scarred countenance and the damaged body of the man who lay before her didn't fit the girlish pictures she had cherished. She knew once again, with that fated certainty she had felt in the country inn, that this was he. She had thought that night she would never be given the chance to fulfill all those dreams, but then, like a miracle, had come Harry's offer.

Unbidden and unwanted, the memory of her half brother's demand intruded. It threatened to destroy the spell her husband had created, just like the images of her first marriage had. Her eyes flicked downward to the broad bandage that spanned the narrow, ridged stomach. Her procrastination had caused that. If she could only get him to agree to do what Harry wanted, then maybe he'd leave them alone. Maybe this time...

"What is it?" Jean-Luc said softly. His fingers touched a curling tendril of silver hair that fell against her downturned cheek. She lifted her head, knowing that she had to ask him. During the long hours she had watched him sleep, she had been able to think of nothing else that would satisfy her brother's demand. Harry was right about that. Only Jean-Luc could undo the damage to Mannering's reputation with the ton. Only he could retract the assertions he had made that day in White's.

"I have to ask you something," she said, wondering what she could say to compel him to do this. Without admitting what had happened before. Without alerting him to their danger. He would try to threaten Harry, perhaps. To frighten him. He couldn't know how ruthless the Mannerings could be when they wanted something. No one could understand unless they had lived through...

"It certainly appears to be very serious," he said, and she could hear the teasing caress of his beautifully accented voice.

"Something very important," she whispered.

"And you're going to ask me while you have me here at your mercy. Unmanned with passion and immobilized with

Stapleton's—'' He stopped suddenly because there had been no answering amusement in her eyes.

''What is it?'' he asked again, all humor erased from the repeated question.

''For Harry,'' she said and watched the slight narrowing of that hazel eye, the small reactive twitch in the still-mobile corner of his lips.

''And what does Harry want from me?'' There was something in his voice that should have warned her. But other warnings had already intruded, far more moving and effective than the possibility of his anger.

''He wants...'' She stopped because, as she had told her brother, she couldn't imagine this man humbly confessing to a lie he hadn't told. Not at White's. Not before those men he despised.

''Maddy,'' he commanded softly.

''An apology,'' she whispered. ''In White's. Before his friends. Before the same people you told about the diamonds.''

The silence grew and she became afraid, aware again for the first time in so long of the power of the man who had just touched her with such gentleness. Under the spell of that gentleness, she had forgotten what she had recognized from the beginning—the aura of danger he unconsciously carried.

Then that damaged mouth lifted in the one-sided smile. Mocking. ''And for what am I supposed to be apologizing to Harry?'' he asked reasonably, but there was nothing reasonable about what was in his face.

''He wants you to tell them that you lied about the diamonds. Or that you're the one who replaced the real stones with paste.''

Again he was still, the lips now stern and taut with the control he was exerting.

''And is that what you want, too, Maddy? You want me to walk back into White's and say, 'Gentlemen, forgive me. It seems that I lied about the actions of one of this illustrious brotherhood'?''

The sardonic disdain was so evident in the question that

she realized, for the first time, what she was asking of his pride.

"Please," she whispered, knowing she couldn't explain why this was so necessary. All the images of that terrible day crowded into her brain. Heart's Fire's agonized screams. And her stepfather's insane fury.

Harry wasn't his father, but she had seen him beat a stable boy into unconsciousness for failing to properly tighten his girth and costing him a fall. His hunting companions had laughed at Harry, and he had taken his revenge on the boy. When she had tried to intervene, he had knocked her to the ground, twice, before the head groom had interfered. Not to stop Harry, of course. He knew the Mannerings too well for that. But to hold her back, to prevent her being hurt. Harry was capable of almost anything. The terrible Mannering rages, she thought, almost welcoming the memory of her half brother's cruelty in contrast to the bloody horror of the other.

"If you do what he asks, maybe he won't bother us," she said, thinking out loud.

"Harry's not bothering me, Maddy," Jean-Luc answered quietly. And then with a deadliness of tone she had never heard before. "Is Harry bothering you, my dear?"

She shivered at the icy threat he managed to inject into that quiet question.

"We have so much," she whispered, not realizing that reminder was the only thing which might make him contemplate doing what Mannering had asked. "And poor Harry… I know you don't understand, but their opinion means so much to him. His place in the ton. It's a relationship he's enjoyed from birth. But now—"

"Is that why Harry came to see you?"

Her eyes widened with the shock that he knew about her brother's visit. But, of course, she should have known. This was his domain, and the servants' loyalties all lay with him.

"Yes," she admitted.

"You didn't tell me then because…?"

"I hated to ask you."

"And now?"

"We have so much," she said again, the key to unlock the hard coldness that had been growing inside his stomach at her first tentative request. "And Harry has nothing. I feel sorry for him."

She hated to lie, but she knew she couldn't chance his reaction if she told him the truth. He couldn't know how merciless Harry could be. She couldn't chance anything happening to Jean-Luc. *God, I couldn't live,* she thought suddenly, *if anything happened to him. Especially if it happened because of me.*

"If I do this, Maddy, I want something in return," he said.

She couldn't imagine what he wanted from her. It seemed that he already held everything she possessed, had ever possessed.

"What do you want?"

"I want you to release me from my promise."

"I don't understand," she said, trying to remember any promise he had made to her.

"I want the freedom to touch you in any way I desire, in any way that I think will give you pleasure. No restrictions. No limits when I make love to you again."

He watched the sharp intake of breath as she thought about what he had asked. He wondered if she thought he was going to do things to her like Fairchild had done. Whatever Fairchild had done to make her react as she had. Whatever had produced that shivering rigidity that had finally defeated him.

"Trust me, Maddy. I won't hurt you. I'll never hurt you. But I need…" He paused, thinking how he could put into words that he needed every weapon in the arsenal of his experience if he were to overcome whatever they had done to her. Whatever all of them had done, he thought bitterly. God, he hated them all, he realized suddenly. The others were dead, but Harry was still alive and able, apparently, to manipulate her into doing whatever he wanted.

Like making her marry a scarred, bastard gambler, his conscience mocked, *who crawled out of the slums of Paris to ruin her life.* And because he couldn't bear it, he banished that thought.

His bitter frustration over having to placate Harry Mannering burned in his gut. He would far rather kill him than apologize to him. He wondered why he'd agreed. Because she asked you, he mocked himself. Because, apparently, you can refuse her nothing. You poor bastard, he thought grimly. Lost because she has violet eyes, and she trembles when you touch her. And because you believe that response is out of passion and not revulsion.

Once more the frightening idea that he might be wrong touched what was left of his heart. He rejected that possibility because he acknowledged, to himself at least, that if Maddy were false, then nothing else really mattered. If she were not what she seemed, then there was nothing left anyway. Nothing that he wanted in what would be the remaining dregs of his life. And at that frightening admission, he knew that he was truly lost.

"Yes," she said softly, pulling him back from that dark reality. "Whatever you want."

Instead of touching her, instead of again putting them back on the brink of sure failure, he lifted her fingers and brought them to his mouth. She shivered as his lips brushed across the back of her hand.

She didn't understand whatever was in the glittering eye that raised quickly to her face when he felt that flicker of motion. But he watched as her lips moved into a smile.

She could not have denied him anything when he touched her as he had today. She had even forgotten his promise. But he, apparently, had not. He had asked to be freed because he would never break his word to her. She smiled at the irony of granting him permission to do the things that she now knew she wanted more than life itself. And because she had acknowledged to herself, if not to him, exactly how much she loved him.

Jean-Luc had steeled himself to keep the appointment she had made for him with her brother. Harry had even arranged it so that he should be admitted at the door. All he had to do with ask for Lord Mannering, who was expecting a guest.

Even if the staff recognized him from his previous unannounced visit, they would never go against the instructions of a member.

At the hour when the club would be full of the afternoon crowd, he presented himself, as totally controlled as when he had played cards with Harry. He had wanted to strike him that night for the studied contemplation of his ruined face. And he had restrained himself. He could do it again. In his profession one wasn't allowed emotions. That was a lesson he had learned as a child, and it had made the adjustment to his life as a professional gambler much easier.

His eyes searched the crowded room for his brother-in-law and finally found the fair head in a crowd of gentlemen that looked very like the ones with whom Ned Stapleton had come to his club. He became conscious again of the now-familiar ache in his side. Another debt he owed these bastards, he thought bitterly, making his way with that unconscious air of leashed power."

Excuse me, gentlemen,'' he said softly to the group that surrounded Harry.

The animated murmur of the men he had addressed suddenly stilled and the resulting silence spread through the room like the ripples from a pebble thrown into the unruffled surface of a standing pond. Again, something alien and dangerous had invaded these protected confines, and they all were aware of it.

"I have something to say to Lord Mannering, and I believe that you all should hear it.''

The silence was total again except for the clock with the cherubs.

"I was mistaken about the necklace,'' he said, watching the slight smile of satisfaction play about Harry's lips. The viscount's blue eyes were full of derision, but Jean-Luc continued because Maddy had asked him to do this. He would carry out her wishes and then leave, free himself from the contamination of the Mannerings, once and for all. Free them both.

"Mistaken?'' Harry asked mockingly.

"The jeweler who made the initial evaluation of the stones tested only two of them. The only two, it seems, that had been tampered with. The only two that had been replaced. The others are genuine. So I've come to apologize and to return this," he said, handing Harry the case in which he'd had a jeweler place the Mannering "diamonds."

Harry allowed his eyes to drop to the outstretched hand that held, unwavering, the price he had demanded. Then his brows arched in disbelief.

"And you think, that after what you've done, you can simply hand over the stones and 'apologize'?" Harry challenged angrily. "After forcing my sister to marry you? After accusing me of lying? Do you honestly believe that these gentlemen and I intend that you should be allowed to get away with that?"

"Don't push your luck, Mannering," Jean-Luc warned quietly.

"Don't threaten me, you French bastard. You may be able to threaten my sister, to make her marry you without my knowledge or consent, but I warn you it won't work here."

"You have your apology. You have your necklace," Jean-Luc said, placing the jeweler's case on a nearby table. He moved to leave, and felt Harry's hand on his sleeve.

Suddenly furious, he turned back. Harry struck a backhanded blow across his right cheek. The gold signet the viscount wore broke the fragile, damaged skin at the corner of his mouth.

"You'll meet me for this," Harry said.

Jean-Luc touched his thumb to the welling blood. He held his hand out so he could see clearly the evidence of that blow. And he knew, without any doubt, that Harry's target had been deliberately chosen. He concentrated again on control. He had never wanted to kill a man as badly as he wanted to kill Harry Mannering. His wife's brother.

"If you need a second, I shall be honored to be allowed to make the arrangements," a quiet voice spoke at his side.

His gaze moved to meet the unusual silver eyes of the handsome man who had spoken. He was as dark as Jean himself, tall and elegantly dressed, and he had stood watching the confrontation, leaning on a silver-headed cane he held in his right hand.

Jean-Luc knew he shouldn't be surprised at Avon's intervention, given the duke's sources of information. Dominic would certainly have been aware of his arrival in London and of the gossip surrounding his marriage. He wondered with sudden amusement what the men gathered around them thought about the Duke of Avon's offer to serve as second for a French gambler. The Regent's spymaster and Jean-Luc's former cell mate in a French prison waited with that distinctive quirk of one arrogant brow for his answer.

"I appreciate the offer, your grace, but it won't be necessary. I don't intend to accept the challenge."

Avon bowed slightly, accepting that decision.

"I hope you know that, if at any time in the future, you have need of my services in that capacity, you have only to ask."

Jean-Luc's nod acknowledged the duke's generosity, and then he allowed his eyes to return to his brother-in-law's shocked face. No one could have anticipated Avon's move. The duke was one of the wealthiest and most nobly born men in England, a man few of the members of his own club would have felt free to ask to serve as second. And the thought of his grace making the offer he had so willingly made to a French gambler would certainly cause a ripple in the confined world of the *beau monde*. No one in London was aware of the bond that was between them, a bond that Jean-Luc would never have sought to bring to the attention of ton, but one that Avon, apparently, had no qualms about publicly acknowledging.

"So you refuse to meet me," Harry finally said into the stunned silence. "I should have known better than to expect you to settle this like a gentleman. My mistake. I should have had you horsewhipped instead."

"The mark of Cain, Harry," Jean-Luc said softly.

"Cain," Harry repeated blankly, the allusion lost on him. For the first time Jean-Luc smiled with honest amusement.

"I don't intend to kill my *good* brother. I don't think Maddy would like that."

He nodded politely to the still watchers.

"Gentlemen, I bid you good day."

He turned and began the long journey out of this world he never intended to enter again. But before he left, something in what Harry had said made him turn around and face his brother-in-law again.

"And, Harry," he said softly, his warning clear to them all, "whoever you send to horsewhip me... You be damned sure they bring a very big whip."

They watched in silence as he retrieved his hat and left as arrogantly as he had before.

The considering eyes turned at last to Avon, who had not moved since his offer had been politely refused.

"My apologies, your grace," Mannering said. This was one man it was better not to alienate, but his curiosity was too strongly aroused by what had just happened to let it go. Things had definitely not gone as he'd planned, and part of that was Avon's fault. "But I didn't realize you knew Gavereau."

Those cold silver eyes rested on the viscount's face a long moment. Finally Avon said, "Our acquaintance is of long-standing. And very important to me. However, I suspect there are a great many things you don't know about your brother-in-law, Mannering, which is surely a shame. And probably dangerous, as well. Gentlemen, I, too, bid you good day."

Avon turned and, with the marked limp he had borne since birth, moved to the door, leaving them still without an explanation.

Chapter Eight

Maddy had returned only a short time before from Madame Darnet's, and an air of feminine clutter created by scattered dress and hat boxes pervaded the darkly masculine chamber. She was trying on a pale satin straw bonnet with a wide rose ribbon that was supposed to tie at the side. She was standing on tiptoe, futilely attempting to gauge the effect in the clouded shaving mirror of the washstand. She had realized belatedly that this small square was the only looking glass the room possessed. There had been, before today, no reason to notice the lack of a full mirror, but with the wealth of new and highly becoming garments that the French modiste had created, the long-forgotten pleasure in being fashionably dressed demanded a proper vehicle for appreciation.

She heard the door open behind her, but wanting to dazzle her husband with the transformation of his poor relation, she made one last adjustment of the bow that nestled charmingly against her cheek.

"You need a proper mirror," she said lightly, her fingers busy with the ribbon. "I can hardly—"

Her voice stopped, for she had remembered the simple and obvious reason this room possessed no looking glass. The quality of the silence behind her thundered painfully in her heart.

She turned, her fingers still touching the brightness of the bow, but its importance was forgotten in the realization of the unthinking cruelty of that remark.

He was leaning against the frame of the door, still dressed in the dark blue coat and the striped silk waistcoat he'd worn to White's. Pantaloons stretched tightly over the muscular shape of his long legs, and she felt again that sudden ache in her body. *Because you want my mouth there,* he'd whispered, and she knew it was true. She wanted him so much, and instead of telling him that...

The single eye was focused on her face. There was, however, despite what she'd just said, no display of emotion in the serene calmness of his features. As controlled as he had been this afternoon when he had faced her brother.

"I'll have Ling see to it," he said softly.

"No," she said, "it doesn't matter. I didn't—" She stopped again and allowed her fingers to fall. "I'm sorry," she whispered.

"Because I don't want to look at my reflection shouldn't mean you must be deprived of the enjoyment of looking at yours. It would be a shame to be denied the pleasure of admiring that bonnet. It's charming."

"You were right," she said, grateful for his reprieve. Seeing the puzzled crease form between his brows, she explained, "About the ribbon. This is the one you chose. And Madame Darnet and I..."

"Insisted I was wrong," he finished.

"And you are always right," she teased, smiling.

"I hope," he said, but there were echoes of something she didn't understand in the quiet seriousness of that answer.

"How was your meeting with Harry?"

She had blocked out the images of that confrontation throughout today's session with the modiste. And now she didn't want to ask, didn't want to know how the "apology" had gone, but she knew that it was better that they openly discuss the unpleasantness of the situation Harry had caused. She should have told him earlier about her brother's visit. Things that were hidden, even innocent things, could lead to distrust. She, herself, had enough distrust of Harry's motives to color everything between them, and she knew that it would, if she were not very careful.

"I gave back the necklace, properly apologetic," he said, the mockery strong in the pleasant timbre of his voice.

"And so it's over."

"Is it, Maddy?"

"If Harry has his apology…" She paused, questioning his hesitation to assign Harry to their past.

"But Harry didn't appear to be satisfied with my apologies. It seems that Harry had other things in mind. Other objectives that you, apparently, had forgotten to tell me about."

She shook her head, trying to understand what he meant. He was watching her so strangely.

"I don't know—"

"I think your brother wants to kill me, Maddy. Something that you failed to mention, perhaps?"

The quiet suggestion about Harry's intent was a realization of all her fears and suspicions.

He waited for the shock to appear in the violet eyes, for the stunned denial that Mannering could possibly contemplate such an action. But instead, moving behind the dark, dilated pupils was an emotion that was not disbelief. And not surprise.

He felt the cold coiling in the pit of his stomach. God, Maddy, tell me you didn't send me there to die, the arrangements all made for me to be shot down by your bastard of a brother in some gentlemanly tableau of murder.

"I don't know what you're talking about," she said softly, but to a man who made his living reading others, that lie was as evident as if she had just confessed her complicity in whatever Mannering had intended today.

He released the breath he'd not been aware was frozen in his lungs and forced himself to breathe. Forced himself to accept what he had seen in her face. Forced his brain to form the next question, and then his mouth to utter it.

"Did you know Harry intended to compel me to meet him? A challenge issued in front of all those blue bloods who call themselves his friends?"

He watched the slow, negative movement of her head, the soft tendrils of her hair, disarranged by the bonnet, moving against her neck.

"No," she whispered, her eyes held by the intensity of his.

"How good a shot is Harry, Maddy? Good enough to accomplish what he wants?"

She waited a long heartbeat.

"Yes," she whispered finally.

"Yes," he repeated, smiling slightly. "I suspected as much."

"When…" she began and then paused. He saw the rasping intake of breath and waited, and finally she finished the question. "When do you meet him?"

"Never," he said and saw the shock that he had waited for, had hoped for before, appear, only now, in her eyes.

"I refused the challenge, Maddy."

"But…" She shook her head again. "I don't understand."

"I refused to meet him. I told him no, and then I left."

"But how can you refuse? If he challenged you, then…" The idea that a gentleman had the option of refusing to meet an opponent who had issued a public challenge was totally foreign to her upbringing. To be forever branded as a coward…

"He made his ridiculous challenge, and I said 'No, thank you,' and then I bid them all a good day," her husband said sardonically, watching her face. "It was as simple as that."

"Why? Why would you refuse?" She knew he wasn't a coward. She was as certain of his courage as she had once been of her own.

The one-sided smile lifted in mockery of her question. So much a product of the world that had produced those who, today at White's, had looked at him with that same stunned disbelief.

"Because I don't intend to stand in some empty field and let Harry Mannering shoot at me, Maddy. Despite what you want."

"What I want?" she asked, bewildered. And then realizing exactly what he had said, she repeated his phrase louder, furiously denying, "What I want? God, Jean-Luc, you can't believe that I want—"

She stopped the rush of accusations, and her hand slowly lifted to her cheek. Feeling against her fingers the satin streamers that had, only moments before, seemed so important, she pulled at the bow, finally ripping the bonnet off. She threw it as hard as she could, but it fell almost at her feet, its lightness making the gesture ridiculous. A child's tantrum.

She put the heels of both hands against her temples, pressing hard, her eyes closed. Slowly her fingers curled into fists. She breathed deeply once, and then again. Seeking control.

He watched, wondering if she were this good an actress. But of course she is, he mocked himself. All the hesitant shyness, the delicate shuddering reaction to his hands and mouth, the soft moaning pleasure when he had suckled her breasts. All an act. All of it carefully orchestrated to make him believe just what he had begun...

"And you think because I asked you to go today, that I knew what Harry wanted?" she said.

"You tell me, Maddy, what you wanted when you sent me to White's today, if not a public challenge you and Harry thought I couldn't refuse."

"I intended to get Harry out of our lives," she said furiously. "I thought—"

"Was this the plan from the beginning?" he interrupted harshly, not wanting to hear her fabricate more lies. After all, he had read the answer in her first response. She had known very well what Harry had planned. "If Harry shoots me down on the 'field of honor,'" he mocked, "you would have accomplished it all. Harry's debt canceled by our marriage. His reputation restored by my confession today. And with my death, your freedom regained. Harry even took care to help your redemption back into the good graces of the ton. His noble sister, willing to sacrifice herself to save her brother. A poor defenseless woman forced into a vulgar marriage, wed without her brother's knowledge, in order to save the family name."

"Stop it," she said fiercely. "Stop it. That's not the truth and you know it. You have to know it, Jean-Luc," she said, and the intensity of that desperation held him a moment. "You have to know that's not true."

"I know your bastard of a brother wants to kill me. And I know that you knew that, too. Beyond that, Maddy, I'm not really sure what else I know."

"I didn't know about the duel. He asked me to get you to apologize. He wanted his name cleared. But the other…"

"Then why, my darling," he asked, the endearment a bitter mockery, "were you not surprised when I told you? Why wasn't it a shock to you to think that Harry intends me harm?"

"I didn't—"

"Damn you to hell, Maddy, don't lie to me again. I saw your eyes. You damn well knew Harry wants me dead."

"I knew Harry hates you. You knew that. And Stapleton—" She stopped suddenly.

"Stapleton?" he repeated, and finally she had surprised him. The name had caught him totally off guard.

"I knew Harry had gotten Ned to hurt you," she said softly, her anger lost as she remembered the blood and his hand clinging to hers as Ling set that endless row of stitches.

He straightened away from the door and took the three steps that separated them, the forgotten bonnet crushed beneath his gleaming Hessians.

"You think…" He paused, trying to make sense of what she'd just suggested. He remembered the scene downstairs. The man was blind drunk. He'd stake his life on the reality of that. He was too accustomed to judging the level of inebriation of his patrons to have been fooled. Stapleton had fallen like a tree with one blow. "He was a drunk, Maddy. Drunk and defending…" He stopped because he had also remembered that Stapleton's attack had been made in defense of Maddy. Made against this marriage they all believed she'd been forced into. "That's all he was," he finished. "And Harry wasn't here."

"You don't understand. You don't know Harry," she whispered.

"Explain it to me," he said, and against his will he wanted to believe whatever explanation she would make.

"He told me to make you come, to make you apologize—"

"To *make* me," he interrupted, mocking. "And how were you to accomplish that?"

"To...deny you." She stumbled over the admission, and the soft rush of color stained her skin. "Until you did what he wanted."

She lifted her eyes to his, watching her so intently. She noticed for the first time the cut beside his mouth, but she fought the urge to touch the bruised and broken skin. She caressed that hurt only with her eyes. And then they flicked back to meet his.

"But I didn't. I was afraid to ask you. Then Ned stabbed you, and I knew it was Harry's message. To tell me to do what he had asked."

"What's his hold over you, Maddy? How can he control you? How the hell can he pull your strings, and you still jump to do his bidding? How the hell can he still get to you while you're living under my protection?" The anger threaded through his voice, his accent thickening with his emotion as she'd never heard it before.

"I told you," she said, not knowing what else he wanted from her. She'd told him the truth. All the truth, and he only seemed angrier than before.

"Tell me again, damn it. I don't understand. What does Harry do to make you obey?"

And, seeing no way out, she told him.

"He hurts things," she whispered, and her eyes fell. All she could bear to tell him. Or to remember.

"He...hurts things?" he echoed, his bewilderment clear. "What kind of things?"

The silence lengthened until he thought she wouldn't respond.

"Things I care about," she said finally, and her voice was only a breath. "Things I love."

"Things," he repeated softly, still without the least comprehension of what she was talking about. No one had ever worried about his well-being, so her concern for him was unprecedented in his life, and, therefore, incomprehensible. "Things like what, Maddy? I don't understand."

"Like you," she said, the thready whisper even lower than before.

"Like me?" he repeated, the idea of what she'd just suggested holding him motionless.

"Stapleton was a warning. If I didn't do what he wanted, then…he'd hurt you even more. I hoped if you went today, if you did what he asked, that he'd leave us alone. But there must be something else he wants," she said, thinking out loud. "I should have known, but I hoped…"

Her faltering explanation faded because she knew nothing more than what she'd told him. Only a long familiarity with the way Harry's mind worked. A brutal familiarity with the Mannerings.

She raised her head and met his gaze, and she didn't understand what was in his face. He hadn't made any response to what she'd said. He was so still. And she knew with sudden despair that he didn't believe her. The Mannerings were going to win again, and she, as always, would lose. Not again, damn it, she thought, finding a shred of the courage they had stolen from her. Not again.

"Why didn't you tell me?" he said softly.

"I thought you'd be angry. That you'd threaten Harry and then…" Her fear of what revenge her half brother might devise stopped that whisper.

Suddenly he was fighting to control his amusement. He looked down briefly, wondering how he could convince her that he could take care of any threat Lord Mannering posed to either of them. She was afraid of her brother. Damn it, he should have known. But she had seemed so brave, his Maddy, that he'd never thought that simple fear would be enough.

"But it's not for yourself that you're afraid," he said, speaking that sudden realization aloud.

She didn't answer, but her eyes didn't leave his face.

"I wish you'd told me, Maddy. I wish you'd trusted me to—"

"It wasn't that," she interrupted, and he waited a long time for whatever else she had to tell him. "But I couldn't bear it if anything happened to you. Especially if it happened because of Harry. Because of me."

She saw, but didn't understand, what occurred then in the dark features of her husband's face, in the hazel eye. His lips tightened, but he didn't speak. The acknowledgment that she cared about him was too precious to touch. It would be guarded in his soul and taken out to examine further only in private. There was nothing he could say in answer to what she had given him. He had come expecting the revelation he thought she had made at the beginning. Expecting that she was as guilty of wanting him out of her life as her brother was. And instead...

"I'm sorry," he said. So little to offer against the enormity of his mistake in doubting her.

"I should have told you. I knew it was wrong, but... You don't understand."

"It doesn't matter, Maddy. Nothing matters but what's between us. Forget Harry. It's over. I promise you. You don't ever have to be afraid of the Mannerings again. But Maddy—" he caught her chin and forced her eyes to meet his "—no more lies. No more omissions. You have to trust that I can take care of you. And I can. I will. You let me worry about Harry from now on."

In the face of his demand, she was left no choice but to nod. He held her gaze a moment longer, aware of the doubt that was still in the beautiful violet eyes. But since that doubt was, she'd admitted, because she was worried about his safety, he allowed his lips to lower to meet hers. They trembled beneath his touch and then they opened, again sweetly welcoming. The kiss was brief, a promise and not a fulfillment.

He raised his head and smiled at her, that beloved crooked smile.

"I'll buy you another bonnet," he said.

She shook her head, trying to find an answering smile. He

didn't know the Mannerings, but she did. And she wondered what it was that Harry still wanted from her husband.

Maddy was deeply asleep by the time Jean-Luc slowly climbed the stairs that night. She had intended to wait up for him, but the bed had stretched invitingly, and she had slept so little the night before, worrying about the meeting she'd arranged between them. She'd intended only to rest, to close her eyes for a few minutes, sure that she would hear him and wake up. Or if she didn't, perhaps he'd touch her into wakefulness.

She had helped him change that afternoon after he'd smilingly refused her request not to go downstairs tonight. Again, after that scene in White's, he knew that he had to make an appearance. The rooms below would be too crowded with the curious to allow only the supervision of his staff, as competent and as carefully trained as he knew them to be. He was the one they would be coming to see. The cowardly Frenchman.

He had fought a duel shortly after he had opened the casino because he had been accused of cheating. That had been a professional necessity. A business imperative. But he considered the practice a ridiculous charade that proved nothing of guilt or innocence. So he had refused a meeting he considered only a ritual of the idiotic codes that governed this society he despised. And then the Duke of Avon had made his unbelievable pledge. Jean-Luc had known that he would be the center of interest in the salon. The target again of the considering glances, bolder and more insulting tonight because he'd refused Mannering's challenge.

The night had been as abhorrent as he'd anticipated, he thought, as he stood in the darkened bedroom slowly removing his formal evening attire. Finally he was nude, except for the broad swathe of bandaging around his narrow waist, his scattered clothing the only disarray in the silent room. All Maddy's new dresses and bonnets had been carefully put away.

He moved to stand beside the bed, looking down on the sleeping figure of his wife. As he watched the gentle rise and fall of her breathing, he rotated the right shoulder and turned his neck slowly from side to side, trying to ease the deep ache that was the result, tonight, not only of the old burns, but also of his tension, a reaction to the hostility that had emanated from the throng in the casino below. They hated his guts, and after Harry's success today, they had felt far freer to express their animosity.

He didn't know whether he should be glad or sorry she was asleep. He was so tired, bone-weary, and every one of his injuries, old and new, hurt in an increasingly demanding chorus. It was probably just as well she was sleeping so soundly, he thought, but against his will he felt the throbbing hardness of his body grow as he looked down on the slender legs, their slim length fully revealed by the rucked-up position of her rail. The corner of his mouth deepened at the contrast between the high, buttoned neck of that maidenly cotton nightgown and its unintended but sensual disclosure of her lower body. And then his throat filled and tightened, unconsciously echoing what was happening in his groin, as he thought about what she had said today.

Things I love, she had whispered. *Like you.*

He had made no corresponding confession, but he knew that it was true. And he knew how vulnerable his feelings for her made him. A vulnerability he had never wanted, but one he could not, in honesty, deny any longer.

He cared for her far beyond the incredible desire for her body that he had felt from the beginning in that fire-lit room of the inn.

She stirred in her sleep, and his mind came back to the present, back to *this* darkened room where he had the right to touch her, to claim her, to satisfy the aching demand of his body in the warm, honeyed silk of hers.

Her fingers brushed at a long strand of hair that lay across her face. It gleamed briefly in the moon's touch like platinum, and he waited, hoping now that she would wake. But her hand relaxed again into sleep, and her mouth parted on a sighing breath. He wondered if she were dreaming of his lips moving over her body, softly suckling against those responsive rose-tipped breasts. But he knew, given his physical condition, that if he woke her tonight, she would only, once more, lie unfulfilled under his straining body while he found his solitary release. And that was something he intended would never happen again.

His dark fingers found the strand of silver and allowed its live warmth to curl around their touch. He bent and put his lips gently against the fragrance of the curl that wound his fingers as surely as she was wound into the very fabric of his soul. He closed his eyes against the sudden, unfamiliar prick of tears. And then he stood erect and allowed the soft tendril to uncurl, freeing his finger, and wished that he could uncoil as easily her hold on his heart.

He had always known that this marriage would hurt her. It had been, given who and what he was, inevitable. Now he knew that the danger was just as great, perhaps greater even, that it would hurt him. And he hated the idea of exposing his heart to the kind of agony this afternoon's doubts had inflicted.

His fingers were tracing the alabaster smoothness of her thigh, moving upward to where the whiter expanse of material stopped. She turned in response to that touch, no longer on her side, but on her back. The leg he had stroked bent, the knee raised. And his fingers moved to caress that which she had denied him before, in the bath. With his long years of experience in these arts, he knew exactly how to touch her, exactly how to give her pleasure she had not dreamed of, could not, in the brutality of her first marriage, have envisioned as existing between man and woman.

He felt the ripple of reaction against his fingers even before the violet eyes slowly opened and fought to focus.

Maddy had thought it was a dream. She had been remembering what he had said about wanting his mouth there, and when she had felt the shattering glide of his thumb she had thought it was his tongue, moving as he'd suggested, across the most intimate part of her body. But when she had opened her eyes, he had been looking down on her, his dark face as still and composed as it had been this afternoon. All of what he was feeling as effectively hidden.

She thought that she should move, should close her legs against the incredibly intimate invasion of her husband's hand. But she didn't want to. She wanted what he was doing. And so she lay, languidly acquiescent, and allowed him to touch her. When he realized that she had tacitly given him permission to continue, the corner of his mouth had moved slightly, and then, never interrupting the sensuous rhythm of those knowing fingers, he had carefully lowered himself to sit beside her on the bed. She heard again his revealing release of breath when the pain occasioned by that careful movement had eased.

"Relax," he commanded softly, and smiled at her. She didn't return the smile, but her body shifted slightly in response to the feelings that had begun to glide upward from the place he was stroking. Slipping into her body like flickers of lightning, warm and jolting against nerve endings that were suddenly, for the first time in her life, being made aware of their intended function. Aware of why they had been created and placed in this location.

She closed her eyes against the sensations, and unconsciously her legs drifted farther apart, inviting what he was doing, allowing him greater access.

He wanted to bend and put his lips over hers, to feel the deep breaths that were beginning to move in and out in her involuntary response, but his aching side denied that urge. He continued the slow, relentless strokes until finally he turned his hand to slip long, hard fingers into the hot wetness he was creating. He felt her jerk against that invasion, and he whispered again.

"Shh, my beautiful Maddy. Just relax. Just let me..."

She moved then, pushing down into the movement of his fingers and, unwilling to allow her that control, he removed his hand and watched her eyes open again to find his face.

"Please," she begged softly, and took a deep breath as he began again the caress she sought.

This time he held her eyes as he increased both the tempo

and the pressure of what he was doing. He felt his own response build as her breathing quickened and her body arched in unspoken demand. Finally her eyes closed and she moved uncontrollably under his touch, all inhibitions lost and forgotten in the strength of her response. He watched as the shivering tremors lessened and then ceased, her breathing still as rapid as if she had run a race.

Her eyes opened slowly, the pupils wide and dark, to meet his, and again he smiled at her. And he delighted in the shocked response as he allowed his fingers to begin the sensual caress all over again. And then again.

She was the one who pushed the confining material away from her aching breasts and caught the other dark hand, guiding it urgently to her nipples. She had talked to him then, his name torn from her mouth as her body arched and lifted under his controlling fingers. Finally, after a long time, he had allowed her peace, allowed the gasping breathing to still in the otherwise silent darkness of the room. And he waited.

When she was capable again of thought, she raised trembling fingers to touch him, to find the painfully engorged fullness that he had ignored while he gave her pleasure.

Her touch was far too soft and tentative to do anything more than to add to the slow and exquisite torture he had already undergone in watching her.

"Do you want to…" she began hesitantly, not knowing the words to finish the invitation.

"More than you can imagine," he said softly, smiling, "but I don't…" He found himself reluctant to admit to the level of pain and exhaustion he was dealing with. "I think we'll wait for that until another night. When I'm not so damned…" Again he hesitated, and finally, giving no explanation, he finished. "Go to sleep, Maddy. We have lots of nights."

She felt him carefully stretch out beside her and heard his soft sigh when his body was at last allowed to rest against the comforting mattress. She could still feel how hard and rigid his desire had been under the caress of her fingertips, steel covered by the soft, hot velvet of his skin. There must be a way to grant him release. A way to allow him to reach fulfillment without causing him any pain or any effort.

Perhaps she could stroke him, as he had… But she knew that his satisfaction depended on the enclosure of her body, not on the caressing movement of one finger. She knew so little of what he had shown her, but from the experiences of her first marriage she knew that much, at least. The problem was how to arrange for her body to envelope the hard, long length of his without putting any strain on that row of stitches.

And somehow into her head came the possibility. When she began to take off the nightgown, his eyes had opened again in the dimness of the room, wondering what she was doing. He really had not had any idea until he had felt the touch of her knee against his hip and then the movement of her body over him. With the sudden realization that she was kneeling above him, the dull ache was replaced by a leap of blood, so that he was again full and hard and wanting.

"I don't know…" she whispered in the darkness, and then his hands were moving to accomplish what she had offered, the incredible offer she was making.

Her hips lowered slowly over his, the tight, hot wetness that he had so lovingly created in her body enveloping inch by inch the aching need in his. He waited a moment, savoring the sensations, and then using his hands against the slender waist, so small that his long fingers could almost span it, he encouraged her to move, to lift, raising that incredible soft sheath of warmth. And again. And…

The explosion was so sudden and unexpected that she might have pulled away had his hard fingers not been holding her. His head twisted on the white pillow, the brutal scars and the dark patch turned toward her, and then only the perfect, beautiful undamaged side visible as his body arched beneath hers. Contorted as if in pain. She wondered if she had been wrong to try this. He was probably going to tear the stitches, she thought, but she lost that thought in her fascination with what was happening. So quickly, she thought in amazement. Not like…

Eventually the eruption had stilled, and he had pulled her

down to lie against the dampness of his chest, their bodies still joined. She felt the softening of his body within her own as his hands moved slowly along her spine and over her smooth buttocks.

"That was so quick," she said, still surprised by the contrast with the endless pain that she had endured while the old man tried to...

She felt the laughter move through his chest and stomach.

"Damn," he said softly in response to what his sudden ironic amusement had cost in the aching gash in his side. He could feel again something besides Maddy's warmth surrounding him, and the cut hurt like hell. He suspected that he'd torn at least a few of the stitches, and he really didn't care.

"I'm only glad you weren't waiting on me to satisfy you. Given the lack of control I just demonstrated," he said, smiling into the darkness and turning his face to drop a kiss on the top of her head that rested against his scarred cheek, "you'd still be suffering, my darling."

"I've never..." she began and then paused, hating to remind him that he hadn't been the first man to touch her, hating to bring the thought of the old man's fumbling ineptitude into his bed. So different from before. So different from what she had endured, all that she had known before his touch.

"I know," he said softly, his lips finding her temple and nuzzling the sweat-dampened tendrils there. "But you will. Soon, my angel, I'll show you what it should be like between man and wife. Together."

"Is that better?" she asked, her fingers caressing the small hard bud of his nipple. He read clearly the doubt in her voice.

The crooked smile lifted again in the darkness above her head. "A hundredfold," he promised softly, and felt the small shiver of response in the body that rested against his.

"That's impossible," she whispered, and he felt the negative movement of her head against his chest. "I don't believe you."

"I'll never lie to you, Maddy. Why don't you believe me?" he asked, his tone still teasing.

"Because I'd die," she said. "Even now… If you did what you did before, I think I'd die."

"I promise, Maddy. A hundredfold better. And you won't die, my darling. You'll only think you have."

Chapter Nine

"Good morning," her voice said softly from somewhere above him.

He opened his eye to find her smile. She was already dressed in a white sprigged muslin that somehow deepened the subtle shade of blue in her eyes. He closed his lid against the glare of the strong afternoon sun and knew that it was late. She'd probably been up for hours.

"What time is it?" he asked, reaching out to find her hand, his eye still closed. He felt along her fingers, slender and relaxed in his hold.

"Time you were awake. Ling's coming to rebandage that."

He reopened his eye and carefully raised his head enough to see the bloodstained cloth over his stomach. No wonder he ached this morning.

"Sit up," she said, lifting her pillow to prop behind his shoulders. "I brought you breakfast."

Obediently he raised his body enough to allow her to place the pillow behind him. He opened his mouth and gently nipped the tip of her breast that had moved too close when she'd leaned over him. He felt her start of surprise.

"Stop it," she hissed softly, backing away in embarrassment, but he knew she wasn't angry. He caught her hand again and used it now to pull her down to sit beside him on the bed. She was careful to avoid the stained bandage.

"Kiss me," he said, tugging her closer.

She dropped a quick peck on his lips, but he grabbed her around the waist and pulled her down against him. He couldn't quite prevent the soft grunt of pain as she fell against his side. But her mouth settled over his, and he kissed her very thoroughly, only releasing her when he realized her struggle wasn't feigned.

"What's wrong?" he said, hating the sudden doubt. Maybe she only liked him to touch her in the dark when she couldn't see....

"Your beard," she said, her fingers pushing against his chin. "It hurts."

He examined the alabaster skin and saw clearly the red burn his whiskers had caused.

"Well," he suggested softly, not allowing himself to think again about the possibility of her revulsion, "there's no beard here." He lifted the scarred profile to rub against the smoothness of her cheek. She turned her head after a moment to nuzzle the rough texture with her lips, a very wifely touch, and then she sat back.

"How do you shave that?" she asked, nothing but curiosity in her voice.

"Very carefully?" he suggested, one dark brow lifting slightly.

And was relieved to hear her laugh.

"Luckily, I don't have to. There really aren't any whiskers there. I suppose..."

His voice stopped, and she knew that he wasn't going to tell her anything else. But it had been a beginning. A relaxation.

"Go away," he commanded softly. "I have to get up, and..." He paused again, for some reason not wanting to confess that he needed to relieve himself.

He saw by her sudden quick amusement that she knew exactly why he wanted her out of the chamber.

"And you're too shy to do that in front of me," she teased.

"Get Ling," he ordered gruffly, carefully sitting up on the side of the bed. "I need to get dressed, and if he's going to rebandage this…'' His eye fell on the tray she'd placed on the small table at the head of the four-poster. The slightly fishy aroma of whatever was on the plate beside the pile of eggs and toast fingers suddenly made him queasy. ''And you can take whatever the hell that is back to the kitchen. Tell Ling I said to bring me up something edible.''

He put his hands on the bed and pushed up, his eye closed with the effort, so that he didn't see what was in her face. And by the time he was upright and again in control, she had picked up the laden tray and was moving through the open door. He never even thought about the force with which it closed behind her.

He had pulled on last night's dark, formal trousers and was standing by the window when Ling silently brought his usual breakfast chocolate and roll into the room. He could smell the familiar yeasty aroma through the clean cloth Ling had wrapped it in.

''First food or bandage?''

''Do whatever you're going to do to this and get it over,'' he ordered, moving to sit on the unmade bed. Ling made no comment about the blood or the broken stitch. He gently rubbed salve into the long gash and then rebandaged it with the strips of cloth he'd brought up.

Jean-Luc leaned back against the stacked pillows and allowed the Chinaman to place the tray on his lap.

''What the hell was the other?'' he asked, only idly curious, as he broke open the roll, washing down the first bite with the fragrant chocolate.

Ling watched him eat with satisfaction and then shook his head. ''Kippers. Something of English.''

''Something dead,'' Jean-Luc said. ''Don't experiment. You know what I like.''

''Lady fix. *Hearty English breakfast.*'' Ling carefully echoed what he'd been told.

And saw the dark fingers pause in midair. The hazel eye lifted suddenly to the inscrutable dark ones of his servant.

''Where is she?''

"In door, not crying."

"Not crying?" Jean-Luc repeated carefully.

"Not crying maybe," Ling tried again.

The soft profanities were not in Ling's vocabulary, French or English, and it was probably just as well. They were certainly nothing anyone would have occasion to use in polite conversation.

The bed was suddenly empty, and his boss had disappeared down the stairs, barefooted and, more surprisingly, still barechested, as well. The Chinese servant ate the rest of the roll and drank the remainder of the chocolate that had been left in the cup. There was, after all, no need to let all this morning's food go to waste.

Jean-Luc found her in the open doorway of the kitchen that looked out on the back alley. The sunshine was pouring over the herb garden Ling had planted there. He slipped his arm around her waist and pulled her against the warmth of his bare side, immensely relieved when she leaned into his embrace. He touched his lips to her hair. And the fragrance of it moved him back to last night.

"I'm sorry," he said softly. "I didn't know that you'd fixed breakfast. I can never manage much when I wake up. A roll, maybe, but..."

She turned to face him, smiling, and he realized Ling had been right. She was no longer crying. But the ridiculous scrap of lace that masqueraded as a woman's handkerchief was still balled in her hand.

"It doesn't matter. I don't suppose you married me to cook for you, either."

He looked down, at a loss. He no longer knew why he had married her. He couldn't remember when he had *only* wanted her body. Because now he wanted so much more.

"I didn't marry you for any of the right reasons," he said finally.

Her hand touched his, and he took her fingers. They stood a few moments in the sunshine without speaking. Ling's kitten came to twine his small body around their feet.

"But..." His voice hesitated again, and she didn't rush him

or question. Another thing he liked. She knew when not to talk.

"I was wrong about not wanting you to be all those things. The things that wives are supposed to be," he said.

She nodded and leaned back against him. He held her a moment and then, turning, he lifted her chin and kissed her. Her lips opened beneath his, and finally he raised his head and smiled at her.

"Cor," a soft voice said in awe.

He turned and found one of the kitchen boys watching, the child's wide, dark eyes rising with shock to his face at his sudden movement.

"What are you looking at?" Jean-Luc said. "Haven't you ever seen anyone kiss before?"

"'A course," the boy said scathingly. "I wasn't watching you kiss 'er."

"Then what the hell are you looking at?"

Jean-Luc heard his wife's soft giggle at his question and even took a second to enjoy the sound he had never heard before. He wondered how long it had been since Maddy Fairchild had giggled. Maddy Gavereau, he corrected silently.

"Them," the kitchen boy said, pointing.

It was only with the child's remark that Jean-Luc realized he didn't have on a shirt, the marks of the burns and the extensive damage to his shoulder, which he had always hidden, clearly revealed to the entire kitchen staff. Only the boy had been brave enough, or unkind enough, to comment. They all were looking at him, however, eyes carefully sliding away when he met their looks and then coming back in horrified fascination.

"Get back to work," he growled at them and watched as everyone scattered to find make-believe tasks around the vast kitchen.

"What a shame," Maddy said, *sotto voce,* behind him, the laughter still lurking under the words. "Now you've frightened everyone to death, and it's so hard to find good staff these days."

He turned to find his wife standing with one hand pressed

carefully against her lips, but he could see their corners quirking behind the screen of her fingers.

"If you had seen your face," she said, giggling again.

And finally in the pleasant acceptance of her amusement, which held no trace of discomfort over the child's comment about the scars, the mobile corner of his mouth lifted.

"Come back upstairs," he invited softly.

"Why?" she asked, daring him.

"Because my feet are cold," he said challengingly. "Maybe *that's* why I married you." He turned and almost stomped through the silent kitchen, every member of the staff busily engaged in some demanding activity. He could hear Maddy's occasional giggle as she followed him up the stairs. And after a while nothing was cold, not even his feet.

"No," Maddy protested, again.

"Hush," he whispered, allowing his tongue to move with deliberate slowness.

"Jean-Luc, please," she begged. He caught her hand that had raised to push him away.

"Shh, Maddy. You've forgotten your promise. I did what you asked. In front of all those arrogant fops." He blocked the memory of the faces that had watched him make his polite apology to Harry Mannering. Because she had asked him to. He had never understood it before, but he knew he was as much her slave as his mother had been slave to... Again the deliberate moving away from anything but the here and now. Away from anything but Maddy's body and the pleasure he wanted to give her.

"No," she repeated, but this time it was only a token protest. He could already feel the relaxation of the tension that had held her. Despite her shocked, vehement protests and blushing struggle when he'd laughingly pulled up her skirts and pushed her down on the side of the unmade bed.

"And besides, don't you know it's bad form to say no to a man who's on his knees before you? Never give him such an abrupt denial. Don't they teach you anything in London, Maddy love?" His tongue caressed between the soft phrases, and he could hear her breathing change, deepen, her body begin, against her will, to respond to what he was doing. "You must ask my father," he mimicked, "or, this is so sudden. Or, you do me too great an honor, sir. I'm quite bereft of words." He mocked the conventional phrases every debutante was taught.

His tongue continued to move, echoing all that he had shown her before, but the intensity of sensation was increased. Tenfold. A hundredfold. She vaguely remembered his words and wondered if this was what he had meant. And wondered why the hot, sweet warmth of his mouth caressing her was so much more demanding and satisfying. When he had touched her before, child that she was, she had thought there could be nothing more pleasurable than what he had given her then.

"Are you bereft of words, Maddy, my darling?" he whispered.

"Don't talk," she begged softly. "Please, don't talk."

And finally, his mouth having shattered her again and again so that she was broken into a million pieces, and none of them capable of denying, any longer, anything he wanted, she lay boneless against the tumbled sheets. Her body was half on and half off the bed, her skirts tangled around her waist.

Wanton, she thought. This is what they mean by that word. This is what it feels like to be wanton. Uncaring of the fact that I'm half-dressed and that I have just allowed a man... And would allow it again, she thought honestly. *Allow?* her sense of humor mocked, and she smiled to herself at the thought that she might try to prevent him.

"A very smug, self-satisfied smile, Maddy," he said softly, easing down beside her on the bed.

She turned her head to look at him. He was lying on his left side, his head propped casually on his palm. So dark and beautiful, she thought, smiling at the idea that she could think that. He would never, by anyone else's definition, be considered beautiful. But to her he was. More beautiful than any other man she'd ever seen. Far more beautiful than her fantasy lover because he was real and warm and so human.

Thinking that, she lifted her fingers to touch against his

cheek. Her hand was heavy, relaxed and drained so that she almost lacked the strength to complete the gesture.

She touched the scars, wondering how she had ever thought they could diminish his attractiveness. And then the velvet patch. And was surprised that he allowed that invasion.

He was watching her face and whatever he saw there made him resist the urge to move, to turn away from the gentle brush of those small fingers.

"What happened to this?" she asked, too relaxed to guard her tongue.

He turned his head to kiss the caressing hand, but he didn't answer. She waited, admiring the strong pure lines of his profile, his face as it had been the first night, only the stark, unmarred perfection of the left side revealed. The silence stretched so long, she was surprised when he began to respond to that unthinking question.

"We had held. The emperor had told us that we were the key. We were the point on the line where the main thrust would be made. He had told us that. Challenging us, I realized later, but at the time, because we worshiped him…"

His voice faded, the memories so strong that she knew he was there again, on that long-ago battlefield, no longer even conscious of the present. She held her breath, determined not to break the spell. From the first, he had told her nothing.

"We were celebrating our victory when we realized that the hut where we had placed the wounded was on fire. A stray cannonball. And we could hear…"

He swallowed, and her eyes followed the hard movement down the brown column of his throat, under the scarred skin. A small muscle jumped beside his mouth.

"It was too late. We knew that, but we could still hear them… The heat was unbelievable, but somehow I reached the door. I broke through. I don't know how. I put my shoulder against the door, but it was on fire and I could feel… That's the last I remember. When the door fell in, the fire just seemed to leap out…."

The halting story stopped, but his fingers gripping hers

more clearly communicated his feelings than anything he might have added.

"It's all right," she whispered. "You did everything you could."

She knew there was no comfort for the regret of that failure. His gaze finally raised to find forgiveness and acceptance in the violet eyes. He had never been able to forgive himself, but he had told it all to Maddy, and he could read no condemnation in her face. He deliberately loosened his hold on the fingers he'd crushed and lowered his mouth to her hand.

"I need you so much, Maddy," he whispered, the movement of his lips against her palm. As far as he could go in admitting to the growing love she was creating in him, feelings that made him too vulnerable, too much in her power.

"I know," she said, thinking of the intensity of the need that he'd revealed last night when she'd given herself to him. And loving him, she moved, as she had then, to grant him the relief that she thought he sought.

Because he wanted her, he didn't question what she was doing. He didn't explain that he had meant something very different from the physical ache that she was beginning to ease. Something far beyond his body's needs.

And later when she again rested against the sweat-sheened skin of his chest, she knew that she was lost, her soul no longer her own, but his. Bought with a gambler's chit. His as surely as any marker that changed hands in the crowded rooms below while she waited each night for him to join her here. Content to wait.

She helped him dress every evening to go downstairs, but he never told her of the increasing hostility, of the diminishing numbers who came to play in the once-crowded rooms. Night after night he left her safe and unknowing in the world of pleasure he'd created around her to descend into an atmosphere of contemptuous stares and ever-more daring whispers.

As the rumors swirled through the narrow world of London society, the hatred they engendered was increasingly reflected in the attitudes of the men who came to the casino each night. He could feel the building tension as the days passed.

Someone was fueling the fires of outrage about his marriage to Lady Madelyn Fairchild, and he knew, of course, who that person must be. He was well aware of Mannering's animosity and recognized the fine hand of his brother-in-law in the campaign. But attributing Harry's gossip only to his hatred, he never even wondered what the viscount hoped to accomplish with the carefully planted whispers. And he never shared his growing sense of danger with Maddy.

With her he buried the smirks and the half-heard insults. In her body he found release for his growing frustration, and in giving her pleasure he soothed the strain created by the tightrope he walked below stairs each evening. He taught her with endless patience the things that pleased them both, carefully at first, limited by the slowly healing reminder in his side of the *ton's* opinion of this union, this *mésalliance*.

And as his body healed, he felt, too, the gradual healing of all the old wounds of the spirit. He allowed her to breech the walls whose construction around his emotions he'd begun in his childhood. Allowed her finally where no one else had been given complete admittance—into the shadowed recesses of his heart.

"You lied to me," she said softly.

He could vaguely feel the gentle movement of her mouth against his forehead as, propped on trembling forearms, head lowered, he rested against her. The shuddering breathing eased at last, his body beginning to relax after the culmination of the incredible climb that had taken them both this time. That had lifted them at the same moment and had left them exhausted, travelers who had touched, briefly, a universe beyond this. And had now returned to lie unmoving, except for the faint shimmering response of overextended nerves and muscles.

"No," he said, finding breath somewhere to answer a question he didn't understand. But knowing that he'd never lied. Only by omission. Only by his lack of an open confession of the feelings that he had at last acknowledged, if only to himself.

"No," he said again, finding her mouth with his lips.

"It wasn't a hundredfold," she said when the long, deep kiss had ended, his lips still resting against her own.

And felt his smile.

"Perhaps a slight exaggeration," he confessed.

"No," she said, her lips tracing slowly over his face, touching at last the cloth of the patch he wore. "An underestimate," she whispered. "At least a thousandfold."

"And you didn't die," he said, his amusement clear in the rich voice.

"Are you absolutely certain?" she questioned, sated and exhausted.

She jumped when his fingers confirmed that she was not, after all, near death.

"Would you like me to demonstrate?" he asked softly, the torturer already beginning to put the question.

"Yes," she said, without any doubt or hesitation, and heard in the darkness his laugh.

"How would you like an occasion to wear the lavender silk?" Jean-Luc asked one evening. She was lying on the bed, watching him deftly tie the elaborate cravat. She had been surprised to discover that Ling didn't act as valet, and then she had been glad, assured of the intimate privacy of the chamber they shared. No one but Ling or the boys bringing bathwater ever entered this room, and only at their express invitation.

"Another evening at Vauxhall?" she asked, remembering with pleasure the beginnings of their relationship.

"A dinner party."

She waited, but there was no further explanation.

"A dinner party?" she finally repeated.

"Friends of mine," he said casually, slipping on the elegant black coat. And he hadn't looked at her.

She hesitated, knowing that she really didn't want to go. During the weeks they had spent together, she had forgotten anything beyond these walls, rejected the vast differences that loomed between his world and what had once been hers. His friends, she thought, wondering whom he might classify as friends and exactly what kind of party they had arranged. And she hated herself for the sudden doubt. Just like Harry and the rest. As much a snob as all the rest. Afraid of anything that was different.

"Then I take it the answer is no?" he said quietly, less a question than an affirmation. He was watching the emotions clearly revealed in her face, the controlled mask that he wore below still in place. So different from the expression he usually allowed only in this room.

"I don't know," she said, shaking her head, and then her eyes fell before the slightly mocking smile that touched his lips.

"It's entirely your decision. I thought you might like a change from this room. Your existence at present seems remarkably confined."

She thought he might be teasing, but when she glanced up again at that dark, contained face, she knew that he believed what he'd just said.

She couldn't prevent the small gasp of laughter at that ridiculous suggestion.

"No," she said, still smiling. "I don't want any change."

And was relieved to see the answering smile begin.

"Then I'll tell them no," he agreed, apparently indifferent, and turned to the door. He hated to leave, hated what he knew he would face downstairs, the increasingly difficult pretense that he was unaware of the comments that were still, out of fear if not out of respect, spoken carefully just out of earshot.

He stopped suddenly and walked back to the bed.

"Come here," he commanded softly.

She scrambled to her knees, her arms reaching naturally now to fasten around his neck. He lowered his head to kiss her, feeling his body ache for its containment in hers. He held her a long moment after the kiss had ended, her slender form fitting with familiar ease against his chest.

"Don't wait up," he said, and heard her laugh again.

"You say that every night," she whispered, her lips lifting to touch his chin.

"And every night you're awake. I worry about you," he admitted softly.

"You're supposed to," she smiled. "That's what it's all about."

And slowly he straightened away from her. *That's what it's all about.* The simplicity of it made him smile, but he didn't deny the reality of what she'd just said.

"Good night, Maddy. Don't wait up," he said again, automatically, and forced himself to leave the warm security of her love.

"My name is Stapleton," the handsome young aristocrat said as he joined the table at which Jean-Luc was dealing. The Frenchman had in no way indicated that he'd recognized the viscount from his previous visit, but he'd been well aware of who he was. Aware also that Maddy thought he had been Harry's representative in that attack.

"We've met," Jean-Luc said, his hands never faltering in the deal.

"But we've never been properly introduced," Stapleton persisted.

Allowing his amusement to show, Jean-Luc finally looked up from the cards to meet the Englishman's hostile stare.

"You're right," he said softly. "The amenities are so important. And now we've met." He held the blue eyes a moment, very much like Mannering's, seeing the flush begin to move into the fair cheeks of the Englishman.

"I'd like to see Maddy," the viscount said, his voice too loud, the words forced. He'd fortified himself for this mission. A little Dutch courage to beard the lion in his own den. After all, he'd nursed a sore and swollen jaw for a week after his last encounter with the gambler. However, no one else seemed willing to do anything but talk about the situation.

Again the smile lifted the corner of that damaged mouth, and the hazel eye glittered dangerously.

"My wife," he said deliberately, "is not receiving guests."

"I'm an old friend," Stapleton said.

"Not of mine," Jean-Luc answered quietly, but as it had in White's, the pool of silence was beginning to surround him. It seemed that the players at the nearby tables were all aware of the confrontation.

"We grew up together. My father sold Maddy her favorite mare. A very old friendship. I'm sure you don't intend to prevent Maddy from seeing her old friends." The look in the angry blue eyes said exactly the opposite.

He probably envisions himself in the role of hero, Jean-Luc thought. Perhaps that's how Harry has managed to work him to the fever pitch. Or perhaps there's a simpler explanation. Perhaps he's in love with Maddy.

"I'll be delighted to take up your card," he offered, the essence of politeness embodied in the frigid, accented voice, "and if Madelyn wishes, she is certainly free to renew this 'old acquaintance,'" His mockery was apparent to the listeners.

"I don't believe that will suffice. Not in this situation," Lord Stapleton said, just as coldly.

"In this situation? What exactly is *this* situation?"

"No one's seen Maddy since your marriage."

"I assure you, that's not the case. And now, if you'll excuse me, these gentlemen are waiting to play."

"These gentlemen," Stapleton repeated, his voice as openly mocking as Jean-Luc's, "are as anxious as I to assure themselves of Madelyn Fairchild's well-being."

"As anxious as you all were, I suppose, when she *was* Madelyn Fairchild? I wonder, gentlemen, where your concern was when her stepfather sold her to a man old enough to be her grandfather. Did you ask Fairchild for his permission to view his wife, Stapleton? Or is your sudden concern with her well-being only because she is *my* wife?"

"Whatever else he was, Reginald Fairchild was a gentleman."

"But it was, my lord, the 'whatever else' that should have called that marriage into question."

"We're not concerned with Fairchild. We're concerned with Maddy's safety."

"Her safety," Jean-Luc repeated, smiling. "How noble. I'll express your concern for her safety to my wife."

"My concern is for what you're doing to her, you perverted bastard. We all have heard how you've—"

"You be very careful what you say." Jean-Luc's voice interrupted, scarcely above a whisper. "It's been a long time since I've killed a man, but I don't believe I've forgotten how it's done."

"Someday..." Stapleton began again, but seeing the lethal reality of that threat revealed in that dark face, he hesitated. "Someday you'll have to answer for what you're doing to Maddy. Someday you'll be outside of Avon's protection, away from all your protectors here in the casino, and then—"

"Get out," Jean-Luc said, his hands moving again over the cards with the professional composure he had fought so desperately to regain. "You're no longer welcome here. If you wish, I'll have someone escort you to the door."

"I'll leave, but there are too many people in London who know what's going on. I don't know how you think you can get away with this. Maybe in France, but not here. Not in England, by God."

"Gentlemen, you may place your wagers," Jean-Luc said calmly, ignoring the fury.

"Aren't any of you going to do anything?" Ned Stapleton turned and said to the men at the surrounding tables who were avidly listening and trying to give the appearance that they were not.

"I'm going to take you home before you get yourself killed," said one of the men who had sat silently at the table during the entire episode. He grasped Stapleton's arm and almost pulled him from the room.

The Marquis of Ainsley stood up at their departure and gathered his stake from the table. He looked down at the Frenchman.

"Stapleton's right about one thing, Gavereau. Too many

people are talking. And none of what's being said is pretty. If I were you, I'd watch my back.''

Briefly the hazel gaze flicked up from the cards to meet Ainsley's dark eyes. Jean-Luc was surprised that they held no hostility. But the gambler never verbally acknowledged the nobleman's warning, and he continued the game as if nothing out of the ordinary had occurred.

Chapter Ten

The Duke of Avon's butler had held his position for more than fifteen years, and he had believed himself able to assign, without a moment's thought, the proper social status to any caller who might present himself at his grace's door. But even Hawkins was perplexed by the gentleman who was calling at Avon House this morning. He had asked for the duke, his manner perfectly correct. Nor could one quarrel with the elegance of his attire. But there was something about this particular visitor that had caused an uneasiness in Hawkins's usual imperturbability. French, of course, and the butler found himself wondering if he might have something to do with the duke's work in espionage. There was a certain air of danger...

"I believe his grace is away this morning," Hawkins intoned, carefully walking the line between insult and a simple lack of commitment of his master's precious time. "If, however, you would be so good as to wait...?"

"Of course," Jean-Luc said, recognizing the butler's inability to place him on the rigid social scale that governed the *haut monde*.

"And whom shall I say is calling?" Hawkins inquired politely, avoiding entirely the question of title.

"Jean," the Frenchman answered. He didn't attempt to hide the quick smile at the almost imperceptible shifting of the butler's features.

"Jean," Hawkins repeated carefully.

The gambler nodded, his dark brow lifting in sardonic amusement. At that suddenly familiar gesture, the butler decided that there was only one person in the household at the present who might be able to make a decision as to what should be done about this caller.

Jean-Luc waited alone in the vast foyer with no outward sign of impatience. He had, of course, known Avon's position, but somehow, waiting, surrounded by the evidence of the duke's wealth, made him uncomfortable. The elegance reminded him of a certain hôtel in Paris. Too many memories. He suddenly wondered why he had come. Perhaps because this was the only place in London where he might now be assured of welcome. And because, once the idea had come to him, he had been unable to deny it. He had hoped that today's mission might give Maddy back at least part of the world that she had lost because of him.

The butler's voice spoke almost at his elbow, pulling him away from those familiar introspections that had become increasingly painful during the last weeks.

"Her Grace, the Duchess of Avon, has consented to see you, *monsieur.*"

It seemed that the butler had solved the problem of what to call him. But Jean wanted nothing to do with the Duchess of Avon, and he had already begun to replace his hat in preparation for taking his leave, when a feminine voice spoke from the open doorway of Avon's study.

"Dominic would never forgive me if I let you go. I'm Emily."

The woman who advanced across the wide expanse of marble that separated them was tall and slim. Her red gold hair was dressed in the latest style, and her topaz morning dress had been cut by a master. "And I think you, *monsieur,* are the Jean about whom I have heard so much."

Jean-Luc hesitated, and then, knowing that he had no choice, other than outright rudeness, he moved to accept the slender hand she presented. He kissed it, his Continental assurance in carrying out that gesture in marked contrast to the average Englishman's awkwardness, and looked up to find the ghost of a twinkle in the beautiful emerald eyes. The amusement, whatever its cause, was quickly hidden, but the duchess's smile was as gracious and friendly as her greeting had been.

"It seems," Jean-Luc said, "that yours is a name I've heard before."

"In a French prison," she agreed softly, "as my husband lay dying of fever."

He rejected her obvious emotion, answering lightly, "Not the first prison, I must confess, in which *I* had been incarcerated, your grace, but the only one in which I found my cell mate to be an English duke."

"Whose life you saved," she said, determined to express what she felt, despite his attempt to turn the conversation. There was no amusement in her voice as she made that assertion.

"I assure you—" Jean-Luc began to protest.

"For which you have my undying gratitude. And, of course, my friendship. I don't know if you can imagine what it meant…" At the memory of Avon's condition when, more than two years ago, her brother Devon had brought him home from that terrible mission to France, her voice broke suddenly, the vivid green of her eyes glazed with tears.

"I always cry," she said in disgust. "Dominic says I'm a veritable watering pot. I don't suppose you have a handkerchief?"

Jean-Luc's immaculate linen was put to good use. As he watched her dry her eyes and even blow her very elegant nose, he found himself liking the Duchess of Avon almost as much as he had come to admire her husband's courageous endurance during the weeks they had spent together in France.

"Forgive me," she said, finally smiling again, "but you see, I'm unfashionably in love with my own husband. Not good ton at all. I'm supposed to find him a dead bore, but somehow…"

Jean-Luc found himself answering the smile that acknowledged her own ridiculousness. Her eyes briefly touched on the damaged and unmoving corner of his lips and quickly traced upward over the scarred cheek and the black patch. Her gaze moved serenely back to meet his, and she smiled again. At her total lack of reaction to the scars, he felt himself beginning to relax.

"You haven't come to see Julie?" Emily asked, afraid suddenly that he intended to intrude on the almost idyllic happiness Devon and Julie had found.

Jean-Luc recognized her unease and rightly identified its cause. Her brother's wife was the woman he had once loved. So long ago, he thought, remembering. Long before Maddy.

The enemies he'd made in rescuing the duke had proved too dangerous, so he had left France shortly after Avon had brought Julie to England. London was the only English city large enough to support the casino he'd established, and he'd known the chance of his encountering Julie was comfortingly slight, given the position she now occupied within the closed world of the ton. So different from the life they'd once shared.

"Is she happy?" he asked softly.

The duchess's smile was reassurance enough, but she answered, envisioning tiny fingers and sweetly curving pink toes.

"They have a daughter. A baby whose hair and eyes are as dark as Julie's. They named her Angelique after Julie's mother, but Dev..." She hesitated, realizing that this man could not possibly want to hear her fond-aunt's babble. "For some reason, Dev calls her Gypsy," she finished the story quickly, eager to get past the awkwardness.

"I didn't come to find Julie," he reassured her, smiling again. "I only wanted to talk to Avon."

Relieved, Emily offered, "I don't know that I can help with whatever you wanted to see Dominic about this morning, but if I can, you have only to ask."

"Advice," he said simply.

"I love to give advice, but I don't suppose you want mine."

"Only if you know something about horses," he suggested, not really expecting her to make any claim to expertise. He didn't even know if the duke were knowledgeable, but he knew that Avon would be able to steer him to someone who would be both honest and expert about the world of Thoroughbreds.

But the slow smile with which that suggestion was met gave him her answer.

"Horses?" she asked.

"Suitable for a lady," he said. "For my wife."

"For your wife? But…" she paused, her confusion obvious. "I had thought that you were… I didn't know that you were married."

"I've only recently wed. Here in England. An Englishwoman. And from some comments that have been made, I believe her to be an accomplished rider. I hoped that…"

Some thought began to move behind the lovely features, some subtle realignment of expression, much like the transformation that he had watched in the butler's face when he had given his name.

"*You're* the French gambler everyone—" Emily's unthinking comment was cut off abruptly.

"Is talking about," he finished for her. And waited.

The duchess's slight nod acknowledged her agreement with his completion of her sentence.

"And I suppose what you've heard concerns my marriage," he said, leaving nothing unrevealed between them.

"To Lady Madelyn Fairchild," she whispered.

"Yes."

When the silence moved beyond a natural pause and into discomfort, Jean-Luc allowed a slight smile, controlling the bitterness.

"I understand," he said. "There's no need to see me out. And please don't bother the duke. I assure you that—"

"Horses," she said again as if the last few sentence had not been spoken, and then she nodded as if thinking to herself. "If you don't mind a short walk, and if you'll wait for me to change, I think I know just what you require."

"But…"

"A horse for Maddy?" she suggested softly.

"Yes."

"Yes, I thought so. What a wonderful idea. And I have the perfect... Ten minutes. That's all I'll need. You will wait, won't you?"

"Your grace, I never intended that you should be put to the trouble of—"

"Horses," she said for the third time, already beginning to move toward the huge staircase, "are my passion. Anyone can tell you. And Avon, of course. But that passion you already knew about. I'll only be a moment."

However, not able to resist giving advice, even if it had not been asked for, Emily turned back at the fourth step and met his eyes.

"The things they're saying..." She paused delicately. "The gossip is rampant even among the ladies and, frankly, the stories that are being told..."

"None of them are true. I promise that whatever you've heard about the situation is simply not the truth. When Maddy married me..."

The deep, accented voice hesitated over the explanation. He knew she would never believe what Maddy had told him. Given his appearance, he assumed no one could. No wonder they all thought he had forced her. And continued to hold her by force. To use her as only he knew she had been used before. And instead... The remembrance of what had grown between them threatened to overwhelm him. But there was no way to convince this stranger of the emotions that now bound them more strongly than the vows they had spoken.

"Then why have you allowed the gossips such an open field?" Emily asked, studying his face. "A few public appearances together would staunch all but the most vicious tongues." And then in belated realization of her husband's motives, she said, "That's why Dominic arranged the dinner party. To allow you an opportunity to show the world that—" Again her voice was cut off. "I'm sorry. But I don't understand why you refused."

"I didn't refuse," he admitted. At her puzzlement, he added, "Maddy did."

"But surely, if she knew what was being said…" The duchess stopped, understanding suddenly that the vicious rumors were something he had kept from his wife. "But, of course, she doesn't know. She doesn't know, and you don't tell her. You must realize how dangerous your situation is. I heard that Mannering challenged you. He won't be the last if the scandal continues. Your wife was very popular. You must convince her that your appearance together is in everyone's best interest."

"She's ashamed, I think," he said softly. "Ashamed of what I am. Of appearing in public in my company. Among her friends. And perhaps even…" This time it was his rich voice that hesitated. Unconsciously his fingers made their habitual reassurance of the placement of the patch. "But in private… As long as we're alone… I swear to you that Maddy's happy. And that she wants for nothing."

The duchess waited a long time for any other information that he might wish to add, but Jean-Luc had confessed more than he had ever intended to reveal about their situation. He stood with his gaze resting on the skilled fingers that held the elegant beaver hat.

"How disappointing," the duchess said quietly. He looked up to find her eyes moving again over his features. "The ladies would be so vexed. No dark degradation or sexual captivity. Only a love story. And one *they* couldn't possibly understand. The other makes for much more titillating conversation, for shocked and excited whispers hidden discreetly behind their fans." There was an undercurrent of bitterness in the soft words.

"And you believe you *can* understand?" he questioned, trying to read whatever was in her voice.

"Because of his limp, they call my husband Cripplegate. Behind his back, of course. It would never do to offend the powerful Duke of Avon."

Their eyes held, and he read in hers compassion and understanding. When she spoke again, the darkness was cleared from her voice.

"I'll only be a moment. Tell Hawkins if you'd like anything. I promise you I have just the mount…"

Her voice faded as she almost ran up the huge stairs and disappeared into the upper reaches of her husband's Mayfair mansion, leaving Jean-Luc to wonder if the Duchess of Avon might, indeed, understand Maddy's ability to care for someone like him.

"I don't understand all the secrecy, and I've told you that I really don't—"

"For me, Maddy. Surely I haven't asked you for so many favors that you would refuse a simple request." He caught her shoulders from behind as she turned away, and he pulled her body against his.

"No, of course not. You've asked for nothing, but you refuse to tell me anything about the purpose or the destination."

"Just trust me, my darling. A short carriage ride. Is that so much to ask?"

"I just don't want—"

"But I want. For me, Maddy," he said, touching his lips to the silver-gilt tendrils that had escaped the pile of loose curls.

"Unfair," she accused softly, turning her head so that her cheek rested against the softness of his raven hair. "You take unfair advantage of all my weaknesses."

"I know," he breathed against the small depression formed by her collarbone and then caressed it with his tongue. "And I hope you continue to be weak where I'm concerned."

"Are you describing the state of my knees or of my morals, sir?"

"I'm not sure there's a difference. As I remember, they have both, on occasion, gotten in my way."

Laughing, she turned her body in his arms so that she was pressed against his long length.

"I notice the past tense," she teased.

"Is that what it's called in English?" he said in mock

astonishment as he molded his aching body against hers. "What an interesting construction."

Her fingers moved over him as she whispered, "Indeed it is. And trust the French to know exactly how to use something without knowing the proper name for it."

Laughing, he carried her back to the wide, unmade bed and they were, in consequence, late for their appointment.

He had known by Maddy's face that he'd been wrong. But he couldn't understand how terribly wrong. Not even when she'd raised shocked, wildly dilated eyes to his.

"No," she'd whispered.

The groom was turning the duchess's beautiful mare, putting her through a formalized pattern of movements designed to show off all her delicate breeding to the best advantage. The small, elegant head, the huge, darkly intelligent eyes, the incredibly fragile legs that would prove so tireless when called upon by a beloved rider.

"No," Maddy said again, and he could see the shimmering tremble that had begun to move through her entire body. "Oh, God," she whispered as the boy began to lead the Arabian closer to where they were standing. She turned and stumbled back in the direction they had come. Unsuspecting, she had allowed Jean-Luc to lead her to the duke's stables, past the groomed lawns and neat fencing, to the spotless paddocks.

He caught her long before she had reached the carriage. He turned her to face him, relieved to find she wasn't crying. And then, reading what was in the violet eyes, he had known that what he was seeing was far worse than tears, pain beyond the comfort of that easy release.

"Maddy," he said softly, at a loss. He had been so sure that she'd be pleased. He'd wanted to give her something she'd enjoy. The dresses that Genevieve continued to supply had been greeted with smiling gratitude, but they were obviously unneeded in her continued and determined isolation.

He thought suddenly of the navy habit that Ling was to bring upstairs while they were gone. So it would be there when they returned. He'd made arrangements for the stabling of the mare close enough that Maddy could ride whenever she wanted. But instead of giving her pleasure...

"I told you," she accused bitterly. "I explained to you," she said, her shoulders twisting in an attempt to escape his hold. "Why don't you understand?"

"What's wrong? What's the matter? I thought you'd be pleased. She's yours. You can—"

"No," she said violently, her hands pushing against his. "She's not mine. She can never be mine." Her eyes were suddenly attracted to something past his shoulder, dilating again, and Jean-Luc looked behind him to find the puzzled groom leading the mare toward where they stood arguing in the sun.

Jean-Luc's hands had relaxed enough with that distraction that Maddy was able to pull away. She ran, faster than he would have believed possible in the thin kid slippers, ignoring the uneven ground. Again he caught her easily, given the vastly superior advantage of his longer stride.

But when he stopped her this time, she hit at him, her small fists pounding ineffectively against his broad chest. Bewildered by the fury that was driving her, he grabbed at her flailing hands. He caught the right wrist easily, the unthinking strength of his grip hard enough that it would leave bruises on the fair, almost transparent skin. Her left struck then at his face. She was sobbing now, the immediate shock that he could be so stupid, could do this to her, having given way to anger. And with the expression of her rage had finally come the tears.

"Why don't you understand?" she said, hitting at him again. He turned his head slightly, avoiding the force of the blow. Her hand had, however, achieved an unintended swipe against the cloth of the patch, so that it moved. He reached to straighten it, the instinct so ingrained that his fingers automatically began that self-protective gesture even in the midst of trying to deal with the unleashed emotions of his wife. Seeing that familiar movement, she caught at the ribbon that secured the patch. Again he dodged, but she ripped the whole thing away, revealing for the first time the blind, clouded eye enclosed in its misshapen socket.

The impact of what she had done held them both motionless a moment. As her hand fell slowly to her side, the dark material of the patch formed a sharp contrast against the pale muslin gown.

He took a deep breath and deliberately released the wrist he'd held. He forced himself not to turn away. She had wanted to humiliate him. Retaliation for whatever he had done to make her so angry. He would allow her the satisfaction. She had wanted to expose what lay beneath the cloth, and now it was revealed. He controlled his breathing and watched her face.

Her appalled gaze fell finally from what she'd just uncovered. And when she spoke, all anger had faded from her voice, but the dark bitterness was still apparent.

"You hide your past. You keep it carefully covered, so no one can see how you've been hurt. So no one will know what's been done to you. You even hide it from me. But I told you about the ugliness in mine. I didn't hide. I told you."

Despite what he was feeling, he responded to the quiet desperation. The accusation. The pain of that whisper. God, Maddy, he thought, wondering... "What did I do?" he asked softly, his fingers touching under her chin to force her eyes up. He saw her gaze lock again on the damaged eye and then move finally to meet the other.

"It was the horses. I told you," she said.

"I don't understand. Tell me again," he said patiently.

"He hurt my horses," she whispered. And then, of course, he knew. *He hurts things. Things I love,* she'd told him. Because she had included him into that circle, he'd lost the full meaning of that admission in his response to the unexpected confession of her love.

"Your stepfather?" he said, and it was strictly by form a question.

She nodded, the movement perceptible only because he was still touching her chin.

"He's dead, Maddy."

The caustic smile that answered that assurance was more chilling than anything she had said. As if his evil might reach out from the grave and touch their lives.

"He can't hurt you anymore."

She shook her head, remembering the long, slowly healing gash Ned Stapleton had made in her husband's side.

She turned away and began to walk back to the carriage. She was unaware that she still held the velvet patch and its ribbon in her hand.

He gestured to the groom who had been standing, watching them, to take the horse back to her stall, and then he moved to catch up, walking beside her until they were almost to the carriage.

"What did he do?" he asked. He didn't know if he were wise to make her talk about it, but he needed to know as much as she would tell him, so he could find a way to help her deal with it. *You hide your past,* she'd said, but he was honest enough to admit that there had been times when he'd longed to tell her, to explain why it was so hard for him to admit how much he cared for her.

She turned at the question, studying the dark face for a moment. She glanced down at the trailing black ribbon in her hand, and almost as an offering, she handed it to him.

She had expected that he'd immediately put it back on, but he surprised her. He took the proffered cloth, but he made no move to cover the ruined eye.

"Talk to me," he said instead. "Tell me what he did."

She waited a long time, the spring sun strong enough that she could feel its warmth against the back of her shoulders, a contrast to the chill inside. Because she had done to him the unforgivable, she forced herself to answer.

"He shot the first. A mare I'd had from childhood. But it was cleanly done, and… I was heartbroken, but it was done. I thought it was all over. I couldn't conceive that there was anything else, anything worse, that he could do. And so, blindly stupid, I still refused. I didn't want to marry an old man. I knew what I wanted—the man I'd dreamed of for so long. And I was so young. And so stubborn." Her voice hesitated, and she shivered again, but she forced herself to continue.

"I'd always been stubborn. He'd punished me before. When I was younger. When I'd defied him. Once he cut up a new ball gown. And one of the hounds had disappeared. It had been sold. At least that's what he'd told me. Afterward, I wondered... But he'd never done anything like...the horses. He was desperate. He needed the money to save the estate, and then, when he thought he'd found the solution, I refused to marry Fairchild. I thought if I held out, he'd realize that he couldn't accomplish what he wanted. I thought..."

The quiet voice halted, remembering.

"But he'd learned that I could live with death. And so he locked me in my room, and then he took Heart's Fire and brought him under my window. And...he began to hurt him." Her voice was only a whisper.

"I tried to make him stop. I screamed at him that I'd do anything he wanted, but he wouldn't stop. And finally he did, but it was too late. Maybe it was too late from the beginning. Maybe it was his punishment for my daring to refuse to do what he wanted. And when he brought out the next one..." She shivered.

"He's dead, Maddy," he said again.

"I know," she whispered. She didn't tell him that Harry had been at the house that day. He couldn't have stopped his father, even had he wanted to. She knew Harry had some genuine feelings for her, some affection because she was his sister. She had tried to mother him when their mother had died. She'd loved the sad little boy he'd been. But as he'd gotten older, she'd recognized that same streak of cruelty within Harry. When he was angry. And when he was drinking. Her stepfather had been drinking that day. He was always worse...

"He can't hurt you anymore," Jean-Luc said.

She shook her head. There was so much that she couldn't explain. If she told him what she suspected about Harry's intentions, if he realized that she was still afraid of her half brother, she knew that he'd do something. Something that might drive Harry to take action.

He had smiled at her fears before, so confident that he could protect them both. But she'd already seen Harry's long reach touch their lives through Stapleton's actions. She had pushed Harry's challenge to the back of her mind. Trying to deny that it meant something, but she knew well enough it had. Harry would never put himself in danger of a duel unless he were playing for very high stakes. She wondered again what her brother wanted, and she knew that unless he found some other way to bring his plans to fruition, she'd be hearing again from Harry.

"You don't understand," she said. "I don't want the mare. I don't ever want to ride again. That's over and dead. I can't ever do that again. If I even think about horses…" She stopped, swallowing her fear, forcing away the memory of what Mannering had done. Forcing away the image of her impotence that day. She hadn't been able to protect Heart's Fire.…

"I'm sorry," he said. "I only wanted to give you pleasure. I never intended to hurt you or to make you remember."

He was apologizing for something that had been done only to please her. Something he could have had no way of knowing would make her unhappy. There had been, in his actions, no deliberate attempt to wound. And she, on the other hand, had done to him the cruelest thing she could conceive, deliberately and with malice.

Maybe she had lived with the brutality of the Mannering rages so long that it had marked her. What she had done to him this morning was despicable. And she had done it because he was trying to give her a gift, something he had thought would bring her joy.

Her thumb lifted to brush along the drooping lid that half hid the blind eye. He didn't avoid her touch, and so she put her palms on his cheeks and pulled his face down until she could touch her lips against the scarred socket. And then she released him and stepped back, waiting for whatever he wanted to say, knowing that, whatever it was, she deserved it.

"Am I forgiven?" he asked softly.

Feeling the sting of tears, she closed her eyes against the concern and love that was in the quiet question. *Am I forgiven?* she wanted to ask in reply, but she knew she didn't deserve his forgiveness for that assault.

Wordlessly she nodded.

"Then let's go home," he suggested, his voice as caressing as when he made love to her.

He helped her into the carriage, but she held herself carefully erect as the horses began to move. Emotionally drained, she denied the compulsion to bury her head against the dark, elegant coat and feel his hard arms around her. Instead, she sat stiffly in the corner of the coach, consumed by guilt and regret.

"It's over, Maddy," he said softly, watching her. "Let it go, my darling. It's all over, and things are exactly as they were before. Soon we'll be home, and you'll feel safe again. I'll keep you safe. I promise."

She turned then into his chest, his arms enfolding her as if he'd never let her go.

I'll keep you safe, her thoughts echoed. But unlike his, that vow was not spoken aloud, because she knew he still didn't understand.

Chapter Eleven

Maddy and Jean-Luc usually had dinner together—before Jean-Luc went downstairs—much earlier than was the custom in the fine homes of the city. And later Ling would bring up some small repast to break the tedium of the long hours she spent waiting for her husband.

Ling brought the envelope up with her supper that night. Maddy recognized the handwriting immediately. Harry's scrawl. The bile rose so strongly in her throat that she thought for a moment she might really be ill. She swallowed the nausea and sat perfectly still, trying to think calmly about what she should do. She had promised that she'd tell Jean-Luc if Harry bothered her again. And she didn't want to lie to him. She wanted their relationship to be as open and as honest as the secrets they both concealed would allow. She supposed that was ridiculous, but she didn't intend to hide anything from him again. She remembered his anger when he'd returned from White's.

The envelope lay innocently on the tray beside the fruit and cheese. As innocent as a viper coiled to strike. She wondered how she was going to deal with this. And she wondered, of course, what Harry wanted. She needed to know, but if she did, then she'd have to lie again. And into this marriage would come deception and mistrust. She took a deep breath, trying to think. She wished it had never been delivered, that she didn't have to handle this.

Without giving herself time to change her mind, she rose and hurried across the hall to Jean-Luc's office. She dipped the pen in the well and scratched out her own name and wrote, above the marks she'd made, Harry's name and direction.

When Ling returned for her tray, he found that nothing had been touched, but he made no comment. He knew that whatever his master had planned this afternoon had not gone well. He had been sent by the coachman to retrieve the new habit before the boss and his lady had even descended from the carriage.

"Would you see that's delivered, please," the lady asked.

She was standing by the window, looking down into the London street.

Ling nodded, wondering, but again he didn't ask. Unconsciously he shrugged, but Maddy's eyes had moved back to the darkness below, and she didn't see his puzzlement.

During the next two days she waited, almost dreading Ling's arrival every night. But there were no more messages. No attempt by Harry to again communicate, and gradually she allowed herself to relax, to drift back into the cocoon of Jean-Luc's care. Back into the security of the narrow world they shared, the world that was all she now wanted. Just to be left alone.

She was sitting in the chair by the table reading when the door opened. Ling had already picked up the supper tray, and she knew it was too early for Jean-Luc. Unless, as sometimes happened, he had come up before the casino closed. Because he couldn't stay away from her any longer, he'd admitted. Her sudden gladness at that thought must have shown in the eyes that she raised to the shadowed form standing in the opened doorway.

"I've come to take you out of here," Ned Stapleton said softly, seeing and misinterpreting the leap of joy in those beautiful violet blue eyes. He'd always thought she had the most wonderfully expressive eyes in the world. And now she was looking at him as if...

And then her expression changed, the quick anticipation fading to puzzlement and then to something else. Fear, perhaps. Maybe she was afraid for him. Afraid that if that French bastard came upstairs before he could get her dressed and away...

"What are you doing here, Ned?" she asked. She stood up, the opened book falling forgotten to the floor before her bare feet. The sheer cotton of her rail provided little concealment for her slim body, especially with the soft lamp on the table behind her now.

"I've come to take you away. No one else would do anything," he said, moving into the room, "and so I knew that I had to. Don't be afraid, Maddy. I won't let him hurt you again."

"Hurt me?" she repeated.

She looked bewildered. He wondered suddenly if her mind might be unhinged. If only half the things they said were true, then he should be surprised to find her reason intact. But he'd take care of her. No one would ever hurt her again.

"What are you talking about?" she asked softly into the silence.

"The Frenchman. Gavereau. He'll never touch you again, Maddy. I promise."

"Jean-Luc?" she whispered, still trying to fathom what he was suggesting. The images that had driven him to this gallant rescue were so foreign to the reality of the relationship she shared with her husband, she was finding it difficult to believe that he could really think she was afraid of Jean-Luc.

"Come, my dear. I promise you'll be safe. From now on. I'll never let him near you again."

He held out his hand, and unthinkingly she put her right into his outstretched palm. After all, he was a very old and dear friend. However, she could make no sense of his invasion of her bedroom. And, she suddenly remembered, he was the one who had hurt Jean-Luc. Had he come there to attack her husband on Harry's behalf as he had apparently done before?

If so, why was he trying to get her to come with him? And in her nightgown. None of it made sense.

"My God," he said softly. She glanced up at that shocked whisper and saw that his eyes were locked on the livid bruises that darkened her wrist. "My God," he said again, looking up into her eyes.

They were still as wide and troubled as when he'd appeared in her doorway. And since all the terrible stories apparently were true, he didn't wonder that she no longer seemed capable of making a decision. Despite the fact that rescue was at hand, she was still too afraid of that brute and all that he had done to her to try to leave.

He put his arm around her shoulders, but she moved away from him.

"Don't," she said, shocked by the liberty he had just taken.

"I'm not going to hurt you, Maddy," he said, talking calmly as if he were soothing a panicked horse. He put his hand on hers, but again she pulled away. "I'm not the one—"

"I think you should take your hands off my wife, Lord Stapleton. She doesn't seem to be eager for your intervention into our affairs," her husband spoke from the open doorway.

"I really don't care what you think. I'm going to take Maddy out of here, if I have to kill you to do it."

"No," Jean-Luc said, and Maddy could see the small smile tugging at the corner of his mouth.

"Now that I've seen with my own eyes... Now that I have proof, do you think I'll leave her a moment longer under your control? Do you think I'll let you hurt her again?"

"Maddy," Jean-Luc said, "have I hurt you, my darling?"

"No," she denied, wondering again what this was all about. What proof was he talking about? "Of course not. But what in the world—"

"Do you want to go with Stapleton, Maddy?" Jean-Luc's question interrupted her spate of confusion. The hazel eye had never left the viscount's face.

"No," she said strongly. "You know I don't want to go anywhere."

"My God, Maddy," Stapleton exploded. "What the hell

has he done to you? Don't you understand? I've come for you.''

''But—''

''It's you who doesn't understand. Maddy doesn't want to leave. I told you before. Whatever you're imagining, whatever knightly rescue you've undertaken here, you're mistaken.''

''Imagining?'' Stapleton repeated incredulously. And then again, mocking. ''Imagining. As I suppose I've imagined those marks on her wrist. They said you kept her tied. While you... But I never believed... No one, no sane, civilized human being could do that to a woman. But I saw them. Deny these, you bastard.''

He caught Maddy's arm and held it out to the light.

Jean-Luc glanced down at the fragile bones banded by the circling marks his fingers had made. She had kept them carefully hidden because she had known how he would regret them. And because she had known that she was the one who had really done the damage. She was the only one who should bear any remorse for that scene in the Duke of Avon's paddocks.

''No,'' her husband said softly, ''I don't deny that I'm responsible for those.''

He took her hand from Stapleton, who, from sheer incredulity over the brazenness of that answer, didn't intervene.

The Frenchman lifted her wrist, putting his lips against the bruises, olived and already beginning to fade. He was watching her face, but whatever passed between them, whatever silent communication was made, was too subtle for the viscount to understand.

''Get out, Stapleton,'' the gambler said, still holding Maddy's hand. ''I really don't want to kill you.''

''You're not frightening me. I'm not afraid of your threats. That may work with Mannering and with women, but not with me.''

''She's not going anywhere with you. She doesn't want to go. Look at her.''

''Maddy,'' the viscount said rather desperately. Her eyes

were resting on the scarred face of the gambler as if there were no one else in the room.

"No," she whispered, but she never looked at him. "I don't want to go with you, Ned. I'm sorry you came. I don't know why you came, but I'm not leaving my husband."

"You don't have to be afraid. I promise, Maddy."

She turned to him then, shaking her head. "I'm not afraid. I don't know why you *think* I'm afraid. I don't know what you believe is going on here, but—"

"I know damn well what's going on. All of London knows. Everyone knows he's keeping you prisoner in order to…"

His voice faded, and the color rushed under his fair skin.

"In order to what?" Maddy asked, not understanding his reticence.

"To use you," he said finally.

Her eyes widened as the import of what he'd just suggested reached her brain.

"Are you saying that…?" She stopped, unable to find the words to convey the ridiculousness of that accusation. "And all of London thinks…"

"No one would do anything. Not even Harry. So I've come, Maddy. And I don't intend to leave without you."

"Ned," she said, controlling her first impulse, which had been to laugh. To glance at Jean-Luc and to see in his face, in the mobile corner of his mouth, his amusement. To share the humor of this unbelievable situation.

Then the small gun was in the viscount's hand, and that hand was moving slowly to train the deadly eye on her husband's midsection. And nothing was the least bit amusing anymore.

Jean-Luc had been anticipating the movement or something like it since he'd entered the room. His booted foot kicked upward, its speed blurring the arched motion. The gun flew from Stapleton's hand and fell onto the counterpane of the bed. It bounced softly, and Maddy took a breath, wondering how long it had been since she'd remembered to do that.

The viscount was holding his right hand carefully with the

left. Staring defiantly at the gambler as if he expected him to pick up the pistol and put a ball through him.

"Get out," Jean-Luc said softly. "And don't ever bother my wife again. I'm warning you this time, Stapleton, because I believe your intentions were good, but I'll tolerate no more interference in my affairs. Do you understand?"

"You bloody bastard," Ned said, hatred filling his quiet voice. "I'll see you in hell."

"Probably," Jean-Luc agreed calmly. "But not tonight."

He moved across the bedroom and, expertly twisting the viscount's uninjured arm behind his back, Jean-Luc pushed the struggling Englishman out the door and to the head of the stairs.

"I imagine, since you found your way in, you can manage to see yourself out."

He turned back and walked into the bedroom, locking the door behind him.

He waited for Maddy to look at him. He hadn't realized that he'd bruised her that day. He understood now why the gowns she'd chosen the last two days all were fashioned with sleeves that fell over her wrists. He took her fingers and felt their trembling reaction to the scene that had just ended.

"I'm sorry," he said, thinking only about those marks.

"Explain to me what he was talking about," she said, raising her eyes to his.

"About your wrist?"

"About what all of London knows. Explain to me what that meant."

"I don't know, and frankly, I don't care what London thinks. I only care what you think."

"Ned said that everyone believes you're holding me prisoner. That you've kept me tied in order to use me." Her voice rose in sharp mockery. But again, remembering the hatred in the Englishman's eyes and the deadly menace of the pistol he had held trained on her husband's body, she lost that sense of the ridiculous.

"That's an interesting image," Jean-Luc said softly, his own amusement washing sensuously through the dark whisper. "I've never personally thought bondage an aphrodisiac, although I know that some men, and even some women, find that very exciting. Would you like to tie me to the bed, Maddy, and 'use me'?" he asked. He raised the fingers he still held to his lips and caressed them, his gaze considering her face, waiting for the fright and the tension to leave.

She pulled her fingers from his grasp, and he watched her quick intelligence replace her fear. She wasn't about to be sidetracked by his suggestion that they make love. He wouldn't be able to fob her off with an assault on her senses.

"What did he mean?" she asked again.

"He's in love with you. Surely you knew that. He's jealous that you're mine, and, I suppose, he envisioned himself as the hero of this rescue. He probably thought—"

"Don't," she cautioned softly. "Don't lie to me. You made me promise that I'd not conceal things from you, and now, when one of my friends," and, more importantly, one of Harry's, she thought, "has just attempted to kill you again, you're trying to make me believe it's because he's some kind of lovesick suitor. What did he mean that all of London knows you're holding me prisoner? Is that what they imagine about our marriage?"

His lips tightened. He had promised that he could protect her and, instead, he had allowed Stapleton to frighten her. No wonder she didn't believe she was secure. And if he told her what was being said, of the implications for his own safety that the situation held…

"Tell me," she demanded again.

"They think you were forced to marry me. That Harry made you, and that I've kept you prisoner to prevent your leaving me."

"But surely," she whispered, "surely they must realize that in this day and age no woman can be dragged protesting to the altar."

Her voice stopped. She had walked to the altar of her first marriage under her own power, nothing of the brutality that had compelled her obedience allowed to show in the straight, proud carriage of her shoulders and rigid spine.

"Surely they can't believe that?" she argued, but she knew very well that there were so many ways to compel people to do things that were against their will.

He said nothing, because she could never imagine all that was being suggested about their relationship. She had, despite Fairchild's tutelage, no way to conceive the viciousness of the rumors that were rampant in the capital. The dark perversions that he supposedly visited on her helpless body each night.

"They can believe whatever evil their minds can conceive," he said bitterly. "They look at me, and they remember what you look like, and then they know that there can be nothing *but* perversion in our coupling."

"Stop it," she said sharply, hating the word he had chosen for their lovemaking. Hating, too, the pain she heard underlying the mockery. *They look at me, and they remember what you look like.* They *remember* what you look like.

God, she'd been so stupid, she realized suddenly. She had held the key all along to protecting him from this particular threat. Even Madame Darnet had told her. And she had lost that determination in the sensual pleasure of this room, in his hard arms and in the sweet touch of his mouth. She'd not used her power to protect him from their twisted minds and from the sickening corruption they had made out of the love he had given her.

"Because I've hidden in this room," she said. She watched him exercise control over the stern line of his lips. "Because I haven't gone out into public on your arm, they think that you're keeping me prisoner. How could you have let me do that? Why didn't you tell me what was going on?"

"You don't have to do anything you don't want to do. I refuse to let my existence, or yours, be governed by what that circle of arrogant, perfumed fops and whispering old dragons think. If you don't want to appear in public with me, it's none of their affair."

"If I don't want…" she repeated, wondering. And then the full reality of the cruelty she had practiced stuck home. He believed that she was ashamed to be seen with him. And at first she had given him cause. The unthinking remarks at the dressmaker's, hiding her face when he had helped her from the coach, her hesitation to go with him to see the mare. All of those he had interpreted as a reluctance to be seen in public with him. Because he was not of her class or because...

She glanced up to find the uncaring mask carefully back in place. Nothing of the endless hurt she had inflicted allowed to show.

"That's not why..." she began to deny, and recognized, unbelievingly, the bitter smile of his disbelief touch upward. She had not seen that mocking expression since the first days of their relationship, but all along the idea that she found the scars repulsive, that she didn't want to be seen with him because of them, had been beneath the surface of his seeming acceptance of her love. "I would have been proud to go with you anywhere. Why didn't you ever..." she began and saw the sardonic amusement deepen.

"The dinner party," she whispered, remembering. "That's why you suggested that we go to the party together."

"And you refused," he said.

"Because I didn't know your friends."

"And because you were afraid, when you met them, that they would be vulgar and common. Like your husband."

"No," she whispered, shaking her head, but acknowledging to herself, at least, that she had wondered what kind of people his friends would be. Guilty, she thought, but having seen that quickly hidden agony in his face, she could not admit that guilt. Not to protect herself, but to protect him.

"No," she denied, her voice stronger. "I didn't want to leave this room. I only wanted what we shared. There was nothing out there in that world that I remembered with pleasure. Nothing I ever wanted to return to. Only you were important. You comprise my whole world, Jean-Luc. I don't want anything else."

He was watching her eyes. And because there was no deception in that, at least, he found himself once more believing her. Because you want to believe, he mocked himself. Because you want so much to believe her.

"I love you," she whispered. "How can you not know that?"

He held her gaze for a long time, no longer touching her. Trying to read what was in her eyes and in her voice. His years of experience in reading faces seemed useless now. He would stake his life that she was telling the truth. *Because you want to believe,* he again mocked that useless wager. *Because you won't* have *a life if she's lying. At least, not one that you'll want to live.*

His eye fell suddenly before the sincerity in the beautiful violet ones. Slowly he shook his head.

"Not a dinner party," she said finally. She had had to force herself not to touch him. She was so afraid that he would avoid her touch. As he had avoided answering that anguished confession. She had given him the ultimate power over her. I love you, she had said, and he had said nothing in return.

He glanced up, waiting.

"I think it must be the most public place in London. Covent Garden, perhaps. And I shall wear the lavender silk. Will you take me to the theater, Jean-Luc? I imagine no one will watch the stage, but with your cooperation, I believe that I can put an end to these ridiculous rumors. If you'll help me..."

"Maddy," he said, and she watched him swallow, and then again, shake his head. "You don't have to do this," he suggested.

"Yes, I think I do. Because I don't like it when someone points a pistol at my husband's...past tense," she finished softly, forcing herself to smile, to find a shred of humor in a situation that had held only pain.

He looked up, the relieved amusement pushing against his firm lips.

"And I think you mentioned something about tying you to the bed and having my way with you. If you're still willing..." she suggested.

"No," he said. Again he took a deep breath. His hand caught hers, and his thumb traced over the dark marks his fingers had caused that day. "No," he repeated, "I have a much better idea. If you trust my perverted mind to find something that will give you pleasure.''

"You have never given me anything but pleasure," she said softly.

"I'd like…" he began and then forced the words back into his brain. I'd like to give you what you have just given me, he allowed himself to think. But his was a silent admission. I love you, she had said, and he had echoed it in his dark gambler's heart.

Instead of saying the words, he pulled her into his arms, pushing the painful fullness of his body against hers. Her fingers caressed him, familiarly touching. Unable to wait, he unbuttoned the neck of her nightgown and slipped it off her shoulders so that she stood before him, beautifully nude and slightly smiling. She moved back against him, her fingers finding the waist of his evening trousers and quickly unfastening the flap that closed the front. Despite the number of times she had touched him, his breath caught when she freed him from the constraint of the closely fitting undergarment. The cool air of the room touched against his overheated flesh that wanted her, that needed her, so desperately. Uncaring for the first time in their relationship of what she wanted, he lifted her.

"Put your legs around my waist," he commanded harshly, his mouth moving against her hair. His breath was coming in gasps, his need so intense that he couldn't think beyond burying himself as quickly as he could into the sweet, always welcoming acceptance of Maddy. She obeyed with no hesitation, her arms holding tightly around his neck.

He used his hand to guide himself, thrusting frantically into her. He heard her breath rush out, the soft moan, and he was suddenly harder, larger, more desperate. He took two steps, carrying her, until he was holding her against the wall. His breath sawed in and out, mocking the almost frantic movements of his body. Plunging deeply, trying to lose all that had happened tonight in her sweetness. Trying to forget that he had revealed the pain. Trying to remember only her words. *I love you.* And the force of that remembrance drove him also.

He could hear the soft, repeating impact of her body against the wall as he rammed himself deeper and deeper into the hot, wet tightness of Maddy, into her acceptance of who and what he was.

She had never felt anything like his complete domination. Her body was on fire, his heat scalding all along the length of their joining. Everywhere he touched her—her smooth, soft belly against the ridged muscles of his, her aching breasts pressed against the hard wall of his chest under the teasing roughness of his coat, her thighs clasping his driving hips— every inch of her skin that was in contact with him was over-sensitized, her nerves too aware of his need. She wanted to scream, to release the force of what he was causing her to feel. She was too full. Too consumed by him. He was too much, too compelling; too much was demanded of her. She didn't know how to answer this. She only wanted to take him all, to absorb him as he seemed to be absorbing what was left of her will, driving her to wildness with the hard surety of his experience.

Her nails bit into his neck, and he welcomed the pain because he was suddenly afraid that he might be hurting her. He didn't want to ever hurt her. His care had been so exquisite that she should never feel discomfort or...

And now he was treating her as he had seen men treat the women in the house where he had grown up. Once he had wandered out into the hallway in response to this same rhythmic thump against the outside wall of his room. The sound that he couldn't stop produced the memory, sharp and painful. A small, dark-haired boy standing silently in his nightshirt— watching a drunk use one of his lovely, sweet-smelling *tantes* exactly as he was now using his own wife.

His wife, he thought in bitter self-disgust, but nothing could halt the throbbing necessity that was fueling whatever emotion directed his actions. Her teeth caught fiercely at his shoulder, hurting him even through the cloth of his coat and shirt, as she smothered another moan, and in response to that sound, he tried to check the pounding movement of his hips. God, he thought, I'm destroying the trust I've spent these weeks building. Treating her like that old, rutting bastard...

"Don't," she begged, and his heart stopped, his veins all clogged with ice.

He forced himself not to move. He couldn't trust himself to allow any movement because, despite that anguished plea, he wanted only to drive into her again.

Oh, Maddy, my darling, I'm so sorry, he thought, sick with despair over what he had done.

"Don't," she pleaded again. He exercised the rigid control she had never before demanded. But he paid the price. His breath sobbed once, and then he bit into his bottom lip to prevent any other expression of his need. He could taste the blood. His body sagged slightly against the sweat-slick nudity of hers.

And then he heard the soft words whispered against his face.

She begged softly, "Please, Jean-Luc, don't..." Desperate for him, she moved her hips, tightening her legs to raise herself and push down against him. She licked the sweat that was trickling down the dark, unscarred cheek. "Oh, please," she moaned softly. And, with her movement, against his will his body betrayed him. The hard muscles of his thighs bunched and then thrust upward. He heard the soft whimper slip from between her lips. So like the sounds she had always made in response to his lovemaking.

With those memories, the force of his need overcame him again, and he lunged into her relentlessly. Unthinking. Unaware of anything but her body surrounding him. *I love you,* she had said. And he had needed so desperately to believe that she could.

Finally, after endless minutes, it was over, the violence that had never before had any place in their relationship gone, washed away in the hot jets of his seed that he had poured into the receptacle he had just made of Maddy's body.

His Maddy, and he had used her as men had used his mother, with no concern for what she was feeling. Used her just as Fairchild had done. His breathing eased, the gasping inhalations gradually becoming easier to drag into his burning lungs. She was shivering in his hold. His own legs trembled with reaction.

Please, God, don't let her hate me, he silently prayed. But he knew there was nothing he could say. Nothing he could ever do to make up for what had happened between them. Nothing...

"Nothing..." she gasped as if reading his mind. Because he still held her crushed against his body, her mouth moved against the soft velvet of the patch that covered the ruined eye.

That horror of an eye that she had once caressed with her beautiful, perfect lips. His heart hurt with the thought of all he had just lost. The strangled sob caught in his throat, but he knew he couldn't let her see him cry, and he fought for control.

At that strange sound, she leaned her head back against the wall to see his face, still half-hidden by the shadows. Her hair was wildly disordered, clinging in damp strands to her shoulders and gilded tendrils still caught in the sheen of perspiration on his face and neck.

"I had thought," she began again, her own breathing gasping and harsh, "that there was nothing else that you could... Nothing that you hadn't done..."

"Maddy, I'm so sorry—" he began, not understanding her gasping confession.

"But that..." she interrupted his hesitant whisper. "You've always touched me as if you thought I might break, might bruise if you did more than brush your fingers over me, or your lips."

From somewhere in the bitter regret he found a tentative smile to answer her. He had no idea what he could do or say. Holding her body against the wall with his hips, still joined to her, but feeling already the softening effects of his release, he moved his hand from behind her and caught the bruised wrist and raised it again to his lips.

Around the touch of his mouth against her skin, he whispered, "Because that's true."

"But I don't care. And if there are bruises," she said, smiling at him, "no one will ever see them but you. And you can kiss each one and make it well. Because, my darling, I have never experienced anything like that. Despite all that you have made me feel, I never dreamed…"

She stopped at what was in his face.

"Then you don't hate me? You didn't mind?" he asked, unable to believe what she had just said.

"Mind?" she repeated. And her laughter, when it came, was so beautiful. "Mind?" she repeated again, still laughing. "No, my sweet, French, very experienced idiot, I didn't mind. How could you believe that? It was so…"

"So what?" he asked, his relief so powerful, so overwhelming, his legs had begun to tremble again. He didn't want her to know how afraid he'd been. He hid what he was feeling by nuzzling his face into the soft space between her jaw and the curve of her shoulder. He could feel the tangled strands of her hair, damp against his cheek.

"I don't know. So powerful. So undeniable. Elemental."

"It was certainly undeniable. But I never intended to hurt you. Not even to give you pleasure."

"I know," she said, her lips finding his ear. Her tongue traced against the small maze that led to the entrance and then eased inside, caressing.

"I love you," she whispered again. And although she felt the response of his body growing between her aching thighs, his lips never formed the words.

"Come here," she said softly.

"Here?" he asked, finally amused, finally accepting that he wasn't going to lose her. "I couldn't *be* any more here."

"Yes," she said, moving inside, her body caressing inwardly against his growing arousal, although her back was very still against the wall.

She felt his reaction, his head lifting to communicate his surprise. She tensed again, and he reacted to her deliberate teasing.

"Maddy," he warned softly.

"Like you do to my breasts," she said, remembering the

gentle pull of his mouth. And she tightened against him again, controlling muscles she had never before used to deliberately entice him.

"Don't move," she demanded. "Let me see if…"

He obeyed as long as he was able. Letting her control. In bondage, he thought in amusement, and then his body betrayed his iron control, causing him to again plunge deeply and uncontrollably into her.

"Maddy," he said, all that he seemed capable of saying, of thinking.

"I think you're right," she whispered, tightening her thighs and welcoming his motion that surged into her body like the swell of ocean waves. Undeniable.

"Now," she urged again, and once more he obeyed. Lost. Lost in Maddy. Because he loved her.

Chapter Twelve

"I don't intend that anyone shall even remember what's on the playbill tonight," Maddy declared fervently as her husband fastened the last of the tiny covered buttons that secured the back of the lavender silk.

"What do you think?" she asked, turning slowly for his inspection, sorry for the first time that she hadn't accepted his offer to have Ling secure a mirror. She had to be perfect. Madame Darnet had suggested that her beauty might prevent the hurtful remarks she was afraid he'd hear tonight. That it might instead make them wonder why she was so in love with him. Someone that they could never consider worthy of that love.

As he stood watching her pivot, the silk swirling about her ankles like an iridescent rainbow, he couldn't know how elegantly handsome she thought him, the smooth sheen of his evening dress and his hair, gleaming blue black, catching the soft light of the lamp.

When she stopped her pirouette, his lips quirked slightly, and she wondered if he were amused at her question. Or amused that she was so nervous. She only wanted this night to be over, to prove to all of them how much she loved him. And to prove that their vicious rumors were lies.

"I think," he said, his voice and his face now very serious, "that you are the most beautiful woman London will ever have the pleasure of viewing. And I don't want to share you with any of the bastards who will ogle you tonight. Are you sure, my darling, that you wouldn't rather stay at home? The two of us?''

But remembering Ned's words last night and the terror of that the small pistol he'd held, she shook her head.

''I want to go, now, before my hair begins to tumble down from this ridiculous style that I shouldn't have tried. I don't know why…''

She stopped, watching his eyes rise to study the upswept swirl of soft curls and then seeing again the sudden lift of his lips.

''If that happened, then I would never get you back home,'' he said softly.

''Why?'' she asked, smiling at the teasing note in his response.

''Because if anyone else saw you as you were last night, with that glorious hair spread over your bare shoulders and spilling across your breasts—''

''Well, you may certainly put your mind at ease about that,'' she interrupted decisively, before he could again seduce her. She picked up the evening shawl Madame Darnet had designed. It was of the same material as the dress, which fell straight from the raised waistline. Small silver roses decorated the bottom of the gown. She didn't like the fuller, more ornamented skirts, but they were the mode. And that was important tonight. She must look as assured and as poised as she had when, at seventeen, she had tamped down this same almost sick anticipation at facing the critical eyes of the ton and made her debut.

The door was flung open behind her husband, and he turned with a crouching fighter's stance to confront whatever threat had again entered this very private sanctuary.

She saw him straighten, relaxed, at the sight of the kitchen boy who had been so fascinated by his scars.

The child had rushed, panting, into the room and was standing, trembling with emotion, the paleness of his soot-smeared face almost lost in the saucer spread of dark eyes. His shaking finger pointed down the stairs in the direction he had come.

"They got Ling." He gasped out the message he had come to deliver, trusting that the boss would protect those who belonged to him. "Gentry-coves in the alley. Said you was to come or they'd carve him."

Jean-Luc pushed past the frightened child and was running down the stairs before her brain had made sense of the message.

She caught the boy's shoulder, and his eyes turned back from the darkness into which her husband had disappeared.

"Who are they?" she asked.

"Gentry-coves," he repeated. "Nobs."

"Why do they want Ling?"

"They don't want Ling," the boy denied, scorning her slowness. "They want *him.* The boss." And then importantly, he stated, "You'd best stay here, my lady. Where it's safe. I'll protect you," he promised.

The echo of her pledge. And what was probably happening below, while she stood here stupidly gawking at a child, was all that she had dreaded through the long days as she'd awaited Harry's next move. *Nobs,* the urchin's word mocked. Like Harry. And Ned. Like all the men that were going to punish Jean-Luc because of what he had supposedly done to her.

Her limbs unfroze suddenly, and she was running down the dark stairs with as little regard for her footing as he had displayed. Through the deserted kitchen. He had closed the casino tonight, giving the staff the night off in order to take her to the theater. She saw the open door that led to the alley and Ling's herb garden. The Chinaman had probably been dragged through his own kitchens and out into the darkness, someone to use as leverage to get her husband into their hands.

She could see shadows on the kitchen wall, thrown by the torches that they were carrying. Distorted shapes dancing against the dingy whiteness. And over the suffocating pounding of her own heart, she could hear the mutter of angry voices.

"But I can, at least, take a few of you with me," Jean-Luc was saying, his voice not even raised into the din but penetrating in its clarity and, like the men who stood hesitating in the circle of light made by the smoking flames of their torches, she, too, heard the ring of truth in that quiet utterance.

"Which of you shall be first?" His amused question urged them on. And in mockery of the phrase they had heard, night after night, as they'd played in his elegant hell, he mocked their fear, totally in control of the situation. "Gentlemen, come. I believe it's time once again to place your wagers. For some of you, your last wager."

She slipped out of the open doorway to his right. He appeared to be totally relaxed, standing about three feet in front of her, facing the crowd, his back to her.

One of the men held Ling. Even in the darkness she could see the gleam of light shimmering along the knife's blade as it trembled against the servant's throat.

Jean-Luc felt the reaction to her presence move through the men who were confronting the dark mouths of the pair of dueling pistols he held unwavering, one in each hand. He didn't know what had caused that response, and he knew that even if he glanced to the right, tracking the movement of the eyes that had been watching him and had now shifted to whoever was standing in the darkness at his back, he would not be able to see anything. Because, of course, the new player who had just taken a hand in this game was on his blind side. He couldn't turn far enough to see what was happening behind him and make any pretense that he was still watching the men with the torches.

"You're making a mistake," Maddy said softly, and as it had last night, when he thought he had destroyed all that was between them, he felt the icy fear course, congealing, through veins and arteries, paralyzing nerves and muscles with its terrifying coldness.

"Maddy," he said softly, trying not to convey his fear to her, "go back into the casino."

''No,'' she said calmly. ''Not until I've made them understand.''

''Maddy,'' he said again, sensing the gathering anxiety of the crowd. Her presence was making them remember the reason they had found the courage and the outrage to come here tonight. He had had them under his control, his surety robbing them of theirs. But now, her beauty a reminding reality behind him, he could feel their anger growing at what he had supposedly done to her, its force almost tangible in the narrow confines of the alley.

''My darling,'' he said, and heard the uncertain pleading in a voice he was fighting desperately to control. If anything happened to Maddy… He took a deep breath, forcing power into his words. ''Go back inside, Maddy, and wait for me.''

''She doesn't have to obey you anymore, you scarred monster.'' Lord Stapleton's voice came strongly from the shadows. ''Not anymore, not after tonight. I saw the marks on her wrist where you'd tied her and used her. I saw them with my own eyes.''

''Oh, Ned,'' Maddy said, her frightened voice still behind him, ''I told you that he didn't hurt me. It was an argument. I hit him, and he had to hold my wrist. It was nothing.''

''Trying to protect herself,'' someone in the crowd suggested. ''Poor lass, trying to fight him off.''

''No,'' she said desperately. She stepped out of the shadows at Jean-Luc's back, closer to the semicircle of torches that surrounded her husband. He couldn't see her movement, and because of that, he missed the opportunity to catch her arm as she passed and pull her behind the safety of his body. Even if to do that had meant dropping one of the pistols. But she was beyond his reach when finally the straight, slim figure in the shimmering lavender silk moved into his imperfect field of vision. She was walking toward the crowd, and from its heart a figure came to meet her. Lord Stapleton. And despite himself, Jean-Luc felt relief. Stapleton loved her, and no matter what happened tonight, he'd keep her safe.

She was between him and the throng, in the direct line of

the pistols, unless he fired into the fringes that curved at the edges of the semicircle.

"I am not being held prisoner, whatever you've been told. My husband has never treated me with anything but respect. You must understand."

"Maddy," Stapleton said softly, his voice very strained, as if what she was trying to make them believe were somehow painful to him. "You don't have to be afraid of him anymore. That's why we're here. To take you away. To protect you. Come, my dear. You're safe now."

He came closer to her, and she took an instinctive step backward, toward the muzzles of the two pistols, away from that coaxing voice that was only reinforcing to these watching men all the lies that Harry must have been telling them these weeks. Why wouldn't they believe her?

"Ned, please, please, believe me," she begged, trying to compel him by the force of her sincerity to know that she was telling the truth.

Unthinkingly she held out her hand in entreaty, and felt him catch her wrist, hurting the bruised flesh. She twisted, pulling against his hold, knowing now that approaching the viscount had been a mistake. He was trying to shift her from her deliberately chosen position between the mob and her husband. And she had not been able to convince him last night, his obsession with his dark version of her marriage overriding the truth that she had attempted to show him.

"Let me go," she said angrily, struggling against the strength of his hold. "You're hurting me," she said, and in response to that accusation, Ned's fingers involuntarily loosened. That unexpected release caused Maddy to lose her balance. She stumbled backward, reaching instinctively to Jean-Luc to save her. And moving instead against the pistols.

Her husband automatically lowered the muzzles, keeping her from falling by thrusting his body into hers. Providing stability for her stumbling figure. He waited a second, until he felt that she had regained her balance, and then using his left hand, which still held one of the pistols, he swept her behind him, pushing her strongly enough that she stumbled again, falling this time against the open doorway that led to the kitchen.

The moment the dark menace of the pistols had been blocked, a man in the crowd, reacting more quickly than the rest to the confusion, had begun to act. He had removed the heavy whip he carried coiled over his shoulder. It was a weapon with which he was very skilled. And he had been paid an extremely satisfying amount of money to come here tonight and to demonstrate that skill. And the man who had paid him had indicated that he would, for once, be allowed to fully demonstrate just how effective a weapon the whip could be.

"You're not to be deterred, no matter if the others turn squeamish," the blond man had ordered, smiling. The kind of unflinching order his hireling enjoyed best.

The weighted thong whistled out of the darkness just as Jean-Luc turned back to face the crowd. He hadn't identified the sound before its touch did the damage. He never saw the movement of Harry's henchman.

His blind side, Jean-Luc realized bitterly. And like the shock of Ned Stapleton's gash, there was a fraction of a second between the shock of the lash across his face and the pain. But the pain, when it came, was far worse than the other. Because, fighting to force the damaged eye open, fighting to see through the agony and the blood that was pouring from the stripe the whip had laid open across his face, he knew. He instinctively raised his left hand to what had been his good eye, which had just been caressed by the whip's tip, and realized only with the touch of cold metal against his cheek, that he still held the pistol. Reacting to sound alone, since that was all that he now had to go on, he forced the pistol back in line where he hoped the crowd was still standing.

Despite their brief uncertain wavering, the black eyes of the pair of pistols intimidated again. The surging flow of the mob halted, arrested once more by the danger the guns represented. Then the lash struck again, curling this time around Jean-Luc's shoulders. And he had no way to avoid what he couldn't see.

Whoever you send to horsewhip me... You be damned sure they bring a very big whip, he had taunted Mannering. And apparently he was to be repaid for his arrogance.

He knew he should shoot, but unable to see anything beyond a hazy glare when he had briefly succeeded in forcing the damaged lid open to expose the agony of the cut eye, he was afraid. What if Maddy had again tried to put herself between him and the mob?

"Dear God," he heard her say. He tried to open the burning eye, but there was nothing visible now beyond the warm liquid that was streaming down his face. Involuntary tears—or blood.

"Jean-Luc," she said, closer to him now, her hands suddenly on his arm. Pulling him as the whip whistled from the darkness that was all around him. He felt her start of reaction, and he realized with horror that the leather thong must have touched Maddy.

He struggled fiercely to push her away, but he was hampered by the pistols he knew he couldn't drop. They were all that stood between Maddy and the fury of the mob. She threw herself against his chest, and not expecting the sudden weight of her body, he stumbled backward, falling heavily against the wall. The whip whistled again in the darkness, but Maddy was against him, her arms covering, her body protecting his.

He heard her voice, shouting angrily into the darkness.

"Stop it, damn you. Stop it," she sobbed. "Haven't you done enough? What do you want?" she asked desperately. "Why are you doing this? I love him. Why don't you understand? Stop it."

Knowing he had no option, Jean-Luc raised the pistol that he held in his left hand and discharged the ball into the air. The surging movement of the crowd, that he had judged by noise alone, was arrested. There was no sound now, only Maddy's sobbing breath.

"I'll shoot the next man who moves," he said quietly, injecting authority into a voice he had been afraid would tremble. A gambler's bluff that he prayed even Maddy was not aware was only bluff. He held the second pistol unwaveringly in the direction that he hoped was the center of the mob and waited.

"Look at her," a voice from the crowd said finally. And Jean-Luc's finger tightened over the trigger. He had heard that voice before, but it was a moment before he placed it. The Marquis of Ainsley. Stapleton's friend.

"What more do you want?" the voice, sharp with anger and disgust, asked, and received no answer. "What more proof do you need that what you've been led to believe isn't true? Do you intend to flay her in order to *rescue* her?" Ainsley demanded with unanswerable logic. "My God, look at her."

Maddy stared back at them, still protecting her husband's body with her own, the mark of the whip welling dark blood over her white shoulders, which were exposed below the neck of the ruined gown. She was defiant, hating herself as much as them. This was all her fault.

She didn't recognize the man who had stopped the mob by pointing out to them all the obvious truth. She didn't even watch as the men he had challenged, even the one from whom he had furiously wrenched the murderous whip, melted into the shadows of the alley. One by one, recognizing the reality of the situation, they disappeared from the confrontation of their own cowardice.

"Maddy?" Jean-Luc said softly, turning his head, trying to understand what was happening in the darkness. There were no more torches to light the night and the lamps in the kitchen had all been deliberately put out before the men had sent the boy upstairs.

"It's all right," she reassured him, taking Jean-Luc's arm and then lifting her face to touch her lips to his. He started with surprise, not expecting their caress. He pulled Maddy against him, holding her as if he would never let go. She was safe, and apparently the threat no longer existed.

"It's over," the marquis confirmed from the shadows. Earlier, he had seen recognition of his voice break over the bloody features of the gambler. Jean-Luc released his wife. The marquis watched as the gambler's right hand moved slowly along the still-steady muzzle of the gun he held, reversing it to hold out the grip for him to take. Ainsley took the pistol, and then put his hand lightly on the Frenchman's arm.

"Let's go inside," he suggested, knowing they were too shocked by what had happened to know what they should do.

"Is Maddy all right?" Jean-Luc asked, turning his head now toward the Englishman's reassuring voice.

"Other than a stained gown and a slight cut across her shoulders, she's fine. I swear to you that's the truth. I'm sorry that I didn't arrive in time."

"I think you arrived just in time," Jean-Luc said. "You must know how grateful I am. And now..." The calm voice hesitated. "If you'll take Maddy inside," he suggested. His dark, skilled gambler's fingers were groping for the frame of the door. He was infinitely relieved when his knuckles brushed hard against the rough stone of the outer wall, and then he gripped the frame.

"This way," Ainsley said, no trace of emotion in the cultured English tones. He caught the hand that Jean-Luc had lifted to touch the door and put it instead on his shoulder. "She knows," he said softly. And then, "Let me help you. It will be easier for her."

At the small nod that was the gambler's reaction to that suggestion, he turned to the woman who stood trembling in the bloodstained gown in which she had hoped tonight to prove the innocence of her husband to the ton.

"We need to get him inside and send for a doctor," Ainsley said softly. It would be something for her to do.

"Yes," she said. And then, "I know you. You're a friend of Ned's."

"I'm Ainsley," he said again, as patient with her shock as Jean-Luc was, waiting quietly in the darkness. And then seeing no reaction, he explained what he had felt as he'd approached the alley tonight, afraid he was too late to stop what was happening. "I'm a friend of your husband's."

She nodded and led the way into the kitchens. She heard behind her the quiet tones of the marquis's voice directing, guiding Jean-Luc's steps across the threshold and to the kitchen table. Whatever her husband said was too quietly spoken for her to hear. And it really didn't matter. In her heart, which earlier tonight had held such hope, there was nothing. Because again, she had failed. And the Mannerings had won.

The Marquis of Ainsley left as soon as he had placed Jean-Luc in Ling's care. The Chinese servant cleaned the blood from his master's face and gently spread the cut with his salve. He held open the swollen lid, intending to introduce some of the ointment into the damaged eye.

"Don't," Maddy said in horror. They had to wait for the doctor. This was too important for any of Ling's primitive treatment.

"It's all right," Jean-Luc had assured her softly. He'd held out his hand to the dark corner where she stood, outside of the circle of light radiating from the lamp Ling had placed on the table, silently watching Ling care for the injury she had caused.

All my fault, she thought for the thousandth time. She had not noticed the entreaty of the hand that eventually fell to lie quietly again in her husband's lap as the servant worked, examining now the cut across his shoulders and then finally tearing strips of clean white flannel to use as bandage. In her guilt, she was unaware that the injury she had unthinkingly inflicted by her failure to respond to that unspoken request was far worse than what had already been done to Jean-Luc tonight. *All my fault* echoed in her head to the exclusion of almost any other coherent thought.

But she had reacted instinctively when she became aware of the two men standing in the dark, still-opened doorway of the kitchen. Seeing the dim light of Ling's lamp, they had come through the alley. And their dress betrayed them. The expensive elegance that so typified the class to which her brother and his friends belonged. "Nobs" echoed again.

Her fingers had found the pistol Ainsley had left on the table, and it was pointed with an unwavering menace at the Duke of Avon's chest, pointed with as much surety as Jean-

Luc had used to hold the crowd at bay earlier tonight. At least, until she'd interfered.

"My name is Avon," the duke said calmly in answer to the pistol's threat. "I'm a friend of Jean's."

The same words the marquis had used, she thought, briefly wondering at that avowal. Two men, aristocrats like Harry, claiming friendship with her husband. But even with that thought and her mind's acknowledgment of his claim, the muzzle never moved from its intended target.

"I've brought my physician, Dr. Pritchett. I think you should allow him to examine your husband's injury. I know that…" Avon paused, wondering how much she understood, despite what Ainsley had told him when he had been dispatched by Jean-Luc to bring the duke to the casino.

"Dominic?" Jean-Luc questioned softly, questioning what was happening to produce that particular note in Avon's voice.

"Your wife seems to object to our presence," the duke explained carefully.

"Maddy, Avon's a friend. It's all right, my darling," he assured her. He wanted to hold her, to protect her because he knew she was frightened, but the horror of groping his way to find her across the unremembered obstacles of the kitchen held him prisoner in the chair in which they'd placed him. Coward, he mocked himself. Afraid to let her see him now, to see the reality of what had happened tonight. A reality that he, himself, was just beginning to accept. A reality that he feared was too much to ask Maddy to deal with. She'd already been forced to accept so much that was…

"Your wife is holding a pistol on the duke," Dr. Pritchett spoke into the strained silence.

"No, Maddy," Jean-Luc said softly, but she heard his accent, too pronounced, clearly indicating his agitation. "Avon's a friend. I asked him to come. For your protection." He turned to where he believed Avon stood and addressed the duke directly. "I want your word, Dominic. No matter what else happens, I want your promise that she'll be safe."

"You have it," Avon vowed softly. "No matter what," he

repeated the deliberate choice of words the gambler had used. He spoke directly then to Maddy. "I think you should allow Dr. Pritchett to begin his examination. The longer we wait…"

They watched as the barrel of the elaborately chased French dueling pistol slowly lowered. Pritchett was moving across the dimly lighted kitchen to the injured man before that movement had stopped.

The English doctor's thin white fingers were as gentle as a woman's, carefully examining the damage the lash had caused. Both across the lid and then inside the eye itself. His words had been soft and noncommittal, touching on the major danger, inflammation, in "cases such as this," but she had seen the quick meeting of his gaze with the watching silver intensity of the man who had brought him.

He had also removed the patch, glancing with professional interest at the old scars, and then, using the white strips Ling had provided, he wrapped them tightly around Jean-Luc's eyes, directing that the bandage not be disturbed until he himself removed it. None of them found anything to say to break the silence that had grown as he completed his action, its finality seeming to rob them all of any thought of conversation.

Jean-Luc had answered the doctor's quiet questions, although she'd not heard half of what he'd said, his tones as calm and low as his questioner. She was thinking instead that the strip of white was too bright against the midnight hair and the dark skin. Too alien. The blackness of the patch that matched and disappeared into the curling ebony of his hair was right. Not this. Not this stark announcement of impairment.

"Maddy?" he said softly.

She moved then and sank down before the chair in which he was sitting so calmly. He didn't turn toward her, and she found herself hating the aloneness, the isolation. She put her face against his knee, her own eyes dry and burning. She hadn't cried. It was too new. The shock too great. The realization of her guilt and her sense of failure too deep.

His fingers touched lightly over her hair. They began to

move, the pads caressing and comforting against her scalp. Finally she reached up to catch his hand between her two and bring it to her cheek. She held it there a moment, the familiar warmth and subtle fragrance that was his a buffer against to-night's horror. She turned her cheek and pressed her lips into his palm. His fingers cupped her face, his thumb touching lightly under her eye.

"I thought you were crying," he said.

"No," she whispered, "I'm not crying."

"You're not afraid?" he asked, and she could hear the concern. "Avon will see to it—"

"Don't," she said. "I'm not afraid."

Ling pressed the cup of drugged tea against her shoulder, and she turned automatically to answer that demand. She took the delicate porcelain and raised it to her husband's lips. She saw him recoil slightly at the acrid aroma of the liquid she held under his nose.

"Drink it, my darling," she begged softly. And was re-lieved when he obeyed. His long fingers lifted to wrap around hers that held the cup against his mouth.

They helped him up after he'd finished the medicine. She remembered how quickly it had taken effect before. When Ned had...

There had been nothing but pain and injury since she'd married Jean-Luc. She had brought only destruction into his life. She had thought she could escape her own pain by ac-cepting this marriage, this gift that fate seemed to have handed her. She should have known that she'd bring the devastation that was her life into his.

"Maddy," he said. They were at the bottom of the stairs, waiting, because he wanted to say something to her. "Are you coming upstairs?" he asked softly. He hated to ask, but he thought that he wouldn't sleep unless she was safe, unless he was holding her. God, he needed to hold her.

"Of course," she lied. "As soon as Dr. Pritchett has looked at my shoulder." She saw the sudden remembering agony in his dark face, but her words had the intended effect. He placed his hand against the railing, Pritchett and Ling guiding and supporting. The duke limped to the foot of the dark staircase, watching the upward journey. It was the chance that she'd been waiting for. Avon was never even aware when she slipped out the door that led to the alley, the dueling pistol again clutched tightly in her hand.

Chapter Thirteen

Maddy should have known that Harry wouldn't be home, but she had lost all sense of time. It seemed an eternity since she'd dressed with such painstaking care, a hundred years ago that she'd stood in that dark kitchen and watched others care for her husband. But the hall clock in the Mannering town house confirmed it was not yet midnight, and Harry might not be back for hours.

If, however, her brother was anything, he was a creature of habit. When he arrived, he'd go into his father's study and pour a nightcap from the French brandy on the silver tray. Even in the heart of the blockade, that supply had never failed. Harry would come there. And so she went to wait in her stepfather's study, unaware, of course, of the Duke of Avon's frantic search through the dark London streets for his friend's wife, whom he had given his word to protect.

She never knew how long she waited. The images from the alley flickered endlessly in her brain. Jean-Luc had had control. He had tried to convince her to leave, and if she had, perhaps nothing that had happened would have occurred. But in her determination to convince them that they were wrong, she'd refused. And then…

She consciously tried to replace the remembrance of what had followed with memories from the short weeks they had spent together, but the horror of those white strips with which they'd bound his eyes intruded again and again.

"You're out very late, my dear. Or up very early," Harry's voice interrupted mockingly from the shadows.

He had stood watching the still, silent figure for a long time before he spoke. He shouldn't have been surprised to find her here. Not given the account his henchman had made about the events in the alley behind the Frenchman's casino.

He knew well Maddy's courage, which she had demonstrated to the mob tonight. But because she had lived so quietly these last weeks, he had managed to put any question about his half sister's feelings out of his mind. He had never dreamed that she would, as obviously she had, fall in love with the gambler. The violet eyes, darkened by emotion and the deep shadows, rose at his voice, but she didn't answer.

He crossed to the table with its beckoning decanter and poured two generous measures of brandy. He took a long pull on his, and then set it back on the tray. The other he brought to his half sister. His gaze traced the whip's mark on her shoulders, and when he raised the bloodshot blue eyes to study her face, she realized that he had not been surprised by the wound.

"A hard night?" he said mockingly, holding out the tumbler.

She was pleased to see the smile fade when she raised Jean-Luc's pistol and held it, almost touching his chest. He took an instinctive step backward, the liquor sloshing over his hand.

"What the hell…" he began.

"No more, Harry. It's over," she said softly.

She saw the realization move into his eyes, but as she had expected, he denied knowledge of what she meant.

"No more?" he questioned.

"I'm going to kill you. I know now that's the only way to be free. I don't think warning you will be sufficient. You've never had to give up anything you want, and I know that you want something…from me or from Jean-Luc. And tonight, whatever it is you want cost him his sight. So I'm going to kill you, and then it will finally be over.''

"Maddy," he protested, trying to laugh at the ridiculous threat. But the laughter faded at what was in her face. And in her eyes.

"No more," she repeated. The Mannerings had done everything that they would ever be allowed to do to those she loved. In her hand she had the power to protect. She had been such a fool not to have used it before.

"You don't understand," Harry argued, entreaty creeping into his tone. "You are mistaken."

"No," she said, shaking her head. "I am not mistaken. You're the one who sent Ned before."

"No, damn it. I had nothing to do with Stapleton's idiotic attack," he protested, almost the truth, but she continued to speak over his denial.

"But you've been fueling the rumors. That vile gossip. You're the one who set tonight's events into motion. I don't know why, but there is no doubt in my mind that you're responsible. And this time—"

"I wasn't there tonight. I had no part in what took place."

"But you know all about it? Coincidentally, I suppose?" she asked, her tone ridiculing his useless denials.

He paused, and she could almost see his mind working behind the blue gaze, trying to devise the best explanation. The glib excuses.

"Not this time," she warned softly. "There's no way out this time, Harry. I've come to call due all the debts the Mannerings owe me."

The pistol lifted slightly, aligning itself exactly with the center of his chest and his pounding heartbeat.

Again his retreat was instinctive. She didn't bother to question that backward step. He was still well within range of the weapon.

"And who will care for your husband?" he asked, a sudden inspiration. His voice was absolutely calm, the words dropping like stones into the quiet pool of certainty she'd felt after she'd reached her decision. "After they send you to prison for murdering me? Is the gambler to become another blind beggar cluttering the streets? Is that what you're willing to condemn him to? You'll have your revenge, Maddy, but will you enjoy it, knowing his fate was all your fault?''

The phrase caught like a knife's edge against her mind. *All your fault.* As she knew it was.

Harry didn't understand the pain that moved into the wide eyes. He couldn't know that she blamed herself for Jean-Luc's injury. His informant, his hireling with the whip, had not been that perceptive. Harry's words had intended to convey a warning of the guilt she would feel if she killed her brother and was no longer in a position to care for the husband she professed to love. He still couldn't fathom his sister's affection for that bastard, but he no longer doubted what he had been told about her actions in the alley. Not with that unwavering pistol trained on his heart. But his words had made an impact, and Harry was shrewd enough to follow up whatever advantage his wits could devise in this situation. If he could make her believe that there was another way out...

''But it needn't come to that. There's a better way. A way that will allow you to tend your husband without ever again worrying about me. My wants are simple, my dear. And very easy to gratify,'' Harry said.

She watched his lips move into an ironic smile that she didn't understand. But she knew that he had gained the upper hand. That's what happens when you love someone. That love could always be used against you.

''Especially easy to gratify with your husband's present...misfortune,'' Harry suggested softly. With Maddy's help, it would be as easy to accomplish as he had suggested. All these weeks he'd plotted and schemed, hoping to incite someone to kill the Frenchman, and now, with one touch of the whip and with Maddy's willing assistance, he knew he could have it all.

''What do you want?'' she asked, and Harry began to breathe again. He hadn't been wrong. The gambler was the key to manipulating Maddy. He'd thought he'd despised what his father had done to her, but sometimes desperate situations called for actions that one normally wouldn't undertake. As this one certainly did.

"The mine," he said, and then realized by her puzzlement that she, at least, didn't know what he had lost when he'd suggested her marriage to Gavereau.

"The mine?" she repeated. "I don't know..." He could see the sudden remembrance stop her. "In Cornwall?" she asked, unbelieving. "The ore mine on Grandmother's property in Cornwall? But why? There's no way... You know that. We've known it for years. It will never be profitable. Why would you want...?" She shook her head, trying to make sense of what Harry was suggesting. The operation in Cornwall had been worse than worthless, a continual drain of money and men. The seam ran too deep, and the mine was prone to uncontrollable flooding. Even with the pumps...

"Watt's patents have run out," he said, so obvious an answer that he didn't understand why she continued to shake her head. "And there are other designs, new rotary engines..." He stopped, wondering why he was bothering to explain what she didn't pretend to understand. "And with Hedley's locomotive operational now, the ore can be taken by rail to the coal fields at a fraction of the cost of bringing—" He stopped again at her expression. "God, Maddy, it doesn't matter why I want the mine. Just give it to me, and we'll be quits. I promise you. You and the gambler can go and do whatever you wish, and I swear on our mother's grave you'll never hear from me again."

She was watching his face, and she heard clearly the desperation in his voice. She thought of all that had happened because of what Harry wanted. Ned's attack, the rumors and then tonight... Could it possibly have been fixed so simply?

"Why didn't you ask me?" she said, unable to comprehend that this was what it had all been about. "Why didn't you tell me that you wanted the mine?"

That worthless mine, she thought again in disbelief. Harry had reinvestigated the possibility of the mine ever again making a profit when his father had died. He had been so desperate for money then. But at the end of the war, the price of ore had dropped dramatically. She was not aware of the changing market these last weeks, of the international boom that was taking place in the demand for British iron.

"God, Harry, you can have the mine. You could always have had it. Is this what it's all been about? Money? Is that why you've done these things to us? God, Harry, for money?" she whispered, thinking only of the dark, groping hand on the rail of the stairs.

Harry heard the whispered *us,* and knew that he had won. Maddy had allowed herself to be caught in the trap of caring more about someone else than she did about herself. Poor Maddy. So easy to win when your opponent is so vulnerable.

"But the mine is no longer yours to give, Maddy," he reminded her. "When you married, it became the property of your husband. And I did write you, suggesting a solution."

"The letter I returned," she realized. An opportunity to prevent tonight's events, she thought, and I lost it. I would have done anything…

"But no matter how willing you would have been to give up that ownership," Harry said, as if privy to those regrets, "I doubt the Frenchman would have been as accommodating."

"He doesn't care—" she began, and Harry's taunting voice interrupted.

"About money?" he gibed. "But I thought that's why your relationship began. Because he couldn't wait the few weeks it would have taken me to put our finances right. Don't tell me he doesn't care, Maddy. You may be blinded to his true nature, but I assure you I'm not." He saw her quick start of reaction at his unintentional wording, and he smiled. "No pun intended, my dear."

"How?" she whispered, needing this nightmare to end, to finally be over. She would do whatever Harry wanted if she could guarantee he'd be out of their lives. That's all she'd ever wanted. To get rid of the Mannerings forever.

"You get him to sign a bill of sale. Put a shilling on the table before him and guide his hand to the right line on the document and make him sign it."

"And if you think he's so concerned about the money, how am I supposed to convince him to sign?" she asked.

"He's blind, Maddy. He won't know what he's signing. Tell him it's a draft for your dressmaker's bill. He'll never know."

"No," she said, and the pistol straightened from the slight droop she had unconsciously allowed. "No, Harry, I could never do that. I won't lie to him. I couldn't use..." She couldn't bring herself to speak that reality aloud. Wordlessly, she shook her head.

"Then you have no choice. You'll *have* to shoot me, Maddy—and condemn your husband to grope his way through the streets of London. The very dangerous streets. If he doesn't sign the bill of sale, then killing me is your only out," Harry suggested, smiling, sure of her now, "because I intend to have that property. It's not his. It belongs to this family. And I promise you, I will do everything in my power to see that it reverts to us. If you won't do it the way I've suggested, there are many other avenues open to acquire what I intend to have. Don't worry, my dear. You're lovely in black. You were a pleasing picture in your widow's weeds. Very becoming. You probably still have some of those useful garments hanging upstairs. And a blind man is so vulnerable to unforeseen accidents. So many dangers lurk in his darkness...."

He knew he had gone too far when he saw the reactive tightening of her finger. He couldn't be sure about the trigger tension of the dueling pistol. Some men preferred them sensitive to the least pressure.

"God, Maddy, watch what you're doing," he warned, a note of panic creeping in despite his effort to sound controlled.

She looked down on the gun as if seeing it for the first time and then deliberately forced her finger to loosen.

"If I do what you want, what guarantee will I have that you'll never bother us again?" she whispered.

"My word, Maddy. The word of an English gentleman," he vowed fervently.

And he heard the small, bitter laugh. "That's what you promised Jean-Luc. The card game. He asked me later..." But she would never share with Harry anything of what had happened between them. "I want a paper. If anything happens to Jean-Luc, any 'unforeseen accident,' then the mine reverts to my ownership."

"Of course," Harry said, his mind busy with the obvious flaw in that plan.

"And if anything happens to me, it becomes Jean-Luc's."

"Then you intend to tell him about this agreement?" Harry mocked, smiling. "So that he can collect on his good fortune if his young and beautiful wife meets an untimely demise."

"I intend to put the paper you write in the hands of the Duke of Avon, to be opened if anything—*anything,* Harry— happens to either of us. A fatal accident to both will give the property to Avon. If you want to keep your mine, you had better pray nightly for our continued health and safety. You'd better hope my *vulnerable* husband meets with no accident. Because if he does, Avon will see to it that you profit no longer from Cornwall. I don't think you want to tangle with Avon, my dear. He's a friend of my husband's, you know," she said, finally allowing the trace of sarcasm and a slight smile.

"Damn you, Maddy," he said feelingly. She'd learned all that his father had taught her too well. He was only glad that she hadn't taken a hand in what he'd been plotting until now. Because he could still carry this off. He still had her very real feelings, as unbelievable as he found them to be, for that scarred, blind bastard to use against her. "All right, damn you. An exchange. The signed bill of sale for my agreement to your terms. I'll send the document to you for the Frenchman's signature. As soon as I've had my man of business draw it up."

"And I believe *I'll* write out the other. When you've signed it, you can have the bill of sale for the mine."

"Agreed. And I don't think we need this any longer," he said. She allowed him to take the pistol and smiled again as he handled it carefully as if it might explode on its own.

"Was it even loaded?" he asked sarcastically, now that the dark muzzle wasn't pointed at his chest. He laid the intricately chased gun on the table beside the decanter.

"Aren't you glad you weren't forced to find out? And now if you'll excuse me, I have to return home. I need…" She hesitated, knowing that he already knew how she felt, but instinctively wanting to hide her concern for her husband from him.

"Of course," Harry said, smiling. "So much to *see* to. For you both."

He walked her to the entryway, and when he opened the massive door of the town house, they were both surprised by the brightening in the dawn sky. Harry found he still held the brandy he'd poured for her in his left hand.

"A toast, Maddy," he said, taking a long pull of the fiery liquid, grateful that he was still capable of enjoying that simple pleasure, infinitely relieved that he wasn't lying in a pool of blood on the worn Turkish carpet of his father's study.

She turned back, puzzled. He could see the cost of the night in the circled eyes and the pallor surrounding their still-remarkable beauty. He raised his glass in salute.

"To the success of our joint venture, my dear," he explained, euphoric that he was, it seemed, going to get what he wanted after all. And at a very small price. An easily kept promise.

"To our success," she echoed softly. Anything that would ensure Jean-Luc's safety. She'd have made a pact with the devil himself to assure that her husband would suffer no more because of her and her family.

Harry laughed and closed the door, and she was left alone on the stoop. She shut her eyes against the sudden release of the restraint she'd exerted before her brother. She had wanted so badly to pull the trigger. It had been so hard to bargain for their safety when all she had wanted was revenge.

And who will care for your husband? Remembering the question that had prevented her from avenging Jean-Luc, she sagged against the frame of the door. She waited a long time for the vertigo to stop, afraid to open her eyes to feel the blackness threaten again. She had never fainted in her life, but she knew exactly what was happening.

Despite her surprise, she was grateful when the strongly masculine hand grasped her elbow and steadied her swaying figure.

"I've come to take you home," the Duke of Avon said softly. He had finally found her in the last place in London he could have imagined her to be. The last place she should have been if what he believed was true.

Avon was trying to understand what was in her face, in spite of the condemning toast he had overheard, but as always, the duke exercised a practiced control over his features, despite the doubts and suspicions that were beginning to ferment in his mind.

She nodded, her eyes meeting his with complete trust. *I'm a friend of your husband's,* he'd told her. Because of that, she allowed him to direct her to his waiting carriage, which would carry her back to Jean-Luc. She had faced Harry and won. And now she would have to face the man she had injured. The man she loved. The man she would spend the rest of her life caring for in hopes that one day he might be able to forgive her for ruining his life.

Beyond his original greeting, Avon said virtually nothing to her on the journey. She supposed, when she had briefly wondered about his silence, that he was feeling, as she was, bitter anguish at the remembrance of what had happened. And then her thoughts had left any consideration of the duke to picture her husband and to consider what she might do to make the unbearable bearable. Because it must be borne. Her guilt and his... Her thoughts jarred against the unspeakable.

Jean-Luc was of course, still asleep when they arrived. She managed a quick wash and a change of clothes in his office, not wanting to chance waking him by performing those necessary actions in the bedroom. She denied Ling's attempts to see to the cut on her shoulders. She had forgotten it until the sting of the hot water and its soreness as she dressed reminded her. It didn't matter. Nothing mattered but carrying out the arrangement that she and Harry had agreed to. And then they would be free. She hoped Avon would help her take Jean-Luc away from London. She didn't know where they could go. Anywhere away from this city and the viciousness of its gossiping tongues.

She sat most of the day by Jean-Luc's bed, simply watching him sleep. She didn't know how she knew when he was finally awake, but she caught the dark hand that reached out, and felt it close around hers.

"Maddy?" he asked softly.

"No, it's your other wife. The one you keep only for emergencies," she teased.

His lips moved upward slowly in the one-sided smile, and she was glad. She could do this. He would never know what she felt. She'd never reveal any of the guilt and remorse. Only the love. And her acceptance.

"Are you all right?"

"Of course. I told you last night," she said, injecting a smile into her voice. She took his fingers and guided them over the bruised cut that tracked across one shoulder and the top of her breasts. He traced gently, following the line. And then he allowed her to recapture his hand and lower it to rest in her lap.

"Satisfied?" she asked, bending to touch her lips to his forehead above the swatch of white cloth.

"I don't think so, but if that's the best you have to offer..." he said suggestively, and she knew that he was trying, too. That he was also hiding the cost.

Answering that teasing challenge, she placed her lips over his and felt them open, welcoming. His fingers tangled in her hair as his tongue invaded. Nothing had changed. Her body responded as always to his touch, the sensual sensations coiling upward. The hot moisture already beginning, preparing for his entry. Her breath becoming shallow and too rapid. Her knees beginning to tremble at the thought of him moving against her, into her. Taking her with him to the place where only they had ever been.

His thumb brushed across her nipple, its hungry flesh separated from his touch by the sheer muslin of her gown. He

moved his nail tantalizingly back and forth against the growing hardness. She groaned, and his palm cupped under her
breast, his hard fingers kneading into her softness.

"Touch me," she breathed into his mouth. "I want you. I
need you so much," she whispered, her own hand pushing
under the sheet to find that he was nude, and that he needed
her as much as she needed him. She caressed and felt his
shivering response.

His fingers began to fumble over the buttons at the back of
her gown. She never thought to help him. And her tongue
continued to meld hotly with his until he pulled away from
her in frustration. She unwillingly opened her eyes, slightly
disoriented by his reaction.

"Damn it, Maddy. Take it off. I can't…"

"What's wrong?" she said softly. She had been lost in the
familiar spell of his lovemaking.

"I can't undress you. I can't manage the damned buttons.
Take it off. I want you."

Realizing that his anger and frustration made no sense, that
he'd undressed her so often before in the dark, laughingly
dealing with buttons and laces, she knew this was only one
of the barriers that they would have to overcome. Every hin-
drance would loom larger; he'd blame every problem on his
blindness. But that didn't matter now. Only to give him what
he wanted. What they both wanted.

She stood up too suddenly, hurrying to do as he'd ask. And
the darkness that had threatened at Harry's engulfed her. She
caught at the post as she had the night she'd had too much
champagne. This was almost the same giddiness. After the
supper at Vauxhall. And with that remembrance, she gagged,
the thought of that night's rich food suddenly repugnant. She
began retching, trying to control herself, as she stumbled away
from the bed and to the closed door. She could hear Jean-
Luc's voice raised questioningly behind her, but she couldn't
answer him. She reached the hallway before the spasm of
nausea had its inevitable result. After it was over, she leaned
weakly against the wall, exhausted and still dizzy. Ling must
have been upstairs for he was there before her head had

cleared. He forced her down on the floor of the hallway, pushing her face between her folding knees.

"Breathe," he ordered softly.

She caught his hand and held on until the darkness had passed, concentrating on answering his whispered questions.

"What is it? What the hell's happening?" Jean-Luc's furious voice broke finally through her efforts to remember. "What's going on?" he demanded again.

She looked up to find him standing, beautifully nude and still slightly aroused, in the open doorway. She watched his strong Roman nose wrinkle against the unpleasantness of the hallway, and she closed her eyes at that evidence of his disgust.

"Go back," Ling said, rising and guiding him back into the bedroom. "Accident. Lady sick. All right now. You make trouble."

She listened to the explanation fade as Ling led him back to the bed. She closed her eyes and rested her head against the wall behind her.

Another target for Harry, she realized belatedly. *And I thought I was so clever. So damned clever.*

She began to laugh at the naïveté that had made her believe she could ever escape. There had been no provision in their agreement for this eventuality. And she laughed again. She could hear the shock in Ling's voice as he chided her for that rising hysteria. But she couldn't help laughing. It was so ironic. Nothing ever turned out as expected. At least not in her life.

Jean-Luc lay rigidly in the bed he'd been led back to, ordered to like a child, listening to Maddy's laughter and to Ling's sharp admonitions against it. Neither of them wondered what was moving through his mind or guessed at the dark images he was creating to explain her sickness and that nearly hysterical laughter. Because what he believed was so different from the reality the two people in the hallway were dealing with, they didn't stop to worry about his uncharacteristic acceptance of Ling's commands.

They couldn't know the reason he had assigned to his

wife's illness. Despite her words, despite her attempt to act as if nothing had changed, this, he supposed, was her reaction to his sightless, inept lovemaking. And despite Pritchett's assurances, the cold fear began to grow. What if he were always condemned to this endless darkness? And more frightening even than that, what if Maddy found that she couldn't cope with that possibility?

Ling had installed Maddy on the small cot in the alcove off Jean-Luc's office. She realized now that this was where her husband had spent the first two nights of their marriage—so long ago.

The nausea had begun to fade with her stillness and with the tea Ling had brought her. But its cause must still be dealt with. She should have known this would be the result of their almost constant lovemaking, but she'd never conceived during the five years of her marriage to Fairchild, and she had simply put the possibility out of her mind. But, of course, the differences between her first husband and Jean-Luc made that denial ridiculous.

She was carrying his child, and despite the timing of that discovery in the midst of trying to protect them from Harry's greedy ruthlessness, she savored its pleasure. She knew that she couldn't tell him yet. He had so much now to deal with. And he didn't know, of course, that she was dealing with her brother. She knew that this pregnancy would only worry him. So she'd wait until they were more secure. Until they'd left London. And if he wondered about her illness this morning, surely there had been enough in the past twenty-four hours to cause such an unbalance in her usual good health.

Obeying Ling's command, she had slipped out of her dress as soon as the door had closed behind him. She now slid her hand under the blanket he'd provided and moved it over the slight mound of her belly. She couldn't tell any difference, but Ling's questions had left no doubt.

She smiled at the thought of a son with hazel eyes and dark hair. Or a daughter. She crossed her arms over her breasts and hugged the images to her heart. Deal with Harry and then leave London. Disappear. Avon would help, she hoped. Especially now. Once they were away, she'd tell Jean-Luc. She closed her eyes, smiling as she thought about his reaction, and eventually she drifted into the sleep she'd missed during the long dark night that had passed.

Chapter Fourteen

Ling woke her the next morning and insisted that she drink the bitter tea he'd brought. Apparently his herbal concoctions again worked, for when she rose to dress, she found that there was no giddiness and certainly no nausea. She was hungry. But since she had eaten nothing the day before, that was hardly surprising. Ling brought her toast and a soft-boiled egg, and when she had finished, he suggested that she might take in the boss's breakfast.

"Plenty worry," he advised. "You tell soon."

"Soon," she promised, taking the small tray from his hands and making her escape to the room across the hall where Jean-Luc was waiting. In her self-centered concentration on the wondrous secret she didn't yet intend to share, she had never stopped to consider what he might be feeling about her desertion last night. She hadn't realized that it was the first night they had slept apart since he'd carried her out of the bath.

He was sitting at the table before the opened window. His face was lifted into the warmth of the morning sun, the faint breeze gently stirring the dark hair.

She stood silently in the doorway a moment, enjoying the purity of his profile and the strong spread of broad shoulders highlighted against the light. His hand rested loosely on the table, the curve of his fingers relaxed and graceful in their supple strength, and she could almost feel them touching her skin, smoothing across her breasts or tangling in her hair as he pulled her down to him.

Her body responded as it had yesterday, wanting him. Even more. As if the child she carried drew her also to the man who had shared in its creation. She smiled at the idea of her body being more in tune to his because she carried his child. She had always belonged to him. Even before she'd met him. He was the lover of her girlhood dreams, and she, more fortunate than countless other dreamers, had found the reality. A reality that exceeded the mythical imagery of her desire.

"Good morning," she said softly.

He turned to her voice, and even the bandage couldn't intrude on her pleasure in being with him this morning. The guilt was beginning to fade with the thought that she'd finally taken action. Soon it would all be over, she repeated, a silent litany, and he'd be safe.

"Ling said you were better," he said. Don't press, he urged himself. Whatever she can deal with. Or you'll lose her.

"I'm fine. A reaction to everything… I didn't sleep and I forgot to eat. It was nothing," she lied.

"And last night?" He couldn't stop the question. None of the decisions he had reached in the long, lonely hours of the night, the primary one not to force her to stay if the blindness was permanent, could prevent his asking where she had been when he'd needed her. Needed her so much to keep that frightening darkness at bay.

"Ling put me to bed in your office. And I fell asleep. I'm sorry," she whispered, knowing what that simple inquiry implied. He had wanted her, and she'd failed him. But soon she'd be free to explain, and he'd understand. "I brought you breakfast," she said, attempting to put them back on a more normal footing. Pretending that nothing had changed.

She walked across the room and placed the tray before him. Judging what she was doing by sound alone, he had moved his hand out of her way. She waited a moment, wondering what she should do to help him.

"Where's Ling?" he asked, sensing her hesitation.

"I don't know. In the kitchen, perhaps, but I can help you as well as Ling."

"No, damn it, that's not why I married you—"

She laughed, interrupting the expression of his reluctance to accept her help. The shock at her amusement stopped his words.

"I never thought I'd hear *that* again," she said, still smiling. "All those reasons why you *didn't* marry me. Be careful, Jean-Luc, or you'll have to decide all over again exactly why you did."

"Damn it, Maddy—"

"Chocolate." She broke calmly into the heart of his furious protest. "And a roll. That hardly seems enough."

As she talked, she lifted his hand, and he was too surprised by that action to resist. She carried it to touch the top of the porcelain cup that held his usual morning beverage. His fingers automatically closed around the rim, and she removed her hand and began to break the roll into bite-size pieces.

"Ling didn't send any jam, but maybe he decided that we shouldn't try that until we're a little more coordinated at managing this," she said matter-of-factly.

The silence from the other side of the table was ominous, but she ignored it. Finally the dark fingers moved carefully down the cup he was touching, and then Jean-Luc lifted it and brought it to his mouth.

She allowed a small smile at his surrender.

He found the saucer with his other hand and carefully replaced the cup after he'd drunk. Without any hesitation, she touched his fingers again, and she allowed her to direct them to the plate where the small pieces of roll waited.

She watched him eat, finding nothing distasteful about the slight uncertainty of his movements. She could see the concentration on his face, and so she didn't talk to him, unwilling to become a distraction in the new skills he must master.

When he'd finished, the relieved relaxation of his body was almost visible. He sat back in the chair and again turned his face into the warmth of the light streaming in through the window on his right.

"Pritchett's coming back tomorrow," he said.

"Really?" she said, knowing that it couldn't matter.

"There's no pain now," he told her, reassurance, he believed, that what the doctor had thought must be true. If there were no inflammation, then the cut on his eye shouldn't affect his vision. He'd still been able to see that night. At least before the swelling of the damaged lid and the blood had obscured his vision.

But because, in her shocked reaction, she had not heard half of what Pritchett had explained to his patient that night, she read nothing into those words beyond the simple statement.

"I'm glad," she said.

"Maddy?" he whispered, turning back finally to face her.

"I'm still here."

"Do you think…"

"What is it, my darling?" she asked as his question faltered and then died.

"You seem too far away. Almost as far as last night."

Don't beg, damn it, he cursed himself silently, hearing the entreaty in his own voice, but he waited and hoped that she'd finally come.

He heard the creak of the chair she'd been sitting in, the soft movement of the material of her gown, but he was still unprepared when she eased down onto his lap. Overcome suddenly by the very smell of her, the familiar warm sweetness of her clean body, the delicate fragrance that he didn't realize was his own soap that she used because she enjoyed the aroma of his skin on hers, he felt again the ridiculous prick of tears. God, she could unman him by simply touching him. He'd never cried, not since he was a child. Since his mother had taken him that day…

He felt her palm against the smoothness of his unmarred cheek. She turned his face to find his lips and pressed her opened mouth against them.

She could taste the chocolate, sweet and dark, like Jean-Luc himself. And then his tongue was moving against hers, stirring memories, hot and hard, demanding both control and response.

"Maddy," he breathed, his hands finding, without any remembrance of his blindness, her softness. He didn't allow himself to think about what had happened yesterday. He only felt and savored the small hands that clung to his shoulders, communicating their need with the increased pressure of their fingertips, the nails demonstrating her body's urgency. He could feel himself growing hard, his arousal pushing up into her slight weight.

He slipped one arm under her knees and the other to support her shoulders. Not stopping to consider the difficulties of what he intended, he rose, easily lifting her slender body. The small table tipped as her hip bumped against its edge. She felt the soft blow, but the crash of the table and the shattering sounds of the lamp and of the china that had been on the breakfast tray came before she had registered its meaning.

Jean-Luc froze. He lifted his head, his mouth suddenly deserting hers, and only then did she realize what had happened.

"It's just the table," she said, dismissing the entire incident until she saw his face.

"Sweet mother of…" he ground out softly.

"It doesn't matter. It's always been a bit unsteady. I think one leg…"

"Damn it, Maddy—"

"It doesn't matter," she repeated more strongly. "There was only the tray and a lamp." She lifted her hand to the back of his head to urge his mouth to return to her waiting lips, but he resisted that guidance. His jaw was rigid and a small muscle jumped beside his mouth.

Slowly and carefully he lowered her so that her feet touched the floor. She kept her hand on his shoulder, finally beginning to understand that he was not going to accept what had happened.

"Hell, I can't even…"

Again he stopped. She moved her hand down his arm, never losing contact with him, until she could take his hand. His fingers closed over hers, but she could feel the trembling reaction to the shock that had interrupted his very different intentions.

"This way," she said, directing him around the upturned legs of the table. He followed without protest, and she hated most of all the loss of his easy assumption of leadership in their relationship. Before, she had done whatever he wanted, willingly following his lead. And now...

She blocked that thought and led him to the bed in which they had spent so many hours, relishing their growing intimacy. She placed his hand on the tall post and then moved back to quickly remove her dress and chemise. She took time to push them out of his way with the sweep of her foot. She looked up to find the same tension in his jawline.

She put her hands on his shoulders and lifted on tiptoe to kiss him. There was no response. His lips were cold against hers. She pressed her body along the muscled length of his and knew then that he had lost the hard urgency of desire that had begun this. Determined to overcome any obstacle, she began to undress him. She wanted his skin against her own, no barrier of clothing between their joining.

Finally, when his hands rose to help, she smiled, infinitely relieved. This meant too much to them both to allow any regret over what had changed to interfere with all that had not. The flame that had burned between them from the beginning could not be extinguished by any alteration of their circumstances. *Love is not love which alters when it alternation finds...* She remembered the scrap of sonnet. Nothing here had changed. Nor would it ever.

She led him at last to lie down, but he pulled her to him, and it was again his sure authority, his experienced mastery, that dominated from then on.

There was now no uncertainty in the movement of his fingers, tracing over the familiar landscape of her body. Nor did his tongue need her instruction in its intent or destination. Slowly, skillfully he brought her again to fulfillment. His teeth tenderly teasing distended nipples, pulling gently and then with fiercer demand against a slight soreness she had not yet been aware of. Her breasts were too sensitive, engorged with passion and ripened by her body's ripening. Her breath feathered softly against his ear as he nibbled and suckled. His fingers slipped under the firm globes to lift them, to bring them to his worshiping mouth. His tongue flicked over the reaching tips, and he heard the soft moan of response.

His body reacted to that whisper of sound, and he deliberately dragged the hard evidence of his desire over her stomach. She arched, needing him, needing the return of his mouth to her breasts, the fullness of him between her legs. She reached for him, but he turned away from her hands. Here, his was the guidance, his the direction. And because she wanted that, her hands obeyed, moving instead to the small nubs on his chest that corresponded to her aching nipples. She caught them and rolled them between her fingers, feeling him gasp and then groan aloud. He lowered his body again to brush across her thighs, and she arched upward, seeking him.

"Maddy?" he whispered.

"Now," she begged. "Now, Jean-Luc."

His hands cupped under her, lifting her up into the downward movement of his arousal. She gasped with the hard pleasure of his entry. But she was more than ready, the moisture already welling to ensure his successful penetration. His hips lifted and drove again, and he felt the quivering surrender begin beneath him. She heard his soft laugh of delight in her immediate reaction, and then the vortex surrounded her, the present disappearing as her body involuntarily arched upward, meeting every driving movement of his.

When the shimmering waves of sensation had ceased, the hot lightning that flickered between her thighs releasing her from its sweet bondage, she opened her eyes to smile into the hazel gaze that always was waiting to acknowledge her rapture. And she found instead the unresponsive white of Ling's bandage.

Fighting the limp inertia of her body's release, she lifted her shoulders slightly until her lips found his. She should have spoken first, she realized, when he started against that unexpected touch. And then his mouth opened to receive her. He was still hard and full inside her, so she moved to give him permission to begin again the ancient lovers' dance that they had perfected through so many endless nights. So many hours spent in giving and receiving pleasure. Unhurried and finally uninhibited.

And this time they found the spiral together. And descended slowly as one. Joined. Always joined. Movement matched to exquisite movement, advance and retreat. Endless and too brief.

His fingers were again tangled in the fall of gilt hair. Its perfume invaded his nostrils, which spread to relish that sweetness. And if the other, the lost ability to find her face, softened with passion after their journey, was never to return, he knew suddenly that this would be enough. To smell and touch and taste Maddy and to know again with this sure certainty that she was forever his. How much more of paradise was anyone promised?

He held her too tightly, the feel of her against his damp, panting body so right. So precious. He could bear anything as long as it wasn't losing Maddy.

"I was so afraid," he admitted softly, the confession torn from him, too weakened by gratitude to stop the words.

"Of what?" she asked. Her palms found his cheeks, and she drew his mouth down to caress over her eyes. She never realized that she was echoing the desire of her own heart. To touch him there. To kiss what had been taken from him and to assure him that his blindness didn't matter. He wouldn't want that, and so she found delight in the movement of his lips against her closed lids.

"That I'd lost you. That you couldn't bear this now. That you didn't want me," he whispered. The gentle nudge of his lips over the soft skin was such a contrast to the hard demands his body had made before. Strength and gentleness. Always they had been his weapons in this arena.

"How could you believe…?" She shook her head in amazement that he still didn't understand his power over her.

"No one's ever wanted me," he said, too softly.

She waited, but there was nothing else, no added admission to that statement.

"I want you," she whispered. "I've always wanted you. Since I was a child."

He laughed, and then hearing the echo of her sincerity, he stopped and waited, too.

"I dreamed about you. About what you'd look like. About your touching me."

"Before we met?" he asked, his fingers moving tenderly over the curve of her breast. She watched their hard strength caress.

"Long before. That's why at the inn I knew it was you. And then I cried, and you thought it was because of the scars." She paused, her honesty demanding the confession she'd never shared before. "And I suppose it was. You had been so exactly the man I'd imagined. Before the fire. And I was sorry that you'd been hurt."

"And sorry that I no longer matched the fantasy you'd created?" he suggested softly, but there was no anger in his voice.

"I suppose. Until you kissed me. And then I knew that you did. The other didn't matter. And I tried to tell you that, but you'd gone. And then Harry…" The words froze. Harry again. Because of Harry, she had agreed to trick him, to use the blindness she'd caused, to deceive him.

"And then Harry sent you to me. Remind me sometime to tell Harry how grateful I am. But don't do it too soon."

There was something in his voice that she hadn't heard before. She shivered with the dark promise it held.

"And you didn't believe that I'd come to you because I wanted to come. Because I'd already fallen in love with you."

"You were in love with the man you'd created. That you imagined me to be. How long did it take you to know that I wasn't that man?" he asked, but he was smiling. Confident again with the response of her body that whatever she'd felt at the beginning, she now wanted the man he was.

"I never imagined a man could be so gentle. I knew you were dangerous—" she paused at his soft, laughing protest of that description "—and then instead, you were tender. You made me feel things that I'd never dreamed I'd feel. You knew exactly how to touch me, to hold me.''

"Remind me *not* to tell you how I knew those things," he said, still smiling.

"You never tell me anything," she chided. "You demand honesty and then—'' Honesty that she wasn't giving. She knew she was doing the right thing in carrying out Harry's deception. She knew that Jean-Luc didn't want the mine, but she was afraid to tell him about Harry's requirements. Afraid he'd try to contravene her brother's demands in some way. And denying Harry had already cost so much.

But Jean-Luc had interpreted her hesitation to finish that thought as an order that he finally share something of his life before he'd met her. And when he spoke, all the lost darkness was back in his voice.

"I was born in a whorehouse," he said, with no explanation to soften the effect. "I learned a lot about women there. What they feel. What they desire.''

She could think of nothing to say. He had told her because she had demanded honesty. And she could think of nothing to answer that confession.

"Shocked, Maddy?" he asked, the quiet bitterness clear.

"Jean-Luc…'' she whispered, at a loss.

"So different from the men you've known before.''

"From Fairchild? And my stepfather? And Harry? Then, yes, so different. But not a difference that I would denigrate.'' Her voice was no more bitter than his.

"My mother wanted me, I suppose. Enough to give up the man she loved to bear me. But I was never sure if that was for my sake or because she thought she'd always have a hold on him. She was obsessed with him. And she wanted to bear his son. A son he made clear he didn't require.''

"Don't," she said softly. "It can't matter anymore.''

"I must have been conceived deliberately. She was his mistress and certainly sophisticated enough to prevent a baby or even to get rid of one if she'd wanted to. I think she thought, since he had no children, that he'd want a son badly enough to overlook the fact that this particular son was a bastard.''

"His…" She paused, unwilling even to repeat the term he'd used for himself.

"His bastard?" He laughed again. "But he didn't. He kicked her out. And she had nowhere to go. So she made an arrangement. She sold herself. An agreement to work for the house after I was born. They were willing to wait, even willing to put up with her baby in the bargain, because she was very beautiful. The most beautiful woman in Paris people said. I remember her, how she looked and smelled. So beautiful…" He paused and then after a moment the calm voice continued. "I grew up surrounded by a dozen lovely and loving *tantes.* They were good to me, lavished on me the love they had no one else to give."

"And you never knew your father? Not even who he was?"

"She took me to meet him when I was five. I looked like him. The older I got, the more obvious the likeness. She dressed me in silk and lace, a miniature *aristo,* and told me I was going to meet my father and that I must be on my best behavior. And if he liked me, we'd go live with him."

There was no comfort she could offer for that old pain. The ending of the story was obvious. What an incredible error in judgment to place that burden on a little boy. She could almost picture the child he had been, nervous but excited, too. The promise of a father's love in the totally feminine world he'd grown up in.

"He laughed. I didn't understand why he was laughing. He caught my chin and turned my face into the light and he said…"

"Don't," she breathed again, but she was so lost in the horror of the story that she didn't move. Lost as he was in Paris, in the past.

Jean-Luc smiled at the concern in her voice, touching her breast again with those dark, tender lover's fingers. "It isn't as bad as you're imagining. He said, 'He's certainly mine. The nose would give me away if nothing else.' Then he released me and I thought, because of what he'd said…" He paused again and shook his head. "And he added, 'But why would you imagine I would be interested in your bastard, my dear?' He gave me a louis, and we went home. Back to the whorehouse.''

"And you never saw him again?"

"Once, during the Revolution. After my mother died. I think he knew me, but he didn't acknowledge the relationship.'' She watched the grim line of his lips deepen. "Perhaps it was the occasion.''

She shivered, remembering the dark tales that had come out of the bloodbath that Paris had become.

"God, Maddy, I'm sorry. Ghost stories. And I didn't intend this when I began. Despite... It wasn't all unhappy,'' he said, deliberately lightening his voice. "Few men are raised by a dozen adoring aunts. It did have its advantages.''

His knowing hands moved to show her some of those advantages, and willingly, she surrendered to his suggestion, wanting him to forget the bitter avowal he'd made. *No one's ever wanted me,* he'd whispered. And she moved to show him how mistaken he was.

Avon came that afternoon, and she offered what she believed would make it easier for her husband.

"Send him up here,'' she said to Ling. She turned to Jean-Luc. "I don't mind. I can wait in your office.''

He shook his head, and Ling waited.

"I'll go down. The stairs are hard for him. You stay here and rest. I don't think you've caught up on the sleep you've missed.''

"I wonder why,'' she said, gently teasing.

He smiled at her before taking Ling's arm, accepting his guidance, and she was forced to fight the sharp jealousy that he would allow Ling to care for him in ways that he would never allow her. She watched their careful passage through the open doorway of the bedroom and stood listening to Ling's nearly indecipherable English as he directed his master down the stairs.

Finally she lay down on the bed that she hadn't bothered to straighten and drifted into sleep, never conscious of the import of the conversation that was taking place in the room below. Or of its consequences for her future.

"Harry was certainly the instigator of the most vicious gossip. Tracing the beginnings of rumor is like catching mist, but the inner circle of Harry's friends remember that the first time they heard those stories, they were all from Harry's lips."

"That's only what we suspected," Jean-Luc said. "And Stapleton's attack?"

"Spurred on by Harry's earliest inventions, perhaps, but I think Stapleton acted on his own. He'd been in love with Madelyn Carlton for years. Everyone, Harry included, was aware of how he felt," Avon acknowledged.

"And the bastard with the whip?" Jean-Luc asked softly. The duke, a dangerous man in his own right, was not surprised by the venom exposed in that question. Not considering the circumstances.

"He's left London. But Harry hired him. At least two people saw them together. Mannering's a rather inept plotter."

"Too arrogant by half. Whatever Harry wants, he believes the world owes him. And be damned to anyone who stands in his way."

"As apparently you do. So be damned to you," Avon agreed.

"Even if I am his brother-in-law," the gambler said, mockingly.

"Or because of it."

"What does that mean?" Jean-Luc asked.

"Your wife disappeared the night you were hurt."

"Disappeared?" the Frenchman repeated carefully.

"After you went upstairs. I searched for her all night."

"And?"

"I found her finally in the one place she should never have been, especially considering what we now know." Avon hesitated and then continued with the bitter truth. "I found her at Mannering's town house."

"And obviously you took that to imply... What? That

Maddy was involved somehow with what Harry had planned?''

The silence grew until the Frenchman spoke again.

"I think you're right not to answer that. I don't have enough friends that I can afford to lose one. And he *is* her brother. That was her home. You seem to have forgotten that.''

"Is there any doubt in your mind of Harry's involvement in what occurred here?'' Avon asked.

"No, not given what had happened before. Not given that the man with the whip was his hireling.''

"And don't you believe that she must have known that also?''

"Whatever Maddy knew, wherever you found her that night, she didn't have a part in that attack. She's the one who put an end to it.''

"But not until after...'' The duke hesitated.

"This? You believe they planned this?'' Jean-Luc asked, touching the white strip that still covered his eyes. Disbelief joined the anger that had begun threading through the slight accent as soon as Avon had made his careful suggestions. "This was the result of... Maddy came into the alley, and I tried to get her out of the way, to put her behind me. I turned around just as the bastard let fly with the whip. They couldn't have known that that particular sequence of events. Unless... You can't think her actions were planned that night to achieve just this result. That they wanted to blind me? A little too precarious a plan,'' he mocked.

Avon didn't argue against that denial, but again the silence stretched between them.

"No, damn you. *That* I won't believe,'' the Frenchman said finally.

"Harry and his sister were sharing a toast when I arrived that morning, unaware, of course, that I could overhear the conversation.''

"I assume you feel I should know what was said,'' Jean-Luc suggested bitterly, the hostility thick in the dark voice. But somewhere inside, a sickness was growing and, against his will, he also remembered the knowledge that had been in her eyes the day he'd returned from the confrontation with Harry at White's.

"They drank to their joint success," Avon answered quietly, watching the reaction in the scarred face of the man to whom he owed his life.

"No," the gambler said again. "I'm no Othello. I know Maddy—"

"And I'm no Iago," the duke interrupted angrily. "Damn it, do you think I want to tell you this?"

"You believe she's involved with what's happened," the gambler said, a statement, not a question.

"I believe…" Avon hesitated, unwilling to condemn on the slight evidence he had collected, but knowing that in his heart he did. There seemed no other explanation. "I don't even know what's going on. Why would Harry start the rumors? What purpose could they have?"

"I should think that would be obvious. To get me killed. I refused his duel. And I can imagine how that would have been set up. You spoiled that plan by your offer. He would never have been able to carry out anything underhanded with your supervision of the arrangements. And then the other began. The more gruesome stories about what I was doing to Maddy. He was hoping someone else, someone overly noble or lovesick like Ned Stapleton, would eventually put a ball through my heart."

"And how would your death benefit Mannering? Arrogant Harry may be, but he's not stupid. What does he have to gain by your death?"

"His sister's freedom? Is that the answer you're looking for? Damn you, Dominic, I told you…" The rigid lines of his body conveyed his anger and his frustration at his inability to do anything about it.

"Do you have a better reason? You continue to insist… How can you be so sure, Jean-Luc, that this doesn't all come down to a desire to release his sister from a marriage that he got her into, a marriage that she no longer—"

"No," the gambler interrupted. His hands unclenched suddenly, and he placed them flat on the surface of the table and pushed himself up. "You have a wife, I believe, your grace?" the Frenchman asked, his voice frigidly polite. "Would you believe that she'd plotted to have you killed?"

There was no answer to that challenge for a long time.

"No," Avon admitted finally.

"No matter what evidence was shown you?"

"No," the duke repeated quietly, this time without hesitation.

"And if someone asked you to give a reason for disbelieving her capable of hurting you, of wanting you dead, could you give a reason he would accept for your certainty?"

"Perhaps not."

"But you would still know. Yourself. Without any doubt."

"I'd know. And you're right. You're no Othello."

"Hamlet," the gambler said softly. "At least until this comes off."

The duke watched the fingers lift to touch the white cloth as they had often lifted to the velvet patch. He hoped that Pritchett was right. Otherwise, he knew the revenge that Harry Mannering deserved would be left up to him. And he was afraid Emily would never understand that necessity.

Chapter Fifteen

In the midst of Pritchett's protracted examination of his eye, Jean-Luc began to wonder what bad news the physician was delaying. He had thought only of this moment, and of the suggestion Avon had reluctantly made about Maddy, since yesterday afternoon.

All night he had held her slight form against his heart, listening to her gentle breathing. He had buried his face in the fragrant softness of her hair that drifted over his body after they had made love, the words of the toast she'd made with her half brother running incessantly through his brain. Over and over in the long hours he'd held her he'd remembered, too, what had been in her eyes that day after Harry's challenge. And in the cloying darkness that surrounded him, he'd relived endlessly those minutes in the alley, trying to prove to himself that what the duke had suggested couldn't possibly be true.

"Warm water," the doctor said to Ling, who hovered over his shoulder, a silent spectator since the examination had begun. Maddy had been banished from the room at her husband's request.

"What is it?" Jean-Luc asked. It was so hard not to know what was going on.

"A slight suppuration. I'm going to clean it away and try to open the lid. There's still some swelling, but the outside laceration seems to be healing rather…'' The quietly professional voice had faded as the skillful fingers made their prolonged examination of that laceration.

"Suppuration?" Jean-Luc repeated finally, questioning the silence.

"A discharge. It's not surprising given the nature—"

"Poison," Ling said over his shoulder. "Eye poison."

"What the hell does that mean?" the gambler asked harshly, his sudden fear making him want to strike out at the voices that surrounded him, voices of people he couldn't see. If only he could read their faces, see what was in their eyes when they talked to him. He'd always been able to tell by a man's eyes if he was telling the truth. Or by a woman's, he thought, and then buried the grim remembrance of Maddy's eyes that day.

"A slight inflammation. I told you this was a possibility, given the nature of the wound."

"You told me that *if* there were no inflammation…" Jean-Luc took a deep breath to control his voice. "Does this mean…"

"It means that the eye needs cleaning and then given time to heal. That's all it means, thus far. The body has remarkable abilities to heal, if we let nature take her course."

"Meaning that you don't know anything to do to prevent this *slight* inflammation?" the gambler asked bitterly.

"No, and if I *did* know any medication that could prevent suppuration and discharge, I would hesitate to use it in so delicate an organ as the eye. You may certainly call in another physician, but in my professional opinion your best option is to wait and see." Realizing the inappropriateness of that expression, the doctor amended it. "Wait and let nature heal if she can."

"And if she can't?"

"Then you'll lose whatever vision you have in the eye," Pritchett said bluntly, but his honesty was a kindness in this case. At least Jean-Luc knew he wasn't hiding anything. "But I'm certainly not ready to concede that yet. The discharge is light, and the outer cut is healing so well…."

As he talked, the cloth with the warm water was applied gently to the bottom of the lid, soaking away the brown crust that had literally glued the long, dark lashes to his patient's skin.

The doctor worked patiently, and there was no pain. When he finally lifted the swollen lid, Jean-Luc was aware of the light. There was nothing in focus, the world lost in a hazy glow, but he knew there was light.

"I can see the lamp," he said softly.

Pritchett's fingers left his eye, the lid allowed to close over the inflamed injury. Jean-Luc felt the doctor's hand comfortingly rest on his shoulder.

"And that's a good sign. As I said before, the inflammation seems to be slight. If all goes—"

"*If,*" Jean-Luc echoed bitterly.

"I never lie to my patients. I can give you no guarantees. I'm going to bind this again, and I will reexamine it in three days. Please don't disturb the dressing until I return. Perhaps we'll know more then."

After Ling had shown the doctor to the door, he returned to find his master, elbows on the table and head lowered into his hands.

"Fix eye," Ling said, and watched the dark head rise sharply. "Fix poison. Like others. Like cut."

"How?" the gambler asked, feeling a sudden leap of hope at Ling's calm surety, despite what the English doctor had said.

"Same on cut. Heal 'suppuration.'" He repeated Pritchett's word carefully.

"The salve? Have you ever used it on an eye before?" Jean-Luc asked.

"Your eye. Outside. All heal up. Medicine good. Not poison. English make poison."

The silence stretched a long time, Jean-Luc weighing the narrowing options. And weighing also that scene in the hallway outside the bedroom, despite Maddy's plausible explanation for her sickness. He really had no choice. Pritchett offered no guarantees, his honesty almost brutal, and Ling's skills had never failed him before.

One chance to save what he had. One roll of the dice. Against the odds, he acknowledged bitterly. As the success of this marriage had been from the beginning.

"God, Maddy," he whispered, thinking of all he now had to lose.

And slowly he nodded.

The document Harry had promised had come that afternoon. Ling brought it up to Jean-Luc's office where Maddy had retreated to write, finally, her half of the contract she'd made with her brother. Her husband was asleep in the darkened bedroom, unaware that he had been helped by Ling's potions to the needed rest that had escaped him last night.

"You send back brother," Ling offered.

She glanced up blankly, her mind engaged in making sure there was no loophole for Harry to slip through in the agreement she was trying to compose. She had debated what to do about the baby, but she finally conceded what she had known from the beginning. She couldn't mention the child, couldn't attempt to protect the baby with this, as she was attempting to protect Jean-Luc, because then Harry would know, and there would always be another person she loved to be used against her. And against Jean-Luc.

"No," she said, shaking her aching head. "Not this time. Thank you, Ling. You may leave it."

He placed the envelope on her husband's desk. She stared at Harry's writing, wondering that he would be so careless as to entrust this to servants. What if Jean-Luc…

He's blind, Maddy. He won't know what he's signing, Harry had said, dismissing the intelligence of the gambler. She closed her eyes briefly, unaware of the dark, considering gaze of the Chinese servant.

"You tell boss?" he asked softly.

She looked up, surprised to find him still there.

"Soon," she repeated her previous answer. And then again dismissing him, "Thank you, Ling." This time she held his eyes until he gave the quick half bow that was his usual acknowledgment of instructions and left.

She touched the envelope that contained the bill of sale. *He won't know.* But she would. She would always know that she had betrayed him. Able to deceive him because he was blind. But weighed against that betrayal was all that they might lose. If Harry had the mine, and if they left London, left for somewhere where the Mannerings could never reach them again…

There are no *Mannerings,* her rational mind argued against her memories. No Mannerings. Only Harry. Her stepfather was dead.

Ghosts, Jean-Luc had said. So many ghosts between them. She found the letter opener on his desk and slit the envelope. She read the document and, although she knew she wasn't qualified to decipher the legal language, it appeared to be exactly what Harry had promised. A bill of sale for a worthless piece of property in Cornwall.

And the sooner she had Jean-Luc's signature on it, the sooner they could be free. Free of the taint her past had put on this marriage. Free of the dangers that his association with her family had brought him. No options. No way out but his signature. Give Harry what he wanted—his worthless mine— and then escape.

Ling helped his master with supper after he had again applied the ointment and redressed the damaged eye.

''Where's Maddy?'' Jean-Luc asked.

''Brother send letter,'' Ling said, replacing the dishes on the tray.

''Maddy's brother?'' Jean-Luc questioned sharply, and there was no way that Ling could know the importance of his answer, given in the broken English the gambler thought he had learned to interpret.

''Brother letters come and go. This one come,'' Ling said, wondering at the sudden hard inhalation. His master's hand found the edge of the small table, and he locked the long fingers over the unyielding wood to stop the sudden tremble.

"You need tea?" Ling asked in concern, the tray balanced and ready to return to the kitchens.

"No, damn it. I don't need your drugged tea. I don't need anything. Just get the hell out."

He was still sitting in the darkness trying to make sense of it all when Maddy came in. He could smell her, the familiar fragrance of her body pervading the room in spite of the breeze that had drifted in with the twilight through the opened window. And even in the face of what he now knew, he wanted her. His body betrayed what his mind had finally accepted. What Avon had suspected all along. He had wondered once before if she were that good an actress. And now he knew. A consummate actress.

She'd make a wonderful whore, he thought bitterly, remembering the small, soft sounds she made when he touched her. And the shivering response. A very talented whore. And he knew, of course, that that was exactly what she was. He'd accused her of that at the beginning. Of selling her body for her brother. But what he couldn't understand...

"Do you mind if I light the lamp?" she asked softly.

"Why the hell should I mind? I certainly won't know whether or not it's lit."

His tone was so different from that careful pretense he'd maintained the last few days, that she hesitated, wondering what was wrong. And then she remembered. He had told her, but she had forgotten in making her own plans for their future. Pritchett had come today.

Her fingers trembled slightly as she adjusted the wick and then lit the lamp. His face was still in shadow, turned toward the open window and the slight breeze that stirred the velvet curtains.

Do it, she urged her heart. Do it, and then put London and Harry behind us.

"Ling sent up a draft for you to sign. Something about the household accounts. I told him not to bother you with it tonight, but apparently there's some urgency—"

She knew she was talking too much. But the abrupt cessation of her explanation was wrong, too. She could feel it in the quiet tension that had invaded the room.

"A draft for Ling's accounts?" he asked.

There was something dark in his tone, and she shivered. In his tenderness, she had long ago lost the sense of his power, but for some reason, with that quiet question, her knowledge that he was a very dangerous man was back.

"I can help you sign it," she said. She could hear the strain in her voice and knew by the slow turning of his head that he had heard it, too. She swallowed and closed her eyes. If he looked at her, he'd know...

She opened her eyes and found the blank whiteness of the bandage. Now, her heart demanded. Before you spoil it all. Before you destroy whatever chance you have to get him away from the Mannerings' reach.

She placed the bill of sale on the table before him, putting the pen she'd brought from his office into his lax fingers.

"Everything ready, Maddy, for my signature?" he asked softly. "This *must* be of 'some urgency.'"

She wasn't prepared for the mockery. She didn't understand it. But she knew what Pritchett's visit today must have meant to him. Until today, he, at least, had still had hope.

"You'll have to show me, Maddy," he reminded her softly.

"Here," she whispered, her eyes filling with tears. They didn't prevent her from directing those fingers that had given her so much pleasure in the short weeks of their marriage. As they would again. She knew she could teach him that it didn't matter. She could fight the black depression that surrounded him tonight. But first she had to protect him from Harry.

She watched him sign, realizing suddenly that she had never seen his signature, but it was clear and bold and only slightly slanting across the line she'd directed him to. So unlike Harry's careless scrawl.

She began to breathe again, the relief that it was done seeming to draw all the blood from her brain, so that she swayed against him.

Feeling the curve of her breast brush his shoulder, he asked softly, still mocking, "And now is it time for my reward?

Now do I get paid again with your body? You do that so well, Maddy. You always have. But it must have been easier these last few days, now that I no longer see what's in your eyes. Those beautiful eyes.''

"Do you want to make love?" she asked, understanding nothing but his pain. Finally he was being forced to accept what she had known since that night in the alley. She reached for the precious document and felt his fingers close around her wrist like a vice.

She gasped, struggling against the force of his hold, but he only tightened his grip.

"Now why don't you tell me what I really signed," he suggested softly.

Her heart stopped, the breath that she'd finally felt free to take frozen in her lungs.

"I told you," she began. "Something for Ling. A draft on the household account..."

"Ling!" His shout interrupted the lie and, realizing what was about to happen, she struggled again, trying to break free.

"You're hurting me," she whispered.

"Good," he said evenly, and the dark fingers bit more deeply into her wrist.

"Jean-Luc," she began, hearing, as he did, the note of entreaty against the pain.

"Don't beg, Maddy. The time has finally come for everything that's been hidden, for everything that's been done in the darkness, to be exposed to the light. Truth, Maddy, is what we're after here. And I'll begin with a truth you apparently didn't know. Ling doesn't handle the household accounts. He can't read. So you'll have to tell me, my darling. I couldn't see it, you know. What did I sign?"

And she could think of nothing, no other lie. Ling would be here soon, and he would confirm that he hadn't sent up the document.

"A bank draft for a bill," she said desperately, Harry's ridiculous suggestion all her frightened brain could dredge up in the midst of her fear, a fear that was growing like a poison mushroom in the darkness of the forest floor. "From Madame

Darnet. I had some dresses made. They were very expensive, and I was afraid you'd be angry.''

''Because I have always been so parsimonious about your dress allowance?'' he asked politely. But the fingers bit deeper and she gasped again. ''You'll have to do better than that,'' he said maliciously.

''What you do?'' Ling asked from the doorway, and they both turned in reaction to his shocked voice.

''Get Avon. Send for the duke and then come back. I'm going to need you,'' Jean-Luc ordered.

''What you do?'' Ling repeated again, his dark eyes on Maddy's too-white face.

''Get Avon,'' Jean-Luc repeated. ''Damn you, Ling, I told you to send for Avon. I need his help. I can't… Just get him, damn you, and then come back up here.''

The servant's eyes locked with Maddy's, and slowly she nodded. Ling disappeared into the hall.

Maybe if he knew the duke was on his way, she could talk to him, calm him down by explaining what she'd intended. He'd be furious that she had deceived him, but she could make him understand.

''Jean-Luc,'' she began.

''Don't,'' he said viciously. ''I don't want to hear any more of your lies. When Avon arrives, we'll sort it out. Until then we wait.''

''You don't understand,'' she said desperately.

His laugh was bitter and short.

''You're right, my darling. I never understood. I thought I could read men's eyes and their voices. I thought I could tell when someone was lying. But you—'' He stopped, that mocking, twisted smile touching his mouth. ''God, you're so good. So damn talented at lies and betrayal. Did you learn that from Harry? All those pathetic lies about what your stepfather and Fairchild did to you. Or did they just get tired of your damned deceptions? Did they find you out as I have, my beautiful Maddy? It's been a lie from the very beginning, hasn't it? And now, when I'm—''

He halted sharply, and she saw the deep breath he drew, and she ached for him.

Despite the cruelty of what he'd said, she knew that he was lashing out because of his blindness. He couldn't see, and she had tried to trick him. She deserved his anger, but he was so wrong about the other.

"I never lied to you—" she began.

His laugh interrupted her, bitter and dark, and she flinched against it.

"Damn you," he said, his voice too soft, deadly now with the destruction of everything he had believed her to be. "Damn you for the lying whore you are."

The locked fingers pulled her toward him, and he raised his other hand to strike her. Whether it was his blindness or his memories that prevented the blow, she didn't know, but instead he released her with a jerk, and she stumbled against the small, unstable table before falling hard onto the wooden floor.

The table toppled, the lamp crashing again in a shattering dissonance. The only light now was the glow from the hall and from the rising moon outside the window.

"Hurt baby." Ling's shocked voice came from the doorway. "You hurt baby," he warned, his English this time clear enough to avoid misinterpretation and to penetrate the bitter anger.

"Baby?" Jean-Luc repeated sharply. And then again, after an interval, his tone entirely different, "Baby."

"I didn't want to tell you until—" Maddy began, but his laughter broke against the whispered words. She had never heard anything like his laughter. And she reacted to the horror of what she was hearing.

"Jean-Luc," she whispered in protest.

"And *now,* finally, it all begins to make sense," he said. "God, how simple. I couldn't understand why you'd married me. Why you'd begun all this. What you had to gain by a marriage to someone like me. But, of course, that's the key to it all. You needed a husband, a very gullible husband, to provide a name for your bastard. Someone who would surely leap at a chance to have a woman like you. As I certainly did. No questions asked. God, I'm such a fool. It must be very satisfying to know what a fool you can make of a man who loves you, Maddy.''

''I don't know what you—''

''Stapleton's?'' he asked suddenly. ''Is it Stapleton's baby?'' he suggested again, and for the first time she understood fully what he was saying.

Oh, dear God, Jean-Luc, she thought. But the shock held her paralyzed. He couldn't believe…

''No, of course not. Stapleton would have been only too delighted to marry you. Then who and why? Who could the father be that would necessitate your marrying someone like me—scarred and deformed, a bastard spawned in a Paris whorehouse?'' He paused again, remembering how much he'd revealed. ''Do you know you're the only person I've ever told that story? Because I trusted that you loved me enough to— God, what a fool,'' he said again, his voice etched with acid.

''The baby's yours,'' she whispered. ''You have to know that.''

''At least legally,'' he agreed, laughing. ''Why wouldn't he marry you, Maddy? What could prevent a man from marrying you once he'd had you, as obviously he has? Once he'd tasted your sweetness, why wouldn't he want that wonderfully responsive body, so damned passionate…?''

The silence was too sudden. And she saw that whatever he was thinking had taken his breath. His lips parted, and then he closed them, and she watched as they slowly whitened against the force that he was applying to keep them closed, swallowing strongly against the bile that was climbing into the back of his throat.

She couldn't imagine the thought that had suddenly entered his mind. Despite its horror, he knew it explained everything. Why the father of this baby could never acknowledge his parentage.

Because she loved him, the tears started as she watched his face, watched what was happening in that dark, marred face.

"Harry," he said softly. "Harry, of course. You're Harry's whore as well as his sister."

The words were only a whisper, and before she had made sense of the perversion he'd suggested, before her mind could grasp the incredible idea that he thought she had made love to her half brother, his head turned sharply toward the window, the strong Roman nose that was like his father's lifting against the acrid odor of burning cloth.

"Ling," he said suddenly, his hand groping into the blackness that surrounded him. He could taste the bitter coppery tang of fear in his mouth. Fire.

Maddy blinked to control the tears, but reacting to that movement, she followed his blind stare and found the bottom of the curtain in flames, caught by the slowly spreading trickle of burning oil from the broken lamp.

"Ling," she breathed as he had.

"God, Maddy," Jean-Luc said, starting across the short distance that separated them. He ran into the overturned table and fell against it, preventing himself from going down only by grasping desperately at one of the legs.

"Maddy, where are you, damn it? Answer me," he demanded, the old arrogance of command in his voice.

"I'm here," she whispered, responding automatically, not realizing that whisper would draw him nearer to the danger.

Ling took the groping hand, untangling him from the obstacle of the table, and then tried to turn him away from the spreading flames.

"Maddy," he demanded again, unable to judge how close to her the fire had spread.

"I'm coming," she promised. "Let Ling get you out. Get out, Jean-Luc. You can't help me," she said, unthinking.

Ling pushed against his master's body, forcing him away from the danger. Jean-Luc struggled, but he was disoriented in his darkness, unsure now where Maddy might be.

"Damn it, Maddy," he shouted again.

"Lady coming," Ling said, pushing again against the still-resisting body. "She come, you leave. Now. Lady here."

They were almost to the door, and Maddy knew that Ling would take him to safety.

She put her hand against the floor to push herself up, and found the bill of sale was under her fingers. They closed over the precious document, and she put it into the low neckline of her gown, safe against her racing heartbeat.

Once she was standing, she could see that the fire had only touched one side of the heavy curtains, slowly eating its way upward. She grabbed the pitcher from the washstand and, taking careful aim, doused the burning material. The black smoke poured across the room, pushed back inside by the breeze. Coughing, she pulled the chair closer to the window, climbing carefully so she could reach above the smoldering ruin of the curtain. She ripped the whole away from the window and, wadding it, threw the sodden mess into the street below. She turned to examine the bedroom, and then she took the counterpane off the bed and threw it over the singed boards of the wooden floor. She stamped over the coverlet, smothering any remaining sparks, and then threw it, too, out the open window.

Finally she pushed her hair out of her eyes, not realizing that she'd left a streak of soot on her temple. She leaned against the wall, fighting against the now-familiar dizziness.

Harry's whore echoed bitterly in the swirling darkness. If he could believe that… But it didn't matter anymore what he believed. Because it was over. Whatever he'd felt about her before, she had destroyed with her deception. She'd lied to him, betrayed him, and he couldn't want her now. Not after all that she had cost him. Certainly not if he believed half of the things he'd just said.

She didn't know how long she'd been alone in the dark, smoke-filled bedroom. It seemed an eternity. As endless as the night in the alley. The night she'd blinded her husband. She had only wanted to make up for what she'd done and to protect him against Harry. *Harry's whore* echoed. But she knew with that poison now in his mind… A black perversion her lies had made him believe…

She shook her head against those whirling thoughts, and then, taking one last look around the room in which she'd lived these few weeks, she slipped into the hall and to the top of the darkened servants' stairs that led to the kitchen and the back alley. She could hear raised voices from the front of the house, people responding to the emergency. Avon, perhaps. And suddenly she remembered. The agreement for Harry's signature. She crossed back into Jean-Luc's office where she'd left it.

With the paper she'd so carefully composed clutched in her hand, she hurried down the kitchen stairs and away from the shouting in the front of the house. At least she had the two documents. When she had secured Harry's signature, then he would no longer have any reason to harm her husband. Avon would care for Jean-Luc, and the safest course for them all would be for her to disappear, so that she'd never hurt him again. And so she could protect the baby from the Mannerings. The safest course for them all…

"She's not there. I promise you. The room is virtually untouched. She must have put out the fire before she left," Avon repeated patiently.

There was no response from the man who sat quietly in the empty salon of the elegant casino he had run so successfully. He had long ago decided they were lying. Maddy was dead because he had let Ling lead him away from the reaching flames. Because he had been too much a coward to face the fire to find her and demand that she come with them.

When he had realized that Ling had lied and Maddy wasn't with them, he had had to be forcibly restrained on the stairs, physically prevented by the straining efforts of several of the strangers who had responded to Ling's call, from returning to the room where he had visualized Maddy caught behind that wall of flame that he knew so well, whose agonizing caress he'd never forgotten.

It really didn't matter what lies Avon concocted to save his sanity. He would always know what he'd done. After what he said to her, she'd chosen to remain in that room.

"All right, damn you," the duke said in exasperation. "I'll take you up, and you can see for yourself."

The unfortunate choice of words stopped him for a moment, and then Avon put his hand on his friend's arm and urged him to his feet.

"She's not dead. She's not there. And I'm not lying to you."

But even in the silence of the malodorous bedroom, the gambler's face hadn't changed. The duke watched as he carefully traced over the undamaged objects in the room, each holding some memory of Maddy. His fingers blindly searched for some shred of what had been here, which he had tonight destroyed. And when he had completed that self-appointed task, still there was no release of the tight control in which he held himself.

"She's not here," Avon said again, trying to break through the rigid barrier of whatever emotion was holding him.

And finally, defeated by that continued silence, he again took the Frenchman's arm to lead him back down the stairs.

"There was a paper," the gambler said softly. "On the table. Would you look for it please."

But there was, of course, nothing there. Nothing at all was found of what Maddy had had him sign, despite the more careful search Ling and the duke made after they'd put him to bed on the cot in the alcove off his office.

And it was there, while keeping watch through the long, dark hours over a man he knew didn't sleep, that Avon began to wonder if he might have been wrong, terribly wrong.

"With Harry?" Emily said unbelievingly, watching her husband's face as he told the story, sparing nothing of his role in the tragedy that had been played out last night. "Oh, my dear. Dominic, how could you be such a fool as to believe that?"

"It never occurred to me that that might be the reason she was conspiring with her brother. But Jean-Luc... When she told Jean about the baby, it seemed to him that an...involvement with her half brother would explain everything. Her reason for marrying him, despite..." His voice hesitated over the admissions the gambler, in his grief, had repeated last night before the bitter wall had been put up.

"Despite what he is," she finished for him, remembering the Frenchman's words as he had stood in the foyer of her home that day. Misunderstanding, the silver eyes of her husband blazed upward.

"What he is, Emily, is my friend," he said softly.

"Who's a bigger fool than you if he could believe that about Maddy. Maddy tried to raise Harry after their mother died. And a more unpleasant child I've yet to meet," she said with disgust. "They were always too pinched for funds to have had a proper governess. As young as she was, Maddy probably wiped Harry's nose and tucked him up at night. And she's his sister," she finished, unanswerably and with utter scorn, the vision of her own dearly loved brother in her mind's eye. "She's certainly not going to... Men are such fools," she said with disgust.

"I think the life Jean-Luc's led has exposed him to more depravities than you can imagine exist, Emily. He knows too well the depths humanity can sink to. You can't judge him when you have no understanding of the causes of his cynicism, however destructive it may have been."

"But surely he can't *really* believe that Maddy could ever... He should know better," Emily argued.

"Perhaps," Avon acknowledged, having known himself the kind of jealousy that could drive the most rational man to errors in judgment, "but if she's entirely innocent, as you seem to think, then why did she leave? Why has she disappeared?"

"There must be some rational explanation for Maddy's actions," Emily mused. "For the deception. For her continued contact with Harry. There must be another—"

"What is it, Hawkins?" Avon interrupted, responding to the near-silent entrance of his butler.

"A woman, your grace. She asked to see you. I explained that you were *en famille,* but she was most insistent. So I thought..."

"Maddy?" Emily suggested to her husband's back as he hurried before the dignified butler into the foyer.

But the woman who stood waiting was no one he knew.

"Monsieur le Duc?" she said questioningly.

"I'm Avon," he acknowledged.

"My name is Genevieve Darnet. I'm a friend of Jean-Luc's," she began to explain. "And I have something from Madame Gavereau. Something that I'm to give to you and to no one else."

"Wait," he said. "My wife is in my study. You can tell us both. If you'll come this way…"

"For the Duke of Avon, she said. And you see, your grace, it's to be opened only if something *tragique,* some disaster, happens to Jean-Luc. She was adamant that you understand that. I was not to leave it unless you agreed on your honor that it would remain unopened." She paused and looked expectantly at the duke. Finally, knowing that whatever was in Maddy's envelope probably held the key to all that had happened, he unwillingly nodded his agreement.

Reassured, the Frenchwoman hurried on. "And so I promised to bring the paper, and I gave her some money. She said that Jean-Luc… I think they had argued. I had warned him. But I knew whatever had happened wasn't her fault. And there was something in her eyes…" She paused again, remembering the empty eyes, and shivered. "And so I gave her the money and took the paper. You understand, your grace? A woman understands these things," she said, her hand held out in a gesture of entreaty to the duchess. "She seemed so distraught, and I was afraid…"

"Of course," Emily said, smiling at her. "Of course, I understand." And then the important question, "How much money did you give her?"

"Ten guineas. It's all I had in the shop," the modiste said, relieved that the duchess, at least, didn't think she had done anything so terrible, despite the fact that she was Jean-Luc's friend.

And then Emily escorted Madame Darnet to the front door

with a smiling suggestion that she was herself looking for a new dressmaker. The modiste left, her unease pushed to the back of her practical mind, and Emily returned to the study to find her husband deep in thought.

"Ten guineas," she said softly, and he looked up, the worry clear in the gray eyes.

"How far could she go on ten guineas?" she asked, having no idea of the fares for public transportation.

But her husband knew there was no point in that kind of speculation, and he simply shook his head.

"What are you going to do?" she questioned, knowing him very well indeed.

"I'm going to make sure that our gambler friend doesn't do anything foolish."

"Foolish?" Emily repeated. "Like putting an end to Harry Mannering's miserable existence?"

"I don't consider, my darling, given the provocation he's had, that that would be foolish at all."

"Nor do I," his wife said. "For once, we're in total agreement."

"But I'd prefer he wait until we have some answers, and with my promise not to open Maddy's letter, those answers may eventually have to come from Harry."

Chapter Sixteen

Three months later

"All of them?" Harry repeated incredulously.

"Mortgages bought for a pittance from your creditors, who were very glad to get what they could. Others called due as payment for gambling debts. Quite *legitimate* debts, my lord," Pennington assured his client at the almost inarticulate sound of protest. "You may be very sure that I verified their authenticity. And, of course, since the estate could not hope to redeem...even at a fraction of their worth... I'm afraid I must inform you the Mannering properties are gone, my lord. All of them," Mr. Pennington reiterated. He could not prevent a small note of righteousness from creeping into his voice. He had, of course, warned the viscount of the eventual outcome of his life-style. But the young today...

"Let me see those damn things," Lord Mannering demanded, grabbing the sheaf of papers from the ink-stained fingers of his man of business with such violence that a few of them fluttered to the floor. The small number that escaped his lordship's furious scrutiny were unimportant. There were quite enough of them bearing that name. All the attacks on the Mannering financial house of cards seemed to have been carried out by the same man.

"Gavereau," Harry said softly.

"Indeed, my lord, it appears that particular French gentleman held a remarkable number of your markers. And had held them now for several months. As to why he should choose this particular time to call them due…"

"Because somehow the bastard learned just how precarious, at this juncture, the negotiations for the formation of the company were. And he knew that word of this would get back to the prospective investors, and then… Damn his black soul to hell. We had an agreement, damn him. Those markers were redeemed. And I kept my part," Harry said bitterly. "That's what comes of dealing with someone who isn't a gentleman. That bloody bastard."

"An agreement, my lord? Indeed, this is the first I've heard of it. If it was a legal contract, then perhaps you'd like for me to peruse the document and see—"

"Document?" Harry said blankly. "There was no document, you idiot. My sister. My *own* sister. And how does he repay me? With this treachery. Damn him to hell."

"A family arrangement, my lord? Still you must know that it's far more desirable, strictly from a legal point of view, of course, to have everything in writing. Even within the family."

"The family," Harry repeated bitterly. "God, that French poltroon to be considered part of *my* family. It makes me sick. And given the fact that he's certainly ruined any chance of my getting the backing I need for the venture in Cornwall, I believe, Pennington, that it might be time to carry out my promise to my sister and arrange her divorce."

"Divorce, my lord? Surely not a divorce." Pennington's voice expressed his opinion of that very shocking procedure.

Harry laughed. "Not the legal kind, I assure you. A rather more permanent dissolution of the matrimonial ties, if you take my meaning."

"Indeed, my lord, I don't believe that I do," whispered the shocked Pennington, hoping that he didn't.

"That's probably just as well." Harry laughed again at his own joke. And then he turned from revenge to more practical matters. "Tell me, Pennington, is it true that on the death of a husband, given, of course, that there are no heirs, his property passes directly to his widow?"

"There are exceptions, my lord. If the estate is entailed, for example..." At Harry's negative gesture, Pennington reconsidered. "Then generally, I would expect that the properties would eventually come to the widow, under the control, of course, of the male members of her family."

"Oh, of course," said Harry, smiling. "That goes without saying."

And smiling still, the Viscount Mannering left the office humming "La Marseillaise" under his breath. The Frenchman was not nearly so clever as he imagined himself to be. And whatever promises Harry had made to Maddy he now considered null and void. After all, the gambler, and not he, had violated the original agreement. As for the constraints imposed by the document he'd signed for Maddy... If, by the gambler's death, he lost the venture in Cornwall, he'd at least regain what rightfully was his—all the properties that bastard had stolen from the Mannerings. And he'd deal with Maddy's threats about Avon when he had to.

"Sufficient unto the day," said Harry piously, his usual unshakable faith in his most recent scheme intact, "is the evil thereof."

The trouble with hiring an assassin, as Harry had learned from his quixotic experience with the man with the whip, was that they were expensive and unreliable, despite their assurances to the contrary. Had he brought that off, it would have been an extremely appropriate answer to the Frenchman's taunt in White's, a taunt the gambler had made in front of Harry's closest friends. He could still remember the looks in their eyes after his brother-in-law's humiliating visit.

But given the situation now, there was really no reason to resort to anyone with more experience than himself. After all, how difficult could it be to dispose of a blind man? There had already been one fire at the casino, caused, according to the gossip, by the accidental overturning of a lamp.

The casino had never reopened after the affair in the alley, and everyone was aware of the reason. With the Frenchman no longer able to direct its operation, the entire staff had been released. There was the Chinaman the mob had dragged out that night, and very likely no one else in residence after dark. Only a blind man and his servant. And Maddy, of course.

Harry had considered the wording of his message to his sister a long time. Something that would draw her away during the hours he intended to carry out his plan. Something she could not fail to respond to. He had finally settled on an urgent request from the Duke of Avon. To meet him at a certain secluded spot—near enough to the casino that she could easily walk, even at night, and yet far enough that she'd be safely out of the way. A meeting, he decided, to discuss a threat to her husband's safety. He smiled rather grimly at the irony of that.

Harry carefully printed out the message to disguise his hand and sealed it with the most impressive seal in his father's collection. Not ducal, of course, but in her haste to examine the contents of a confidential message from Avon, Maddy would never realize that. Since she had willingly confronted a violent mob to protect her husband before, she would surely, as vulnerable as he was now, be brave enough to venture out into the London night.

His forced entry into the casino on the night in question seemed almost too easy, but Harry's self-confidence did not lend itself to questioning fate's benevolence. The empty salon was eerie in the silence, its vast proportions and massive furnishings under their Holland covers giving evidence of the owner's previous success. He supposed the gambler had used the profits he had acquired in those affluent days to carry out the acquisition of the few Mannering properties he hadn't won at these very tables. But soon, Harry thought, moving smoothly from shadow to shadow across the lower floor, all would be as it should be once more.

He had reasoned that, to be plausible, the fire must start in the upper story, in the living quarters. He quietly climbed the stairs into the darkness above and was confronted on the landing with two doorways, both open. Upon exploration, he found the one on the right led to a large bedroom, dimly touched with light from the street lamps below. There was no one there, the sheets of the bed smooth and undisturbed.

Harry tiptoed across the hall, the glow of the full moon through the window of the opposing room almost bright enough, now that his eyes had adjusted to the darkness, to give a sense of normality to his passage. He entered with less stealth than he had employed in the bedroom, having already decided that his probably was a fruitless journey, the entire building apparently deserted. Perhaps the Frenchman and Maddy, in the months since the attack, had moved into a more normal residence. He ground his teeth in frustration.

"Who's there?"

The question came from the darkness, and despite his shock, Harry could perceive the shadowed outline of a figure in the chair behind the desk. And recognizing the accent, he knew that he had found his quarry. Alone and unprotected.

"I thought we had an agreement," Harry said, throwing the accusation at the shape hidden in the darkness. He could see nothing of the features of the man in the chair, but he knew he himself was more clearly illuminated by the moonlight.

"And *I* thought our agreement had ended," the soft voice answered.

"Ended? Why would you believe… I had nothing to do with what happened here that night. I hope you're not blaming me for the action of a few firebrands. Maddy was very popular, you know. And the rumors that resulted from your marriage—"

"And I suppose you had no part in those, either, Lord Mannering," the quiet voice interrupted to mock.

"I never…" Harry began and then swallowed the lie. Why was he arguing with the man he had come to kill? Because suddenly, Harry realized, that seemed a little more difficult that he had thought. It was one thing to set a fire and leave, unaware until later of its consequences, like the rumors he'd set into motion, himself carefully removed from their outcome. But he was finding it quite another thing to cold-bloodedly put an end to a man who was calmly discussing their past interactions.

"It's a little late for visitors, Harry. Or did you come to see Maddy? She's not here, you know."

"I know," Harry admitted. "I sent her away."

"Did you?" The small laugh was bitter. "Somehow I thought I had managed that. But perhaps you're right. You always had more control over Maddy than I did," the Frenchman suggested.

There was something in the deadly quietness of the voice that was beginning to bother Harry. Almost as if the gambler were aware of something that Harry had not thought of. Or was waiting for something...

"And how is Maddy?" The question floated out of the shadows.

"Maddy? Good God, how should I know? Surely you would be a better position to... I haven't seen Maddy in weeks. Not since—" Harry paused abruptly.

Not since she had brought the agreement for his signature. But he couldn't reveal that. That would lead to a discussion of the mine, the one valuable piece of his property that the Frenchman had not yet acquired.

"Somehow I would have thought that with the baby..." The suggestion trailed away.

"The baby?" Harry repeated in bewilderment. "I don't understand. What baby?"

Additional proof, the gambler knew, that he'd been wrong. Since Avon had opened Harry's message to his sister, which had given them warning of tonight's attack, Jean-Luc had begun to acknowledge the possibility that Maddy was innocent in Harry's scheming. And perhaps even innocent of...

"The baby Maddy's carrying," the voice explained.

"An heir. My God, is that what you're suggesting? That you have an heir? And why should I believe that? It's very possible that you're simply trying to trick me." Harry apparently then rejected that idea, his anger building, "Damme, if I don't believe you and Maddy would do that just to spite me. Produce an heir. Someone to inherit all that you've stolen from me."

The famous Mannering rage had begun eating at Harry's control. All his careful planning had been for naught. Even if he killed the gambler… If Maddy's child were male, then everything that belonged to the Mannerings would end up in the hands of this French bastard's whelp. Avon would *certainly* see to that. Damn them all to hell. And damn Maddy especially, for falling in love with her husband.

There was absolute silence now from the dark figure in the chair, and finally another question, whose answer would mean a revelation of all Harry's careful plans.

"And why would the thought that I might have an heir distress you so, my lord?" Jean-Luc said softly, but his mind was still working on the salient part of that accusation. *That you have an heir? You and Maddy… You and Maddy…* "You're not by any chance planning to arrange my departure from this world, are you, Harry? I *did* warn you about the mark of Cain."

"You're not my brother, you bastard," Harry denied furiously, "and don't quote Scripture to me like some damned Methodist. We both know what you are."

"You're right, of course. We *both* know exactly what I am. But the question remains. What business do you have here tonight, Harry? If you didn't come to see Maddy, then why don't you explain why you're skulking through my home? I'm sure you have a very reasonable explanation."

"Very reasonable," Harry said with deadly passion. "I'm going to kill you. I should have done it before, only Maddy…" He paused, forced to remember the terms of the agreement that rested in Avon's safekeeping.

"Maddy?" the gambler said softly.

"Nothing, damn you. Nothing."

"Then might I be allowed to know the method by which I'm to meet my Maker?" There was no hint of fear in the question. Indeed, the tone seemed to verge on amusement, and once more the viscount felt a momentary touch of unease, which he forced back by remembering that this time he held all the trumps.

"Your Maker?" Harry questioned with a sneer. "Meet your master, I should think, you charred devil." And enjoying his own wit, he laughed. "Although it appears you've had a head start, I'm going to send you to hell in a most proper fashion, *dear* brother."

"I don't think so," said the Duke of Avon from the doorway behind him.

Lord Mannering turned at the sound of that assured voice. Revealed by the moonlight streaming through the uncurtained window, two men stood in the open doorway of the gambler's office.

"And I shall be happy to testify to the threat you have just made. I would venture to say that you might even be found to have upon your person the materials needed to carry out that threat."

"Testify and be damned," Harry said furiously, the blood pounding like a hammer through his temples. The Frenchman and his keeper. "Be damned to you both. No one will believe Gavereau, given the stories concerning his treatment of my sister. Most of London would consider I'd done a service in killing him. And you've made your championship too obvious, your grace, to pretend to be an impartial witness now."

"And I, Harry?" the Marquis of Ainsley said, stepping from the shadows behind Avon. "Do you suppose they'll believe *me* to be impartial?"

The infamous Mannering black rage overcame the viscount at the unfairness of it all. They were all against him. Aligned with the Frenchman instead of lending their support to one of their own, as any proper-feeling member of the nobility should. Well, he wouldn't go down without a fight, not Harry Mannering.

"He has a gun." The Frenchman shouted the warning, throwing himself across the desk in an attempt to wrest away from his brother-in-law the dueling pistol whose elaborate silver ornamentation had caught the moonlight as Harry raised it to point at the men in the doorway.

Startled by the exclamation, the viscount turned in response as the gambler's body slammed into his. The report of the gun was shockingly loud in the confined space, the trigger obviously as sensitive as Harry had once feared it might be.

"A light," ordered Avon, moving quickly to intervene in the surging bodies that struggled, almost hidden by the shadows covering the floor.

But before Ainsley had managed the lamp on the desk, it became obvious that one of the combatants had already established dominance. The illumination that the marquis's capable hands brought to the room revealed Mannering efficiently locked in the grip of a man whose profession demanded the ability to subdue drunks and troublemakers with speed and power. The viscount had been no match for tactics learned on the streets of Paris and perfected in more gambling hells than even the Frenchman could remember.

"Well-done," said Avon in quiet admiration.

"How did you know he had a pistol?" Ainsley asked the question that had bothered him since the warning.

"The moonlight," Jean-Luc said softly, the still-mobile corner of the scarred mouth raising slightly as he met the murderous gaze of his brother-in-law. "The silver glinted in the moonlight."

"But…" Ainsley began and then halted, his question made ridiculous by the obvious. "I thought you were blind."

"Dominic believed keeping my recovery a secret gave us an advantage in a game the Mannerings have had all their own way far too long."

"The Mannerings?" the marquis questioned, remembering that there was no one left of that line but Harry. "But there are no—"

"Ghosts," agreed the Frenchman, and his fingers tightened reflexively on the muscles of Harry's throat. "Too many bloody ghosts."

"Speaking of blood," said Avon calmly.

"I know," Jean-Luc answered, a note of resignation creeping into his voice. "The bastard shot me."

"Bastard," Harry spat out, still defiant, despite his helplessness. "I'm not the bastard here, you blackguard."

"Do you know, Harry," said his brother-in-law musingly, "in spite of your noble and very legitimate birth, I believe, in this instance, that you might be wrong about that?"

"A fine piece of workmanship," Avon said in admiration of the dueling pistol he was holding. Pritchett had already bound the deep furrow the ball had made in the gambler's upper arm, and the injured member rested, somewhat more comfortably, in a sling. Jean-Luc was sipping brandy as he watched Avon's examination of the pistol Maddy had left at Harry's house the night she had gone to bargain for his life.

"It was my father's," the gambler said.

The duke's gray eyes lifted from the chased silver in answer to the Frenchman's amusement.

"It's engraved," Avon said softly.

"I know. The *Comte de Marivaux.*"

"And he gave it to you?" the duke asked, carefully placing the pistol beside its mate in the rosewood chest.

The Frenchman laughed. "I bought them in a pawnbroker's shop after the Revolution. I decided I was as entitled to own them as any other of his gutter spawn."

Dominic studied the man seated at ease again in the chair behind the desk. The twisted smile had been briefly mocking before the gambler turned his attention back to the brandy, which the duke suspected was necessary now as much for the pain as for its restorative properties.

"He's in London, you know," Avon said finally.

"I know. One of the countless *émigrés.* But I didn't come to England for what you're obviously envisioning as a touching reunion. Meeting my father is an experience I have already enjoyed. I assure you, neither of us wishes to repeat the encounter." He took another deep pull on the brandy.

"And Maddy?" Avon suggested, a topic they had avoided, despite Mannering's many revelations, revelations that the Frenchman had mercilessly extracted in spite of his own injury. There was nothing they did not now know about Harry's machinations and his callous use of his sister to carry them out. And when Avon had finally opened Maddy's agreement, this attack on her husband certainly fulfilling the conditions he'd agreed to, the viscount's last hope to save something out of the fiasco had been destroyed.

"Why do you suppose Maddy would care to meet my father?" Jean-Luc asked, being deliberately obtuse. "Consider the awkwardness. 'My father, my dear. Although he doesn't acknowledge that relationship. Sir, your bastard's estranged wife.' I should think, Avon—"

"Are you going to Cornwall?" the duke broke in, and his tone brooked no more nonsense.

"No, you are. If you will, of course, your grace." The gambler used the formal address with deliberate yet polite coldness. "Or perhaps I should ask Ainsley, if you don't have the time."

"Don't be a fool," Avon demanded sharply. "What do you want me to do in Cornwall?"

"Make Maddy aware of the financial provisions we've decided upon for her future. And for the child's. And of Harry's imminent departure, of course. Knowing Maddy—"

"The child?" Avon interrupted again, and then emphasizing the pronoun, "*Your* child. This is not some—"

"Damn you, I know exactly my relationship to…" The gambler didn't finish that thought. "But you must know, after what I accused her of…"

"Coward," the duke pronounced softly and watched the single hazel eye lift, glittering with anger, to meet his challenge and then drop to the golden liquid in the glass he held.

"Why do you think I should go to Cornwall when we both know—"

"Because you owe her that, at least," the duke said.

"An apology?" Jean-Luc mocked harshly. "For that which is unforgivable? For having uttered the unspeakable?"

"Yes," Avon ordered, without compromise.

And after a long time, the gambler agreed, softly, "Yes."

The fall rains and the condition of the roads running west from the capital made their journey a nightmare. They both knew the wound Harry had inflicted was now inflamed, despite the saltwater poultices Pritchett had suggested, and Jean-Luc remembered Ling's derision of the English doctor's therapeutic strategies. However, the Chinaman himself had disappeared more than a month before. He had remained only long enough after the overheard argument with Maddy to complete his ultimately successful treatment of his master's eye.

They reached the cottage at the end of another miserable day's travel. Even in Avon's well-sprung conveyance, every jolt and pothole reverberated through the throbbing heaviness of Jean-Luc's arm. A misting rain had begun as, following the directions of a helpful villager, the tired horses were allowed to stop before the dwelling whose air of decay and neglect made the duke wonder if they had indeed been directed to the right place. There was nothing remotely aristocratic about the scene, despite the quite elevated social standing of Maddy's maternal line.

"A damned hovel," the gambler gritted, exiting the coach and protecting as well as he could the damaged arm, which, without the support of the sling he'd just removed, protested vehemently. "Why the hell would she come here?"

"Safety," Avon ventured. "You may be sure Harry and his father would not frequent these environs. And through the years, perhaps Maddy found that once out of sight, she was also out of mind."

"You have to get her out of here and back to London."

"Yes, of course. But given the lack of reaction to our arrival, I'm beginning to think there's no one here, which may necessitate a return to the village for additional information. But first things first. We'll get you settled and—"

"There's a fire," the gambler said softly, gesturing with his head to the smoke wafting out of the chimney that leaned precariously against the house.

"Then perhaps I was wrong," agreed Avon. He walked the few steps to the sagging front door and knocked imperiously.

Jean-Luc found he was holding his breath but, as the silence stretched, the only response to Avon's repeated summoning of the inhabitants, he found himself relaxing.

A respite from facing Maddy. As much as he wanted to see her, he knew he had forever relinquished whatever rights he might have to her forgiveness. There was no way to make amends. Apologize, admit what a fool he'd been, give her the papers Avon had had prepared and leave. Remove the stain of what he was from both their lives. Hers and the child. He would not allow the words Dominic had used to enter into his undertaking of this commission. He had forever relinquished those rights also.

Avon touched the handle of the door, which creaked protestingly and then swung inward. The duke limped into the darkness of the interior only to reemerge a moment later.

"Deserted." Avon confirmed their first impression. "But there *is* a fire, and at least you'll be out of the rain."

"I think I should return with you to the village and help—"

"And risk an inflammation of the lungs, as well? Don't be a fool." And then seeing what was in his eyes, the duke amended, "There's a chair. And I won't be long. We may have been misinformed about Maddy's whereabouts, but *whoever* is living here won't begrudge an injured man the use of his fire and shelter from the rain."

"Especially if you grease his palm with enough gold," the gambler suggested, but he had already begun the short journey into the warmth and surprisingly welcoming atmosphere of the cottage. The room was clean and pleasantly arranged, the rag rugs bright and coverlets neatly spread over its threadbare furnishings. And overlying all, the faint fragrance that Jean-Luc would have recognized anywhere, anytime. They had not been misinformed.

Avon had taken his arm to help him to the chair that was cozily arranged near the cheerful blaze, but the gesture was too reminiscent of those weeks when Ling had fought the infection that threatened to leave him forever a prisoner in the dark world Harry had arranged for him.

He gently removed his elbow from the duke's hold and walked to the chair. He sank gratefully into its soft warmth, hating the effects of the fever that sapped his strength, especially at the end of such a long day. He eased his arm against his body, carefully supporting the elbow with his other hand and, almost against his will, rested his head against the worn covering of the chair, closing his eye and allowing himself to savor, for what he was aware was the last time, the subtle aura that was uniquely Maddy's. He never knew when Avon left.

But he was aware when, only a short time later, Maddy quietly slipped into the back door.

Maddy laid the mass of wildflowers she carried on the small table and then shook out the damp shawl she had, in the name of decency, thrown around her arms to hide the bulge of her pregnancy. As if the villagers had never seen a pregnant woman before.

Increasing. In a delicate condition. She remembered all the silly euphemisms the ton used to hide the reality of pregnancy. But as she had been, at the beginning of her marriage, unable to throw off her upbringing and enjoy the freedom her life with Jean-Luc had offered, so was she now unable to go out in public without making some concession to those ridiculous conventions. Even if "public" was the path that wound along the top of the cliffs.

The room had darkened with the dusk, and now only the flames provided any light. She turned to see if she needed to bring in more wood for the evening and felt her heart stop. Against the backdrop of the fire, that perfect profile she had first seen in a country inn two years ago was before her, highlighted again against the darkness.

"I'm not a ghost," he said softly in answer to her gasp.

So many ghosts, flitted through her mind.

"At least not yet," he said, the one-sided smile moving upward briefly. "But if you'll give me a moment of your time, Maddy, I promise that you'll never have to see me again."

And still she waited, hoping, despite that unpromising beginning.

"I know—" he began and then paused "—everything," he finally finished. "Everything Harry did, or made you do.

And how he did it. And I know about the baby.'' The hardest part of this confession that could have no atonement. "I know that Harry... I know that you and he never... There's nothing I can say, Maddy, except I was wrong. So terribly wrong. And I'm sorry.''

"How do you know?'' she asked softly.

"Harry became remarkably voluble—under the right persuasion. He admitted everything.''

"And you believed *Harry?*'' she said. Her laughter was not caustic, but simply amused. "It's ironic that Harry could convince you when I—'' She stopped, as suddenly desperate to make her own confession as he had been. "But then Harry had never lied to you, so perhaps you had more reason to trust his word.''

Misinterpreting that quiet declaration as a reminder of his lack of trust, he closed his eye again. He had not looked at her because he knew if he did, if he allowed himself to remember, he'd never be able to do what he had come to accomplish. To give her the security he'd arranged and then get out of her life. To allow her once more to become what she had been born to be, to return to the circle that had included her since her birth. Until their marriage.

He eased his right hand into the pocket where Pennington's enumerated listing of the properties she now owned rested. He drew the paper out and laid it on the small table that had been placed for the convenience of the chair's occupant.

"These are yours,'' he said simply. "The Mannering estate, cleared of encumbrances. The properties are all in your name, and your ownership is perfectly legal. Pennington will manage them for you.''

"And Harry?'' she questioned, a sudden fear that what he was offering had been acquired at the price of her half brother's life. Although she knew that if ever a man deserved to take that revenge, her husband did. Yet somehow she didn't want Harry's blood on his hands.

"My Lord Mannering has decided to seek his fortunes in the New World. I...arranged for his passage.''

"Harry?" Maddy said, amusement again tinging her voice at the image of Harry among the savages.

She was aware of the responding lift of her husband's lips.

"But the properties? How in the world…" she began, suddenly wondering at the miraculous restoration of the estate. "Or did Harry's mining scheme really have merit?"

Jean-Luc smiled at her justified doubts about her brother's business sense. "In this case, Harry seemed to have stumbled on something that may succeed. Eventually. With careful supervision and some smart backing. Avon has undertaken to oversee that particular venture for you."

"For me? But…"

"By the terms of yours and Harry's agreement, the mine has reverted to your ownership."

"I don't understand. The agreement was very specific, and Madame Darnet had promised that she would secure Avon's word agreeing to its conditions before she entrusted it to him. Avon would never open—"

"Obviously Avon's word means less to him than you imagined," he lied smoothly, having no intention of telling her that Harry had violated their agreement by putting a ball into him. It smacked too much of trying to find redemption by seeking to arouse her sympathies. "We needed to know what Harry was up to, and the agreement gave the first clue as to why Cornwall was so important."

"I see," she said untruthfully. The thought that someone like Avon might break his word was difficult to grasp, so against the strictures that governed their lives. But, too, there were stories of the duke's more clandestine activities, so perhaps…

"Then, I think, that's all. Avon or Pennington will answer any further questions," Jean-Luc said, pushing himself up from the depths of the chair.

"And you?" Maddy whispered.

He had still not looked at her. If he did, he'd never find the will to leave.

"I'm going back to France. I have some investments there I need to reassess," he lied again.

"I see," she said simply.

"Goodbye, Maddy." They were the only words he could allow. And the final truth, "You'll never know how sorry I am."

"Jean-Luc," she said, and at the familiar, Anglicized pronunciation of his name, he felt his vision glaze with tears he determined to control. Before God, he swore, he would not let her see him cry.

He took a step, blindly seeking escape, and stumbled against the small footstool that she sometimes used to elevate her feet as she sat before the fire. He looked down, but not yet in control of the emotions he fought, he still couldn't see what he'd blundered into. He stopped, his face turned away, blinking rapidly to control the despised moisture.

"I'm sorry. I didn't think to help you," she said at his side, her hand cupping under the elbow of his injured arm.

"Don't," he ordered sharply, as much in response to the knowledge that he couldn't bear her touch as to the agonizing jolt of pain.

Her hand fell away immediately, and she stepped back.

"Of course," she whispered and he heard the tremor in her voice. "I should have known that whoever brought you would have explained the arrangement of the room. It's only a stool," she said more calmly, stooping to move it out of his way.

It was only with that gesture that he understood what she believed. There was no way she could have known that Ling's treatment had been a success. And that, of course, explained why she had allowed him to talk to her when he had expected, and indeed knew he deserved, to be shown the door before he could even begin. Pity, he thought bitterly, knowing there was nothing else between them.

He had managed the short, obstacle-free distance to the door, before her voice stopped him.

"And if your son has your father's nose," she asked softly, "shall I bring him to you when he's four or five? Old enough, perhaps, to question why *his* father doesn't want him."

"Doesn't want him?" he repeated unbelieving, her words

like the touch of the assassin's whip against his naked heart. With his good hand he gripped the facing of the small, crooked door. "God, Maddy, how can you say that?"

"Because you're walking away from us both. What else can I tell him?"

"That his father forfeited any right to know him because he didn't know how to trust. Didn't know how to love."

"Why should you have trusted someone who lied to you, a betrayer of the honesty you wanted between us?" she asked reasonably.

The strong muscles of his back lifted with the depth of the breath he took. And he waited.

"Jean-Luc," she said, "please don't go."

He turned slowly, needing to see if what was in her face matched what had been in her voice, and found her smiling at him. She touched the wetness beneath his lashes, and he saw nothing but love in the beautiful violet eyes.

Remembering his generosity in the Duke of Avon's paddocks that day, she whispered, "Am I forgiven?"

Oblation for a sin that was his.

Unable to believe that he was again being offered the paradise he'd lost, he carefully enfolded her in his arms, both arms, ignoring the last reminder of Harry's contamination.

After only a moment he stepped back, and the dark, skillful gambler's hands molded around both sides of the protrusion of her belly. He watched his own fingers smooth over the small mound that held his child, and finally raised his gaze to hers. He smiled into her eyes, which slowly, realization dawning, began to widen and dilate, the rim of violet blue lost in wonder.

She touched the fine white line that traced across the bridge of his nose and his eyelid, the only remaining physical evidence of the nightmare in the alley that she had relived so many times.

"Then Pritchett did manage to—" she began.

"Pritchett be damned," he said, laughing. "Ling's concoctions are far more efficacious than that London quack's."

"That's remarkably reassuring," she said, smiling, "especially since he's offered to deliver your son, or your daughter. When the time comes, of course,'' she added, seeing the sudden concern in his eyes.

"Ling? But how could he know how to find you? Avon and I..."

"I don't know. But he's been here almost three weeks. He never even mentioned that he'd healed your eye. He's working at the inn in the village. He said he had come to be my servant, but of course, living out here alone, allowing him to do that would hardly be proper."

Jean-Luc's sudden shout of laughter caused the familiar rush of color under her transparent skin.

"Oh, God, Maddy, always concerned about the proper conduct. No matter the occasion. I suppose I shall have to be on my best behavior from now on."

"It doesn't matter," she said, smiling, remembering that ghost also. "I've already decided I want to keep you."

Epilogue

"**P**eg a note to the door," Jean-Luc suggested as his warm mouth, moving slowly across the top of her breasts, sent shivers through her.

"And what should I say to the Duke of Avon in this note I'm going to fasten to the door?" she asked, clearly scorning that he would even suggest such a thing.

"Come back in the morning? Go back to London? Anything that will allow us to retire gracefully. And alone," he suggested, expertly unbuttoning the throat of her dress although he was hindered by having to use only one hand. His tongue trailed into the warm fragrance between her breasts.

"But he'd think he's not welcome."

"Unless he's a blockhead," he agreed, "which I assure you, my darling, he is not."

"But he'll take that to mean—"

"Exactly what I intend he should take it to mean. Go away. I want to be alone with my wife. With whom, I might add, I have *not* been alone in months," Jean-Luc reminded her, his lips still moving seductively.

"Three."

"What?" he asked, nibbling along her collarbone.

"Three months," she whispered, her hands beginning to make their own remembering exploration.

"Maddy," he warned in response to her now-expert touch.

"Don't. Not unless you want this to be over before it's properly begun."

"I don't mind. I don't expect, after a delay of three months, that it's going to be…"

"Don't make predictions," he warned softly. "Let me surprise you. Just lock the door and—"

"I *cannot* lock the door against the Duke of Avon who is in Cornwall in the first place because he's trying to help us. That is simply not done, Jean-Luc. Even you—"

"Barbarian that I am," he interrupted, smiling.

"Should know that we have to at least make a pretense of making him welcome. We should really invite him to stay the night, but I don't—"

"No, Maddy. Damn it, that you won't do. He's a sophisticated man, a married man who also is in love with his wife. He'll understand that we need—"

"Don't you dare," she admonished, horrified that he might tell Avon that. "Don't you dare tell him that we *need* anything. I warn you, Jean-Luc."

Fortunately the knock on the door prevented her having to think of a threat that she might possibly find the willpower to carry out. Her knees had been trembling since he'd touched her, and all she wanted was to be in his arms. But he was the one who had mentioned that Avon had promised to return and that they might expect his arrival at any minute. And apparently…

Jean-Luc stalked toward the door, and Maddy flew to open it before he could reach it. The duke stood on the stoop, moisture from the cold rain, which had now begun to fall in earnest, darkening to charcoal the shoulders of his coat and dripping off the rim of his tall beaver.

"Your grace," Maddy began, genuinely contrite that between them they had managed to send Avon back and forth to the village on a wild-goose chase on a night like this. It was very possible that his journey would result in illness if he remained any longer in his damp clothing. "Oh, my heavens, you're drenched. Jean-Luc can build up the fire and you can dry out in no time. Please, come in and—

"Tomorrow," Jean-Luc interrupted the invitation.

The duke had already removed his hat and had been shaking the rain from it in preparation to enter. At the gambler's single word, Avon's silver gaze lifted, filled with amusement, to meet Jean-Luc's. But he turned with a perfectly controlled face to Maddy and began to intone the proper response with a great deal of self-assured charm.

"*Madame* Gavereau, you are kindness itself, but I fear I have urgent business in the village that prevents my acceptance of your gracious invitation until tomorrow, but I shall—"

"Afternoon," Jean-Luc suggested on top of the last few words.

The duke's graceful refusal died as one dark eyebrow climbed to express his opinion of that proposal.

But he replaced his hat and bowed to Maddy.

"Take care of him," he advised softly, and then, before he stepped off the low step into the rain and darkness, his silver eyes, brimming with laughter, met the Frenchman's again.

"Braggart," Avon suggested, smiling, before he disappeared into the darkness.

They stood together in the open doorway until the sound of the carriage faded into the night.

"What did he mean?" Maddy asked, leaning against her husband as he slipped his arm around her waist.

"Do you remember the needs that we weren't going to mention to Avon? Perhaps he was, somehow, already aware of them and was simply suggesting that you do your wifely duty and—"

The back of her hand slapped his flat stomach smartly, and he laughed.

"Stop it," she chided, finally laughing with him.

"Close and lock the door, my darling. I really don't think I'm up to any more interruptions."

He turned back to survey the simple room while she obeyed.

"Maddy, my love," he asked softly, "where have you hidden the bed?'' And then, the thought not to be borne, ''You do *have* a bed?''

''Well,'' she said, watching him begin to shake his head at her hesitation.

''Don't, please, don't tell me that—''

''No, there is a bed. Of course, I have a bed. Only...''

Jean-Luc took another, more careful look around the room and then strode to the curtain that apparently served as a partition to the bedroom.

He pushed back the material to reveal what was, in actuality, no more than a cot. He stood a moment looking down on that disappointingly narrow mattress in its rather fragile-looking frame. Maddy could see the depth of the breath he took.

''Not exactly what I have been imagining,'' he said, but he turned to smile at her. ''Through all these long months. If somehow I ever again—'' He stopped, thinking how close he had come to losing her.

''I never thought that you romanticized about this. I thought only I... I thought that men didn't... What did you imagine would happen if we ever again...?'' she hesitated, watching his face.

''A bed. A real bed. And candlelight. The champagne you liked so well. Only this time...''

''In moderation,'' she agreed, smiling at him. ''And what else?''

''A steaming bath. And you in it. And I'd pick you up and carry you—''

''Hmph,'' said Maddy.

''What did you say?''

''Nothing. Pray continue.''

''A snort, Maddy. I distinctly heard a snort.''

''Well, unless you've brought a winch, I can't imagine your lifting me out of a bath and carrying me any distance. Not anymore.''

''Are you doubting my strength?'' he teased.

''I'd doubt your sanity should you try that now.''

"All right, no tub. No sweeping you up in my arms. As a matter of fact..." Jean-Luc hesitated.

Maddy's eyes fell at that pause, and then she forced herself to look up again.

"I know that I've changed so much," she began, her hand unconsciously smoothing over the bulge that had replaced the slender waist his hands could span. "I don't even know..."

"What don't you know?" he said, moving back to take her in his arms. "You must know that *this*," he said, putting his hand over hers, "makes you only more beautiful."

Again the small doubting sound.

"Another snort, Maddy. Your friends are right. You're becoming vulgar, my darling. It must be the company you're keeping."

She laughed, and then said more seriously, "You can't think this is beautiful."

And her husband, who was indeed very wise in the ways of women, allowed her to see his sincerity in his eyes and to hear it in his voice, so that she was left no doubt. "I think you are more beautiful than you have ever been. More beautiful than you were at seventeen when you were the reigning toast of London. Or at eighteen as Fairchild's bride. Or in a country inn capturing the heart of a man who believed he no longer had a heart."

"At twenty-five," she said, admitting a truth she'd never before revealed, again watching his face. But he only smiled at that revelation.

"Or as my trembling bride. More beautiful even than when I carried you out of the bath the first time, so small and frightened."

"I wasn't frightened. I've never been frightened of you. You've never given me cause—"

"And I won't now. And I'll be very careful, Maddy. I promise. There's no danger to the baby. Not at this stage, at least."

"How do you know all that?" she asked, shocked perhaps, but not questioning his expertise, which she certainly had cause to know he possessed. "Exactly how many pregnant woman have you made love to?"

"Exactly none," he denied. "At least none that I knew of. None that were…" he amended, and then seeing that she was not pleased with that answer, he began again. "I told you that I was raised in a very feminine environment. I learned… things."

"Things," she repeated. And then again, her tone entirely different. "Things. I remember some of those things," she said softly. "But if you'd rather stand around all night talking about your checkered past."

"If I seem to be hesitating, it's because I'm wondering if that bed will even support our weight."

"Our weight?" she questioned, placing her hands on either side of what had been her waist. "Are you trying to insult me?"

"I'm trying to seduce you. And I'm making a damn poor job of the attempt. Maddy, my darling, come to bed with me," he invited.

"I thought you'd never ask," she said, beginning to remove the simple kersey gown. He stood watching as she shed the garment, revealing a serviceable cotton chemise stretched tautly over her pregnancy.

She glanced up to find his eyes on her. Embarrassed still by the heavy awkwardness of her body, she attempted to lighten the too-serious expression that was in his face.

"The poor relation again. I left everything in London the night…"

"I know," he said, remembering what had happened that night. What he'd accused her of and wondering if she'd really ever forgive him. The silence stretched a moment before she spoke again.

"Harry?" she said, remembering also, and he waited for whatever she needed to say to him. Whatever it was, he knew he deserved.

"Harry," she said again, and unbelieving, he heard her giggle. "My God, Jean-Luc, how could you ever think… After everything that we had shared… After you had shown me...everything, how could you possibly imagine that I would... With Harry!'' she said again. And she was still laughing when he pulled her against him and began kissing her with all the expertise at his command. He backed nearer the bed, drawing her with him, still enfolded in his arms, although the injured one was throbbing with renewed agony.

When he felt the edge of the mattress against the back of his legs, he fell back onto the small bed, pulling Maddy's body down on top of him. Desperate now to hold her. To touch her. To drive the remembrance of his anger and the pain he'd inflicted from her mind.

There was a splintering sound from beneath them, and then a resounding crash as the bed gave way. Since there was no great height to the bed to begin with, they did not have far to fall, but they landed with a distinct thud. There was a stunned stillness for a brief moment, the dust from the ancient mattress rising about them in a cloud.

And then the quiet was broken by Maddy's laughter, peal upon peal of it. Laughing still, she rolled off him and onto the arm Harry's ball had hit. His startled expletive was involuntary and heartfelt, but apparently expressive, even in French. Maddy scrambled away from him as rapidly as the shattered bed and her bulk would allow.

He pulled the damaged arm against his stomach, rocking slightly, still cursing, but more moderately. When the unexpectedly vicious pain had eased somewhat, he looked up to find violet eyes locked on his face. Maddy was sitting on her knees beside the fallen bed watching him.

''What in the world?'' she whispered, her concern obvious.

''Harry,'' Jean-Luc said, remembering her laughter at what he'd thought. ''Your damnable brother shot me. Not so funny now, hmm, Maddy? You laughed because I thought that you and Harry... Because the thought of it made me insane, I suppose, but remember that you're the one who put that damned pen in my hand and made me sign away a very valuable piece of property to your brother. What was I supposed to think, damn it? What—''

''He shot you,'' Maddy interrupted, having heard nothing

beyond the beginning of his tirade. And, of course, the other didn't matter. Not in the least. That was over, and they both knew it. "Let me see," she ordered, reaching to unbutton his waistcoat.

"You can't see. It's my arm. I'd have to undress."

"And hadn't you planned to? Or did your fantasies involve taking me from the bath fully clothed."

"I told you, you were nude, beautifully nude, and I—"

"Not me, you idiot. You. Or were you going to wear your clothes again all night? Are we back to the silliness of not removing your shirt because you have a few scars?"

"A few scars!" he repeated, hurt that she would ridicule the effort that he had made to protect her from what he considered to be the horrors of his body.

"If that isn't just like a man," she said, exasperated. "Take off your clothes and let me see what damage you've let Harry do to you this time," she ordered, resignation coloring her voice.

"*I've* let Harry do?" he repeated. "It seems to me that Harry's done whatever he wanted from the beginning. I should have killed the bastard months ago. And instead, because you ask me to, I waltz into White's and apologize to him. I must have been out of my mind."

"Kill my brother?" she asked icily, managing to forget the fact that she had gone to Harry's home to do exactly that.

"Heaven forbid," Jean-Luc mocked. "The dear brother who's stabbed me, blinded me and then shot me. Why ever would you think—"

"He didn't stab you," she denied, attempting to introduce some logic to the argument.

"No, your former suitor managed to do that. Do you have any other suitors lurking around waiting to do me harm, Maddy? Should I sleep not only with my clothes on but also with my pistols?"

"Any *other* suitors?" she asked coldly. "Others like Harry, I suppose. Are you still imagining…?"

"No, damn it. No, of course, I'm not 'still imagining' that Harry… That you could ever…"

"Well, I should hope not," she said, slightly mollified. She eased back off her knees, the position becoming painful, and sat on the floor. She crossed her arms and looked at him.

Suddenly he realized the ridiculousness of the tableau they presented: Maddy sitting on the floor, her chemise stretched tightly across the bulge of her belly, her disordered hair streaming over her shoulders and a smudge of dirt on her cheek; himself, still fully clothed and stretched out on the remains of a collapsed cot, carefully nursing his arm, which he held tightly against his body.

Not at all as he'd imagined it would be.

And then he knew that it didn't matter if their reunion didn't match his fantasies. Or hers. Because they were together. Whatever the situation, that was really all that was important. *That's what it's all about,* Maddy had said so long ago. It had taken him a long time to know how true that was. Marriage. And children. And loving…

"I love you, Maddy," he said softly, the first time he'd told her that. And he could never remember saying it to another soul in his life.

He watched tears well in violet blue eyes surrounded by tangled strands of silver-gilt hair and dirt. He allowed his gaze to trace slowly down her body, over the worn and mended chemise, to where the tightness of the material did more to reveal than to hide the bulge of her belly, made more prominent by the way she was sitting. And he knew that he had been right before. She had never been more beautiful.

"I love you so much," he whispered again, and she saw the truth in his face.

"And I love you," she said. "I always have. Forever. It just took me a long time to find you."

"Well," he said, teasing, "you always have to have things done properly, you know. I, on the other hand, believe in taking action. Action that will lead to somewhat quicker results."

Her lips moved into a smile as she clearly read his meaning.

"Do you have a chair, Maddy?" he asked softly, and her

eyes widened slightly at the thought. "A *sturdy,* straight-back chair."

"A chair?" she repeated, thinking about it. Imagining. And finally, fascinated by the idea, she nodded.

"Ahh," Jean-Luc said. "Now, perhaps, we're getting somewhere."

"Slowly, love," he whispered, his hand on her waist, guiding. "Slowly." His injured arm was resting between their joined bodies, supported by the protrusion of her stomach.

Her toes stretched again, lifting, and she felt the shuddering intensity of the breath he drew. And then, too quickly, another. She knew what was happening perhaps before he did, trying so desperately to hold back for her sake. She leaned into him, her arms tightening around his neck and felt the forces they had created overwhelm him. The strength of his ecstasy surprised her. There was none of the control he had always exhibited. They had barely begun when his body had erupted beneath hers. Not the subtle, patient lover who had dominated his passion with experience, controlling until he carried her with him, as lost in what they were feeling as he.

Instead…

"Maddy, I'm so sorry," he said when his body had stilled. His hand caressed up and down her spine, comforting, because he knew he had left her behind, that he had given her no chance to join him. "I thought I could… I'm so sorry."

She leaned back slightly, to see his face, and smiled at him.

"And *now* will you let me put you to bed? You have a fever, you're in pain and you've been traveling in that condition all day."

"No," he said. "Not until…"

"Jean-Luc," she whispered, exasperated.

"Damn it, Maddy. I don't intend—"

"I know what you intended, believe me. I remember your intentions very well. But sometimes things don't happen the way we intend. It doesn't matter. We have the rest of our lives."

"It matters to me," he said softly.

"I know. And that's one reason I love you. One of the many reasons. But you need to rest. You know you do."

"I need to see you... To watch what happens when... Damn it, Maddy."

"Voyeur," she suggested, laughing.

"You are so beautiful like that. So relaxed. Uninhibited. Finally not concerned with the 'proper thing to do.'"

"I thought that *was* the proper thing to do. For a man and wife. That's what you told me."

"You're exactly right, my darling. And that's why I don't intend that this should... I think I have an idea," he began. "If you'll trust me?"

"I've always trusted you," she reminded him.

"Then turn around."

"Turn around?" she questioned, not understanding.

"And sit facing the other way," he said, waiting for her to visualize what he intended.

Slowly she obeyed, again slightly scandalized by the images his words had suggested, but knowing how skilled he was in devising ways of giving her pleasure, she knew that she wanted this. Wanted him. Any way they could manage.

"Lean back," he suggested softly against her ear when she was once again seated on his lap, this time facing away from him. He carefully moved the injured left arm around her to rest once more on the ledge of her belly, his fingers cupping her breast.

"Put your legs outside of mine," he ordered in that same seductive voice, his accent thickening slightly. And then his right hand traced down over her pregnancy, stretching to reach the place she was waiting for him to touch, anticipating so much the familiar movement of his fingers that knew exactly...

"Knees, morals and now babies," he said softly, his mouth nuzzling against her throat. At the first stroke, her head fell back onto his shoulder, her breath sobbing softly. Her left hand lifted to catch in the raven blackness of his hair.

As the intensity of sensation grew, she writhed in his arms, straining to lift her body closer to the knowing pressure of his fingers.

"Maddy," he said, warning, perhaps, that he intended to be in control.

Her fingers clenched in the curling softness of his hair. Her breath was shuddering in and out, and her body arched uncontrollably.

"Maddy," he said again, the movement of his hand hesitant.

"Now, Jean-Luc," she begged him. "Please, don't make me wait. I need..." And briefly she remembered what she had said about Avon. She wondered what he would think....

And then she didn't wonder about anything at all. There was nothing but the blinding intensity of sensation. Familiar and yet new each time. Different each time. And this...

Gradually she became aware of the dry, fever-induced heat of his body behind the shivering coldness of hers. His right arm was now wrapped around her also. Holding her securely against him. Safe and very satisfied.

She turned her head to put her lips against his cheek.

"Thank you," she said softly, and heard him laugh.

"My pleasure," he assured her, still smiling at her politeness. "My *deepest* pleasure, my darling. Always, my deepest pleasure."

* * * * *